Holding
The Directives

By

Joe Nobody

ISBN 978-0692258248

Edited by:
E. T. Ivester
D. Allen

www.JoeNobodyBooks.com

Published by

www.PrepperPress.com

Other Books by Joe Nobody:

Holding Your Ground: Preparing for Defense If It All Falls Apart

The TEOTWAWKI Tuxedo: Formal Survival Attire

Without Rule of Law: Advanced Skills to Help You Survive

The Home Schooled Shootist: Training to Fight With a Carbine

Holding Their Own: A Story of Survival

Holding Their Own II: The Independents

Holding Their Own III: Pedestals of Ash

Holding Their Own IV: The Ascent

Holding Their Own V: The Alpha Chronicles

Holding Their Own VI: Bishop's Song

Holding Their Own VII: Phoenix Star

Apocalypse Drift

The Little River Otter

The Olympus Device: Book One

The Olympus Device: Book Two

Prologue

"I'm not a soldier or a warrior anymore," the grizzled sergeant whispered. "I'm a zombie herder."

With a practiced eye, he scanned the lines of humanity shuffling forward, waiting their turns for what the locals called, "manna," or food from heaven.

In reality, heaven was a pair of semi-trailers parked on a highway overpass. The manna was pre-packaged rations, occasionally MREs, most times bulk bags of rice, corn, or beans. God was the US Army, dropping the meager quantities from the bridge to those waiting in line below.

A ring of security surrounded the trucks, courtesy of the sergeant's rifle company. The foot patrols were augmented by two escorting Humvees, each mounted with a heavy machine gun. Their primary mission was to deny any civilians the opportunity of approaching the ultra-valuable commodities inside those trailers.

The people of Houston rarely chanced the urge to rush the trucks these days. The combination of "Shoot to kill" orders, and the isolated high ground provided by the overpass, had all but eliminated the riots.

Two hundred meters ahead, perched over the lanes below, he could observe bustling activity as the trucks were unloaded, slight packages of food being released into desperate, outstretched hands below. The unloaders were distributing their cargo in a rush, experience having taught them to "Get in and get out," as quickly as possible. Besides, there were only two semis today, and that could mean trouble.

Returning his gaze to the cued citizens of the Bayou City, he scanned for signs of discord, agitation, or outright disobedience. He'd seen it before - more than once. It took only one troublemaker... one person raising a voice of protest or complaint to spark the fire of insurrection. That meant shooting, cleaning up the bodies, and tons of paperwork. He hated paperwork.

His eyes worked the crowd, noting a young man fidgeting on the

1

balls of his feet, a nervous up and down bounce that bore closer scrutiny. There was a stooped, middle-aged woman mumbling to herself as she crept forward in the line. She too earned a spot on the sergeant's short list of potential troublemakers.

But, for the most part, his gaze revealed nothing more than the typical assembly; a wretched, filthy, thin, coughing, mass... unfortunately representative of the zone's surviving civilian population. Zombies lurching forward on unstable legs, eager to be fed.

He turned to the eastbound lane, the exit route where his men herded the benefactors after they had received their manna from government-heaven.

Here was where the majority of his men were posted, a virtual skirmish line of soldiers scrutinizing with keen diligence as the newly food-endowed citizens scurried away with their bounty. Trouble could start here too, but it would be of a different nature.

Young girls lounged around, rows of their scantily clad, brightly clothed bodies propped against the wide assortment of abandoned cars and trucks. The rusting hulks were leftovers, relics from a time when a desperate population collectively attempted to flee the city and wound up idling on gridlocked freeways until they ran out of gas.

On manna-day, the prostitutes came out in droves, hoping to invoke the world's oldest profession in exchange for food, ration tickets, or other valuables. It was payday, and the girls were working the passersby, hoping to score a generous John or Joan.

Technically, prostitution was against the law, but so were many things that the NCO let pass. Hell, the majority of his men and he had sampled the local wares. Over two years away from home could make a man overlook certain regulations. Over two years of enforcing martial law, of being the grocer, doctor, policeman, social services provider, and fireman to the civilian population could encourage a man to ignore those rules and regulations.

It had all taken a toll. The sergeant's unit was beyond being merely demoralized, racked by desertions, and the constant victim of mounting insubordination. If his troopers wanted to blow off a little steam by spending 10 minutes with a pretty girl, that was just fine with him. "An MRE will set you free," was the motto amongst the troops.

Mingled with the hookers were the scavengers and peddlers, hawking their merchandise for barter to those passing through. The eastbound lane had become a spontaneous marketplace, free enterprise springing up within minutes of the manna's arrival.

He noticed a group of men gathered nearby, the unauthorized meeting drawing the attention of his corporal and two privates. Sighing at the potential sign of trouble, he moved to check it out. "Damn, I *really* hate paperwork," he mumbled, increasing his pace.

Unauthorized assemblies of five or more people were against regulations, and for good reason. Insurrection had broken out in more than one of Houston's 56 districts, and the sergeant wasn't about to let anything get started in his. Rebellion led to more casualties, cremations, and double shifts, not to mention the myriad of forms and depositions the zone's commanders would heap upon his person.

Twenty feet away, he exhaled with relief. His lieutenant was among the group, standing next to a man everyone called Uncle Nate, the civilian representative of District 17. The presence of his commanding officer meant this gathering was authorized. If trouble broke out, the paperwork would be stacked on the LT's desk, not his.

The sergeant could see them all huddled together, each man reading a sheet of paper. It was an unusual sight. Lieutenant James peered up at the sergeant's approach, a curt nod the only acknowledgement of his arrival. Without a word, James passed his subordinate a document, the single page of typeset print clearly of the Army's making.

"The Alliance of West Texas to Assume Command of the Houston Control Zone," was the title. It took only a few minutes for the sergeant to finish reading the article.

"What's this mean, sir?" he questioned the officer.

"It means there's a new sheriff coming to town. It means the US government is pulling out, and this homegrown organization is taking over."

Rumors of the Alliance and the progress in West Texas had made the rounds, but no one really knew what to make of the stories. Now, out of the blue, was this.

"We are going to hold division-wide assemblies in the next few days," the lieutenant stated. "Each man is to be given the choice of staying with the 7th, or transferring to a unit still under the control of Washington and the Pentagon. Staying means swearing an oath to this new government."

Uncle Nate stepped closer, the civilian's expression unreadable. "I like their list of directives," he began, pointing at his copy. "I sure hope they can do better implementing them than what we've seen so far out of DC."

The sergeant gazed down, focusing in on the five items listed. They read:

Energy
Agriculture
Security
Transportation
Communications

Uncle Nate continued, "Says here that, and I quote, 'All of the Alliance's resources are to be aligned in order to achieve these directives.' Do you think they've got more food out in the western part of the state than we have here?"

Both of the military men shrugged. "Only time will tell," the officer offered, "At this point, you know as much as I do."

Uncle Nate decided he wasn't going to receive any additional input, and wandered off, seeking more talkative company. Once they were out of earshot, the sergeant engaged his leader for a more detailed response. "Seriously, sir, what does this mean?"

"As usual, we're the last to know here in lovely suburban Houston. General Zackery is supposed to be holding briefings tomorrow, so I should be filled in shortly afterwards. What I do know is that everyone back at Hood was given this choice a few days ago. Most of the division is staying put... probably no better place to go. But others are leaving. I guess they've had enough fun in Texas."

"How many are transferring, sir? Has anyone said?"

"No specific numbers have been cited, but the scuttlebutt is that not many are heading out. Captain Henning just arrived from Hood, and he told me that there were only a few farewell celebrations in progress. He said he drove through the on-base housing and only noticed a handful of moving vans."

"What about you, sir?"

"I'm staying, Sergeant. I've been hearing about this group out of West Texas for months now. According to a friend of mine from Fort Bliss, there are electric lights in many of the towns out there. He claims that food, minerals, and manufactured goods are moving by the truckload. He believes this new civilian leadership has its shit together."

The sergeant was skeptical. For two years, command had been promising to turn the electricity back on within 90 days. It had never occurred. Examining the thin, sunken-faced wretches passing by, he reasoned that hollow promises made for hollow people. What made the Alliance leadership so sure they could pull off what had perplexed and baffled the best minds in the country since the collapse?

"I'll believe it when I see it," the NCO commented. "I hope those poor bastards from out west realize what they're getting themselves into."

The First Directive - Energy

Like ghostly apparitions from a teen horror flick, the blurry, white images appeared oddly distorted against the background of stark blacks and grays. "Contact," Bishop whispered into his microphone as he adjusted the infrared optic's focus. A slight twist of the control fine-tuned the clarity.

"I've got eight... no, make that nine individuals at 250 meters," he transmitted.

Without removing his eye from the device, his finger found a button and pushed. The image changed drastically, the ghoulish, spirit-like outlines now becoming red and angry. A blinking line of text appeared at the bottom of the display informing him that red now equaled "hot."

A party of demons strolling through purgatory, he mused.

"I'm looking at a work group of some sort," Bishop broadcast. "There are eight people carrying shovels, hoes and rakes, and one guy with a rifle. I can't tell if he's protection for the detail... or its jailer."

"Does it matter?" Major Baxter's cynical, but hushed voice sounded in his ear.

Prick, Bishop thought. *That guy's sphincter is so tight, you couldn't drive in a straight pin with a sledgehammer.*

Bishop continued to ponder the officer's harsh comment for a moment. Regardless of the role of the passing guard/jailer, his presence signaled organization at some level. Little more could be learned from his inclusion in the group.

"I suppose not," he replied. "They're heading away from me, so I'm continuing to the objective. See you at the roadblock."

A few minutes later, Bishop scrambled down a small, roadside knoll, keeping low and quiet as he stalked through waist-high weeds and brush. Again, pausing to orient himself to the surroundings, he mentally reviewed the next phase of their plan – the barricade.

Bishop's head and body were shrouded in a net, the nylon mesh laced with grass, weeds, small branches, and other local foliage. It was heavy, hot and scratchy, but a necessary precaution. Even in the low light of pre-dawn, despite their overwhelming numbers, surprise was always the strongest ally.

Slowly, ever so cautiously, he inched closer to the target. Gone were the days when vigilant mowing teams cropped the grass and errant shrubs from the road's shoulder. These days, the resulting thicket provided good concealment, almost to the edge of the pavement. The undergrowth was integral to the plan, providing means for a takedown without gunplay. Their orders had been clear and firm – don't let them breathe, think, or react. Complete, overwhelming domination would keep fingers away from triggers.

A campfire smoldered ahead, its dying embers and low flicker providing an excellent reference point. Bishop slowed his pace even further; small, deliberate steps interspaced with gaps of time. No matter how well his camouflage imitated the local shrubbery, movement attracted the human eye.

Up ahead was the roadblock, now a common fixture in post-apocalyptic towns and cities everywhere.

Communities had learned the hard way - people were the problem. In the early days of the nationwide collapse, transients began roaming the countryside. Some were simply desperate, needing food, water, or shelter to survive. Others harbored more nefarious intentions.

As post-collapse time dragged on, the population became increasingly desperate. Society's remnants began to realize that help wasn't on the way; that things weren't going to bounce back to normal. Yesterday was no more, its hasty return doubtful.

Many began assessing their available assets and commodities. Everyone from soldiers to priests, principals to city managers struggled with the same dilemma - how to feed and care for their people.

Those who didn't ignored history at their own peril. Throughout the ages, hungry people were unruly people. Underfed populations were notorious for overthrowing kings, governments and local leaders. Empty stomachs led to unrest and revolt. It was a biological reality that many mayors, city councils, and town managers didn't initially grasp.

An education on such matters was soon delivered, however, often via the muzzle of a rifle or flaming embers of a torch.

The vast majority found that food, medical supplies, and fuel were already in short supply. When it dawned on local leaders that they couldn't feed their own families or neighbors, normally compelling, charitable impulses of benevolence evaporated. Additional mouths meant less food for their own. They reacted swiftly, taking drastic steps to shoo away the refugees and vagabonds traveling the countryside.

Over time, many learned that a roadblock was an extremely effective tool. The "anti-Welcome Wagon," it projected a message… a billboard of sorts that advertised, "Look elsewhere for your new address. Keep moving. Looters will be shot." The barricade Bishop was approaching, complete with its armed, tough-looking men, accomplished just that purpose.

A tow truck parked sideways in the road, its girth no doubt intended to intimidate anyone entertaining a plot to barge through. Two pickup trucks bookended the larger, heavier vehicle, their positioning rendering it impossible to drive around the barrier. Sandbagged fighting positions, a large tent, campfire, and several 50-gallon barrels rounded out the configuration.

It was obvious this obstruction had been in use for some time. As he scanned the target with the thermal optic, Bishop noted the stacks of firewood, BBQ grill and lawn chairs. Someone had even hauled out a porta-potty so the guards wouldn't have to dig cat holes.

It was also clear that the garrison manning the facility was bored. Only one of the three sentries appeared to be awake, his level of alertness questionable.

Bishop studied the sentry closely. A full beard, long, unkempt hair and some sort of soiled baseball cap indicated the fellow wasn't part of a well-disciplined unit. Outfitted with an AR15 or similar weapon, but no load-rig, body armor or sidearm, he didn't seem to appreciate the seriousness of his role.

This may be easier than we thought, Bishop judged, keeping a close eye on the guard as he crept ever closer.

The watchman was sitting in a dilapidated lawn chair, shreds and threads of the nylon webbing dangling beneath the seat. Apparently, there was some interesting memory or vision in the blaze, the man's eyes seemingly mesmerized by the flames. Bishop couldn't be sure, but he thought he noticed the gentleman's head nod forward as if he were dozing off. Sleeping bag-covered lumps and the distant rumbling of one guy's snoring pinpointed the other members of the garrison.

Baxter's voice sounded through the earpiece. "Scouts, report your positions."

Bishop didn't immediately respond. He was designated as number three and would wait his turn.

One click sounded across the frequency, closely followed by two more depressions of the sender's microphone. Scout one, two minutes from being in position.

The process was repeated by number two, who responded that he was within one minute of the objective.

Show off, Bishop thought as he pressed a sequence indicating he was still three minutes from being ready. *I'm going to be the last one present and accounted for. Baxter will love that shit.*

He was so close now; any mistake would give him away. Each footfall took time, Bishop allowing his weight to shift forward at a snail's pace. Even the crack of the smallest branch or twig could alert the sentries.

Two clicks and then nothing. Scout number two was in position.

Mr. Sleepy-guard jerked his head up, and for a moment, Bishop thought the guy had heard something. Ready to pounce if the sentry made any move to wake his comrades, Bishop relaxed when the watchman rubbed his eyes and shook his head. *He dozed off*, Bishop realized. *He's trying to stay awake and finish his shift. I've been there a hundred times.*

One click, and then nothing. Scout number one was ready.

Finally, Bishop arrived – less than 20 feet away from the nearest truck. So close, he could hear the crackle of the fire. So close, he could smell the porta-potty. He took a knee and raised his weapon.

Three clicks.

Major Baxter didn't respond at first, his eyes scanning the long row of trucks and men parked alongside the road. There were 21 vehicles in all, each packed to the brim with food, medical supplies, a gasoline generator, and fuel. The Army had even contributed a mobile water filtration system. It was an impressive collection, assembled specifically for the town of Brighton, Texas.

"Make ready to approach the objective, Sergeant Riggs," the officer ordered.

"Yes, sir," responded the NCO, pivoting quickly to rush and execute the order.

For a brief moment, Baxter felt the nag of fear cross his gut. This mission was important, the first of its kind. If it went well, it would become a textbook example for others. If it didn't, the blame would follow him throughout the rest of his military career.

Not that his boyhood dreams of lifelong service to his country were going that well anyway. The United States had dissipated. His unit, division, and base now pledged to an unknown, unproven entity that called itself the Alliance.

He understood the logic of the decision. Food rationing at Fort Hood was depleting morale. Medical supplies were running low. Communications were practically nonexistent. The battalions that did venture out from the central Texas base returned with reports that made even the bravest soldier shiver. Houston and Dallas had hundreds of thousands of dead, and the number was increasing every day.

The great, proud nation, the most powerful country on earth, was starving to death. The leadership was tearing itself apart. The most potent military ever assembled was divided, reunited, and

11

then divided again. It was more than troubling — it was debilitating.

Morale had already registered an all-time low. When the average trooper realized there wasn't enough food to feed his children living at the base, tempers began to rise. Desertions, already an issue, threatened to become epidemic.

And now, this "Alliance." *How long would this last?* Baxter pondered, watching his men hustle to their vehicles. *Was this really the answer?*

To make matters worse, his superiors had insisted... no, forced these civilians down his throat. Twenty of them had arrived at Hood, their pickup trucks filled with food and supplies from West Texas. All of that would have been understandable were it not for their leader - a clown named Bishop.

Undisciplined, brimming with ill-timed humor, and brandishing an unacceptable level of familiarity, Bishop had tried to be casual and friendly. The memory of those first few days made Baxter snort in disgust. Why would such a man think an officer in the United States Army would accept him as a comrade, let alone listen to his bumpkin-like strategic advice?

Sure, Baxter had heard a few stories about the man's antics. These tales, the major was convinced, were obvious exaggerations of secondhand information and most likely self-promoted lore.

The sound of truck engines pulled Baxter out of his analysis, the sergeant's voice booming up and down the line as he ordered the mulling men. "Mount up, ladies! Teatime is over. We've got work to do."

By the time they were ready to depart on the mission, Baxter had filed his second request to leave Bishop behind or have the West Texan replaced. It was then that he finally discerned the true cause for his being burdened with such a clod.

Bishop's wife was important, a key figure in the civilian leadership. The man was politically connected, and that explained it all.

Baxter's thoughts were interrupted by the sergeant's return. "The convoy is ready, sir."

The major nodded and motioned toward the lead Humvee. As he stepped up to enter the passenger side, he scanned back along the long line of waiting transports.

The sight reinvigorated his determination and confidence.

At significant cost and enormous sacrifice, the convoy had been pledged to this mission. Such a gathering of goods was worth its weight in gold, so desperate was the need for the supplies and materials now under his command. Division had determined that here and now, in Brighton, Texas was where the precious cargo would be distributed. They had chosen him to lead the mission. They were committed. It was his duty. He would succeed despite the handicap imposed by his superiors.

Bishop waited alongside the roadway, his ears straining to hear what he knew would be the next phase – the approaching engines of the convoy.

During the wait, doubt grew in his mind. *I'm still not convinced this is the right way to accomplish this initiative. I wish I had raised more of a stink.*

Back at Hood, the military commanders had been unquestionably confident with their plan. "Arrive with overwhelming force and assert our authority," they had proposed. "Leave no room for doubt among the civilian population. Be clear in defining the objective and our intent. The local people will welcome order and control and will respect the show of force demonstrating our capability to implement it."

But Bishop's experience didn't exactly mesh with that line of thinking. He'd toured more post-collapse villages and metropolitan areas than anyone else at the table, and his gut told him the Army's ideas were risky. In the end, the council had voted to accept the military's recommendations. Despite his reservations, Bishop had to support what the Alliance's ruling body ordered. It was the rule of law, part of living in an orderly society.

I need to stop bitching and worrying, he thought. *We're the white hats… the good guys. It'll be fine.*

He then refocused on the pavement beyond the barricade, straining to hear the announcement of the convoy's arrival. Behind him, the two-lane Texas highway stretched into the darkness toward Brighton. He hoped they would be welcomed there. He prayed that the townspeople had fared better than others he'd seen since the economic collapse of the country.

According to the scavenged Texas Visitor's Guide, Brighton was a berg of just over 5,000 people. Like most small communities, many of the locals owed their livelihoods to a single, dominant employer. Condor Pipe and Valve, the town's economic anchor, bumped the tiny municipality to the top of the Alliance's priority list.

Terri and the council were desperately trying to reestablish electricity to the area's major cities. It was the first directive. In the case of Dallas and Houston, that meant reviving the two huge nuclear power facilities that serviced those vast urban areas.

When the collapse had occurred, both of the energy plants had implemented emergency shutdowns. While the residents counted their blessings that those procedures had been executed, both facilities had remained idle and unmaintained since. Complex machinery and electronics, left untouched for over two years, hadn't weathered inactivity well.

When the military had rolled into the metropolitan centers and established martial law, one of their first priorities had been to resume energy generation at the power plants. While much work had been done, the personnel, spare parts, and materials required for such an effort had simply been beyond reach. Not having the resources, authority, or wherewithal to kick-start the supply chain, both of the enormous facilities had remained inactive.

Condor Pipe and Valve had been one of the dozens of manufacturers identified as a critical-path supplier. According to the few surviving engineers, the remote factory could provide the essential cooling conduits and other equipment necessary to repair the rusting, corroded plumbing at both facilities.

Despite the cost and resources required, no one could argue against keeping those nuclear rods nice and cool. Nor was there any doubt that electricity had provided the fledgling West Texas towns at the core of the Alliance a much-needed shot in the arm. Many believed the Alliance would have never succeeded without the windmill-generated energy powering those populations.

Of the five directives, energy was the most critical. With an active grid providing electricity, communication with the masses was achievable. People could find work, locate missing relatives, and exchange ideas. With fuel, transportation was a no-brainer. Voltage meant produce and meat could be preserved, processed, and accounted for. Bishop soon found he had a new assignment.

All of the other directives, it seemed, were easily obtainable if energy were plentiful.

All of this meant reestablishing society, rule of law and a government in the town of Brighton. Isolated from the major metropolitan areas, no one from the military or the Alliance had visited the community since the collapse. No one knew what to expect. Everyone hoped there were still enough survivors to restart Condor and begin generating product.

Bishop's thoughts were pulled back by the low rumble of the convoy. *Let the games begin*, he mused.

Alerted by the sound of 21 engines rolling toward their positions, the guards manning the roadblock were initially stunned. Voices, ripe with both surprise and confusion, soon filled the air. One man had trouble navigating his exit from his sleeping bag, almost falling out of the back of the pickup's bed. The other recently roused watchman originally pulled his boots on the wrong feet. Bishop was reminded of the Keystone Cops, witnessing one guy stumble while the other seemed to have forgotten where he'd left his rifle.

Bishop watched as they fluttered about, scrambling to take up positions. Given the bedlam, he guessed they didn't get much business these days, probably spending their shifts bored to tears and playing poker.

By the time the lead truck stopped 800 meters short of the barricade, the noble defenders of Brighton had attained their assigned positions. Two rifle barrels pointed at the approaching procession while a third man stood in the center of the highway brandishing an AR15. The garrison's effort had been slow and unpracticed.

"I'm not impressed," Bishop mumbled as he prepared to move.

With the sentries' attention focused on the idling convoy, Bishop stood and removed his net-camouflage. In the faint, but growing light, he detected two other nearby outlines performing the same act. On cue, the three scouts moved as one, silently slipping in from behind the unaware watchmen.

The two soldiers with Bishop made for the sandbagged fighting positions, their assignment to neutralize the guards stationed there. The Texan had to admire their skills as he hung back a few steps, watching to make sure the takedown went smoothly.

A few moments later, both Brighton men were slowly lowering their weapons, and then their hands were raised in the air. Before Bishop had passed by their positions, the two wide-eyed watchmen were lying flat on the ground.

Bishop's task was to subdue the man a few steps in front of the roadblock. Cutting smoothly around the tow truck, rifle high and ready, he quietly closed on the oblivious guard. Covered by the low din of the convoy's motors, he stepped to within a few feet of the sentry's back.

"Good morning," Bishop announced, trying to keep a friendly tone.

The man jumped, his instincts ordering his body to pivot and seek the source of the voice behind him. He found the muzzle of Bishop's weapon two inches from his nose and inhaled sharply.

"Drop the rifle, my friend, and you'll get to eat breakfast. Test my trigger finger, and these hollow-points will split your head in half. I know that for a fact."

As Bishop anticipated, the sentry's panicked mind couldn't arrive at a decision. The Texan knew he'd have to ease the process along. "Drop the fucking rifle! Now!" he growled.

The sentry, staring into the coldest pair of human eyes he'd ever seen, didn't hesitate again. A plastic and metal clatter sounded over the background noise of the convoy's engines as the AR15 connected with the pavement.

"I want the prisoners secured, Sergeant Riggs," Major Baxter's voice rang out. "Use the zip ties to bind their hands, and prepare them for interrogation."

Bishop tried to keep the frown off his face, but failed. "Major, a word please."

"What now?" the officer blustered, clearly annoyed at Bishop's interruption.

"Sir, I would recommend treating the locals with respect. They aren't insurgents or criminals – they're just a few guys who were protecting their neighbors and families."

The young officer stepped in close to Bishop, his voice going low and mean. "They were manning an illegal barricade and showed clear intent to engage us. I'm not going to pour them a drink and shake their hands. We need to establish authority and control. Those are my orders."

Bishop's temper swelled in his chest, every cell in his being screaming to punch the overzealous man's face. But he suppressed it, checking his urge, allowing only a low snarl and simmering defiance. "Illegal to whom, Major? How were they to know who they were engaging? As far as these men knew, we were a roving gang of zombies intent on murdering everyone in Brighton. Take a moment and put yourself in their shoes."

Shaking his head in disgust, Baxter pivoted and faced the still-waiting sergeant. "Do as I ordered, Riggs. Now."

Sighing, Bishop moved to the side, watching as the three sentries were bound and then forced to their knees. The major moved to stand in front of the frightened men, his voice thick with a condescending tone. "Who is in charge of Brighton?"

Two of the prisoners glanced at the third comrade, clearly indicating which of them was in charge of the blockade. Bishop had to hand it to the captain of the guard; the man had a little grit. "Who wants to know?"

"I am Major Baxter, commanding a detachment from the 1st Combat Team, 7th Cavalry, United St...," the officer hesitated, unsure of how to continue. After an uncomfortable pause, he finished with, "The Army."

"Well, Major, I don't believe you," the now-recovering sentry responded. "The Army I know wouldn't act like sneaky thieves, stalking freeborn Americans in the night."

Bishop barely managed to subdue the snort of laughter that formed in his throat. He was beginning to like the head sentry. Baxter, on the other hand, saw no humor in the response.

There was now enough light to see the major tremble with anger, the officer's weight shifting forward while his hands balled into tight fists. "I asked you a question! Who commands Brighton?"

Bishop, thinking Baxter was about to strike the captive, was at his limit. Inhaling deeply, his foot lifted to take a step toward the aggressive officer, physical confrontation written all over his face. Before Bishop's boot managed the first step, the sergeant stepped in.

"Major!" the older, seasoned veteran barked. "Sir!"

Somehow, the NCO's voice managed to penetrate Baxter's ire. Almost as if the subordinate had slapped his superior's face, the major turned and glared at his second in command. "What? What is it, Sergeant?"

"Sir, we can't locate the keys to this tow truck. With your permission, I need to attach a towline and pull it to the side. It's the only way to open the road."

"Smooth," Bishop whispered under his breath, knowing the real reason why the sergeant had interrupted. "That was some very quick thinking."

Baxter, however, didn't appreciate it. His voice thick with indignation, he replied, "So? What's your point, Sergeant?"

"Sir, the captives are kneeling directly in front of the wrecker's tow hitch. I can't attach a tow rope while they're there."

Baxter's head snapped toward the locals, then back to his man. For a moment, Bishop thought the officer in charge was going to rip the sergeant a new one, but he didn't. "Very well. See to it," and then the major was off, storming toward the command Humvee as if he had important matters that required his immediate attention.

Bishop watched as a couple of troopers helped the prisoners to their feet and then herded them to the side of the road. As soon as the bound men were settled, he sauntered over and took a knee beside them.

"I'm not with the Army, fellas," he began. "Our illustrious commander is a little on edge this morning. Give me something to work with, and I'll make this right."

The head guard eyed Bishop with a hint of suspicion, but still probed, "What do you want?"

"Does the tow truck still run? And if so, where are the keys?"

The man snorted, nodding his head. "We start it every now and then to let someone pass. The keys are over the sun visor. Where else would they be?"

Bishop chuckled and then smiled at the sentry. "Give me a minute to get this all straightened out. Please don't hold it against Baxter. The major's under a lot of pressure these days."

"Good luck pulling that two by four out of the guy's ass," the man replied.

Bishop hustled over just as one of the soldiers was arriving with a Humvee. "Sergeant," he shouted over the engine noise. "One second, please."

"Yes, sir?"

Bishop pointed to the tow truck's cab, motioning for the NCO to follow him over. Climbing up, Bishop opened the door and pulled down the eyeshade. He caught the falling keys in mid-air.

Smiling, the sergeant took the ring. "Thank you, sir. I wasn't real sure our little Humvee could move this behemoth anyway."

Satisfied with the progress on clearing the roadblock, Bishop took a deep breath and moved off to find Major Baxter. It was time for a serious discussion.

He found the man addressing some of his troops, the group clustered behind the command Humvee. Standing to the side, Bishop just stared at the major until he was noticed.

"Yes?" Baxter barked, looking annoyed.

"We need to talk, Major. We need to have a little chitchat before we enter town."

Bishop was surprised at the officer's reaction. Instead of acting as if he were being pestered, the man actually reared up – almost as if he wanted to get a few things off his chest as well.

"Let's take a walk," Baxter replied, nodding towards a game path leading into the bordering woods.

"Let's," Bishop agreed.

The two men marched into the underbrush, both remaining silent until they were out of sight. Baxter turned and poked his finger into Bishop's chest. "I am sick and fucking tired of your constant interference," he began. "You have done nothing but seek to undermine my authority, question my every decision, and degrade my command's performance. I want it stopped, and I want it stopped right now."

Bishop took a half step closer, bringing his face in tight with the irate officer. "You are the epitome of why I was happy to leave the Army, Baxter. You are thickheaded, unwilling to accept advice, and so wrapped up in your command structure and discipline that you wouldn't know a good idea if it slapped you up the side of the head. I want you to open your eyes and ears and take advantage of those who have experience. You're going to fuck this mission up and get people killed if you don't."

20

"What sage advice, Bishop? What experience? The only reason why you are here is because your wife is some political bigwig back home. Sure, you've galloped here and there with your fancy rifle and civilian kit. Hell, I'll even accept the stories of your shooting it out with some starving refugees and common thugs. But that don't buy you shit in my store, mister. I play in the big leagues. My men and I play for keeps, and we don't need some overpaid night watchman trying to tell us how to go about our mission. We are professionals, highly trained and disciplined. Get the fuck out of my way, and let me do my job."

Bishop backed off, the move necessary to avoid butchering the asinine man standing before him. With a calmer voice, he tried to reverse the direction their conversation was heading. "Major, if we were in Iraq or some other combat zone, I would bow to your wisdom, training, and experience. But we're not. We are in America, dealing with Americans. They don't give a shit about martial law, military justice or any of that. They care about security, where their next meal is coming from, and how to keep their kids from getting sick and dying. If you roll into this town like a conquering army, they will resist to the core of their being. They will stall, play dumb, and sabotage anything we try to accomplish. I'm only suggesting a slight modification to your perspective - a minor adjustment to treat civilians with respect and put yourself in their shoes before reacting. Is that so much to ask? Does that slight courtesy endanger the mission?"

Baxter snorted, "Treat the civilians with respect? Now that's rich... really rich. I've seen how your type treats women and children. When I first graduated from the Point, I worked with contractors in Iraq and Afghanistan. You hired guns would piss off the locals, rambling through towns like cowboys in from a cattle drive. Then, after they were all riled up, the natives would take it out on my men. We became the targets of those you and your type incensed. So I don't think you have any basis to be schooling me on how to treat noncombatants. I can do without that type of advice."

Bishop had heard the same debate a thousand times. The attitude was common in the military. Private contractors were mercenaries, selling their honor, loyalty, and gun to the highest bidder - milking the government agencies that hired them for every last penny.

The Texan knew the major and he weren't going to settle the issue here and now. Short of one of them beating the shit out of the other, this wasn't the place and time. Even if he did teach the young officer some manners, doing so would jeopardize the operation. Troops don't respond well to seeing their commander all bloodied up. If the well-conditioned officer happened to get the better of Bishop, Baxter would feel completely empowered to do as he pleased.

Bishop also understood the resentment. Regular military men, like the major, had been fighting and dying for their country while their families back home barely made ends meet. Private contractors were making thousands of dollars a day, buying new cars and living first class. Army and Marine deployments meant 13 months away from home and family, while the guys in Bishop's trade were flying back to the States several times a year.

It was a big part of the reason why so many contractors remained anonymous about their past. After a few bad apples had made headlines, Bishop had seen men in his profession treated like scum. When the US government had thrown some of the bigger security agencies under the bus in order to salvage political reputations, public opinion had been blemished even further.

Bishop decided to play his trump card. "Look, Major, you and I are not going to settle this debate here. So let me remind you of your orders. You are to handle security; I am in charge of negotiations and civilian relations. The generals back at Hood were very clear on that point. So why don't you adhere to your wonderful, unyielding discipline and follow orders? I'd prefer to work with a partner during this little adventure, but if you want to play hard ball, I'm more than willing to get on the radio right now and have your sorry ass relieved."

Baxter clearly wasn't prepared for Bishop's threat. For a moment, he considered the statement a bluff. "Your dick isn't big enough to swing that far."

"Want to try me? You said yourself my wife was some bigwig. Do you really want it on your record that you were relieved from a command before the mission even got started? I've tried to earn your respect, but clearly, your prejudices aren't going to allow that. So I'm going to assert my authority. I'll let you know when I need your help."

And with that, Bishop pivoted and marched off, leaving Major Baxter with a stunned look on his face.

The Texan exited the underbrush and made a beeline for the three prisoners. In a flash, Bishop's fighting knife flashed in the early light, cutting through the nylon ties securing the captives' hands. The two soldiers standing guard started to protest, but one look from Bishop quelled their words.

"Get these men some water," he ordered, not wanting to give the troopers a chance to gather their wits. Turning to the three recently freed locals, Bishop watched as they rubbed the circulation back into their wrists and bodies. "Thanks," their leader said.

"No problem," Bishop replied. "Now I know we all got off on the wrong foot, so here's the deal. We took you down all sneaky-like in order to avoid an accident. Guys get spooked. Soldiers get nervous. Sweaty fingers squeeze triggers, and then bad shit happens. Get it?"

After digesting Bishop's words for a moment, the leader said, "Okay, I'll buy that for the time being. Still, why did Mister Hard-ass over there act like he wanted to send us to Guantanamo?"

Bishop shook his head, knowing his response was coming at a critical point in the newly established relationship. "You can't really blame us. We've seen it all, dude. Dictators running towns as if they were the reincarnation of Stalin or some shit. Gangs of escaped convicts overwhelming local governments and ruling like land barons from the Dark Ages. Think about it. We have no clue what's going on in Brighton, so we assume the worst. You would do the same thing in our shoes."

The message seemed to resonate with the former captive, his head nodding north and south. "Okay, I can run with that. Why Brighton? Why now? Why after two years does the government show up and claim they're here to help?"

Bishop smiled, but shook his head. "We're having a conversation, so now it's my turn to ask a question or two. What are conditions like in town? How many folks are still alive?"

23

Bishop saw a flash of fear cross behind the sentry's eyes. After a nervous glance at his mates, he said, "Do you know about the war? The Repos?"

Bishop's face wrinkled into a frown. "War? What war?"

The leader stared hard into Bishop's eyes for just a moment, and then relief seemed to unfurl his brow. "We've lost a ton of folks. Starvation, bad water, and contagious diseases took a chunk of the population early on. Then it was the raiders. People called them bandits, marauders, and ghouls. They'd hit at night, mostly around the edges of town. As time went on, they got braver. Nobody was safe."

Something about the man's response troubled Bishop, the Texan's instincts bristling with a feeling that he was being told a half-truth. His first reaction was to press, but he pushed it aside. Baxter had already came across as Mister Hard-ass, and Bishop didn't want to repeat that mistake.

Bishop said, "I hear ya. Other areas have reported the same, my friend. So let me guess, you guys organized, set up roadblocks like this one, and protected your loved ones?"

"Yeah, that's about it. Even with that, we kept burying people. The elderly didn't have a snowball's chance in hell. No medicine, no medical equipment. When doctors did show up for work, they were helpless. The young suffered, too. The antibiotics ran out after two months. After that, even a little scratch or minor cold could kill a kid.... some adults, too."

Bishop grimaced, trying to show sympathy and understanding for the man's horrible memories. "We've all been through hell. Let's hope it makes us stronger, that there was a reason why this all happened."

"So why are you here now? What has changed?"

"People began regrouping in West Texas. We got lucky, and circumstances allowed us to start rebuilding. Now, we're taking control of the entire state. Hell, we might even recreate the Republic of Texas out of the ashes. But for right now, we're trying to save as many people as we can and restart the recovery process."

The man turned and looked back at the long line of trucks, his expression showing confusion. "But why Brighton? From what you say, there are many places that could use help. We're in reasonably good shape compared to refugee accounts I've heard about recovery nationwide. Why here?"

"Because of the Condor factory. We need to bring it back on line. We need the products it produces in order to repair a couple of nuclear power plants."

Understanding crossed the guard's face. It all made sense now.

"Well, as soon as you're ready, why don't you and I take a truck into town, and I'll introduce you to the mayor. He's my brother-in-law."

Bishop was a bit skeptical. "Why just you and me?"

"We had some rogue national guardsmen roll through a few months after the collapse. They said they were in charge, and that the president had declared martial law. Ends up they raped a bunch of the women and killed anyone who questioned their absolute rule. We drove them off, but not before they did a lot of damage. A bunch of soldiers pulling into the main square might not get the reception you guys are expecting."

Bishop grunted, nodding his agreement. "Okay, my friend. I'll take a ride into town with you. Let me explain what's going on to the major."

The man extended his hand toward Bishop. "Red... Red McCoy."

The handshake was accepted. "Nice to meet you, Red. They call me Bishop."

"I don't approve of this... not at all," Baxter announced. "I could quite possibly end up with a hostage situation, and that might delay or endanger the entire operation."

25

"That's an excellent point, sir," Bishop responded, trying to show the Army officer some respect. "But I don't see any safe way to go about this. If what Red said is true, we could get people hurt or killed by just rolling into town. I'm willing to accept the risk, sir, with your approval."

The major didn't like it, but he had to agree with Bishop's logic. There wasn't any foolproof method, no tried-and-true protocol. "Okay. But keep in touch via the radio as much as possible. If they get clever, let them know we're still coming in."

In other words, you'll let them kill me, just so long as you achieve your objective, Bishop thought. *How cute.*

A few minutes later, Bishop and Red were driving one of the barrier's pickups into town. "My brother-in-law, Lewis, is running the show. He lost his wife, who was my sister, and their two children soon after the economy tanked, and like your major back there, he can be a little difficult to deal with. You're doing the right thing by coming alone."

"How does the town feed itself?"

Again, there was a slight hesitation in Red's response. "We're lucky, I guess. Brighton is surrounded by some pretty productive farms and ranches."

"But you said you lost a lot of people to starvation?"

"Not at first. After it became clear that the electricity wasn't coming back on, the farmers would bring food into town and barter. Before long, we ran out of goods to trade. They wanted things like fuel, medicine, ammunition… a whole list of stuff. We drained gas tanks, scavenged what we could, but it wasn't enough. It took a long time for everybody to pull together and work to feed the survivors."

Bishop didn't buy it. Too many of the young man's responses just didn't seem to track. Red's previous mention of a war drifted back into the forefront of his mind. He wondered if his host's statement about the long time it took for everybody to pull together might not have been a little more violent than what he was being lead to believe. "So what would you guess the town's population is now?"

Red grimaced. "We lost thousands. We dug graves with a bulldozer... it was the only way." After a brief pause at the morbid memory, a forced chuckle signaled a change in subject. "It's still amazing to me how creative people get when they're desperate. One old fool tried to make fuel out of the fermenting corn. He blew his house to smithereens. He survived, but no one tried it again. Another guy made some pretty good rot-gut whiskey, but with very little sugar available, even the supply of moonshine was limited."

"What about the Condor plant?"

"When the fuel ran out, we started having trouble with fires. Without a fire department to respond, we lost more than our share of houses and businesses. One of the Condor warehouses burned as well, but I'm not sure what was stored in it – if anything. You'll have to ask the mayor and his crew about that."

"What did you do before the collapse?"

Red's voice became sad. "I molded young minds. Elementary school math teacher."

The truck entered the outskirts of Brighton. Bishop turned his attention to the passenger window, trying to absorb as much detail about the small berg as possible.

As they drew closer, the open space between structures lessened, the density of civilization increasing as they neared the center of town. The first commercial building was the VFW, its WWII artillery pieces standing guard in front of the building.

As they passed, Bishop began to notice the common hallmarks of a post-apocalyptic habitation. Makeshift rain catches were perched beneath most downspouts, comprised of anything from 50-gallon barrels to old coolers repurposed for the critical task of collecting runoff water.

Stacks of firewood were abundant; trees were not. Clothing dried outside on lines, the billowing colors swaying in the morning breeze. Even at the early hour, windows and doors were open to allow the circulation of air and light. It was summertime in Texas, and heat stroke would soon be claiming its share of victims.

Those same porches were often adorned with a multitude of

buckets, baskets, and jugs. Something about the scene sparked a memory from the first days at the ranch with Terri. The two had just bugged out of Houston and badly needed vitamin C to avoid scurvy. The most commonly available source of the antioxidant was pine needle tea.

They had traveled across the desert floor and into the mountains, climbing until they reached the tree line. The needles were abundant and easy to gather, but shipping their significant harvest home created a substantial challenge.

On their next trip, Terri brought along a plastic clothesbasket, which was soon filled to the brim with green, life-giving pinion needles. The two had learned an important lesson. From Bishop's vantage, the citizens of Brighton had apparently received a similar education. Anything and everything that could assist the human hand in collecting, transporting, and traveling with cargo was evident. A woman strolled to a neighbor's yard, shopping bags filled to overflowing with what looked like collard greens. Behind her, a child steered a wagon stuffed to the brim with similar edible foliage.

There were other signs as well.

It was barely 20 minutes after sunrise, yet every occupied property was already surrounded by activity. The citizens had adjusted their work schedules around dawn and dusk, adopting the noon siesta to minimize heat exposure. Without air conditioning, the stifling heat and humidity had become a prominent dynamic in their lives. *Another reason to look forward to Christmas*, Bishop mused.

It wasn't just the temperature that forced people to become early risers. Natural sunlight also played a role in most folks' daily routines. If Brighton were anything like Meraton, candles were expensive and often in short supply. Oil lanterns and the fuel necessary to light them were more valuable than anything other than firearms and ammunition. The best way to conserve those precious resources was to adjust the workday to respect the rise and fall of the sun.

After another mile, Red slowed the truck and turned into the city square.

Like most county seats, the center of Brighton was dominated by a large courthouse. Three stories tall and constructed of huge limestone sections, these buildings were originally designed to house the county sheriff, jail, clerks, elected officials, and of course, the courts.

Surrounding the grand old building was the square. Brick storefronts lined the streets on all four sides of the courthouse, their offering everything from small appliances to aspirin. A small café sat next to the bookseller, both of the locally owned outlets dwarfed by the independent furniture store.

To Bishop's eye, it was the classic small town square, typically a friendly place that normally hummed with neighborly smiles and greetings. But not today. Not in these times.

The stores weren't open, and Bishop was reasonably sure it had nothing to do with the early hour. Small piles of leaves cluttered the streets here and there. A few sections of sidewalk sprouted significant weed-beds rising from the expansion cracks.

There were only a few cars parked in the town's business center, all of the windows covered with a layer of dust and grime. Some smart-ass, long ago, had possessed enough energy to write, "Wash me" across the back glass of one late model sedan. Now, the scrawled text was barely legible, almost completely obscured by a new layer of dirt.

The municipal grounds were completely overgrown, thigh-high weeds competing with bushy shrubs that had once been manicured with pride. Bishop noted several bullet holes in the limestone façade, many of the darkened windows void of glass.

Red continued driving, bypassing what Bishop had assumed would be the center of any government still functioning. Two blocks further, the driver parked in front of a smaller, modern brick building.

"Welcome to City Hall," Red announced.

It made sense. Scanning the immediate vicinity, Bishop could tell this was the hub of local activity. The small lawn in front of the parking area didn't need to be mowed; the grass was well worn by indigenous foot traffic. Men and women meandered throughout the scene, a few with children in tow. Two police cars were parked in the small lot; both appeared to be functional.

"Why don't you stay here for a bit while I go in and explain what's going on? I know it's a bit rude, but these are crazy times, and you just never know how people are going to react."

Bishop understood. "That's cool. I'll be right here."

Red exited the truck, actually looking both ways before he crossed the road. Bishop noted his new acquaintance nodding at a man strolling down the sidewalk, then shouting a warm greeting to another idling by the front door. A moment later, he disappeared inside.

Bishop opened the passenger door and stood next to his ride. He still had his rifle and full load gear, so he decided to stay close to the truck in order to avoid attracting any attention. Something wasn't right in Brighton, Texas, but he couldn't put his finger on it.

"Stop it," he whispered, scolding his suspicious nature. "These people have endured the apocalypse. They're going to act weird. Quit seeing a boogeyman in every shadow. You're getting as bad as Major Baxter."

The two armed men stationed on both sides of the mayor's office nodded as Red approached. "He's in a meeting," the older guard greeted. "Are you sure you want to interrupt?"

"This is important... very important," Red responded as he reached for the doorknob.

Amy Sue was present and accounted for, at her normal post in the reception area. Her toothy smile automatically flashed before she'd even looked up to see who was coming through the door.

"Hello, Red," she said. "I thought you were on roadblock duty this morning?"

"I need to see Lewis," he responded. "It's urgent."

"Well, he's meeting with Mr. Winfrey and the sheriff right now. I'm not sure how long he'll be tied up."

"This is more important… believe me Amy Sue… I need to see him *now*."

Shrugging her shoulders, the secretary pushed her chair back and sashayed around the desk. She knocked lightly on the door leading to the inner sanctum and then pushed it open a few inches.

"Mayor, Red is here, and he insists it's urgent."

A gruff voice sounded from inside, "Tell him I'll be finished up here in a few …."

Red rushed past the surprised woman and entered the office. "This can't wait, Lew."

The mayor's headquarters was impressive for a town the size of Brighton. A large, darkly stained, walnut desk monopolized the room, its size and positioning designed to project power and authority. Behind the monument-sized workspace stood three colorful flags; beyond them, the bureau emblems of the United States and Texas bookended a central design embroidered with the city seal.

One wall was covered with framed photographs, most displaying a smiling Lew shaking hands with a myriad of celebrities, national politicians, and professional sports figures. A huge map of the town hung opposite, the streets, landmarks, and city facilities highlighted in a rainbow of colors.

Red noticed none of this however, his attention focused on the two gray-haired men sitting in the leather visitors' chairs. "I'm glad you're both here. You'll want to hear this as well."

"What's wrong, Red?" the man behind the big desk asked. "I've never known you to come barging in here like this."

"We've got company," Red began, and then proceeded to inform the gathered men of the morning's events.

"And he's waiting outside?" Lew asked.

"Yes. I talked him into coming by himself. The rest of the military

31

is parked by the barricade. If they don't get word in an hour, the asshole officer in charge is going to come rolling into town."

"Shit," the mayor muttered, standing to peer out the window. "Just when things are starting to go well, this crap gets dumped in our laps."

Mr. Winfrey spoke next, "Are you sure they don't know anything about the war?"

"I don't think so," Red answered honestly. "From the questions Bishop was asking, I don't think they have a clue about our recent history.

Lew spun around, his focus falling on the sheriff. "What occurred here was perfectly legal, gentlemen. There was a countywide emergency declared, and duly elected officials executed extreme measures to ensure the survival of our citizens. There's nothing more to it."

The sheriff grunted, "You keep telling yourself that, Lew. Soon, you might even believe your own tale. I know we did what we had to, but if the truth ever sees the light of day, it's not going to be pretty."

The mayor's face blustered red. The man pointed his finger at the local lawman and tilted his head forward as if preparing to issue a scolding.

Red didn't give him a chance, "I don't think this guy, or these Alliance people, give a rat's ass about what happened here. They want Condor up and producing product. As least that was my impression."

The room became quiet, all four men occupied by their own thoughts.

Winfrey's composed voice finally interrupted the silence. "Whatever we decide, I don't think it wise to leave our guest outside cooling his heels. Red, go escort the man in. We'll decide what to do before you get back."

Nodding his agreement, Red quickly left to retrieve Bishop. As soon as he was out the door, Winfrey continued. "Your brother-in-law might become a liability, Lew. We need to keep an eye on him. As far as the Army goes, it sounds like they are coming into town, whether we like it or not. I suggest you welcome them with your best pre-election smile and then stall. That will give us time to assess the situation and determine our next move."

Lew agreed. "As usual, you're right. I'm glad you never wanted to be in politics, Winfrey. I probably would never have been elected mayor if you'd thrown your hat into the ring."

The older man smirked, "Why would I want to engage in such activity? Being the president of the biggest bank in town is more than enough for me, Lew. I have plenty of influence as it is; my ego requires no more. Besides, politics is a messy affair. I'm very content right where I am."

Before Lew could reply, Amy Sue knocked again on the door. "Sir, Red is back with a visitor."

"Good! Good!" the mayor replied with exaggerated cheer. "Please, show him right in."

Bishop felt a little out of place. Still wearing a full combat load on his vest, the slung battle rifle, bush hat, and fighting knife somehow seemed inappropriate for what was essentially a diplomatic meeting.

After handshakes and introductions, the mayor indicated Bishop should take a seat, an offer the Texan declined.

"I don't want to appear impolite or uppity, Mr. Mayor," Bishop began, "But I left a significant number of very nervous, very well-armed men back at the blockade. I want to return there as soon as possible before anxious thoughts fill their minds."

"Completely understandable, sir," Lew answered. "What is it exactly you want from us? Red gave us a quick overview, but that only left a partial understanding of the situation."

"I'm here to offer you a chance to rejoin society, Mayor," Bishop answered. "I represent an organized group of communities stretching across the state. We have elected a government, established rule of law in dozens of towns, and we are now striving to kick-start a recovery in Houston, Dallas, Austin, and San Antonio. We need the Condor manufacturing facility up and running as soon as possible. We are willing to offer a

33

considerable amount of assistance to facilitate that event, as well as help you and the local leaders with whatever issues may be troubling your fine city."

It was Winfrey's turn to speak. "What type of assistance is available?"

Bishop tried to remember who the older man was, the introductions occurring so quickly. *Ah*, he thought, *the banker. Maybe Terri and he can meet sometime and tell old loan jokes or something.*

Dismissing the thought, Bishop answered the question. "We have food, fuel and some medical supplies. We can offer help with security, some transportation needs, and initially, small amounts of electricity. But most importantly, we can open up trade between Brighton and the rest of the Alliance. We've found trade has done more to advance recovery than any other single effort."

"But we're doing fine," Lew responded. "We could always use medical supplies and fuel, but our people have full stomachs, and the sheriff here has done an excellent job maintaining law and order."

Bishop was perplexed by the mayor's statement. He had always imagined that any community would be happy to jump on the Alliance bandwagon. He had contemplated having to convince the town's leaders that his mission wasn't hostile, and that democracy was still alive and well in Texas. But to be shunned after giving his sales pitch wasn't something he'd anticipated.

"Are you saying you don't want our help?" Bishop frowned.

"No... no I didn't mean exactly that," the mayor replied.

Again, the banker interrupted. "You must pardon us, sir. This is all a surprise, hitting us completely out of the blue. Of course, we are interested in what you and your new government have to offer our citizens. While our elected officials have done an excellent job given the extreme circumstances encountered, there is always room for improvement."

That guy is powerful, Bishop noted. *He's the real authority in this room.*

The sheriff picked up where Winfrey had left off, "Why don't we have them pull their trucks into the square, Mr. Mayor? They can occupy the courthouse if they need a roof over their heads or somewhere to work. I'm sure it's a mess, but it would beat pitching tents."

Lew seemed to agree. "That's an excellent idea, Sheriff." He then turned to Bishop and extended his hand, "I'll have Red escort you back out to the roadblock. He can then guide you and your convoy back into town. I propose that you set up, at least temporarily, in the courthouse. After you've had a chance to settle, we'll schedule a meeting and get the process rolling. Would that be acceptable?"

Bishop agreed, looking at his watch. "Thank you gentlemen, I look forward to working with you."

An hour later, the convoy pulled into downtown Brighton. Bishop, riding in the second vehicle behind Baxter's command Humvee, was surprised at the number of people who turned out to watch the parade.

For the most part, the population looked reasonably healthy. He'd seen much, much worse. Most of the men wore longish beards; few sported short hairstyles. The women looked plain and unadorned, makeup evidently no longer available or in vogue. Still, most of the people appeared reasonably put together, recently bathed and adequately clothed.

Bishop didn't note a single heavy person among the crowds of onlookers, but that was to be expected. "There's nothing like an apocalypse to encourage weight loss," he teased with the driver.

But the locals weren't starving either. Bishop spotted children scampering about, playing next to their parents, the display of energy unlikely if malnourishment was common. The people looked healthy enough, the vast majority between 20 and 50 years old.

35

A few of the younger men were armed. Bishop spotted sidearms, hunting rifles and a couple of shotguns. As they ventured closer to the main square, he noticed four men with badges and AR15 rifles standing on one corner. "The sheriff's deputies," he guessed.

Despite no sign of starvation or abuse, there was still an odd demeanor about the local population. Bishop kept trying to figure it out as they passed, but couldn't quite put a finger on it. Something was just a little bit off.

It finally dawned on him as they turned to enter the square. Not one person had smiled or waved at the convoy. Again, the reaction wasn't what he'd anticipated.

While Bishop hadn't expected a tickertape parade or the local marching band to greet their arrival, he found it odd that such a display of men and material entering town did not seem to invoke at least a little optimism. *That's it*, he thought. *It's almost as if they're sorry to see us.*

For a moment, Bishop was troubled by the reaction. Why weren't people at least friendly or curious? Soldiers, in any procession, normally elicited a positive response. Americans were normally proud of the military.

Then Bishop remembered Red's recounting of the rogue guardsmen who roughed up the town. *Maybe that's it*, he considered. *Maybe they're waiting to see if we plan to do the same thing.*

Red's escorting pickup parked in front of the courthouse, the remainder of the convoy pulling into spots all around the large building. "Don't forget to put a quarter in the meter," Bishop harassed his chauffeur. "We don't want to piss off the locals by trying to avoid a ticket."

The private laughed, "Will do, sir."

Before Bishop could exit, Baxter was at the door. "What is wrong with these people?" the officer asked. "I felt like I was driving through Kabul with all the hard looks thrown our way."

"I agree, sir. I felt a hostility as well. I'm writing it off to the town's previous bad experiences with men in uniform," Bishop

36

answered.

"Well, I'm not taking any chances with security. Can I count on your men to help with guard duty?"

For once, Bishop had to agree with the aggressive man. "Yes, sir. We can pull our share. Just have the sergeant let me know the duty roster, and I'll provide the headcount."

Red produced a ring of keys, eventually finding a match for the makeshift padlock securing the chained doors of the courthouse. Bishop pointed to the nearby bullet holes. "What happened there?"

Red seemed a little embarrassed. "When the food started running out, we had some folks get pretty upset. A few of them decided they needed to take matters into their own hands and tried to take over. Fortunately, they were small in number, and order eventually prevailed."

Bishop assessed the visible battle damage with a keen eye. "Fortunately."

With both Bishop and Baxter in tow, they entered the dark, moldy smelling structure. "All of the local government has been moved over to City Hall. You can use this entire building if you want. There's no water, and obviously no electricity, but it will keep the sun off your head. It was built before there was air conditioning, so if you open the windows, there should be a reasonable breeze. Some fresh air might help with the stuffiness."

A few minutes later, Red was off, leaving the new arrivals to their own devices. Baxter wasted no time, issuing orders for placement of vehicles, assigning sentries, and designating office space.

Bishop's sixth sense was on full alert, a combination of the reception they had received and the up-close view of the bullet damage to the building they were now occupying. He paid special attention to Baxter's deployment of security.

And as much as he hated to admit it, the officer did an excellent job. Like a spider weaving a web, the major layered their security. Starting with the likely avenues of approach and ending with a two-man overwatch position on the courthouse's top floor, the

Texan had to acknowledge Baxter knew what he was doing.

"My compliments on the security arrangements, Major," Bishop said. "Excellent work."

Baxter didn't know how to take the compliment, his expression puzzled as he vacillated between sarcasm and sincerity.

Bishop smiled, "Seriously, I'm not fucking with you. Nice work."

Acknowledging Bishop with a curt nod, Baxter hustled off, apparently unhappy with the placement of a nearby Humvee. Bishop stood and watched the officer's exit. Eventually shaking his head, he then set off to make sure his men were doing their part.

As he rounded the corner, a woman holding a small child on her hip came into view. She was across the street, innocently watching the soldiers as they unpacked equipment. Her hair was similar in color and length to Terri's, the baby not much older than Hunter.

Bishop paused for a moment, the scene making him yearn to hold his own wife and child. The tightening of his chest was unpleasant, and resentment began to build. "Why can't I manage to stay with my family?" he asked the empty air. "Why does life keep separating us?"

Bishop's morning was filled with unloading boxes, dusting off old chairs and setting up a basic space to sleep. By 11:30, it was already over 95 degrees outside, the air thick with humidity.

He had found a cozy first floor office, the stenciled sign indicating it had previously been occupied by the county clerk. It had all the available modern conveniences, including one window that actually opened, rows of filing cabinets full of musty smelling papers, and less than a half inch of dust on every surface. The in-suite commode smelled worse than the old files, but closing the door seemed to block the fouler aspects of the air.

After cleaning the remaining foliage out of his survival net, Bishop located two large screw hooks that he judged would hold his weight. He whispered an apology to the absent clerk, then screwed the large threads into a pair of opposing doorframes and strung the net as a hammock using some paracord from his pack. It was the envy of the establishment, many of the soldiers offering him significant barter for the contraption.

Even Major Baxter commented on his ingenuity. "I'm going to have to get me one of those nets," the officer had remarked. His almost friendly demeanor quickly dissipated with his no-nonsense order. "Here's the schedule for guard duty. Please have your civilians show up at their assigned posts at the designated time."

As Bishop scanned the handwritten document, he noticed Baxter wiping the sweat from his brow. "I would recommend you limit physical activity between 1200 and 1800 hours, Major," Bishop suggested, proud of himself for thinking to use military time. "Without air conditioning, everyone in Texas works early in the day, rests during the hottest hours, and then finishes up around dusk. We can expect the locals to be the most active during these times as well."

Baxter nodded his agreement. "Makes sense. But I'll tell you what doesn't. I can't figure out why the local government moved out of this building. I walked by the new city hall, and from a tactical point-of-view, this construction is far, far superior. The battle damage on the exterior indicates there were some episodes of violence locally, yet this facility remains mostly intact. Why abandon the easiest building to secure? Why give up the high ground?"

Bishop had wondered the same thing, but hadn't thought it was a critical mystery to solve. "Maybe they figured the violence was over. Maybe the city building was easier to keep cool with generator electricity? I'm with you though, this place sure would be easier to defend and secure."

The two men approached the front steps, both secretly hoping there would be more of a breeze outside. There wasn't. Wading through the weeds, they settled for the shade of an ancient oak. Bishop wondered briefly which had been there first – the courthouse or the tree.

39

"What time are we to meet with the city leadership?" Baxter asked.

"Seven… 1900 hours, sir. It should start cooling off by then."

"Roger that," and then Baxter was off, some unknown task pulling the officer away.

While the newly arrived soldiers settled in, the mayor called a staff meeting. Like all of their recent gatherings, the event was held in Lew's crew cab pickup, engine running and air conditioning blowing full blast.

The truck's interior had become a popular gathering point since average temperatures had begun to sizzle. The inside of any building was stifling at best, an oven at worst. Before fuel had reached the ultra-critical state, they had succeeded in cooling the mayor's office with a window air conditioning unit, but now there wasn't enough gasoline left to run the big generator.

The only bearable spots in the entire county were Lew's truck and a couple of the police cars. The truck was far roomier and the obvious choice.

"I'm down to a quarter tank," the mayor noted as the attendees settled into their seats. "We need to make this quick. I don't think that's enough fuel to last us through the summer."

Mr. Winfrey, as usual, spoke first. "I don't know about you gentlemen, but I haven't been able to find a single scenario where I'm comfortable with our guests remaining in town. Furthermore, I can't see any advantage in joining this new government. I can, however, see a lot of disadvantages should we decide to become part of this so-called Alliance."

Lew grunted at the banker's eloquent way of putting things. "Disadvantages? What a nice euphemism, Mr. Winfrey. I think 'prosecutions' would have been my term of choice. I do, however, have to agree with your assessment. We don't want these people

40

here. They won't understand our past decisions and will no doubt condemn us for the tough choices we had to make. I, for one, have no desire to deal with that."

Everyone turned and looked at the sheriff, signaling it was his turn to voice an opinion. "I agree. We don't want or need them here. That being said, I would like to get my hands on the equipment and supplies they brought with them. With all of that gasoline, we could hold a staff meeting every day and not worry about it. What a windfall."

Red spoke up from the back seat. "They're not just going to hand all that stuff over. We would have to take it from them, and I don't think that will be so easy."

"We've had to acquire supplies and critical items before," the sheriff responded, his tone carrying an edge. "The concept of using violence to achieve our goals isn't new to anyone in this truck."

Shaking his head, Red snorted at the lawman's comment. "These guys aren't a bunch of farmers and naysayers. You're talking about a whole lot of bodies on both sides."

"We've dealt with bodies before too, Red," the mayor responded. "Besides, we're better organized and prepared this time around."

Winfrey sighed, the older man making his frustration clear. "Why is it that you men always think of violence first? Let's just ask them to leave... tell them we're not interested... tell them the Condor plant is beyond salvaging. While I agree that their equipment and supplies would be nice to have, we were doing just fine before they arrived, and we'll do equally well after they are gone. Besides, confiscating their provisions would initiate an investigation from their leaders... and that is something we want to avoid."

"And if they don't leave? What happens then?" the sheriff asked.

The banker rubbed his chin for a moment before responding. "Then we'll cross that bridge when we come to it."

"So we are in agreement then?" the mayor said. "We will simply refuse their offer and ask them to leave us alone?"

"I'll go along with that," the sheriff concurred. "But... I think we should start preparing for the worst case. If they decide not to cooperate, we may need to convince them to move on."

"Then it is settled," Winfrey replied.

"In conclusion, gentlemen, I'm afraid we must decline your most generous offer. The Condor plant is beyond repair. Most of the workforce hasn't survived the collapse, and it would be deceitful for us to represent otherwise. While our people would welcome the goods and services you have proposed, we have nothing to trade... no value to offer in return."

Bishop was stunned, barely managing to keep his chin from physically dropping. He glanced across the conference table at Major Baxter and found the same unbelieving expression on the officer's face.

"But... but, sir," Bishop stammered, "We are offering so much more than electricity, medical supplies, and other essentials. Surely you must understand that Brighton, as a community, would benefit from the trade, inclusion, and security that come with being part of society as a whole."

Again, Bishop noticed all of the local eyes riveted on the banker. "Yes, young man, we understand that. But our people have suffered badly at the hands of strangers. Even if a factor of trust were to be established, the demise of civilization has taught us some very hard lessons. Now, more than ever, we know that you don't get anything of value unless you have something of equal worth to exchange. Our community is poor, barely feeding its own. We have nothing to offer in trade for what you propose to deliver. I wish it wasn't so, but the fact remains. Maybe not today, but at some point that inequality would breed trouble."

Before Bishop could form a counterpoint, the sheriff cleared his throat. "In addition," the lawman began, "we would like to politely request that you and your men leave town. The presence of so many heavily armed strangers is making our citizens nervous. It is a distraction that we don't need. All of your food and equipment might also be a temptation for some of our more desperate residents, and I'm all about prevention. If someone makes an attempt to loot your convoy, it would be an incident all of us would regret."

Baxter's reaction was predictable, "While I respect your concerns, sir, I assure you we've taken appropriate security measures."

"I'm not worried about someone actually getting away with raiding your possessions, Major. I'm worried about burying one of our own, and then the follow-on reaction from the community. We have order in our town, but just barely. The last thing any of us need is an encounter that turns violent."

Baxter realized his error and simply nodded at the lawman.

"I need some time to consult with my superiors," Bishop said, not being able to come up with anything else. "I will communicate our intentions tomorrow morning."

And with that, the meeting adjourned.

As Bishop and Baxter trekked from City Hall back to the courthouse, neither man could believe what had just occurred.

"I just can't accept their reaction," Bishop said.

"I never anticipated this," Baxter agreed. "Of all the scenarios we mapped out, outright rejection was never one of them. Unbelievable."

"I suppose it isn't so outlandish. Out in West Texas, we've had more than a few individuals who wanted nothing to do with any size, shape, or type of government. I guess Washington's failure put a bad taste in a lot of people's mouths. There is a small part of me that feels the same way," Bishop mused.

"But look at these people. Yeah, they're eating, but that's about it. I haven't seen so many lifeless eyes since I watched a zombie movie. What about hope? What about improving the quality of life?"

Bishop nodded his agreement, but didn't respond.

As the two men mounted the courthouse steps, Bishop paused, the thought of returning to the stuffy, damp-smelling building unpalatable. "I'm going to take a walk and try to clear my head."

Baxter started to protest, but then changed his mind. "Let me assign someone to go with you. No one should be wandering around alone."

The Texan waved off the concern. "I've got my weapon. I'm not going far. I need solitude."

The major shrugged his shoulders and turned back to enter the building. "Up to you," he mumbled as he passed through the threshold.

Bishop waited until the officer was out of earshot and shook his head. "Really, Major, your heartfelt concern for my well-being is touching. Really, it is. There's no need to waste so much energy trying to talk me out of going by myself. I'll be okay," he whispered sarcastically.

Shaking it off, Bishop turned and scanned the area. Sighing loudly, he randomly selected a direction and began walking.

The blocks passed quickly, his mind cycling over the next move. The Alliance's engineers had identified secondary supplies for the needed components, but they weren't easily accessible. One was in Oklahoma, the other in Illinois. "Might as well be in China," Bishop mumbled.

During the planning sessions, several contingencies had been tabled, most assuming that the Condor facility had been damaged or would require significant resources to reinitiate production. None of those scenarios had involved outright rejection by the local authorities.

Bishop had also been prepared for Brighton to be in a state of complete anarchy, with zero organization and few remaining survivors. Before the meeting with the mayor and his council, that had been the worst case anyone had considered. Now, he had an even more complex problem. He could take the Condor facility by force, probably bring in enough reinforcements from Hood to hold the ground against anything the locals could throw against it.

But that still didn't solve the problem of the workers, foremen, and specialists required to produce product. If Lew and the other local leaders wanted to play hardball, they could make the effort extremely difficult and fraught with risk. And besides, annexing territory by conquering the native population was not the Alliance plan.

Bishop paused for a moment to cross a street and get his bearings. An old man, shuffling along the sidewalk with a cane, drew his attention.

The old gent was an unusual sight, not only in Brighton, but anywhere else Bishop had traveled. Without medical professionals, prescriptions, and community support, the elderly hadn't fared well.

Bishop watched as the man progressed slowly, his feeble stride determined, yet unstable. "You have grit," Bishop whispered. "I'll give you that, old timer."

The subject of Bishop's attention turned, intent on crossing the street. The Texan watched as the man struggled with the curb and then proceeded to amble over the pavement. Deciding to be a Good Samaritan, Bishop waited and then offered a helping hand.

"Thank you, son," the soft voice responded. "It's not often someone offers to help an old soul these days."

"You're welcome, sir," Bishop responded as he made sure his new friend negotiated the curb successfully. The task accomplished, the Texan turned away and began to consider his route back to the courthouse.

He started to step across the street when something hard poked him in the back. The sensation was immediately accompanied by a rather young-sounding voice. "My cane is chambered in a .308 Winchester, and my finger is on the trigger. It shoots pretty well. At pointblank range, it will blow a nice hole through your fancy body armor. Turn around slowly, and walk with me."

A river of emotions flooded Bishop's head. He was pissed at himself for having fallen for the old man's disguise and letting his guard down. He was also scared.

As he turned, he observed the feeble outline of the old body transform and grow. Right before his eyes, the stooped, semi-crippled frame rose to its full height and spread its girth. Bishop found himself beside a healthy, good-sized fellow. The cane-gun wasn't shaking anymore. The gunman's breathing and eyes were steady and confident.

"What do you want?" Bishop asked.

"Not here," came the reply as the mugger's head pivoted to check the area. "Pop that magazine out of your rifle, and clear the chamber," he ordered.

Bishop hesitated for a moment, not wanting to comply. A sharp poke from the gun-cane made him reconsider.

"Now your sidearm," the voice commanded. "Hand it over to me."

Again, Bishop did as instructed.

"Walk with me... pretend you're trying to help me down the street," said the voice.

Bishop nodded, and then found himself hooking arms with a surprisingly muscular limb while the muzzle of his own pistol poked firmly against his ribs.

Staying in character, the abductor hunched over and hid his face as the duo shuffled along the sidewalk. "You're such a nice young man," the guy whispered. "Helping an old fella along. More young people should be so polite and accommodating."

At least he has a sense of humor, Bishop thought. *If he didn't have a gun stuck in my ribs, I might actually like this guy.*

A half block later, the voice hissed, "In here," and pulled Bishop inside an abandoned store. The captive could see the rusty chain securing the front entrance had recently been cut.

As soon as they entered the darkened building, the escort stepped away and rose to his full height. Squaring his shoulders and stretching his spine, Bishop was looking at a man probably in his mid-30s. The guy was clearly in good physical condition, far from feeble.

"Sorry to do that to you, but you never know how someone is

46

going to react. There are eyes and ears all over this town, and it wouldn't go well if the mayor and his boys were to catch me."

Bishop, assuming he was being robbed for his kit and gear, didn't know what to say. He managed to come up with a single word. "So?"

"So, I need to talk to you. I figure you're the head honcho of that outfit that rolled into town this morning. I've seen you meet twice with Winfrey and his gang of cutthroats, and thought you might want to know the truth about Brighton, Texas."

Again, articulation escaped the Texan. "So, talk."

"Not here," came the response. "Besides, you wouldn't believe what I've got to tell you anyway. I need to show you… to prove our version of the events, and to do that, I'm going to ask you to come with me voluntarily."

Fighting back a rising fury and cursing his own stupidity for getting bushwhacked, Bishop wasn't in a verbose or particularly diplomatic mood. "Go with you *where*?"

"I don't want to say, just in case we're captured en route," replied the stranger. "I will guarantee you won't be harmed. I also promise you'll be free to return to your people in a few hours."

Bishop tilted his head, obviously pondering the request. "What if I say no?"

The hostage-taker smiled and then lowered Bishop's pistol. Flipping the weapon around and then offering it grip-first to his captive, he responded, "Then you're free to go."

Still thinking it through, Bishop was curious. "Is there really a .308 cartridge in your cane?"

The stranger smiled, holding up the crutch and working a small mechanism in the handle. Sure enough, a shiny brass cartridge fell into the man's hand.

"Damn," Bishop whispered. "I almost decided to test you on that. I thought you were a common street mugger trying to bluff."

"That, my friend, would have been a mistake on your part," the guy responded with a grin. "If the sheriff's men had caught us

47

fighting in the street, I would probably be dead by now. You would most likely be joining me in hell shortly afterwards. Lew's boys don't believe in leaving any witnesses."

So far, the village of Brighton had offered nothing but anomalies, inconsistencies and glitches. Maybe the little trip his abductor proposed was really the path to enlightenment. "Okay, my curiosity is getting the better of me, overwhelming my commonsense," Bishop said. "I'll go."

To Bishop's surprise, the stranger pointed at Bishop's rifle and then tossed over the magazine he'd removed just a few minutes before. "I'd reload that weapon if I were you. You never know when someone might try to rob us... or worse."

As the two men exited the building, the stranger resumed his off-Broadway role, bending slightly at the waist and hobbling along. Bishop, trying to play his part, hooked arms and pretended to be assisting the old gentlemen.

As the two passed by the occasional pedestrian, Bishop received more than the normal number of smiles and nods, the citizens of Brighton obviously pleased to see the young helping the old.

"I wonder if I'll get a merit badge for helping you cross the street." Bishop mumbled.

"If you can't eat it or shoot it, then who gives a shit?" came the hushed reply.

Before long, they were passing through the outskirts of town, open spaces becoming more common than homes or businesses. Another mile, and Bishop's new friend shook off his helper and announced, "You're cute as hell, but I'm spoken for."

Bishop snorted at the one-liner and retorted with one of his own. "So can you tell me where we are going yet, or is my blind date still a mystery?"

"We're getting close. We have to cut off the road before that next hill. There's a Brighton roadblock immediately over the rise, and I'd prefer to avoid it if at all possible."

The two men angled off into the woods, eating up the distance and circumventing the sentries on the road. After passing by the danger point, Bishop's guide led them along the edge of what had once been a large field of some now unidentifiable crop. The hike was easier, and they trekked the distance quickly.

"Our first stop is right up here... about another half mile."

The two men approached a farmhouse from the rear, the back porch obscured by waist-high weeds. As they closed in on the abode, Bishop detected several windows were broken out, bullet holes splintering the surrounding frames. The back door was completely missing, black stains of smoke and debris everywhere.

"Looks like there was a firefight," Bishop noted. "Quite a serious one at that."

"This was the Colbert's farm," the actor stated coldly. "Burke Colbert's great-grandfather traveled to Texas from Germany in the 1800s and settled this land."

Bishop strode up the private road, his gaze taking in every detail of the now-empty structure. Someone had poured hundreds of rounds into the home. Not only was there a significant number of entry wounds in the old house's frame, the driveway and sidewalk were littered with empty shell casings.

"The Colbert family held out for four hours. Eventually, our illustrious sheriff and his men got tired of wasting ammunition and upped their game with gasoline firebombs. That was the end of it."

"Why?" Bishop questioned, trying to keep his voice and thoughts neutral. Experience had taught him that there were always two sides to every story. "What did the Colbert family do? What crimes were they accused of?"

The stranger shook his head slowly, "I know you don't have any reason to believe a word I say. That's why I brought you out here. I'll answer your questions in a bit, but first, I want you to walk around and look at the front of the house."

Bishop obliged, continuing to the front of the farmhouse. When he turned the corner, he inhaled sharply at the scene that confronted him.

There, nailed to the wall as if they had been crucified on their veranda, hung four skeletons.

Birds, insects, and the elements had picked the bones clean, only a few shreds of clothing covering the deceased. Bishop turned to his tour guide, his expression a mixture of disgust and sadness. "Why?"

The stranger didn't answer immediately. He ambled closer to the first skeleton and pointed to the scrap of faded, red and white checked cloth dangling from the pelvic bone. "This was Martha Colbert. She was my Sunday School teacher back when I was a kid. This fabric is from her kitchen apron. She always wore one around the house."

He took another few steps and pointed to the next corpse. "This was Mike Colbert. We graduated from Brighton High School together. He was the captain of the football team and one of my best friends."

Motioning Bishop closer, his guide reached up and lifted a belt buckle dangling from the body's waist. It read, "Texas Division II State Champions – Brighton Tigers."

The stranger then lifted his own shirt, an identical award adorning his belt. "We all got one," were his only words.

Bishop started to turn away, but his host spoke again. "Before we go, I want you to see one more thing. Look at the skulls. Look at the wounds. Do you know what that means?"

After a moment of studying each of the four victims, Bishop shook his head in agreement. "Yes, I know what that means. They were executed. Shot in the back of the head. I've seen it before… too often, as a matter of fact."

"So you asked me what crimes the Colbert family was accused of. A fair question. But does it matter? Even if they had been axe murders on a rampage, did they deserve to be executed and then have their cadavers crucified to a wall?"

"No," Bishop responded. "Nobody deserves that. But why? Why would a bunch of deputies and the sheriff do this? What possible motivation could they have for such cruelty?"

"I've got one more thing to show you, and then I'll answer all of your questions. We have to trudge a few more miles, but I promise… if you want to know the truth, it is worth the effort."

Bishop stared hard at the man next to him. "I want to know the truth, but your little mystery game is getting old, my friend. I don't even know your name."

"My name is Evan Condor."

"Of Condor Pipe and Valve?"

"Yes, my father started that business. I was the plant manager before everything went to hell. Dad was grooming me to eventually take over so he could retire."

"That plant is the main reason why we came to Brighton."

"I know. We have our spies, Bishop. I know what Lew and those other criminals told you. That's why I sought you out. I'm hoping you and those soldiers can set things straight… bring justice to my hometown."

"Did you ever consider just striking up a conversation with me? Why all of this cloak and dagger shit?"

"Because I didn't want to get you and your men killed. If Lew and his thugs even get a hint that you know what's been going on around here, they'll attack, and even more people will die. Besides, I wanted to judge you for myself. I had to make sure. There is something else I need to show you. Will you come with me?"

Bishop agreed, his mind trying desperately to process the influx of information.

The duo continued along the road, the blacktop surface making travel easy. After a few minutes, Bishop had to ask. "Aren't you worried about someone coming down the road and catching us out in the open?"

"Naw," came the immediate response. "You're in my territory now. We're as safe here as in a lover's arms."

"You don't know my wife," Bishop chuckled.

"By the way," Evan said, "I believe the plant can be restarted, regardless of what Lew and the others told you. It's been a few months since I was there, but with electricity, some repairs, and a decent workforce, we could probably begin manufacturing most of our inventory."

"Now that's the best news I've had all day," Bishop replied.

They soon came to a lane, twin tracks of worn dirt leading into a thickly wooded area. After they had traveled a few hundred yards off the pavement, Evan looked to his left and waved. Bishop was startled to see an arm appear from behind a strand of short bushes. A sentry, and a well-hidden one at that.

The path meandered with a myriad of twists and turns, finally delivering the men to a massive, but somewhat dilapidated barn. Part of the roof had caved in, the rest of the shelter looking like it would soon follow. Faded white and red paint covered much of the now-scrap lumber, rotted ends of broken timbers protruding here and there.

"Welcome to my headquarters," Evan announced.

Bishop peered around, wondering what he had missed. There were the remains of a few other outbuildings, not enough of the smaller structures left to identify their original intent.

In the distance he spotted the exposed foundation of what he guessed had been the farmhouse. Other than that, he couldn't see anything that even remotely resembled an HQ.

"No offense, but I'm not impressed," Bishop said.

"Good," Evan replied, and then motioned for Bishop to follow. "Come on, I will show you where we live."

The two men strolled to the rear of the barn, circumventing a pile of old boards that had once been a wall. Evan stopped and pointed at the ground.

The entrance looked like it belonged to a common root cellar.

Two doors, mounted on a concrete frame, were positioned just above ground level. Bishop was still skeptical. He'd visited his fair share of such underground storage units, and they were typically inhospitable - quite small and cramped.

Evan rapped three times on the steel door and then pulled it open. A bright light flooded up from below. "After you," he offered.

Bishop moved to the top step and instantly sensed that this wasn't the average cellar. He stepped down, entering a huge underground room, almost as large as the barn above. There were overhead lights, ventilation fans, and a stereo playing soft country and western music.

There were also a couple of dozen people scattered around the facility. Cots, chairs, boxes of clothing and an eclectic collection of mismatched furniture dotted the room.

"This was built during Prohibition," Evan explained. "The man who owned this farm was a terrible businessman, always on the verge of losing his land to the bank. It was rumored he had a drinking problem as well. The Great Depression and a lack of booze evidently doubled the gentlemen's problems, so he turned to a life of crime. According to some local rumors, this was the largest moonshine operation south of the Mason/Dixon. The revenue agents never found it."

"Wow," Bishop said, still amazed by the size of the complex.

"Later, in the 1950s, a new owner converted it into a bomb shelter. My grandpa was one of the contractors that worked on revamping the place. It supposedly once held enough food and water for the man's extended family to survive a nuclear attack."

"That was all the rage back then," Bishop commented, "I remember seeing those old films, featuring duck and cover. The government even passed out pamphlets describing how to build a proper shelter."

Evan indicated Bishop should follow, the two men passing through one of the many doors leading from the great room. "There are over a dozen storage areas and sleeping quarters. We've even got four functioning bathrooms. It took us a bit of work, but we managed to get the well working again. The lighting system is all DC powered. We scavenged some solar panels and hooked them up some months ago. Burning candles didn't work out so well."

The passage led to a small, cinderblock-lined room. With just enough space for a single cot and a chair, Evan began removing his disguise. While he changed, he began spinning the sordid story of Brighton, Texas.

"For the first week after the terrorist attacks, the electricity came and went several times a day. It was really nothing more than an annoyance at first, pissing folks off because they couldn't watch the news. Brighton was practically a ghost town in those early days, every mother's son glued to the television, digesting a steady diet of video feed covering the fires raging in Houston, Atlanta, and eventually Washington, DC."

Bishop's host shook his head at the memory, recalling the fear and uncertainty that gripped the nation.

"And then the power went out and didn't come back on. The first day, it wasn't any big deal. By the end of the third day, people were really starting to get concerned. The town's two grocery stores were stripped to their bare shelves. Every gas station ran out of supplies. Some people tried to leave town, most heading off to relatives or friends. The vast majority returned a short time later, full of stories about the grid-locked interstates and bandits preying on stranded motorists."

Bishop sighed, remembering those first days of confusion and fear. "My wife and I were living in Houston at the time," he said. "We had no idea what was going on. Without television or radio, no one knew anything."

Evan's gaze focused on an empty piece of air, his voice monotone as he recalled the painful memories. "Our locals, as well as the refugees started camping out at the supermarkets, sleeping in their vehicles, waiting on any delivery truck that might be bringing food. None ever came."

Condor stopped his narration for a moment, pulling on a pair of work boots that seemed a better fit than the loafers he'd worn to town. "After a week, people were getting desperate. The camps moved from the grocery stores to the courthouse. People started demanding the county officials do something... anything to get food into town. It was the local county agent who came up with a solution. He went to the farms and ranches surrounding Brighton and spread the word that the folks in town were starving. Most of the ranchers responded, many loading up grain, pigs, cattle and chickens and hauling them to town. A farmer's market was set up at the high school, and it worked pretty well for a month or two."

"What happened?" Bishop asked, considering the similarities with Meraton and its fledgling marketplace.

"The growers wanted fuel, medicine and other valuable items in exchange for their food. After a while, all the tanks had been siphoned, the local pharmacies cleaned out. Guns, ammunition, clothing and other perishable items were also traded, but gasoline and diesel were the primary currency."

Bishop could see what was coming. "And the town wasn't producing any more of those items. The people were spending, but never replenishing their coffers."

"That was exactly what was happening. A sizeable constituency of people complained to the county and city officials. On one hand, the farmers said they couldn't continue to grow and transport food without fuel. On the other side, the people were starving and didn't believe their rural neighbors should be so greedy. In a matter of weeks, there was a serious divide, Mayor Lewis and his crew leading the townsfolk, the elected county officials siding with the farmers."

Bishop thought back to Red's early statement about a war. It all made sense now. "So when did the shooting start?" he asked, the question surprising his host.

"I don't know really. Dad and I were trying to keep people from looting the plant. Some asshole must have spread a rumor that we had huge tanks of gasoline at the facility. We had people poking and prying around, many of them beyond caring if they damaged private property. When we heard the shooting start that morning, Dad left to try to go make peace. He never came back."

As the memory grew in the son's mind, Bishop watched Evan's expression change from stoic to melancholy... eventually brewing into a seething fury.

"He was a patriot. A leader in the community. I begged him not to go, but he kept pacing back and forth listening to the gunfire. He kept telling me that it wasn't right for Americans to be killing Americans. Eventually, I couldn't hold him back any longer, and he left."

"I'm sorry," Bishop said. "Did you ever find out what happened to him?"

"No. Never did. What I do know is that the rural side lost. The battle raged for almost an entire day. I sat at the plant, listening to the gunshots, worrying about dad. When it finally stopped, a passerby told me that Lew and the city-men had won the day, and that all of the county officials were dead. I didn't find out my father had been killed until that evening when one of our workers brought me his body draped over a horse."

Bishop remembered the bullet holes at the courthouse, and it all made sense. Before he could finish his train of thought, Evan's voice again filled the tiny room.

"Their next move was actually conceived by Winfrey, the banker. I guess the town's citizens were full of victory, but still without food. Someone told me that after the celebration began to wear down, Lew and the other leaders were worried that the people were going to turn on them. Winfrey came up with the solution."

Bishop frowned, not quite understanding what Evan was implying.

"Oh, it was all wrapped up in a pretty, legal package. Most of the farms had mortgages and loans at the bank. Winfrey, sensing the entire town was about to slide into the abyss of anarchy, claimed that the farmers hadn't been making their payments. He whipped up the emotions of the populace, his rhetoric turning their rural neighbors and friends into the villains – redirecting their anger in any direction but toward Winfrey and his friend the mayor. It worked. Two nights later, the first vigilantes attacked the Colbert farm, demanding they surrender all of their livestock and grain in order to pay their debt. The Colberts, of course, didn't agree. You saw the results."

"Now I understand," Bishop whispered. "Now it all makes sense."

But Evan wasn't finished. "For months, they picked off individual farms and ranches. They would haul the looted livestock, feed... even bags of dog food back to town. Everyone would eat until it ran out, and then they would all gang up and go knock off another farm."

"Why didn't the farmers fight back?"

"At first it was only the operations that owed Winfrey money that suffered attacks. The others tried to reason with Lew and his crew. A few of them brought supplies into town and just donated them... giving away truckloads of food to placate their neighbors. Their charity slowed the "Repos" down, but it was never enough food."

"Repos? I've heard that word used somewhere before."

Evan smiled at his use of the slang. "Repossessions. That's what we took to calling them. The people in town weren't evil or criminal – they were just desperate. They needed some prodding. When Lew or the banker saw supplies were getting low and frustrations were high, they would hold a meeting on the square and stir up a bunch of the men into a frenzy. The sheriff would pitch in, using the bank's debt as justification for a 'repo posse.' They made it all sound legal and moral. It was several months before the farmers started banding together and fighting back."

Evan finished buttoning his shirt, now fully transformed from elderly citizen to young man. He sat down on the cot and pointed back toward the main room. "I'm going to crash on this cot for a while. I've not slept in two days. I brought you here so you could interview those people out there. They are the farmers and ranchers who escaped the raids. Altogether, there are about 200 of us. We've fought Winfrey and his henchmen to a draw, but it won't last. We're outnumbered and outgunned. I'm hoping those soldiers and you can make all this right. Wander around, talk to those people out there, and satisfy yourself that I'm telling you the truth. When you're done, find a big guy named Frank. He'll escort you back to town."

Bishop nodded, and the two men shook hands. "One last question before I go. What are the town's people eating - now that you have stopped the Repos?"

Evan snorted and stared down at the floor. "Lew has work gangs... some are composed of actual criminals... prisoners from the jail. But quite a few of their 'slaves' are men captured during the raids. The mayor and his lapdog, the sheriff, run a sort of debtor's prison. They use those poor souls to farm the properties that were taken over by the bank – the ones closet to town. They are basically using forced labor under the guise of a homegrown justice system."

The group I saw in the thermal optic when we first arrived, Bishop thought. *Another piece of the puzzle.*

Bishop didn't need a lot more convincing. Evan's story made sense and was supported by observations he'd already noted. It also resolved several unanswered questions that had been so troubling.

After talking to a few of the refugees, the Texan found Frank, and the two men set off for town.

"We need to hurry. It will be dark soon, and they start working the fields just before dusk," the escort explained.

Bishop returned to the courthouse with just enough light left to identify Major Baxter standing on the front steps, talking with the sheriff. "Where the hell have you been?" the officer snapped.

"I helped an old man back to his house," Bishop answered honestly. "He invited me in for some tea, and time just got away from me."

"Old man?" the sheriff inquired, his tone thick with doubt. "I'm not aware of very many old timers around town. Where does he live?"

"I'm not sure," Bishop answered. "I got a little lost on the way back. His house was out in the countryside, just beyond the edge of town."

"We've had people out looking for you," Baxter stated. "Don't wander off again."

"Yes, sir," Bishop responded, acting as if he were worthy of the scolding. "I'm exhausted, gentlemen. If you'll excuse me, I'm going to hit the rack before it's my turn at sentry duty."

Bishop started to pass between the two men when the sheriff reached out and grabbed him by the arm. "I wasn't finished with my questions," the lawman hissed.

After learning the truth about Brighton, Bishop was already disgusted just by being in proximity to the man. Something about the hand squeezing his arm ignited a firestorm of wrath inside the Texan. In a blur of motion, he found the lawman's thumb, bending it backwards until the grip on his bicep was released. A simple twist, side step and push sent the sheriff to his knees, his arm helplessly pinned high against his back.

Bishop's pistol was pressing hard against the man's ear. "Don't you ever lay a fucking hand on me again, you piece of shit. I know your kind. Say your prayers, little law-bitch."

A slight whimper sounded from the sheriff's throat when Bishop cocked the hammer of his pistol.

Baxter was momentarily stunned by the speed and violence of the action. "Bishop. Bishop, stop! What are you doing?"

But the Texan's only response was to pull his victim's arm higher, a loud pop signaling he'd dislocated the sheriff's shoulder. The man howled in pain, the outburst followed by a low whine of misery.

"Are you finished praying yet? I don't hear you asking for forgiveness, *Sheriff.*"

"Bishop!" Baxter shouted again. "Stop this! Are you fucking crazy?"

Baxter bent lower, getting his face in close to Bishop's, in hopes of driving his message through. What he saw in the Texan's eyes made the soldier recoil.

The major would never forget those coal-black pools, the dark stare of an emotionless predator about to terminate his prey. There wasn't rage... or anger... or any sentiment at all. It was as if Bishop was a machine, a cold, mechanical killing device without humanity or conscience. In all the wars and campaigns of his military career, he'd never seen anything like it.

"Bishop. Stop. Please," Baxter tried again, his voice now a hushed plea.

Something changed in Bishop's posture. Like someone snapping out of a trance, his head briefly tilted, and then he exhaled audibly.

Bishop lessened the pressure on the lawman's limb, sending a signal that he was about to free his captive. Baxter recognized movement, realizing too late that the sheriff was reaching for his sidearm.

Before Baxter could say anything, the Texan's boot whizzed through the air, a vicious kick landing square against the sobbing lawman's head. The blow sent the crippled man reeling down the courthouse steps where he landed with a thud. His pistol bounced a bit further, clambering another few feet on the concrete.

Baxter stood with his mouth open, temporarily flabbergasted. Before he could recover, Bishop made eye contact with two soldiers who had been observing the encounter. "Get him over to the medic," the Texan ordered. "And then I want him arrested and detained. If anyone from Brighton comes around looking for him, we have no idea of his whereabouts. Do you understand?"

"Yes, sir," both of them snapped as they hustled to help the disabled lawman.

Bishop watched as the two privates reached for the sheriff, and then turned to address Baxter. "Major, I need to have a word with you, in private. Right. Fucking. Now."

Baxter started to protest, but then thought better of it. Had the Texan gone insane? Somehow, the major sensed that wasn't the case. Curiosity replaced the fear he'd experienced while looking into the predator's eyes. "This had better be good," he mumbled as he followed Bishop inside.

On a rooftop two blocks away from the courthouse, a stunned deputy jerked his face away from the binoculars. "Holy shit! Did you just see that?" whispered the observer. "He just kicked the sheriff's ass."

"Yes, I saw it," responded the other, pulling his eyes away from his own optic. "You'd better hightail it downstairs and let the mayor know. Something's going on."

"You're right. Do you think he's still at City Hall?"

"Now how the fuck would I know where he is? Go find him."

Standing quickly, the recently deputized young man made for the service hatch on the roof. Five minutes later, he was dashing toward City Hall.

Bursting into the reception area, he discovered Amy Sue tidying her desk, preparing to head home. "Where's Lew?" the excited man barked. "One of the newcomers just kicked the sheriff's ass right on the courthouse steps. I think they're holding him prisoner."

Lew was also ending his day. Recognizing the frantic deputy at his office threshold, the mayor was immediately concerned. "Slow down, damn it. Just slow down, and tell me exactly what you saw."

Within minutes, the deputy blurted out what he had witnessed from the rooftop. The mayor was clearly disturbed about the development. With a sigh of apprehension, he instructed, "Bring Mr. Winfrey to join me here immediately. On the way back, share with him what you observed."

As soon as the deputy had rushed out, Lew approached Amy Sue's desk. "Send out the word. Gather the men," he ordered. "Gather them all. I'm afraid we're going to have a long night."

It took Bishop 45 minutes to recount his journey and what he'd learned. When he had finished, Major Baxter shook his head in disbelief. "I knew something was wrong here. It just felt off. Are you 100% certain?"

"Yes," Bishop responded. "I'm as sure about this as I can be of anything in this crazy world. What I didn't see with my own eyes, I had multiple witness accounts. We're dealing with a bunch of evil sons-ah-bitches. A group of murdering, out of control bastards."

"Well, at least I understand why you lost your temper with the sheriff. What you just told me about the inhumane treatment of these ranchers is about the best justification I've ever heard."

Bishop frowned, "I didn't lose my temper, Major. I wasn't mad at all. The sheriff's still breathing isn't he?"

For a moment, Baxter wondered if all of the stories he'd heard about the Texan were actually true. After the mini-drama he'd just watched, the tall tales were suddenly more believable. Clearing those thoughts from his head, he looked up and asked, "What's the next move?"

"Evan thought the plant could produce product with a few weeks of work, some spare parts, and electricity. Depending on how many of his key employees were still alive, he thought it was doable."

"And the mayor and his crew?"

Bishop rubbed his chin, the dilemma obvious. "We're not invaders, Major. On one hand, we're nothing to these people. We have no authority or right to stick our noses in. It would be easy enough to arrest the mayor and his lackeys... take them out of circulation. But then what? What if the people side with their leadership? We can't kill the entire town."

"And on the other hand?"

Bishop chose his words carefully, "On the other hand, I feel a moral authority. There's right and wrong. We're Americans, and that sets a precedent for freedom and liberty. What Lew and the banker are doing is wrong."

Baxter processed those words for a few moments before responding. "Seems straightforward enough. We have to take down the local leadership. Like you said, it's doable."

Bishop stood and began pacing the room, something still troubling the Texan. "Before we go acting all high and mighty, are we sure? You don't know how many times I've thought things were black and white, only to find several shades of grey in reality. Surviving in a post-apocalyptic world seems to blur the distinction between good and evil even more."

"I don't understand. It all seems pretty cut and dried to me. I just asked if you were sure, and you said 'Yes.' Are you changing your mind?"

Bishop stopped and grinned at his poor choice of words. "Sorry to confuse you, sir. I'm absolutely sure of what Lew and his henchmen have done. What I'm not so certain about is the true depth of the mayor's crimes. He did feed his people. You could argue that he utilized the available resources to provide greatest benefit to the most needy. Is that really so bad? Would you or I have done anything differently?"

"So what are you saying, Bishop?"

"It would be easy for me and a couple of your best shooters to walk over to City Hall, spray down the security and then give Lew and his boys an injection of high velocity lead. A simple enough solution to the problem. But that would make us judge, jury, and executioner. Would we really be any better than the men we are eliminating? From what I've heard and seen, we would be acting in the exact same manner, killing off the few so we can help the many. It just doesn't sit right with me."

Baxter was impressed. He'd originally thought Bishop nothing more than a hyped-up country boy. The man's depth was raising the major's level of respect.

"I've got it!" Bishop declared. "Instead of killing them outright, we'll arrest them and hold a trial. A jury of their peers. We'll even let them have representation like the constitution allows."

The major brightened at the concept, relief replacing the ill feelings he was having over the thoughts of ordering his men to kill non-combatant civilians. He then had an even better idea. "A military tribunal! We can have officers from the Judge Advocate General's office come up from Hood. They will get a fair shake, and *then* we'll march them all in front of a firing squad."

Bishop liked the idea. "We've got a plan then, Major. Let's start working out the details of tomorrow morning's take down."

But before Baxter could react, the sergeant came busting through the door. "Major! You'd better get out here. Something's going on. Something big."

"I've got movement," one of the Army sentries reported, his voice barely carrying over the rush of scrambling men. Peering again through his night vision, the specialist focused on the gable of a nearby building. "I've got two men with rifles taking up a position on top."

"I've got the same over here," shouted another. "No! Make that several men on the rooftops. They're all over the place!"

Bishop looked at Baxter and said, "Welcome to the Alamo, Major. I think Lew and Mr. Winfrey don't appreciate our detaining their friend the sheriff."

"Alamo, my ass," the officer spat. "I've got enough firepower to hold this building *and* go out there and lay waste."

Bishop grunted, nodding toward the north. "Don't be so sure, Major. I think we've got a lot of company coming."

Baxter followed Bishop's gaze to the spot where a yellow and red light illuminated the darkened street. A few moments later, several hundred people came rolling around the corner, dozens of torches filling the night with a menacing glow surrounded by black swirls of smoke.

Still, the officer wasn't impressed. Keying his radio's microphone, he directed, "Bring the Humvee with the 50 caliber up to the front steps of the courthouse. Do not... I repeat... do not fire on any civilians unless I specifically order it."

Bishop nodded his agreement with the tactic. One of their military vehicles was equipped with an M2 machine gun mounted in a roof turret. The belt-fed weapon was capable of enormous firepower, able to spray deadly streams of lead at 600 rounds per minute.

They heard the Humvee's motor start as the crowd drew closer. Bishop moved to a corner, watching the soldiers execute the major's order. He inhaled sharply as a flickering light arched through the air, the projectile landing on the Humvee's hood and exploding in a ball of red flame. Another Molotov cocktail soon followed, and then a third.

The men in the Humvee would have been fine if they had just driven through the flames. From inside the military transport, the two young soldiers were overwhelmed by the wall of fire surrounding their ride. The driver, an inexperienced private, panicked and slammed on the brakes. Thinking he was going to be baked alive, the terror-stricken young man opened the armored door and tried to climb out.

Rivulets of burning gasoline leaked in via the open door, the heat and smoke adding an additional element of bedlam to the interior. Both the driver and passenger tried to escape, their clothing catching fire in the surrounding pools of burning fuel. They were completely engulfed before they made it five steps away from the now-doomed vehicle.

Bishop, outraged at the attack, raised his rifle and snap-fired several shots at the window where the gas bombs had been launched.

Twinkles of light began flashing from every rooftop surrounding the courthouse. Bishop dove prone as dozens of bullets cracked over his head, solid thuds and thwacks wounding the limestone façade behind him. Rolling to his right, he fired again at a vague outline of a rooftop shooter.

Without thought, he rolled left just as the ground erupted in geysers of dirt and grass.

Scrambling for the cover of the building, Bishop zigzagged as dozens of rounds chased him across the front of the courthouse steps. Stinging limestone shrapnel whizzed through the air, biting his skin and pelting his body. He dove the last few feet, hitting the marble floor hard and tumbling onto the landing.

An orchestra of return fire thundered through the courthouse halls. Soldiers and the men from West Texas responded to the attack with a deadly volley of their own. Shouts, orders, and battle cries bounced off the walls, Major Baxter's orders booming over the din, directing his men get their asses into the fight.

After catching his breath, Bishop found an open spot near the major. "The Humvee with the Ma Duce (M2) has been destroyed, sir. Both men inside are dead."

"Shit! Our radio was in that vehicle. We don't have any way to call for help." Baxter said. "Now what am I supposed to do with that mob?"

Bishop followed the officer's gaze toward the approaching throng of civilians. There were at least three hundred of them, their surreal, collective anger illuminated by the flaming torches brandished high in the air. Bishop raised his rifle to study the crowd, quickly identifying at least two women at the front.

"Damn... there are families in that group," he informed the major. "I hate this shit."

Ducking as a bullet snapped through the open window, Baxter looked helpless. "What the hell do I do with this? Order my men to fire on civilians?"

Bishop shook his head, even more disgusted with the local leadership than he had been before. "Order your men to fire above their heads, sir. See if that disperses them."

Baxter took the suggestion, turning to order the nearby soldiers to carefully fire over the advancing mass.

Again, a volley of fire roared from the courthouse, dozens of rounds flying a few feet above the horde. The oncoming wall of people hesitated for a moment, but then continued in its resolve to overrun the building.

"Shit," Bishop said. "Fire at their feet, sir. A few rounds may bounce up and hit some legs, but that beats the alternative."

The major issued the order, a barrage of lead punishing the earth just in front of the approaching throng. Bishop spied a couple of people go down, and again the front of the crowd paused. The advance only halted for a minute, however, the throng ignoring the obvious warnings and continuing to march forward.

The Texan did not want to shoot civilians. He already suffered enough nightmares for any two men, and firing on misguided people wasn't in his playbook. He was beginning to understand why the farmers had lost the first battle that had taken place on this very spot.

The ammunition stored in the burning Humvee picked that moment to start cooking off, a booming chorus of pops and bangs causing the oncoming wall of humanity to hesitate. When the stricken vehicle's fuel tank exploded in a ball of fire, the irate citizens of Brighton actually backed away.

Bishop heard an unusual sound, for a moment thinking Baxter had his radio turned up so loud he was hearing the officer's earpiece. But that wasn't where the mechanical-sounding voice was coming from. Using his rifle optic, he quickly scanned the mob and identified the source. A young man wielding a bullhorn was cajoling the horde to storm the courthouse.

The Texan knew that most riots were sparked and fueled by a few key individuals. His training at HBR had covered the topic of agitators and the fact that they were almost always a critical ingredient in any uprising. Regardless of the initial cause or purpose, disturbances needed the occasional push in order to gather momentum or else they just seemed to fizzle out. Bishop had just spotted one of the motivators.

He centered the holographic red dot on the bullhorn and squeezed the trigger. The man operating the amplification device jerked his head away, an expression of shock and pain on his face. After briefly examining his damaged tool, he again raised it to his lips and began egging the crowd to storm the building and expel the intruders.

I guess that dumbshit didn't get the message, Bishop thought, adjusting his aim a little closer to the man's face and pulling the trigger again. He never saw where the round connected - a storm of bullets slapping the window frame and forcing the Texan to pull back. But the mechanically enhanced voice was silent.

"Give them another volley high and low," Bishop yelled to Baxter. "I just took out one of the ring leaders."

Again the soldiers opened up, grass and dirt flying into the air and pushing the now-leaderless mob back.

This time Baxter let it go for almost twenty seconds before calling a cease-fire.

All eyes in the courthouse were fixated on the milling multitude, but they didn't reform. Instead of advancing, Bishop spotted people pointing and talking, but no one moved in their direction.

"They've stopped the crowd," Red observed. "I'm not sure how, but they did."

"No matter," replied Lew. "Let's go ahead with the next phase."

"I'll see you in a bit," the nervous man mumbled as he turned toward the stairs leading down to a basement beneath City Hall.

Taking the narrow descent two steps at a time, he reached the concrete floor quickly. Reminding himself to maintain an air of confidence and authority, he eyed the 60 men lined up against the walls and waiting for their orders, taking a moment so his voice wouldn't squeak.

"For those of you who weren't with us the last time we had to retake the courthouse, the plan is very simple," Red called out.

"There is an emergency tunnel connecting this basement with the old boiler room in the target building's lower floor. It is narrow, low, and damp, but we know it is clear. I want each of you to keep your weapon unloaded while we're passing through. I'll be in front with a flashlight. When you get to the stairway leading up to our target, load your weapon then, and not before. Is that clear?"

Sixty anxious faces nodded their understanding.

"They won't be expecting us - surprise will be on our side. I'll be the first through. We need to get as many of our people out of the tunnel as quickly as possible. The last time, we learned that lesson the hard way. So the first few of you who exit, don't start shooting unless it's unconditionally necessary. When you hit the top of the stairs over there, just keep going. Don't hesitate; don't pause. The more of us that can get out of the opening and into the fight, the faster this will end. Do you understand?"

Several voices sounded off, all of them making it clear they understood.

"The snipers we have posted around the courthouse will begin shooting in five minutes. They should keep everyone's attention focused outside the building. We'll hit them from behind, and then we can all go home to our families. Any questions?" Red asked, his eyes searching every face.

There were none.

"Okay, follow me."

And with that, he purposely strolled to a rusty metal door set in the basement wall. Turning the handle quickly and hoping no one could see his shaking hand, Red reached in his pocket and pulled out a flashlight.

A whispered prayer formed on his lips as he stepped through the threshold, bending at the waist to accommodate the low ceiling of the tunnel.

Bishop and the major monitored the crowd for a few minutes, both men wanting to make sure the mass outside no longer posed a threat.

"It looks like we did it," Baxter announced, the rare smile forming on his lips.

"Yes, sir, it sure does," Bishop replied. "But, not to rain on the victory parade, I don't think this is over. We still have a bunch of shooters up on those rooftops."

"Surely they have to know they can't push us out of here just by sniping at us. I bet they fade away into the night," the officer replied.

"Maybe," Bishop responded. "But I wouldn't if I were them. I would have them open up and keep our heads down. While we were distracted, I'd hit this building with a full infantry assault. Nothing fancy... no envelopment or diversions... just one big, hardass push to get inside the building."

Baxter threw a doubtful glance at Bishop, opening his mouth to disagree. But the words never left the major's throat.

Dozens of rooftop rifles opened up at the same moment, every shooter surrounding the courthouse pouring round after round into the already tortured windows and doorways.

Over the background of pummeling lead slamming into walls, floors and contents, Bishop managed to get Baxter's attention. "They'll be coming, Major. I can't tell you from where, but I'll bet my left nut they're advancing on us right now."

Keeping his head down, the major seemed uncertain of what to do. "We've got all four sides covered," he finally announced. "We'll reinforce once we figure out where their primary attack is coming from."

"Major, I don't want to tell you your business, but I've got a different idea. Let me take four of my men and head to the center of the building. We'll be a quick reaction force. When you figure out which side they're coming from, I'll take my squad and hit back hard."

Baxter thought about the suggestion, eventually nodding his

head. "Do it. And good luck."

Bishop rose up and proceeded down the line of defenders, tapping the random man on the shoulder and yelling, "You're with me."

After he'd gathered four of the West Texas contingency, he led his squad to the center of the building where they took cover beneath a wide staircase leading to the second floor. Despite being away from the outward facing walls, the stray bullet occasionally found its way, cracking through the air or smacking a nearby surface.

Bishop joined his crew, the group squeezing into the tight space while waiting on the major's command to move out.

"Hey, Bishop," the man furthest back called. "Can we move a couple of the cases out of the way? Jonesy and I are gonna have to get married if he gets any closer back here."

Laughing, Bishop nodded. "Sure, pass them up."

A moment later, the man behind the Texan grunted, hefting a thick wooden crate. Bishop glanced down, noting the military stencils on the side of the container, "US Army M67 HE-FRAG: Count-20."

"Well looky here, boys," Bishop said. "These might come in handy. Our friends brought along some fragmentation grenades. Everybody grab a couple."

"There's a different kind back here, Bishop," someone said. "These are smoke grenades from the look of it."

"Grab a couple of those, too. You never know."

While the explosives were being passed out, Bishop took a moment to check on the major. Chancing a quick dash out from his cover, he spotted the military man still focused on the front side of the building and keeping low.

"I just know they are going to hit us any moment," Bishop whispered to himself, angling for a position where he could observe the commanding officer. "I'll wait here for the major's order. Every second is going to count."

Taking a knee and praying a ricochet didn't come his way, Bishop kept his eye on the officer 40 feet to his front, ready to throw the quick response team into the fray. A cool stream of air touched the back of the Texan's neck, the almost-breeze a pleasant sensation compared to the rest of the muggy, smoke-filled atmosphere.

"I wonder if someone opened a window... or maybe the wind suddenly shifted," Bishop announced to no one. "Damn that feels good."

But it felt too good... too cool. *Now where in the hell is that coming from?* he thought, instinctively turning to see if he could identify the source.

There was no obvious origin. Glancing quickly to ensure there was no change in the major's status, Bishop turned and scurried around the corner, head pivoting right and left to find the source of the breeze.

He followed a corridor, passed a few doors, and then encountered a wall of pleasant, sweet, cool air. It was almost chilly! But where was it coming from?

The gloomy, low-light conditions hampered his search. Eventually, he recognized movement in a darkened doorway, initially believing some of the major's troopers had retreated to this area of the building. He heard a voice, a man directing, "Go! Go! Go! Come on! Get moving!"

Bishop stuck his head through the opening, thinking some of the soldiers were inside. He examined what appeared to be a heavy equipment room, rusted pipes, valves, and tanks littering the area. It took a moment before he realized that there were too many warriors to be the major's men. Another moment passed before he recognized Red, the man he'd taken down at the roadblock.

Now what the hell is he doing here? the Texan's mind scrambled to answer. *How did he get in... inside?* His eyes adjusted to the darkness. He spotted the tunnel, men pouring out of the opening.

Bishop's rifle came to his shoulder in a flash, his finger tightening on the trigger as the tiny red dot of his optic found the lead man's chest.

72

Over and over again, he fired, his weapon hammering a cadence of devastating bullets into the invaders. Center. Pull. Center. Pull.

Bodies were flying, diving, and scampering everywhere, screams and shouts of warning filling the confined space. Curses were lost in the roar of Bishop's carbine, the yelps and howls of the wounded lost in the chaos. As he swept the room, it occurred to Bishop that invaders were still streaming out of the opening. Pivoting on his heel, the narrow doorway appeared behind the red dot of his optic.

His first two rounds struck center mass of a man on the top step, the kinetic energy and shock pushing the already dead man backwards into the line of his fellows, knocking another back into his peers like a string of falling dominoes. For a few moments, no one in the tunnel seemed eager to ascend the stairs.

Repeatedly Bishop fired into the opening, the familiar nudge of the M4 against his shoulder comforting in the confused mayhem of the fight. He worked his aim downward, waist high, spraying right and left.

The men in the tunnel suffered badly. Traveling at over 2800 feet per second, the 68-grain hollow points spit out of the M4's muzzle slashing organs and smashing bone. Even the shots that initially missed human flesh generated havoc, the whistling lead bouncing off the concrete walls and slamming into the men further back in line.

With the tunnel-exit holding the Texan's focus, the survivors of Bishop's initial sweep recognized an opening. One brave soul rose from behind his cover, centering his sights on Bishop's chest. He started pulling on the trigger.

Bishop sensed the movement, desperately commanding his body to get low. Something slammed into the Texan's left side as he hit the floor, the sledgehammer-like blow sending streaks of pain circling his rib cage. He rolled left, snapped three shots, and then rolled again. A shriek of misery told him he'd found the shooter.

From the tunnel came more sounds of suffering mixed with curses of frustration. Bishop imagined the men down there, trying to push the dead and wounded out of their way so they could join the fight… so they could seek revenge.

73

His discovery had taken the intruders by surprise, but they were recovering quickly. Bishop saw the white flashes of muzzle blasts and knew he couldn't stay where he was. He crawled backwards, making for the door, his rifle maintaining a steady, rhythmic bark, covering the retreat.

Once in the hall, Bishop tried to stand. His left side was throbbing, breathing difficult. He was sure he'd taken a round to the chest. Time to get back to his own people and warn them of the breach. Time to get some help.

He kept the tunnel-room to his front, stepping backwards and retracing his original route. The attackers were becoming more aggressive, the occasional pursuing head appearing, always followed by three or four hastily aimed shots flying in Bishop's direction. The volume and rate of the harassing fire was increasing every second.

He knew he wasn't going to contain the incursion by himself. Bishop turned and ran.

Finally reaching the main section of the courthouse, Bishop was waving and racing toward his men. "They're inside! They're inside!" he screamed, "Get help."

Confused by their leader's words, Bishop's squad didn't react at first, hesitant to leave their secure hide. When Bishop slid past them, like a baseball player swiping second base, they were still confused. The hailstorm of bullets chasing the Texan's flying frame made his warning horrifically clear.

The four of them rushed to his side, taking up positions and raising their weapons. They didn't have to wait long for clear targets to appear.

A dozen men stormed the main rotunda, their weapons firing wildly as they spread out through the complex. Stunned at the appearance of so many enemy within the walls, it took the men from West Texas a few nanoseconds to react.

The interior of the courthouse erupted in complete bedlam. Bishop's squad opened fire, rifles blazing into the attackers at pointblank range. Lead, smoke, and thunder filled the air. Men were screaming, warning, ordering, crying, and praying - but no one could hear them.

Some of the invaders surprised the soldiers stationed throughout the courthouse, others falling prey to the military's weapons. It was a rolling, confused, fur ball of combat - enemy and friend on all sides.

Realizing surprise was no longer with them, more and more of Red's people rushed forward to join the fray. Soon it was Bishop's five against 20. Less than a minute later, it was 30, and they kept on coming.

Bishop sensed they were about to be overrun, his mind demanding his body seek cover from the blizzard of death flying all around him. Forcing the panic down, he began shouting for his men to retreat. "Go to the major," he ordered at the top of his lungs. "Move to the front… get to the Army's position!"

He chanced sticking his rifle around the corner, blindly squeezing off a dozen shots to give his men cover as they retreated. Chunks of exploding plaster and wood responded, nipping, stinging masses of debris tearing into his arms and hands.

Pushing aside the pain in his chest, Bishop gathered his strength and rose. He began a rearguard action, walking backwards half bent at the waist, his weapon sweeping the doorway, waiting for a target to show. Through the haze, he spied the outline of a man at the corner, his weapon shoulder high and not more than 10 feet away.

Both men fired at the same moment, a searing, tearing pain ripping through Bishop's thigh as he watched his target's head jerk back from the impact of his own shot. Bishop fired constantly, not letting off the trigger until the attacker fell.

The muscles bearing his weight no longer answering his commands, Bishop's leg buckled beneath him. After landing on his already pounding left side, the Texan managed to scramble prone, firing a few shots in a desperate move to keep the invaders from charging through the doublewide opening.

It took every ounce of willpower he could muster, but he forced his body to move. Every nerve in his body seemed to be howling in protest as he began to push his torso backwards in a clumsy motion that was a half crawl, half scuttle. After the first few movements, he felt something warm and wet beneath him, one

75

hand slipping on the slick marble floor. He grimaced at the red liquid - he was crawling through his own blood.

After what seemed like a hundred-mile trip, he reached the next dividing wall. In the mayhem, he almost shot Baxter, the major and several men approaching from behind. The officer started issuing orders, positioning his men to counter-attack.

For the first time since the mission began, Bishop was actually happy to see the man. "You okay?" the major asked.

"I'm hit, but still functional. There are 30 or more of them forming up in the rotunda. Most have ARs and AKs. They came pouring out of some tunnel. I suspect it leads back to City Hall. Now we know why they let us have this building."

"Let's see if we can slow them down a little," the officer replied.

About then, Baxter noticed the blood all over Bishop's clothing. Without even asking, he turned and yelled, "Medic! To me!"

A young specialist sprinted over, a large bag secured across his chest. "Where are you hit?" the kid asked, his hands starting to feel up and down Bishop's torso.

"My left ribs and the back of my left leg. The leg hurts worse."

"Roll over... let me take a look."

Bishop did as he was told, the movement sending burning hot streaks of agony through his lower body. For a brief moment, he was positive the leg had somehow caught fire, and even more convinced that every rib on his left side was broken.

Examining the wound as best he could, the specialist cut away part of Bishop's pants leg. It took him a moment to realize his patient had taken a load of buckshot from a scattergun.

"You've got four or five pellets in your leg. Judging from the bleeding and the size of the holes, I'd guess it was about a #3 shot. You'll live, but it's gonna hurt like hell when somebody digs those out of there."

After rummaging in his kit, the medic squirted a cool feeling liquid onto the wound and then proceeded to wrap the leg with a large bandage. "I've sprayed a topical antibiotic and painkiller on the area. This bandage is soaked in a fast clotting agent."

"And my ribs?"

"I can't tell if they're broken, but your armor stopped the bullet. You're one lucky guy."

Bishop smirked, "I don't feel so lucky."

Baxter returned just then, the officer breathing hard. "There's good news and bad news. The good news all of our people are accounted for. I've lost five KIA (killed in action), four wounded. We also have three civilian KIA, another three wounded. We hold the west side of the building; they hold the east. The rotunda is no-man's land."

"And what's the bad news?"

"The snipers have stopped shooting."

Bishop's head snapped up, the officer's words making his eyes open wide. "We have to get out of here, Major. Get our men to the Humvees and leave. All of those shooters are on their way here - you can bet on it. There's no way we can hold this building."

The expression on the major's face indicated he had already considered Bishop's prediction. "I agree. That's what I would do if I were them."

Turning to the sergeant, Baxter shouted, "We're pulling out. I want as much security as you can muster around our transports. We're leaving town."

"Yes, sir!"

Bishop struggled to his feet, the effort inviting waves of pain-induced nausea to surge through his gut. "My guys and I will act as the rear guard. We'll keep those boys from the east side off your back while you get our transportation ready."

"Are you sure? You look like shit."

"Thank you, sir," Bishop laughed, and then pulled his thermal imager from his kit. "This should help me see through the smoke and dust. We'll hold as long as we can, but I wouldn't waste any time."

Nodding his understanding, Baxter was off. Bishop could hear him barking orders as he hustled to the west.

Motioning to Jonesy and the other civilians, Bishop shouted, "Any non-driver stay here with me. All drivers head out with the Army people. Get your trucks ready, we're blowing this pop stand."

Several heads nodded their understanding, and then over half of Bishop's crew scurried out. He was left with six rifles, counting himself. They wouldn't be able to hold off a determined assault for long.

"Form up on both sides of the arch leading to the rotunda," the Texan ordered.

A few moments later, they were in position, three men on each side of the doublewide opening. Even though the fight was in a fleeting lull, the thick smoke hanging in the air made it nearly impossible to see the enemy's side.

Bishop flipped on the thermal, and the world changed to a flurry of psychedelic colors and shapes. He adjusted the various settings, finally choosing "white = hot."

With a quick scan, he could identify at least a dozen men on the east side – or at least parts of them. Like his own squad, the men of Brighton were all behind cover, only the occasional arm, shoulder, or pair of eyes peeking around a corner.

Bishop was just fine with that. He could care less if they decided to just stay put. The longer Baxter had to get their retreat organized, the more of them would make it out alive.

Over three minutes passed, the two sides watching each other like two tomcats separated by a screen door. Bishop thought he heard a motor start outside, but couldn't be sure. Once or twice, he heard Baxter's voice booming some order, but couldn't make out the words.

"Come on, Major," Bishop whispered. "We ain't got all night here."

When the gunfire erupted behind him, Bishop jumped. His first thought was that somehow his foe had managed to get around behind him, but then he realized it was the Major's team in front of the courthouse. What started as a few random shots outside turned into a volley before growing stronger still. Less than a minute later, it sounded like the Army men were engaged in a pitched battle.

"Oh, shit," Bishop whispered to himself. "The rooftop shooters are trying to surround us. This isn't good. That means our friends on the east side of the building will probably…"

Jonesy, from the other side of the arch hissed, "Bishop," interrupting the Texan's train of thought. "I've got a bunch of guys moving over here."

Bishop scurried across the opening, barking, "Make a hole… make a hole," as two shots zipped through the air. Replacing Jones at the edge of the arch, he raised his rifle and scanned with the imager.

The Brighton boys were definitely active, a large group of them gathering for a rush. Bishop started to raise his rifle when he felt a tapping on his shoulder. Bishop turned to find a wicked-looking smile on Jonesy's face, one of the fragmentation grenades in his hand. Bishop nodded with a smile of his own.

In a flash, both men armed themselves with the explosives, the pins free and clear. Jonesy counted one… two… three, and they both tossed at the same time.

It seemed like an eternity before the concussion shook the wall at Bishop's back. Taking a deep breath, the Texan peeked around the corner and spotted some men still moving. He began firing.

The men from West Texas made the rotunda a living hell. With a man high and another low on both sides of the arch, the four rifles kept up a steady, deadly rate of fire as their foe tried desperately to cross the open area.

But the fighters from Brighton weren't the only ones suffering. It didn't take the assaulters long to realize they only had to concentrate their fire on the arch's frame. Horrendous volumes of bullets began impacting where Bishop's men were hiding, each round chipping away the wood and plaster that was keeping the West Texans alive. Bishop saw one of his men take a hit in the arm from a bullet that had penetrated the thick wall, another falling to the floor after exposing himself around the corner.

Both sides struggled, both fighting the choking, blinding cloud of gun smoke, powdered plaster, and debris that filled the air. Blood from the dead and dying made the marble floors as slick as ice. In the rare lull, the pleading, desperate cries of the wounded could be heard through ringing ears.

Bishop's magazine ran dry. He rolled out of the way and was quickly replaced by another shooter. After slamming home a fresh box of pills, the Alliance negotiator slapped the bolt release and was ready to rejoin the fray.

He had one frag grenade and two smoke canisters left. *No sense in carrying this thing around*, he thought, and a moment later, another explosion rocked the building. There was a momentary lull, and then it all began again.

We can't hold this position any longer, he realized. The walls that had protected them just a few moments before were crumbling, whittled away by the relentless pounding of hundreds of bullets.

"Fall back! Fall back to the front door," Bishop screamed over the roar of the battle.

Again, Bishop's arm arched in a throwing motion, this time a popping hiss sounded instead of an explosion. Thick, obstructing smoke began to fill the rotunda.

After seeing his men begin to move toward the front door, Bishop began spraying random shots into the dense fog generated by the smoke grenade. He had no idea if he was hitting anything, but thought it might deter the more eager souls on the other side.

Once he was sure all of his men were clear, Bishop turned and ran like the wind to their fallback position, traversing the 40 feet in a limping gallop.

After taking cover beside one of the entrance columns, he chanced a quick glance outside. A sickening sensation filled Bishop's core when it occurred to him that Baxter's men weren't in their trucks, but rather behind them. All of the visible soldiers were shooting across the courthouse lawn, most of them using wheels, engine blocks and any other suitable cover.

The sergeant appeared at Bishop's side, his breathing labored from exertion. "The major's been hit. He's taken a round to the chest, but the doc says he'll make it. There must be a hundred enemy out there, hiding in every nook and cranny. We're surrounded. I don't see any way to get us out of here."

Bishop moved further outside, using the overgrown hedges as concealment. Taking in the perimeter, he thought the scene resembled one of Dante's paintings. Two of the Humvees were burning, as were several of the pickups. Men were prone, some shooting, some withering in agony. Just below, the medics had found a relatively safe nook to establish their triage. At least a dozen wounded were there, surrounding by the litter of emergency aid. Adhesive tape, bandage packaging, and bloody scraps of cloth were scattered everywhere.

"How many men are left fighting, Sergeant?"

"We're down to less than 20, sir," came the report. "Ammo is holding out, but I don't know for how long."

Before Bishop could respond, a wave of weapon fire erupted from behind. The Texan didn't even have to look – the men from the rotunda were pressing forward again. *They are the hammer*, Bishop thought. *They are going to pound us into the anvil.*

Jonesy and his men would slow them down, but couldn't hold forever. *We have to get out, or we are all going to die right here in Brighton, Texas.*

Visions of Terri and Hunter entered Bishop's mind. He then thought about the men that had traveled with him from West Texas. He knew many of their families. Just a few days ago, he'd been shaking hands and hugging spouses, promising to bring the men back alive. Their intent had been noble, and now all this... this carnage.

We weren't conquerors, Bishop contemplated. *We weren't here to impose our will or to take advantage for our own benefit. We came here so we could help millions of others.* This just wasn't right.

"Sir?" the sergeant's voice sounded, cutting through Bishop's fog.

"We've got no choice. We have to bust through, or we'll all die right here. We need a diversion or some sort of cover."

"We'll never make it off this square," the NCO said. "Even if we did get the men into the trucks, they would shred us to bits before we made it a single block."

Bishop thought about making a mad dash on foot, but the wounded ruled out that option. He thought about surrender, but was reasonably confident the mayor had no intent to take any prisoners.

"I don't see any other option," Bishop finally announced. "Order the wounded loaded into the back of the safest trucks. We'll use the smoke grenades to cover their loading, and then it's pedal-to-the-metal until we bust free. Hopefully, some of us will make it through."

"But, sir, I'm not even sure any of the trucks will run. They're pretty shot up."

"There's no choice. Do it."

Just as the sergeant turned to execute Bishop's orders, a new wave of bedlam sounded from the buildings surrounding the courthouse.

Bishop's first instinct was that the Brighton men were moving to close the pinchers of the vise, but the amount of incoming rounds didn't seem to increase.

He scrambled to a nearby Humvee and went prone behind the back wheel. From that vantage, Bishop raised the thermal optic and began searching for an answer. Whatever was happening out there, it was increasing in intensity. More and more reports of rifles and shotguns rolled across the landscape, but the Texan sensed his men weren't the target.

Around a corner, just down the street, three Brighton men rushed toward them, their heads darting back over their shoulders as if they were being chased by the devil himself. Several muzzle flashes appeared, all three of the runners falling to the pavement. "What the hell?" Bishop mumbled, trying to make sense of it all.

And then the pitch of the distant battle increased, an ever-building number of shots echoing through the town square. More men appeared, scurrying away from the courthouse. Shouts filled the air, frightened voices competing with the discharge of so many weapons.

"Sir!" a nearby soldier yelled, "I've got some guy over here waving a white flag."

Bishop scrambled for a better vantage, raising his optic to study the signal. He identified only one man, brandishing a flag and then scooting down the sidewalk to duck into the next doorway. "Hold your fire," Bishop ordered. "Let's see what he's up to."

The flag bearer moved again, now closer, just across the street from the courthouse. "Come on in!" Bishop screamed as loud as he could manage. "Come on... we won't shoot."

Zigzagging across the lawn, Bishop recognized Frank before he reached the perimeter. It all fell into place and made sense – Evan and the famers were joining the fight.

Panting hard from his run, Frank sat on the ground next to Bishop and tried to catch his wind. "We're hitting them from the south," the big man reported. "Evan didn't want your men shooting at us, so he sent me to warn you. He also wanted me to tell you that we're running low on firepower and see if you guys can spare some weapons and ammunition."

Bishop took a moment, visualizing the situation in his head. The Texan didn't hesitate. "Sergeant! Sergeant!"

Pounding footfalls announced the NCO's arrival. "Sir?"

"Take 10 men, the weapons from the wounded, and as much ammo as you can carry. Go with this man. He's with the cavalry, and they're here to save our sorry asses."

Three minutes later, Bishop watched as Frank led a squad of soldiers back to his own forces. Bishop picked another five soldiers and said, "Come back inside with me. We're going to get these guys off our backs. It's time for a little recoil therapy."

The rising sun offended Bishop's eyes, but physical exhaustion discouraged much activity. Adjusting his hat instead, he decided to pull another mouthful of tepid water from the Camelbak tube draped over his shoulder.

The reflection of his own movements drew his eye to a storefront glass window. There he scrutinized the image of a bloody, ragged man sitting with his back against a mailbox. Bishop managed a smirk at the poor fellow's state. Filthy streaks of black and grey covered his face, the dirt-darkened skin competing with the raccoon-like circles under the emotionless eyes.

Every inch of the gent's clothing was covered in mud, dirt... and blood. There were multiple holes and rips in his shirt, one sleeve barely attached by a few dangling threads. *What a pitiful wretch you are*, Bishop whispered to the reflection. *You look like day-old shit warmed over.*

Unable to tolerate his appearance any longer, Bishop decided to study his surroundings instead, curious what the new light of day would reveal. It didn't take long to conclude that Brighton and her people hadn't faired any better than the wretched soul reflected back to him.

The majestic courthouse, once the center and pride of the community, looked like a disaster zone. It had started in there, the fight eventually boiling over into the streets. Still smoldering Humvees and pickup trucks lined the pavement and lawn. Soot-blackened patches of bare earth dotted the once-green grounds. And then there were the bodies.

The dead were scattered everywhere. Empty, hollow faces returned the Texan's gaze. Corpses were lying in grotesque, unnatural positions, their limbs at odd angles, twisted in impossible configurations. There was a man draped over a car's hood, both of his arms nowhere to be seen. Another rested against a nearby light pole, the top half of his torso a good six feet from an orphaned pair of legs.

The worst were those who had burned. One charcoal-black form was reaching for the sky, as if last night's stars would pull him from the flesh-consuming flames. Another appeared as though he had simply laid down to take a nap while being roasted alive.

Shaking his head, Bishop decided to look toward the heavens, hoping the glance would at least provide some salvation from the carnage and destruction that surrounded him.

But that wasn't the case.

He found himself enveloped by the remnants of battle. Columns of smoke rose into the morning blue. Already the vultures were circling, the scavengers preparing for a banquet of human flesh. There was no respite for his tortured soul. There was no vista that offered relief. Bishop decided to simply close his eyes.

It didn't help.

The darkness of his lids was illuminated with mental pictures from his short-term memory. Dying men, screaming wounded, the vibrating dance of a man being riddled with bullets.

He saw Jonesy fall, replaying the moment when a fist-sized hole of gristle and bone appeared in the man's chest. He recalled the look of fear and helplessness as his friend slid down the wall, a smeared trail of blood and tissue left behind. Bishop could still hear his final plea. "Tell my wife and kids I love them."

There were so many dead. So many images. Frank's head nearly severed from his body, a point-blank blast of a shotgun to blame. A man dragging himself across the street, leaving a trail of intestines and gore behind.

Bishop shook his head, self-preservation demanding the parade of memories be halted - or his remaining sanity would disappear forever. *Maybe lucidity isn't all it's cracked up to be*, he pondered. *Maybe going crazy is the way out.*

Unable to bear the thought of sitting and torturing himself any longer, Bishop made the difficult decision to stand. He had to go somewhere – didn't he?

Using his rifle as a brace, he managed to achieve a knee, every cell of his body protesting the move.
And then he was on his feet, staring at his weapon.

"Are you loaded?" he questioned the carbine. He didn't wait for an answer. He didn't care.

The first step was a pure, scathing hell of pain. The next was worse. But he kept on putting one foot in front of the other,

85

something drawing him back to the courthouse.

After half a block, his joints loosened, blood flowing to aching muscles and tendons. He'd never been so tired, so uncaring, so... disinterested.

Had they won? He didn't care. Had any of his men made it out alive? He didn't know and was too exhausted to check.

A sudden bout of introspection forced his legs to stop moving. *Why are you so indifferent? Why so apathetic? Have you finally lost it? Have you finally snapped?*

The questions were troubling, any answer or admission seemingly beyond his mental reach. *Move your legs, Mr. Shell-shocked. Keep moving those boots.*

His eyes were drawn to two men stumbling toward him on the sidewalk. They were armed, their weapons barely supported by weak, lethargic hands. Something in the back of Bishop's exhausted brain told him he should be concerned. There was no way of telling if the approaching men were friend or foe. He didn't care, and it soon became obvious that the strangers didn't either.

They passed each other without making eye contact, the soulless shuffle and passing of empty men, hollow shells who were beyond fighting... beyond loyalty to either side.

A woman appeared, sleepless red eyes darting up and down the street. "My husband," she said in a voice near panic. "Have you seen my husband?"

Bishop couldn't answer. Words were simply outside his grasp.

He continued his trek, his wounded left leg only slightly more painful than its unharmed mate. And then he found himself in front of the courthouse, staring blankly at steps littered with men.

For a moment, Bishop thought they were all dead. Some were soldiers, small parts of their uniforms still recognizable through the mud and gore. Others were strangers, lying here, sitting there, with closed eyes and drooping heads. A few faces belonged to his Alliance neighbors, their bodies strewn among the battle scene. As he watched, a couple of them moved... the scratching, stretching, and yawning sure signs of life.

Bishop shuffled over, the sound of actual, living humans seemingly out of place in the dreamlike aftermath of the longest night he could remember. He forced his legs to move again, following the sound of voices, hushed conversations, and rushed words that seemed to be coming from the other side of the building.

One of the medics was still at it, pressing a canteen of water to the parched lips of an injured man. Two women were there as well, both trying their best to comfort and mend. Bishop spied the slumbering young specialist who had bandaged his leg hours before, an audible snore rising from the lad's exhausted frame.

Bloody clothing, piles of used, red bandages and a carpet of trash dotted the area. One of the women tore off a section of her skirt, using the fabric to triage a man's bleeding arm.

Bishop remembered his blow-out bag, fumbling to unhook the still-full medical kit from his vest.

"Hey," he called to the Army medic as he tossed the pouch. "This might help."

Bishop tried to count the wounded, but gave up after reaching the number thirty. The line of men lying on the ground stretched around the corner, and he just didn't have the energy to further scrutinize the situation.

He stumbled back to the steps and began climbing, the movement hampered by the dried blood and cardboard-like bandages wrapped around his thigh. He passed men he'd never seen before; some of them most likely had been shooting at him a few hours ago. He didn't care, and neither did they. After gingerly negotiating the ascent, he entered the courthouse only to be greeted with more carnage.

Bodies, limbs, and pools of now-purplish blood were everywhere. The musty interior boasted a new odor – a bouquet thick with copper, feces, and urine overwhelming the once stale air.

The Texan ambled forward, stepping over the dead, careful not to slip in the small rivers of blood and piss that crisscrossed the floor. *If I fall, I won't be able to get back up*, he mused. *They'll think I'm one of the dead and bury me. Maybe that wouldn't be so bad.*

His journey took him to the rotunda. The worst of it had happened here.

Bursts of the night's battle flashed through his mind like a bad slideshow. At one point, in this room, it had degraded into hand-to-hand combat. Bishop shuddered, looking down at the fighting knife strapped across his chest. A thick crust of a red, scab-like substance covered the handle and guard. The butt of his rifle was worse, bits of flesh and human hair matted in every crevice of the stock.

He had to stop before entering, but the pause wasn't due to any remorse, respect for the dead, or flood of memories. Bishop hesitated because he couldn't see an open path through the mass of dead men covering the travertine tile.

Here, the bodies were clustered and entangled, evidence of the vicious, close-in fighting. Both sides had wanted to hold this room. After a while, that desire hadn't been tactical or strategic. There wasn't any good reason or special value associated with this tiny hunk of Brighton, Texas real estate - it had simply become personal.

Mankind can be so stupid, Bishop thought as he tentatively stepped into the worst of the killing zone. After watching friends die... after hearing the screams of agony, victory, and death for so long, men lose all sense of self-preservation and continuity of thought. The battle that raged over the rotunda had devolved into nothing more than a competition... a game... a contest of wills worthy of human sacrifice. And sacrifice they had.

Bishop stepped around two bodies on the floor, the dead men locked in an embrace of violence - a dance of death. One man's hand still wrapped around the knife sticking in the chest of his foe. The stab victim's fist clenched a pistol, its muzzle still aimed at the knife wielder's heart. They had died together, both men's faces still painted with their final act of fury and rage. *For what?* Bishop thought.

The West Texan grimaced. He knew the answer to the question. He had been a player in the same contest just a few hours ago. Now, in the light of day, he regretted it, understood the madness of it all. What made it worse was the realization that the punishment for being a participant would last the rest of his life. Maybe longer.

Two women appeared, both straining under the burden of the stretcher they carried. *A moaning teenager being carried to the medics.* They were followed by an elderly man, his bloodstained frock and dangling stethoscope indicating he was a physician. *Plenty of work for you today,* Bishop thought.

The Alliance negotiator finally made it to the clerk's office, only slightly surprised to find the space undisturbed. Closing the door behind him, Bishop leaned his rifle against the wall and began unbuckling his load rig. The Camelbak came off next, soon followed by the body armor. The equipment reeked of his own sweat and stress.

A small, fleeting relief crept in, the lightening of his body's load providing a momentary sense of weightlessness and newfound freedom.

I should clean my weapon, he thought, pulling off his shirt. The material was matted, stiff, and crinkly with old perspiration and… and other things once human. The still-cool air felt good against his skin.

I should go find that doctor and have him look at my leg and ribs, he considered. *But the doc has better things to do right now.*

Bishop eyed the net-hammock, still hanging right where he'd set it up. A moment later, he perched on the homemade bed, suspended by the soft mesh, gently swaying back and forth like a child in his mother's arms.

I should take off my boots, he pondered, but leaned back and closed his eyes instead.

"Bishop? Hey, Bishop? You still with us?"

It took a moment for the Texan to blink away the crust of sleep and grime, the blurry image of a man standing over him finally coming clear. For a moment, he was still leaning against the mailbox, but then it came back quickly.

"Hi Evan. Nice to see you made it."

"Same back at ya. We've been looking all over for you."

The word "we" prompted Bishop to glance over Evan's shoulder, the sergeant's filthy face managing a slight smile. "Damn... it's like a high school reunion," Bishop mumbled.

Like an angel from heaven, the NCO held out what could only be a steaming cup of coffee. "I thought you might appreciate this, sir."

Bishop smiled, "Why, Sergeant, if I wasn't already a married man..."

Bishop swung a leg over the edge of the hammock, the move causing him to inhale sharply from the pain. With the help of his two visitors, he managed to stand.

"You've been hit," Evan observed, noting the blood-soaked leg. "You better get that looked at."

Glancing out the window, Bishop tried to judge how long he'd been sleeping. "What time is it?"

"Zero nine thirty," the sergeant replied.

"I've been out for three hours. Seems like days," Bishop noted, reaching for the cup of joe.

"It's all over now," Evan said. "We won... if you can call it that. Mayor Lewis has disappeared, along with one of the sheriff's patrol cars. We captured that bloodsucker Winfrey, though. So, as things stand right now, we have managed to detain two of the most selfish opportunists – the banker and the sheriff."

It was all too much, too fast for Bishop. He sipped the coffee, the strong, bitter brew helping clear the cobwebs as it slid down his throat.

"How many did we lose?" Bishop finally inquired, looking directly at the sergeant.

The NCO stared down at the floor tile, his hoarse voice filled with remorse. "There are still eleven of my men alive, four critically injured. Twelve of your guys made it through, six needing better care than what we can provide here."

"Twelve? That's it?"

"Yes, sir. The major is still alive, but barely. He needs surgery, as do several of the others. We are trying to salvage enough transportation to move them back to Hood. A couple of the local doctors are doing their best to stabilize the critical ones... trying to get them to a place where they can be moved."

"Very good, Sergeant. It sounds like you've got it all under control."

"We'll give you a few minutes to get your shit together," Evan said, as the two visitors moved toward the door. "I'd get that leg looked at as soon as possible."

Bishop thanked both of them for the wakeup call and, more importantly, the coffee. "Let me find a clean shirt and get my shit in a single, neat bag. I'll be out in a bit."

He spent the next 30 minutes washing his face and body, pouring the bottled water from his pack to accomplish the task. "You don't want to frighten the women and children," he whispered, digging a clean shirt, socks, and pants out of his bag.

He scrubbed as much of the blood and gore off his equipment as possible. Next came his weapon, the carbine receiving a quick field strip and lube.

When he finally emerged, Bishop was far from a new man, but projected a much better appearance than the haggard soul who had entered the clerk's office a few hours before. Frowning at the thought of a trip through the courthouse again, he was surprised to discover he wasn't the only thing in Brighton that had cleaned up a little.

Dozens of volunteers were busy outside his temporary room, removing the dead and searching for additional wounded. While the effort wasn't completely finished, he found the rotunda passable and not nearly as heartbreaking.

He emerged on the front steps, the view of the courthouse lawn completely changed from before. People were moving around, seeming to have some purpose or goal. The only thing that separated the scene from a typical day in any Texas community were the charred piles of burned out vehicles and the rows of bodies laid out on the grass.

Many of the dead had been covered with sheets. Men with clipboards walked among the deceased, taking notes and occasionally bending to search a body for identification. There were scores of dead, with more being delivered to the makeshift morgue every minute.

Someone had set up a couple of tent-like awnings to keep the sun off the wounded. Dozens of the town's citizens hustled here and there, assisting what appeared to be a mixture of doctors, EMTs and other healthcare professionals tending to those who were still alive.

Evan was in the middle of it all, the man's energy and determination enviable. Bishop watched as two more wounded were delivered on stretchers. A table had been set up nearby, three of the surviving soldiers giving blood.

Bishop's eye was drawn to activity near one of the large trees that dotted the courthouse lawn. Two men were there, each lobbing a rope over a low branch. The Texan inhaled sharply when he noticed one end was tied in a hangman's noose.

He didn't feel any pain as he bounded down the steps, determination in his stride as he approached the rope-throwers.

"What are you doing?" Bishop challenged.

One of the men turned, looking Bishop up and down as if he were stupid for asking such a question. "We're getting ready to have a hanging," he replied. "We're going to string up the banker and the sheriff."

"I don't think so," Bishop replied, tightening the grip on his carbine.

The two hangmen exchanged glances, troubled expressions on their faces. "Look mister… we're just following Evan's orders."

Before Bishop could respond, Evan was standing beside the Texan. "Is there a problem, Bishop?"

"Yes. Yes there is. Could I have a word with you? In private."

The two men strolled a few feet away, Evan clearly not

understanding why Bishop was upset.

"Stop this, Evan. Stop it right now. This isn't right," Bishop said.

"I don't understand. You of all people know damn good and well what those two men did. They deserve to die."

Sighing, Bishop shook his head. "Yes, they probably do, but not this way, and not today. There needs to be a trial, an impartial judge and jury. If you hang them before that, justice won't be served. You'll be no better than they are."

"How can you say that? You saw what they did. They tried to kill you and all of the soldiers, too. How can you defend them?"

Bishop put his hand on Evan's shoulder, his face full of compassion. "I'm not defending them. I'm defending the system. Rule of law doesn't mean replacing one leader with another. It means restoring a system that has worked for over 200 years. Have a trial. Give them the same shake you would want if the situation were reversed. Then hang them from the highest tree in town if they are found guilty. I'll even help hoist the rope if it's done in a fair, just way."

Watching Evan's face closely, Bishop knew this was a critical moment for both the town of Brighton and the Alliance. How the man reacted would be an important indicator of his future leadership.

"You're right," Evan finally admitted. "I'm sorry... I just have loathed and hated for so long. I've buried so many friends and neighbors."

Bishop smiled, relieved his new friend still possessed reason and humanity. At that moment, the Texan was sure Evan was going to be a great leader for the people of Brighton.

Without hesitation, Evan moved back to the two hangmen and ordered the ropes be taken down. It was a small, but positive event that helped offset the pain, suffering and misery Bishop knew would dominate so many lives in the coming days.

It was a ragtag lineup if Bishop had ever seen one.

Only four of the military vehicles were salvageable, three of the civilian pickups. He surveyed the remnants of what, only three days before, had once been an impressive display of strength and authority.

No longer. Even the units judged capable of making the trip back to Fort Hood looked more like candidates for a junkyard than any semblance of a military force. Bullet holes, dented fenders, missing window glass and numerous scorch marks were testimony to their experience in Brighton. The men didn't look much better.

The pickups were filled to capacity with wounded, some in critical need of surgery and treatment unavailable locally. Other casualties could ride in the cabs, their arms in slings, heads in bandages and legs supported by crutches.

The sergeant appeared at Bishop's side, "We're ready, sir. We managed to salvage enough gasoline and diesel to make the trip back. One of the pickups is questionable, but I've got a rope along. We may end up towing her into Hood."

Bishop nodded, 'Thank you, sergeant. Get the men loaded up."

The Texan then turned to Evan and extended his hand. "In a few days, the Alliance will send in more people. I have the list you created and will get some experts hustling to gather what you need. It may take us a bit, but we'll be back."

The local nodded and smiled as he shook Bishop's hand. "I'll do what I can to get the plant ready. We'll repair the generator you're leaving. There should be enough fuel to prepare the facility. We'll be ready when your people return."

Bishop started to turn, and then paused, one last thing on his mind. "Evan, you may already know this, but I've got to say it anyway. Your first priority now is to heal... to bridge the divide that still exists here in Brighton. If you are fair, compassionate and equal handed, then it can be done. If you allow vengeance, retribution, or hatred to control this town, you'll never recover. That's the end of my little speech. Good luck."

And with that, Bishop limped down the stairs, making a beeline for the lead unit of the convoy without as much as a glance back.

They rolled out of Brighton in silence, the sergeant behind the wheel, Bishop gazing out of the passenger window.

"Where do you think we went wrong, sir?" the NCO eventually asked. "Don't you believe there was something we could have done better? I feel like there should be some payoff for all of the men we lost... that they shouldn't have paid the ultimate price for nothing. There has to be something salvageable out of this whole mess."

"We should get some of the parts necessary to restart the nuclear power plant. I suppose we should feel some sense of accomplishment over that."

Shaking his head in disagreement, the soldier expanded his thought. "No offense, sir, but I don't remember fighting for the factory in Brighton. I don't recall anyone trying to stop us from reaching it, or saying it was off limits. My point is we went in without any intelligence, local knowledge, or concept of what was happening on the ground. That's why we lost so many good men, sir. That's why those citizens back there will be burying their fathers, husbands, and brothers for weeks."

"I feel exactly the same way. If I have anything to say about it, we'll never make the same mistake again. We were arrogant, full of a righteous belief that we were on the side of good and right. But there isn't any black and white left in our world. Nothing, it seems, is that simple."

They continued, eating up the miles in silence. Bishop shared the sergeant's looming sense of dread, despite being able to report, "Mission accomplished." The price had been too high, the cost, perhaps, unnecessary.

The Texan also faced a serious session with a surgeon. He fully expected the removal of the buckshot still in his leg to take him out of action for quite some time. It would be his third time in convalescence since the world had gone to hell, and he wasn't looking forward to it.

"I'll promise you one thing, Sergeant. I swear upon my father's grave that we are going to change our protocols and tactics. I don't care if I have to personally beat every general and council member over the head with a bat, we are going to learn from this and get better. I owe it to our dead. Never again."

The NCO scanned his passenger's face, considering the words. He'd heard it all before, skepticism and doubt creeping into his thoughts. How many politicians had said the same thing about Vietnam, Iraq, and Afghanistan? How many men had died in those long, bloody wars, only to have the United States pull out and allow the enemy free reign?

But the man beside him wasn't a politician. He was a warrior, a kindred spirit with conflict and death.

Glancing again at Bishop, the sage old NCO reconciled his internal ambivalence, arriving at a conclusion. *I believe this man. He is committed to making a difference. If these Alliance people have more like him, this will all work out.*

The Second Directive – Agriculture

Terri sat in the council chambers, slightly annoyed at the continued droning of the presentation she had endured for the last 45 minutes.

Flipping the handout, she rapidly evaluated the page of graphs indicating the gross food tonnage that would be required once the Alliance had fully integrated the territory formally known as the state of Texas.

"And so you can see our needs will increase exponentially over the next 90 days. The number of individuals under the protection and governance of this body will increase by approximately 9 million, or roughly six times the Alliance's current population," the logistics specialist from Fort Hood stated. "In summary, given known conditions and anticipated harvests, there is no foreseeable set of circumstances that will allow for our projected agricultural output to meet that need."

Thank God, Terri thought. *He's finally finished.*

But the torture wasn't over yet. As soon as the presenter took a seat, General Owens stood and cleared his throat. "We are facing a huge issue," the military commander began. "As I understand it, the success of the Alliance here in West Texas can be attributed to an understanding that keeping the citizenry fed has to be a priority. If that same insight isn't applied to the new territories, civil unrest could erupt, and the entire region could slide back into anarchy."

Pete spoke first, "What are they eating now?"

The question caught the military men off guard, the two senior officers exchanging puzzled looks. "Sir, I'm not quite sure I understand the question."

Nick jumped in, "The councilman wants to know what those 9 million people are eating now... today? What did they eat yesterday? I think it's a fair question, gentlemen."

Terri lifted her handout and added, "Your numbers do not seem to take into account the existing food supply. This presentation makes it appear that we will have 9 million hungry souls magically appear out of thin air, General. While these numbers are staggering, I don't believe we're starting from scratch... from zero. All of those people back in Houston and Dallas have to be eating something today and tomorrow. Where are they getting food right now?"

Owens nodded his understanding. "Right now, the military is drawing down on existing government supplies and emergency military rations, as well as trucking in food from the few productive, rural areas that are operational. To date, thousands of head of cattle have been slaughtered in the surrounding ranges. We have been depleting the bovine population at an alarming rate. Given no outside sources of feed and a lack of veterinary care, the herds can't be replenished quickly enough to meet the demand."

"Oh that's great," DA Gibson announced, rubbing her temples. "Just wonderful. So what you're saying is that we inherited all those people right when the food was running out. Perfect timing."

Terri wasn't happy either. "Why is this just now coming to light? We have worked for three months to establish our directives. Energy first, followed by agriculture, transportation, security, and communications. An enormous amount of time and brain power went into establishing those priorities, and what I'm hearing today is that we got it wrong."

"Madam Chairman, command and control of the military zones has been marginal at best. Our teams have only now successfully integrated the hodgepodge of units administrating martial law in Houston, Dallas, Austin, and San Antonio into a unified command. Before now, no one had a clear picture of how critical the food situation had become."

Terri shook her head in disgust. For a brief moment, she longed for Bishop's input. That desire was quickly thwarted by additional frustration when she realized her husband had been directed to do a job... a very dangerous job... that was no longer the first priority.

Several conversations broke out at once around the table, small clusters of the military's representation wrangling the controversial update with different council members as the whole governing body rehashed the news. Terri stood and meandered to a nearby window, the view affording some measure of calm.

After a few minutes of solitude, she pivoted abruptly and raised her voice, overriding the din. "I can't speak for all of you, but this update puts a tremendous weight on my shoulders."

The room grew quiet, all eyes turning to watch as she slowly strolled around the conference table. "I feel responsible for all of those people. The women and children... the elderly... all of the survivors that we find suddenly thrust into our care."

Her eyes moved around the group, making contact with the seated representatives. "But," she continued with emphasis, "I don't think we can take this all on our backs. I don't believe there is anything the people in this room can do to fix this alone. It was the citizens of Alpha, Meraton, Fort Stockdale, and the Rio Grande Valley that allowed the Alliance to succeed. I believe it will be the people of Houston, Dallas and the cities lying in the central corridor of this state that will enable that continued success."

Most of the council members had seen Terri like this before. She held their rapt attention as her tour of the room ended where she had started. After reaching the head of the table, she continued. "So my proposal is this; I want every vacant lot planted with a garden. I want a rabbit hutch in every backyard. I want any boat still afloat to be designated for fishing. I want to bus the thousands of unemployed, unoccupied men and women out to the countryside and have a shovel or hoe available for every empty hand. We have a food emergency - so let's grow food. We have three growing seasons here in Texas. We have 90 days before things get critical. We can handle this, but we had better be burying some seeds."

Several voices erupted at once, most of them protesting the complex, nearly impossible logistics involved in such an initiative. It was General Owen's declaration that eventually demanded the floor.

"While that is an extremely noble concept, ma'am, I'm not sure how realistic it would be. Out here, in the rural portion of the state, people have the skills to raise their own food. In the metro areas just east of us, I'm not so sure that is the case. Where would they get seeds? Where would they get the breeding stock? Who would teach them how to grow and harvest?"

It was Pete that responded. "General, we have the people here that can get this started. I'm sure most of our citizens wouldn't mind contributing a chicken here, a rooster there, or a pair of rabbits. We have ranches and farms with expertise. What we don't have is the organization to spread such knowledge, nor do we have the wherewithal to support such an initiative. The only entity that has that in place right now is the military."

Owens shook his head, "Sir, we don't have battalions of gardeners. We don't have platoons of rabbit ranchers. Our average soldier is 19 years of age and volunteered to earn college money. I'm not trying to be obstructive, just realistic. The military doesn't have the skills to implement such a protocol."

Nick wasn't convinced. "General, I know you have extensive training facilities at Bliss, Hood and the other bases. Don't you have the organizational skills in-house to train thousands of men and women on the latest weapons technology, defensive tactics, and other knowledge of warfare? If the civilians provided the know-how, couldn't we redirect some of that enormous educational capability?"

The military commander had to consider Nick's questions for a moment. His expression made it clear he was approaching cognitive overload while absorbing a proposal that would completely repurpose his warriors. "You're correct in that we can train many people very quickly. I suppose we could just as easily start churning out recruits with the skills to raise goats and chickens as opposed to teaching them to clean a rifle."

Terri's voice sounded from the head of the table, "Plowshares," she said in a low tone that drew every eye. "We'll beat swords into plowshares, spears into pruning hooks. Just like the Bible says."

General Owens was still skeptical, his orderly mind trying to sort it all out. "Of course the men under my command will do everything in their power to execute this council's wishes, but do we really think it will be enough? We have several operations already in progress, and I don't want to lose the momentum we've already established. As we all know, resources are thin."

Terri smiled at the commander, "I don't think anyone is suggesting we convert battle tanks into farm tractors, General. But the concept of using the organization, discipline, and infrastructure of the military to implement an emergency program of victory gardens makes sense. The American people have done it before."

"Digging for victory," Pete recalled. "That was the British catch-phrase during World War II. Both the US and the Brits had extensive programs for civilians to grow vegetables. I've seen the posters, and I can still hear my grandmother brag about raising squash on the roof of her apartment building in Philly. I've read that in 1944, half of all the produce consumed in the United States was grown in private gardens; even the urban areas made substantial contributions."

Diana added, "I don't see that we have any choice. According to the briefing we just received, we risk losing everything if we don't do something quickly. A plan to convert firing ranges and combat schools into classrooms for Agriculture 101 doesn't seem so outlandish given the circumstances."

"We need every vacant lot filled with vegetable gardens. We need every field planted with something edible," Terri stated. "I don't care if we have to build tent cities next to the farms and plant every row by hand. We need action like the Work Progress Administration back in the first Great Depression. We need food, and thousands of tons of it."

United in their resolve, the council discussed ways to pool its resources to accomplish this initiative, as well as plans to get the new territories to "buy into" the innovative survival strategy. The vote was unanimous to initiate an emergency agricultural program.

After optimistic handshakes, a few hugs and hasty parting conversations, Terri left the chambers exhausted and thinking of Bishop. She knew he'd agree with the change in priorities while at the same time being frustrated with the circumstances.

Her footsteps echoed off the walls as she sauntered along the marble floors of the Alpha courthouse. An unusually quiet morning, she found the sound oddly unsettling, a reminder that the once lively building was now largely empty. "You're not

101

alone," she whispered, trying to suppress the doubt that seemed to accompany every major decision. "Leaders throughout history probably felt the vise of isolation squeezing their chests."

She paused for a moment, peering up at a painting that had caught her eye some months ago when she had first been elected to head the council. It was a large, nicely framed print of Howard Christy's, *We the People*.

The scene depicted a gathering of the Founding Fathers, constructing the Constitution. Above them were several spirit-like images of common, everyday colonists, apparently overseeing the work being done to create America's new foundational document.

When Terri had first scrutinized the artwork, her initial assessment had been that the people were watching their leaders closely, intent on making sure the needs of the citizenry were being addressed. Lady Liberty was among the onlookers, depicted in an angelic glow as she observed those great men working so diligently, creating a revolutionary new type of government.

But after studying Christy's classic a few times, she had changed her mind. The people weren't overseeing, demanding, or even anxious. They were there to support the men who were framing a new direction for this land - lending their prayers, dreams, souls, and collective goodwill to ensure the success of those who would ultimately influence the destiny of their new country.

"You're not alone," she whispered to herself. "Like those great men working so hard to define the role of government, you have people willing to do what it takes for us to succeed. We have thousands and thousands of brilliant, dedicated minds all striving toward the same goal. You've got it easy compared to the men in that picture, and they made it work. Lincoln and Roosevelt both had problems that make yours seem like child's play. They overcame. Quit being a sissy and get the job done."

Her spirits slightly elevated, Terri continued her trek through the hall, turning the next corner where she was greeted by the sounds of playing children, their small voices and laughter uplifting her mood even further.

The nursery door was bookended by Butter and Slim, the two security guards glancing up and smiling as she approached.

Mr. Beltran had insisted both men leave the ranch and join Nick's security teams after Terri's election to the council's chair. "We all have to do our part," the distinguished rancher had declared. "Both of these men are capable, loyal, and trustworthy. You'll need folks like these to help rebuild the country."

"Everything okay, Miss Terri?" the always cheerful Butter asked.

"Yes. Everything's just fine. How has Hunter's morning been?"

"From the sound of things, all of the children are having a good time," Slim responded.

"We need to get going. We have a long trip ahead of us, and the council meeting lasted longer than expected. Are the guys all packed and ready?" Terri asked.

"Yes, ma'am. Our gear and personnel are all loaded up and ready to go," Slim replied.

Terri entered the makeshift day care center, the repurposed room furnished with community donations for Alpha's most diminutive citizens. A shelving unit housed old drums, buckets of broken crayons, and Matchbox cars. An assortment of books filled one full row, sporting a hodge-podge of family favorites including several Dr. Suess stories and some picture books for the newborns. An older man in the community had carved a couple of stick ponies for the "cowboys in training" to get a little practice. One adult was supervising the tots while two preschool engineers built a Lego city. Another worker gently rocked an infant that had cuddled into the older woman's embrace. Both of the grandmother-types greeted Terri with sincere smiles. "Good morning, Miss Terri," the baby snuggler offered in a hushed voice. "Hunter's had a busy morning. He downed some mashed sweet potatoes while watching the older children build a little town and finally fell asleep to The Cat in the Hat."

The architect supervisor turned to comment as Terri passed, "We were just discussing his progress. He is so alert and strong. I believe he'll be sitting up on his own in the next few days."

"Really?" Terri quizzed. "Isn't he a little young for that?"

"Five months is a bit early," one of the ladies responded, "But both your husband and you are athletic people, so it's not unheard of. He is such a happy little boy. We both enjoy our time with him."

Terri smiled and thanked the two babysitters, and then strolled into the adjoining room. Here, the blinds were pulled to maintain a dark, quiet place for the children who needed sleep.

Hunter was snoozing, hardly noticing as his mother gently scooped him up and held him close. Sighing with relief, she gently swayed side to side while humming softy. *You're growing like a weed*, she thought. *Every time I pick you up it seems like you've gotten bigger. Your dad will really notice the difference when he gets back.*

After whispering a sincere, "Thank you," to the two kind souls charged with caring for her child, Terri exited the nursery to find Butter waiting for her return. Slim was nowhere to be seen, but that wasn't a concern – she knew instinctively that he was making sure the exit was clear.

"How's the little fella doing?" the huge ranch hand inquired in a hushed voice.

To answer the question, Terri turned slightly to let her bodyguard see Hunter's closed eyes.

Butter's face lit up with an enormous grin as he reached up, lightly caressing the newborn's cheek. "He needs his rest," the big man whispered. "Growing is hard work."

And you should know, Terri thought. It never ceased to amaze her how gentle and affectionate Butter was with Hunter. Towering at least 6'4" and weighing close to 260 pounds, she had initially been concerned when her new security man had shown more interest in playing with her son than guarding him. *There's a super-sized child inside of him*, she had eventually decided.

Not only was Butter extremely tall and muscular, he was the only man in Alliance territory who had gone hand-to-hand with Nick and not been bested. An undefeated state champion wrestler, it was rumored Butter was well on his way to the United States Olympic team before the collapse occurred.

When they had first met, Terri assumed her protector had earned his nickname due to his blonde, butter-colored hair, but Slim soon set the record straight. "He slaps butter on everything. Ever since we were kids… butter on breakfast cereal, butter on steak, butter on grits…. Heck, I am shocked he's not one big ball of butter fat."

The irony of it all wasn't lost on Terri, especially after several months of fighting to regain her pre-pregnancy figure. *There isn't an ounce of fat on that guy*, she thought, envious of such a metabolism.

No sooner than Terri and her guardian reached the courthouse's side exit, Slim appeared at their side. "Everything's in order, Miss Terri," he announced. "It looks like another bright and clear day… good weather for a road trip."

Slim held the door open for Terri to pass, his eyes always darting right and left as if he expected some threat to materialize out of thin air. Next to Butter, the dark-haired ranch hand appeared tiny – almost harmless. She knew that was an illusion.

Slim was actually an average size fellow with a wiry build and brown eyes that never seemed to focus on any one object. Looking like he would be more at home in a saddle than guarding a dignitary, he was hardly the type anyone would visualize as a security professional. That was a misconception as well.

Over time, Terri had found that Slim was the truly dangerous one of the pair. He was incredibly fast and accurate with a pistol. So impressive were his skills that even Bishop, Nick, and the Darkwater contractors had solicited his training and advice.

The man was also uncannily observant. More than once, he'd shocked Terri by noting some minor detail that she had missed. Nothing seemed to escape his scrutiny.

When Terri discovered that Slim had worked at the Department of State, protecting American diplomats and VIPs all over the world, his demeanor, habits and skills all made sense.

About the only thing Slim seemed to fear was Hunter. More than once, she'd had to pull the infant away from Butter, his inexhaustible enjoyment of playtime interfering with meals and naps. Slim, on the other hand, shied away from any contact with the baby. It was almost as if the man was scared he'd break the child. The dichotomy was amazing and often humorous.

With Hunter still sleeping, Terri and her escorts strode across the courthouse lawn toward a waiting line of idling vehicles. There were six in all, a carefully selected assortment of civilian, law enforcement, and military transports. Terri's objective was the second of two large, class-A motorhomes, one of which had become her traveling office and abode. In front of her "home on wheels" sat a military Humvee, one of Sheriff Watts's squad cars, and another camper that was used to house her companions. Behind, two civilian pickup trucks rounded out the entourage, their beds stuffed to the brim with fuel cans and boxes of supplies.

"Our first stop is Austin, ma'am," Slim noted. "We'll be on the road for approximately five hours. Is there anything else you need before we roll out of Alpha?"

Terri shook her head, "No. No, I think Betty and I packed everything we needed last night."

"Good. The military representatives arrived early this morning and are all set. Sheriff Watts has assigned one of his senior deputies to accompany us and work with any law enforcement we might encounter. We've got two engineers, one representative from the rancher's guild, and of course, my team."

Terri scanned up and down the line and sighed, wondering if they were utilizing the Alliance's resources in the most effective manner.

Obviously, the trip was necessary. The folks in the big cities in the central part of the state had been made aware of the federal government's voluntary withdrawal from Texas. However, few of the officers running the military zones knew much about the Alliance or its leaders. Everyone on the council had agreed - it was time for a series of face-to-face meetings. The planning for the excursion to the eastern part of the state had begun several weeks ago. Tomorrow, Nick and Diana would be making a similar journey to Dallas and Fort Worth.

It was more than just showing the flag. A long list of objectives had been identified for the trip. The leadership in West Texas needed firsthand knowledge of what conditions were like on the ground. The huge population centers east of the Hill Country needed to have representation on the council. A thousand things had to be accomplished in order to enable a recovery and improve people's lives.

At first, Terri had envisioned a variable all-star team of Alliance expertise descending upon their neighbors in need. She had visualized hoards of engineers, farmers, ranchers, and mechanics invading the big cities and projecting a message of "We're here to restore order to your lives."

But, as the council had learned more about the true conditions in the east, her desire to save the day began evaporating. In a matter of weeks, she realized that plan was utterly unrealistic.

So now, instead of making a big splash, they were going to stick a toe into the troubled waters of their fellow Texans.

"What's the total number of people going on the trip?" Terri turned and asked Slim.

"All told, we have 16 hardy explorers setting sail with us today, ma'am," came the response.

"And how many of those are dedicated to keeping Hunter and me out of trouble?"

"Seven, ma'am."

Almost half, she thought, disgusted at the use of valuable assets.

At first, she'd protested the continuous rings of security that Bishop and Nick insisted surround her. "Who would want to hurt Hunter or me?" she'd argued. "It is a waste of resources to have men guarding us all the time. Besides," she added, patting the 9mm pistol that was always on her belt, "I can take care of myself."

While no one doubted Terri was quite self-reliant and skilled to boot, Bishop wouldn't budge. "You are the face, voice, and icon of the Alliance. There are always going to be people who disagree with what we're doing. By its very nature, the act of governing often generates anger and ill will. You can't please everyone. In addition to that, there are still dangerous men roaming Alliance territory. Sheriff Watts can't ban every outlaw and desperado. What happens if one of these rogue individuals decides to take Hunter or you hostage? It's happened before, hasn't it?"

So she had agreed, deciding to make the best of it. Terri had to admit it was nice to have them around when Bishop was away. But half of their personnel? Wouldn't it be better to take along more experts?

"I don't need that many bodyguards, Slim," she protested. "This is getting ridiculous. We should be utilizing those limited seats for people who can help our friends back east."

Slim shook his head. "Ma'am, we've been through this a hundred times already. I beg you, Miss Terri, please let me do my job. If nothing else, put yourself in my shoes. If something happened to you or the baby, would you want to be the guy who had to tell Mister Bishop?"

Terri waved him off, knowing she wasn't going to win the argument. "Okay, okay. I'll quit bitching about it. Let's get going."

After making sure she managed the motorhome's steps and was out of earshot, Slim turned to Butter and remarked, "She's so damned headstrong. One of these days she's going to let that confidence override commonsense - and that is going to get her, and us, into trouble."

Butter nodded, accustomed to his friend complaining about Terri's strong will and excessive determination. "I know," he consoled his co-worker. "But remember what Mr. Beltran said when he asked us to take this job."

Nodding after some thought, Slim had to agree. "The boss was right... as usual."

After watching Butter head forward to one of the waiting transports, Slim mounted the steps and slid behind the motorhome's steering wheel. He peered back into the cabin and spotted Terri sitting in a lounge chair, a seatbelt already fastened across her lap. The baby was secure in his crib. "Getting underway, ma'am," he announced, and then shifted the transmission.

As the convoy rolled out of Alpha, Mr. Beltran's words echoed through Slim's mind. "That woman is special, boys. She has the right combination of grit, love, mountain lion, and commonsense all wrapped up in one soul. Protect her. Keep her safe. She's our best hope and deserves the chance to see it through."

Terri glanced away from her never-ending stack of paperwork, Slim's usual activity at the helm drawing her attention. Her driver was pressing his radio earpiece tightly, a sure sign something important was being broadcast.

She tried to hear his response, but the words were undecipherable. Intuition told her something was wrong.

It became apparent that she wasn't going to have to wait long to find out what was going on. Slim looked up into the mirror and said, "Miss Terri, please remain seated. We're making an unscheduled stop."

"What's going on, Slim?"

"We just received a broadcast from Fort Hood, ma'am. The convoy is pulling to the side so you can be briefed."

"Bishop," Terri whispered, throwing a worried look at Betty. "Something has gone wrong with Bishop."

A few moments later, she felt the trailer's momentum slow as Slim let off the gas. Another seemingly endless minute passed before they navigated to the shoulder and stopped. Terri's seatbelt was off in a second, and after a glance at Betty and Hunter, she was striding toward the coach's door.

Slim beat her to it, blocking her exit. "Ma'am, please wait just a moment. Colonel Jefferies is on his way back from the lead Humvee and will fill you in immediately."

"Is he alive?" her worried voice asked.

Slim's eyes flashed surprise at the question, yet again amazed at the woman's level of perception. "Yes, ma'am, Mister Bishop is alive. All that I know at this moment is that his unit suffered extreme casualties, and your husband is in surgery at Fort Hood."

Terri stood motionless, her face filling with a thousand questions. Betty was there, pulling Terri close in a supportive embrace. "How bad is it?" the older woman asked.

Before Slim could answer, a knock sounded on the door. The guard unlocked the latch, admitting the military officer.

After removing his hat in respect, the colonel explained, "Ma'am, I just received a broadcast from Fort Hood on the long range com. The unit assigned to secure the manufacturing facility at Brighton, Texas has returned to the base with over a dozen wounded, including your husband. At this time, he is in surgery. That is all I know at the moment."

"How far away are we from the base?" Terri asked.

"Three hours, ma'am, give or take."

The Chairwoman of the Alliance Council reappeared, replacing the frightened, concerned wife. "Well what are we waiting for, gentlemen? Our itinerary has just changed. Take me to Fort Hood."

Slim's natural aversion to any deviation from the plan showed on his face, but before the security man could voice an objection, Terri's stare bored into his eyes.

"You were going to say something, Slim?" she challenged, her tone making it clear the effort would be wasted.

"No, ma'am," he answered wisely, and then turned to the colonel. "Please inform the base commander of our anticipated arrival. I'm not sure how long we'll be staying."

"I'll brief the rest of the convoy as well," the officer noted. "I'll also let the commanders in Austin know we've been delayed."

The colonel started to turn for the door, but then paused. Turning back to face Terri, he said, "We have the finest battle-trauma surgeons in the world at Hood, ma'am. I'm sure your husband will be okay."

Bishop was lying on his stomach, and it was pissing him off. His groggy mind registered the discomfort of the unnatural position, but was unsure what to do about it.

Deciding that his side, back, or even a fetal arrangement would be more comfortable, his brain sent the signal to roll over.

Somehow, despite the anesthesia, his arms answered the confused command, and he began to rise.

A firm, but gentle hand pressed down on his back, easily defeating the weak effort. "No you don't, mister. You need to stay off your back for a bit."

Bishop wanted to protest, but only managed about the weakest, nonthreatening growl he'd ever heard. It was almost funny.

Somewhere, off in the distance, he heard a new voice. It was talking about him, so he abandoned the effort to roll over, instead focusing his attention on what was being said.

"He had four pellets of buckshot in his left thigh," a male voice reported. "There was some initial infection, minor muscle damage, and several skin lacerations."

"So he's going to be okay?" came a familiar voice.

I must be dreaming, Bishop thought. *That sounded like Terri.*

"Yes, ma'am, he's going to be fine. We had to dig around in there to remove the lead, but it was pretty straightforward. He's going to be sore for a while, but after the staples come out, he will eventually regain full use of the limb. He had multiple contusions, lacerations and some severely bruised ribs, as well."

"Thank you, doctor. When can I talk to him?"

111

"He should be coming around any minute now. But, I have to warn you. From the reports I've heard, his physical condition might be the least of our worries."

"What do you mean?" came that female voice again.

Damn, Bishop thought. *They must have given me some really, really strong happy juice. I could have sworn that was my wife.*

He drifted away from the rest of the conversation, choosing instead to dream about Terri and his son. They were all at the ranch together. It was nighttime, and mom and dad were showing Hunter the stars. His baby blues rivaled the stars' twinkle.

A rustle beside him ended the daydream, then a sweet scent registered through the haze. The aroma was familiar, warm, and inviting. He felt a soft touch graze his cheek... a kiss.

The narcotic fog slowed his recognition, his brain failing to connect the dots. *That nurse's hair smells just like Terri's*, he decided. *Nice of her to kiss me though. What a wonderful bedside manner.*

Then reality dawned, Bishop's eyes fluttering open. "Terri?"

"Hey, babe. How are you feeling?"

Bishop's throat was dry, his voice cracking. "Terri, what are you doing here? When... why..."

She brushed his hair, leaning in to kiss his forehead and massage away the growing worry line there. "I was on my way to Austin. We heard on the radio that you'd been hurt. I thought I'd stop by and make sure you weren't chasing any nurses around."

He moved his hand, reaching for her. She accepted the offering with a glowing smile, squeezing him gently.

Emotion boiled up inside the Texan. He was so happy to see his bride, so thankful she was there. Tears started streaming down his cheek, embarrassing sobs that he couldn't seem to control.

Terri didn't speak or move, she just held onto him, letting him work it out. Finally able to control his voice, Bishop stared at her with the saddest eyes she'd ever seen. "Things went so terribly wrong. It was so bad.... the bodies... dying men... we can't let

112

that happen again."

"I heard, baby. I'm here, and we'll work it out. I'm so sorry this happened."

She watched as Bishop's eyes lost their focus, the terror on his face indicative of some horror being relived from vivid memories. She felt the shiver roll through his frame, and then he began sobbing again.

After he had recovered, she bent close and whispered, "I love you, Bishop. With all my heart and soul, I love you. I'm here for you. We *will* work this all out together. I promise."

For three days, Bishop remained bedridden at the doctor's behest. Terri brought Hunter in as often as possible, the infant seeming to give his father as much comfort as anything.

On the fourth day, the couple began walking short distances, the circulation and exercise prescribed to accelerate Bishop's healing.

When it was just the two of them, during the quiet hours of the day, Bishop would speak of Brighton. His recounting began with short, snappy sentences, and then he'd stop, anger and frustration causing him to pull back into the recesses of his mind.

Over time, he began to extend, including more and more details about what had gone wrong, why people had reacted the way they had, and why the killing had been so intense.

Terri had been briefed on the mission's outcome from the senior officers at Hood. She had seen the reports filed by the surviving soldiers. She knew it had been a terrible experience for all involved. She also understood that Bishop had been in the center of the whole ordeal.

It was on the fifth day that General Owens stopped by to visit Bishop in the infirmary. Terri was at her husband's bedside when the senior officer entered the room.

After pleasantries and greetings had been exchanged, Bishop got serious. "General, we can't use that same strategy again. We have to come up with something different."

Trying to placate the wounded man, Owens nodded politely and smiled. "Of course my officers will modify our procedures and mission profile, sir. I know they're already working on improving the defensive capabilities for the next mission. There have even been some discussions on including some armor with each group. We'll be better prepared next time."

Terri was surprised when Bishop sat straight up in the bed. For a moment, she thought he was going to physically accost the visitor, so intense were his eyes. "No, sir. We're not going to do any such thing. There's been another victim from the collapse, one I didn't realize until Brighton... a causality that none of us considered, but now we know."

Owens was slightly taken aback, not familiar with anyone questioning his authority or decisions in this way. "I don't understand?"

"The Army, sir, or at least how the public looks at the military. Before the collapse, Americans respected and honored those who served... those who sacrificed for their freedom. That perspective is the causality. It didn't survive the downfall."

Owens frowned, the expression making it clear he couldn't process what Bishop was trying to tell him.

The Texan, frustrated by his inability to form the words, tried again. "Civilians looked at the military to protect their freedom... their way of life. But that freedom no longer exists. Liberty died with society. The pursuit of happiness perished with the apocalypse, or more accurately in the months and years that followed the downfall. People can no longer live the way they want to live. Their definition of being free is only a memory, a fading image of something they'd experienced long ago. They are now slaves in their minds – indentured with servitude to hunger."

"Okay. I follow you so far, but what does that have to do with my soldiers and the uniform? We didn't cause the collapse. We're

114

blameless," the general shrugged.

"Few people think the Army is responsible; that's not the point. What I'm trying to say is that you can't defend something that no longer exists. In their minds, freedom is an illusion. There's no nation to defend, no constitution to uphold. When we paraded into Brighton, we represented something that was so far from those people's reality, we were nothing but a ruse. They had already been deceived enough and wanted no part of a military intervention."

Owens disagreed. "While I think I see what you're saying, is it wise to change our strategy based on a single incident?"

Bishop looked down, dismayed. "You've read the reports, sir. Didn't it strike you as odd that the locals could gin up the population so easily against us? The agitators were shouting phrases like, 'Remember Katrina,' and 'Remember Waco,' during the riot. The vast majority of their people took up arms against their own Army. They fought and died in droves. Not because of a few crooked leaders or some big lie – but because we represented something so foreign to their reality it was as if the Chinese military was rolling into their homes."

Owens nodded, "Yes, I read the reports. But do you really believe that attitude will be prevalent?"

"That attitude is completely understandable. We weren't there when they were suffering the worst of it. No one showed up to help or lend a hand. Now, the average person is suspicious and has no faith in any authority beyond the men and women who survived the hard times beside him. We are foreigners in our own land."

The general shook his head, not wanting to accept Bishop's explanation. "That may have been true in Brighton, but I don't think it's reasonable to assume that example as typical. I'm going to recommend my officer's modifications to the council."

Bishop smiled, "Sir, your men and you are brave, noble, and extremely skilled at what you do. But no one has ever tried to rebuild the American society after a collapse. I would prefer to work with you and your planners, but as an equal. If that is unacceptable, then I will make my own presentation to the council, and quite frankly, sir, it will involve using a minimum of military assets for first-approach missions."

Terri grunted, a sly grin creasing her lips. "Sounds like you're fired, General. But then again, you never really wanted the job in the first place – right?"

"Isn't that ultimately up to the council?" the confused officer responded, trying to tread carefully.

"If you want to debate my husband in front of the council, General, that is your right. I'll even recuse myself from the proceedings. But you will be creating an unnecessary political divide. What's the harm in listening to Bishop's ideas? What possible negative consequences can come from his experience and vision?"

Owens extended his hand to Bishop, "Welcome aboard, son. I look forward to working with you."

After the officer had left, Bishop glanced at his wife and said, "Now we know how that man got promoted so quickly. He's open-minded and fair. Things are looking up."

According to the map, the town was called Riley. Bishop had never been there. Just west of the Oklahoma border, a little south of Amarillo, the remote Texas berg was listed as having just over 2,000 residents – pre-collapse. He hoped at least half had survived.

It would be another hour before dawn, their original plan allotting time for any potential complications along the road. But there hadn't been any major obstacles, downed bridges, or blocked pavement... a pleasant surprise and positive harbinger for this critical assignment.

Four men had been chosen for the objective, the debate among the Alliance leadership raging between smaller and larger groups. Bishop had argued passionately for this specific configuration, the disaster at Brighton, Texas still fresh on everyone's mind. Too many had died there. Bishop still moved with a slight, but perceptible limp in the early hours after rising.

In a way, the Texan felt like a lab rat. His mission was, in so many ways, the opposite of what the Alliance had attempted at Brighton. Instead of overwhelming force and the quick establishment of authority, they were to leave a small footprint, gather information, and remain inconspicuous to the local population. They were here to scout, gain an understanding of the local situation, and establish contacts if an opportunity presented itself. The Alliance leadership, with a realistic assessment and solid intelligence, could then react with whatever was necessary to integrate the community. It was a slower process that didn't meet the timetable of desperate people needing help, but fewer would die.

Cory was selected for his mechanical skills and overall good nature. Bishop knew the man could fight if the need arose. Kevin had grown strong, tall and wide, his skill with a sniper rifle unparalleled among the ranks of Alliance shooters. Nick had taught the boy well, rounding out the natural gifts provided by God - a sharp eye, steady hands and the patience to only squeeze the trigger.

"Boy?" Bishop whispered, glancing at his best friend's son. "He could probably kick my ass. I wonder what the hell Nick is feeding that kid. I'll get Terri to put it on the grocery list for Hunter."

He dismounted from the pickup, immediately heaving gear from the bed. Bishop was pleased that every man went about his business quietly and professionally. Still, they were all nervous. The unknown did that to men – even those who had been carrying a rifle to survive the last few years.

Kevin sauntered over, his pack and rifle resting easily on his shoulders. "I'm too keyed up to rest," the kid stated honestly. "I want to head off and find a good observation point. This land is pretty flat, and it might take me a while to locate just the right vantage."

"Not by yourself, you're not. You know the rules. No one works alone."

Kevin nodded, "Yes, sir. Cory said he doesn't feel like sitting around either. He's going to go with me if it's okay with you."

"Okay. That will work. You keep me posted on the radio. I'm hiking into town at first light, and I need to know you have my back. Good luck."

With a nod from Cory, the two men hustled off into the darkness. Bishop watched as they snaked their way down a line of short oak that had taken root along an old fence. There was a stand of taller trees in the distance, sitting on top of the rare undulation in this part of the state. It was an area where they hoped to find a good observation point – a vantage that would allow them to bring most of the small town beyond into the optic of Kevin's long-range rifle.

Bishop sensed footsteps behind him, pivoting to find Grim returning to the truck. "Are those two off already? Little eager are we?"

"It's their first time out like this," Bishop chuckled. "They're both so charged up I am surprised it took them this long."

Grim laughed, "Yeah… I still remember my first mission. Talk about a ball of raw nerves. It's only by the grace of God that I didn't accidentally shoot somebody."

Bishop patted his friend on the shoulder and smiled. "Everything go okay setting up the cat's eyes and trip wires?"

"Yes, sir. We're as secure as a baby in a crib. Unless we both fall completely asleep at the wheel, no one is going to sneak up on us."

"Good. I hope we're not here more than a day or two, but there's no way to be sure how long this will take."

"Why don't you catch a quick nap? I'm going to start gathering firewood. We both could use a cup of coffee before we stroll into that town."

The suggestion made Bishop yawn. "Sounds good."

Pacing back to the pickup, Bishop paused for a moment and scanned his surroundings. All around the perimeter were small, twinkling pinpoints of light – the cat's eyes.

Illuminated by a series of infrared lights resting on top of the cab, each small dot was actually a tiny reflector, not unlike the safety units found on bicycles. While the unaided human eye couldn't see the infrared spectrum of light, the material in the cat's eyes could.

If intruders wandered between the reflectors and the truck, their presence, speed, and direction would be easily detectable.

He was confident that Grim's installation of the trip wires was professionally done as well. The Darkwater contractor had years of military and private experience. So much so, Bishop knew his second in command could take over if something happened to him. Dismissing the thought until a better time, he climbed into the cab and laid back against the headrest.

He was sure Grim had identified the likely avenues of approach and layered them with alarms. They were using noisemakers only, as it wouldn't be good to kill or maim one of the locals before they'd even had a chance to introduce themselves. Very undiplomatic, to say the least.

"Diplomacy?" he whispered to the empty truck. "Is that going to be our best approach? Do I use a soft touch with patience and kind words? How about strength? Should I go in like a bull and let them know up front who's in charge? Threaten to kick all their asses if they don't join the Alliance and do as we say? That didn't work out so well in Brighton, but this isn't the same place or people."

He closed his eyes to rest, the countless meetings and strategy sessions back at Hood flowing through his mind. Everyone had a different opinion, each person anticipating, no dreaming, what the team would encounter.

Some people dismissed all the planning, claiming any isolated group of people would welcome the Alliance with open arms. They claimed that Brighton was the exception, perhaps the only one of its kind in the entire state. Others pointed to the situations Bishop and the contractors had encountered in Arkansas, situations where violence occurred without a word being spoken.

Eventually, the debate ascertained the truth. No one really knew what the team would find in the sleepy town of Riley, Texas. It might be like Meraton, or it might be like Brighton. Or it might have its own personality. There was simply no way to know.

"That's why I'm here," Bishop whispered to the empty cab, tapping the dashboard for emphasis. "The council expects me to think on my feet... to make decisions on the fly. There's no manual for rebuilding a nation after an apocalypse – I'm just going to have to play it by ear."

Bishop finally had to admit he was too keyed up to rest. Opening his eyes, he scanned the perimeter, wondering if he should go help Grim with the firewood. He'd watched the contractor stroll off to the north, but couldn't detect any hint of his companion now.

In the rearview mirror, something drew his eye. The cat eyes... one of them had just blinked out.

There it was again. And then another.

"Oh shit," Bishop whispered, his hand moving to the pistol holstered on his leg. His rifle was still in the bed, as was the rest of his kit.

He pushed the button on his radio. "Grim, unless you circled around the south, I've got company coming in. At least two, maybe more."

"It's not me, Bishop. I'm 200 meters to your north. Would it be the kids?"

Before Bishop could respond, Cory's voice sounded across the airwaves. "We're 500 yards west of the truck. It's not us."

"Shit," Bishop said, just as Grim added, "I'm on my way in. Kevin, you and Cory stay put. Even if you hear a protracted gunfight, stand by and wait for instructions."

"Yes, sir."

Bishop could see them now, ghost-like shapes moving along the same route he'd driven the truck an hour ago. They had cut up through some thick scrub, probably bypassing Grim's booby traps.

He could make out three distinct shapes, but understood there

120

might be more. He started to reach for the night vision, but realized objects in the mirror were closer than they appeared. And they were coming fast.

Bishop was pinned, no doubt about it. They were too close for him to jump out and reach cover. Still, if they were hostile, his chances inside the cab weren't very good either.

"Is there anyone in the truck?" a voice hissed.

"How the fuck would I know? You got a flashlight handy?"

"Hell, no. You know we haven't had a working battery for over six months. Very fucking funny, dude."

"Well then how would you expect me to know if there was somebody in the truck?"

They're kids, Bishop realized, judging the young, bickering voices. *But cautious kids.*

He watched them fan out as they approached the rear of the pickup, his eyes darting from mirror to mirror, trying to keep track of each one's position. He remained still, knowing any movement would give away his presence inside the cab.

A few moments later, they were close enough for him to see their rifles in the low light. Memories of a pre-collapse job in Africa reentered Bishop's mind. *Kids can be extremely dangerous and violent. They haven't developed a conscience just yet. Desperate kids are even worse.*

The leader finally made it to the bed and glanced inside. "I told you idiots that I heard a truck motor. There's some sort of equipment in the back," came the whispered voice. "Looks like a bunch of food and camping equipment."

"Food? Jimmy, are you sure?"

"Shush! If they're around, they'll hear you."

"Let's take the food and get the hell out of here," came the nervous response.

But the leader wasn't so sure. He took a few steps forward, raising his rifle and looking hard inside the cab. Bishop's grip tightened on the pistol.

The kid finally made out Bishop's silhouette against the seat. "Who are you?" came the clear, surprisingly loud challenge.

"My name's Bishop, and you should put that weapon down."

The kid's head pivoted right and left, looking for any reason why he should follow Bishop's suggestion. "And why should I do that?"

"Because there is one of the meanest sons-ah-bitches, you've ever seen right behind you. He likes to eat and won't take kindly to anyone messing with his food supply. That… and the fact that I have a .45 caliber automatic pistol aimed right at your head."

The kid chanced another glance right and left, but didn't see any threats.

Bishop didn't give him time to think. "Seriously, son. We mean no harm, but if you keep pointing that pig gun at me, my friend isn't going to like it much. Lower the weapon, and let's talk."

"I don't think so," replied the now-shaky voice. "I think you're by yourself and are trying to bluff your way out of this. Why don't you throw down your pistol and get out of the truck? Then we can talk."

Bishop's eye was drawn to a shadow behind Jimmy. If the kid hadn't been pointing a rifle a Bishop's head, he might have felt sorry for the young man.

Another high-pitched voice sounded from the back of the truck. "C'mon, Jimmy… just shoot him, and let's take his stuff. He's just another trespassing bum who'll probably try and steal our food and guns anyway."

But Jimmy didn't answer. His eyes were wide as saucers because Grim's fighting knife was across the lad's throat.

While Bishop couldn't hear what Grim whispered in the boy's ear, he had a pretty good idea. The rifle lowered slowly until it was pointing at the ground. A slight "thud" announced its impact with the turf.

"Guys. Guys. I… errrr… I think you should come over here,"

Jimmy stammered.

"What's wrong Ji...," one of the others started to ask as the youths rounded the truck. Jimmy's problem was obvious - he had a very nasty-looking new acquaintance.

"Both of you! Drop your weapons, or I'll slice off this one's head and shit down his throat. Go on now. Put 'em down."

But they didn't. Bishop had to hand it to the youths – they had mustard. Again, with weapons pointed at Grim and his captive, they moved to flank their target. Bishop decided to add to their tactical difficulties.

Opening the truck door, he emerged still holding the pistol, but with both palms up and signaling for calm.

"My name is Bishop, and I'm a Texas Ranger. We're here to see if the town of Riley needs help. Parts of the state are in a full-blown recovery."

"Bullshit!" the kid responded. "Anybody could say that. Why would the Rangers come here after all this time? You're a liar."

Despite the cockiness of the response, Bishop could tell his little account had partially resonated with the young male's mind, seeding doubt.

"Tell you what," Bishop said. "We'll turn your friend loose. We'll even let him keep his weapon. You guys back out of here, and fetch whoever is in charge. Tell them we'll meet them on the edge of town to talk... and only talk."

Even in the dim light, Bishop could spot the kid's eyes darting back and forth... first Grim, then his hostage, and finally the guy making this unexpected offer.

"Look, son, I don't take kindly to being called a liar," Bishop said, his voice near a whisper. "I let that go. I heard you suggest shooting me and stealing my food. I've cut men in half for less than that. I'm making the rare exception here. Take advantage of it, and live another day. I've only got so much charity flowing through my veins."

"Okay... but... but... you let Jimmy go."

Bishop nodded at Grim, who pulled away the knife and gave the kid a gentle shove towards his friends. He immediately reached down and grabbed the discarded rifle, working the bolt until it was empty. He handed the weapon over and growled, "You can have your ammo back tomorrow – if your stupid ass lives that long."

Jimmy took the long gun and stepped closer to his friends. They started backing out when Bishop stopped them. "Wait. I was telling the truth. We're really here to help. Can you have whoever is in charge meet me at the edge of town just after daybreak?"

"That would be my uncle, Shane," Jimmy responded. "He's been the big dog in Riley since the mayor died. I'll give him the message."

Bishop nodded, and then added, "Jimmy, tell him there are more of us than just the two you see here. Advise him not to get any clever ideas. Even if he got lucky, and took out my team, hundreds of other men would follow, and they're not nearly as nice as I am. Do you understand?"

"Yes, sir. I do. I'll tell him."

Bishop and Grim watched the threesome fade back into the night, the cat's eyes indicating that they followed the same path out as they had used coming in.

"Do you think that was a good idea… letting them go so they could warn the others?" Grim asked.

Bishop grunted, "You're always such the optimist, Grim. That's what I like about you."

"You may be right; you may be wrong. You've given away the element of surprise, and I don't think that's a good thing."

Bishop stared off in the direction of the town, knowing Grim had a valid point. "Our purpose is to save people, Grim. Not wipe them out. If we wanted to bulldoze down that village, then you're spot on. But that's not what we're here to do. Besides, I don't think shooting the youth of Riley would endear us to their leadership. We didn't have many diplomatic choices here."

"That's why you're running this show," Grim responded, his voice friendly. "I lost all my tact and social graces years ago. Besides, that kid was skinny as a beanpole. He only had three shells in a rifle that holds five, and the bolt didn't feel well oiled, so I don't think we're up against a well-tooled fighting machine. Least I hope not, because now they know we're coming."

The weeds were approaching Jimmy's waist as he crossed the yard. For a moment, he recalled the smell of freshly mowed grass, a chore that once commanded most of the lad's Saturday mornings. *"Maybe there are some positive aspects to the apocalypse,"* he mused.

The flickering light from the kitchen window answered his next question. Shane was awake, probably cursing up a storm over his lack of cigarettes. In the morning, his mood was always foul without his nicotine-induced, tobacco fix. In the evening, it was the lack of beer that elicited yet another string of curses. The thought evoked a grunt from Jimmy. There hadn't been any smokes or brew for over a year, and still his uncle bitched and moaned about it almost every day.

"Shane, it's Jimmy. Coming in," he yelled halfway across the yard-turned-pasture. These days, it wasn't good to surprise anybody.

He entered the back door and leaned his rifle against the wall. Before he could say anything, his uncle spoke up. "You're back early. Did you guys get a hog already?"

"No, we ran into some strangers before we even got to our hunting spot."

Shane immediately went on alert. "Everybody okay? What strangers? Where?"

The answer came rushing out of Jimmy's mouth. "We heard their truck down by the old Wheeler place. We tried to sneak up on them, but they caught us. This guy… his name was Bishop or something like that. He said he was a Texas Ranger and was coming to Riley to see if we needed help. He wants to talk to you

125

at the edge of town after the sun comes up."

Shane held up his hand to silence his nephew. Drawing a pistol from his belt, he peeked out the blinds toward the backyard. "Are you sure they didn't track you back here?"

"Shane, they had no reason to follow me. They had plenty of food and gas cans in the back of their truck. I think this guy was telling the truth."

"Do ya now?"

"They could have killed us easy. One of them got the drop on me from behind. He had his knife right here," Jimmy said, pointing to his neck. "But they let us go. Even let me keep my rifle. If they were raiders or hobos, they wouldn't have let me keep the gun."

Shane had to think about that statement for a minute. The kid had a point. "How many of them were there?"

"We counted two, but Bishop said to tell you that he had more men – just in case you had any thoughts about being… what was the word? Oh, yeah, 'clever.' I believe him. They had bulletproof vests and battle rifles. When the big guy had a knife at my throat, I felt a bunch of clips on his vest."

The older man started to ask another question, but then paused. After another glance out the window, he began pacing the kitchen floor.

"What type of truck did they have?" he finally asked.

"It was just a regular looking, pickup truck. One of those newer models with two rows of seats. There was a camper shell over the bed, but the tailgate was down. That's where I saw all the supplies and gear."

"So it wasn't an Army truck or a Humvee?"

"No. But… the truck was clean, Shane. That's how we spotted it so easily. It sparkled in the starlight, chrome wheels and all. It looked brand new. Who squanders water washing a pickup? Who would waste the soap?"

"Did they wear uniforms?"

"Yes, but I couldn't tell what the patches said."

Again, Shane began pacing, his hand scratching the full beard at his chin.

"Go and roust the Herbert twins. Then go over to Walt's place and have all of his clan meet me at the gas station. Rustle up as many of the rats as you can. Hurry now. Have them come quick. I'll be waiting for our visitors at the Shell station. Have them meet me there."

"What are you going to do, Shane?"

"Go on now," the older man snapped, not wanting to admit he didn't really have a plan. "There's no time to gab. Get going."

Bishop's earpiece sounded with Kevin's voice. "I have a clear field of fire all the way to the brick building to the east. I can cover you as long as you stay between that structure and the gas station."

"Got it," Bishop responded. "How secure is your position?"

"I'm up in a tree with Cory patrolling around this little slice of woods. There are 500 meters of open field on all sides, so no one can get close to us. We're secure."

"Okay. So this is going to happen just like we practiced. If Grim and I go prone, start shooting. If I drop my hat, start shooting. If you see people trying to sneak up on us, or a large number of armed people trying to flank us, I need to know. Other than that, you will have to use your judgment. You'll do fine. Good luck."

"Yes, sir. My dad told me before we left that I was to make sure you got home okay. I won't let you down."

Funny, Bishop thought. *Nick said the exact same thing to me about you.*

The sun had fully cleared the horizon, announcing what

appeared to be a clear, sizzling hot day. Glancing at Grim, Bishop questioned, "Are you ready?"

"Let's do it."

And with that, the two men began hiking toward the distant berg.

Bishop had selected a chest-rig full of magazines for this first encounter. With a blowout bag (medical kit), 12 full pillboxes, and fighting knife, his choice of kit wasn't good for anything other than combat. A Camelbak full of water and small bag of jerked beef were his only survival supplies.

Grim took one side of the road, Bishop the other. Taking the lead, the ex-contractor stayed 10 feet in front of Bishop, eating up the distance with a steady pace.

Ragweed, grass and a variety of overgrowth bordered the two-lane state highway leading into town. Bishop didn't like it, but they really didn't have much choice. Kevin, their over watch, would have seen anyone setting up an ambush. Or so he hoped.

The foliage began to thin as the two approached the first buildings, Mother Nature a little less successful reclaiming the concrete and asphalt associated with sidewalks and vacant lots. Bishop was glad, their vantage improving with every step.

A pre-collapse atlas from the library in Midland Station had given the team a good indication of the community's layout, the primary residential section on the far side of downtown. Riley had one main street, two churches, three gas stations, one school, and a handful of small businesses.

The first structure along their route was the Shell station, a weather-faded sign advertising DVD rentals available in the convenience store.

"I wonder if they have that latest Sci-Fi blockbuster out of Hollywood?" Bishop asked Grim.

"Funny."

The Alliance men managed another few steps before a warning sounded from ahead. "That's far enough!"

Grim stopped his forward progress, turning his head slightly so

Bishop could hear his low words. "So much for our over watch."

Walking up to parallel his teammate, Bishop remained on the opposite side of the road. He couldn't help but sneak a quick scan of the landscape for the closest cover. "We just want to talk," he yelled back in the general direction of the challenger.

"Then talk," came the reply.

Bishop hesitated. Standing exposed, unable to get a visual on the town's spokesperson wasn't the dynamic he had in mind. He decided to establish control. "I like to look a man in the eye when I'm talking to him. Come on out; we only want to have a conversation."

Kevin's voice sounded in Bishop's ear. "I've got two men with rifles moving on your right, 400 meters away. They are making for that church."

A figure appeared from the station's corner, a younger man, perhaps in his mid-twenties. He was bone thin and filthy, worn clothing hanging from sloping shoulders. He had an SKS rifle across his chest, with what looked like an old belt serving as the sling.

As he slowly stepped closer, Bishop examined the dark shadows under the guy's eyes. Stringy, greasy-looking hair rounded out the appearance of a man who wasn't having the best years of his life.

"The two men on your right have made it to the church," Kevin reported. "I have a very clear picture. They're younger than I am... maybe 12 or 13 years old."

Bishop didn't acknowledge Kevin's report, instead addressing the man at the gas station. "My name's Bishop. My team and I have been sent here to see if this community needs help."

"Sent by who? The government? The Feds? The Army?"

Bishop smiled at the man, trying to heed Terri's advice about being friendly. "There's been a new, local government formed. We call ourselves the Alliance. Most of Texas south of here is part of this new group. Together, we have been able to establish stability within our area that we believe others need. We established trade, giving folks access to food, medical care, security, and much more. So we are spreading out, town by town. Neighbors helping neighbors. What's your name?"

"Shane. I'm kind of the default honcho hereabouts."

"Well, Shane. It's a pleasure to meet you. What's your status here in Riley? How many people are still around?"

The local ignored Bishop's questions, instead firing one back of his own. "How do I know you're not just another raider or highwayman? We've had our share of fast talkers show up. All of them... every single one was a con artist, thief or murderer. Why should I believe you're any different?"

"You shouldn't. I'm not asking you to, at least not at first. Like I told that young man this morning, we only want to talk."

Shane shook his head, the expression one of confusion more than disbelief. "If you're what you say, why didn't you just roll into town with food and soldiers?"

"We've found that can be very dangerous. Some places don't want help. Some towns are controlled by men who don't want any outsiders around at all. We aren't invaders, Shane. We're your fellow citizens and friends. We've found it best to show up with a few men, just enough to protect ourselves while establishing contact and communications. If that goes well, then I can send a message and start helping your town integrate into the Alliance."

Kevin's voice interrupted. "Bishop, I have two more armed men approaching from your left. They are 250 meters out, riding bicycles and working their way toward the Shell station."

Grim didn't like it. Turning away from the man directly in front of them, the former Darkwater operator took a knee and raised his weapon, scanning for the new arrivals Kevin had just reported. The move made Riley's honcho jumpy.

"What's he doing?" Shane demanded, backing away and raising his own weapon. "You said you just wanted to talk."

"Settle down," Bishop said calmly. "We have a sniper watching over us. He's spotted some men over by the church and two

130

others coming up behind you. My partner is just being cautious."

Bishop regretted the use of the word, "sniper," wishing instead he'd said "lookout." Shane was clearly freaked out, his gaze darting across the horizon, trying to find the hidden shooter. All the while, his near-panic legs were pumping backwards.

"Shane!" Bishop commanded, trying to halt the local's retreat. "You're fine. We are *not* going to hurt you. Chill out."

But it was too late. Without hesitation, the town's representative turned and fled, quickly disappearing around the corner.

Bishop walked over and took a knee beside Grim, trying to keep his eye on the distant church and the gas station at the same time.

"Damn it! I hosed that up royally. That one word freaked that guy out. Sniper. What was I thinking?"

Grim shook his head, "Don't be too rough on yourself. That dude was about as skittish as a Bible salesman calling on a whorehouse. Did you see how thin he was?"

Bishop nodded, "Clearly they aren't eating well. Did you catch a whiff of the body odor? I don't think we have to worry about them sneaking up on us."

The two Alliance men stayed put for several minutes, holding out hope that Shane would rethink his withdrawal and reappear. Kevin's voice came across the airwaves, "I've got more movement back in town. They're being careful now, staying in the shadows and scampering around. More guys on bicycles heading your way."

Grim wasn't happy. "I don't like this. We're too exposed. Terri will kick my ass if I let you get shot out here in Bumfuck, Texas. Let's head back to the truck."

Bishop had to agree. "Let's do it."

The two men executed their egress, each covering the other in a maneuver called bounding, one leapfrogging past as the other covered his movement. Twenty minutes later, they were back at the truck.

"Kevin, we're back at base camp. Any more activity inside the city limits?" Bishop broadcast.

"Not much. I finally got a good angle on two more of the riflemen. They were young like the others – maybe early teenagers. One of them wasn't much taller than the rifle he was carrying."

Bishop considered the report for a moment, trying to make sense of it all. Weren't there any adults in Riley? It would surely make his job easier if there was someone a little more seasoned to deal with. *Maybe the older men are staying back, waiting to see how things go down*, he reasoned.

"Stay put for 30 more minutes. If you don't see anything new, come on back in. They know where we are, so I want to move before they build up enough courage to come and visit us. We'll head to site B."

Grim shook his head in disgust. "It took me almost an hour to set up all those cat's eyes and trip wires. Now I have to do it all over again."

Bishop smirked at his friend's griping. "Old age getting to ya, buddy? This apocalypse is hell for guys like you, huh? Serious lack of ibuprofen and Absorbine Jr.®

"Screw you, *sir*."

"Would I be the first blonde you ever had?"

Both men chuckled at the response.

Grim got serious again, scanning the area and then heading off to retrieve the team's early warning devices. "I'm on it. Make sure our observers report in via radio before they come rambling through the woods. I wouldn't want to shoot one of them by mistake."

"Roger that," Bishop acknowledged. "I'll go with you. No sense in just standing around here."

Still trying to catch his breath, Shane leaned against the building that once housed the post office. The sound of footfalls caused his head and rifle to jerk up in the same motion, but he quickly relaxed – it was only the twins.

"What happened," one of the boys asked. Shane could never tell them apart, but it didn't matter.

"They saw you guys coming in," he hissed between breaths. "Next time, be more careful. You could have gotten me killed."

"How did they see us? We stayed in the weeds," the other said.

"They claimed to have a sniper. That might be bullshit, but somehow they knew you were coming in."

The sound of wheels rolling over gravel grabbed their attention, several more boys with rifles riding in from the north. Jimmy was leading them.

The reinforcements helped Shane settle down and regain his composure. "They claim to be Texas Rangers, but I've never seen a cop who wore an Army uniform like that. Their equipment all looked military. I think they're just a bunch of looters, hoping we've got food or guns or stuff."

"What are we going to do?" asked one of the boys, his dirty face filled with fear. "My older brother got shot the last time the raiders came by. My pa got killed the time before that."

"Your pa died of the sickness, Willy. He went plum crazy like the rest of them did," one of the others challenged.

"He did not!" the smaller kid shouted back, shoving the accuser.

The other boy threw a punch that missed, and a few moments later, both were rolling around on the ground fighting.

Shaking his head in disgust, Shane reached down, pulling one and then the other up by the belt. "Stop it! Both of you... stop it right now. We have very dangerous men nearby, and it's no time for fighting. Now knock it off, or I'll kick both of your scrawny asses."

Breathing hard and staring at one another, both boys did as they

133

were told.

"Now listen to me... all of you," Shane began. "This is some serious shit. Even if those guys really are Rangers, we've all done some things that would put us in jail. Maybe even lethal injection. I don't think they are cops, but we can't take the chance. I say we retreat to the catacombs and wait until they get tired and leave."

None of the gathered throng liked the idea, several moaning at the thought. "The catacombs? Gosh, I hate that place, Shane," one of the older boys challenged. "There's nothing to eat down there but the corn, and that place is creepy. Why don't we just go out and kill them all?"

Several of the others agreed with the challenger, many voicing their opinions at the same time. Shane lifted his hands to quiet the crowd, "Shut up!"

After the protests had died down, Shane peered over the top of the gathering. "Now listen to me, and listen real good. I've spent time in jail, and it's no fun. You boys wouldn't last a week inside. If we hide, they'll leave in a few days, and then things can go back to normal."

"But what are we going to eat and drink?" someone from the back asked.

"I've got an idea on that," came the knowing response. "I think we can steal the stranger's food after we hole up in the catacombs. Hell, they might even have some cigarettes or beer."

"What was that bullshit about being a Texas Ranger?" Grim asked.

"I couldn't think of anything else," Bishop grinned. "They were just kids, and when I was that age, the Rangers were heroes. I used to listen to bunkhouse stories about their exploits. The ranch hands were always going on about how brave and fair the

Rangers were."

Grim laughed, shaking his head. "I think somebody watched too much television. From what I recall from my history books, the Rangers were a bloodthirsty bunch, barely on the right side of the law."

"Yeah, I think you're right. There were periods when they got a little out of control, but overall, the people of Texas respected them. Before the collapse, their organization had transformed into more of a crime scene investigation unit, doing fancy forensics and stuff like that. But the lore continued."

Grim thought about Bishop's response and then shrugged his shoulders. "Hell, you can tell the locals you're Santa Claus or the Tooth Fairy for all I give a shit. Whatever works."

"Well now, that's the problem, isn't it? What does work?"

Grim got serious for a moment, "I don't know what happened in Brighton. I wasn't there. But you came back looking like somebody had hollowed out your insides with an ice cream scoop. I know you, I've seen you fight and deal with shit that would drive another man to his knees. To see you like that is kind of freaking me out. So I'm taking this seriously... I'm following your lead. I've got your back, whatever you decide is best. But... and I've got to say this right up front... if I see this going wrong, if I think this is going bad, I will pick your scrawny ass up and carry you out of here kicking and screaming. You can fire me later."

"Thanks, Grim," Bishop said. "You know that means a lot to me. I'm still sorting out what happened in Brighton... still working it through. You'll be the first to hear my exaggerations and lies when I'm ready."

Before the contractor could respond, Kevin's voice sounded over the airwaves. "I've got a lot of movement in town. It's as if the people are darting around, trying to stay out of sight. But they're up to something."

Bishop keyed his microphone. "Are they heading toward us?"

"No, I don't think so, but I can't say for sure what they're doing. I don't see any indication of a threat, or any sort of movement toward our position."

"Keep me informed," Bishop responded and then looked at Grim. "We need to get in there and find out what's going on."

"Not during the daytime, we're not. You need a little shuteye, some food, and some down time to think. That town ain't going nowhere. We can go poke around after dark when we have the advantage."

Bishop smirked at the response, "So you're my babysitter now?"

"Damn straight. I am here to keep your sorry ass alive, brother. Besides, you know I'm right about waiting until it gets dark."

Bishop sighed, admitting Grim was indeed correct. "You're spot on with going in later. Besides, we need to put eyes on those grain silos. If they're empty or rotten, there's no sense in hanging around."

"Now you're talking sense," Grim responded, happy a disagreement had been avoided. "Now that you're in such a congenial mood, why don't you take a little siesta? I'll wake you up in four hours and take my turn."

"Now that is the best suggestion you've made all day, Grim. Make sure Cory and Kevin both get some rest too."

Jimmy mentally checked his assignments, his mind flashing an inventory of faces that he needed to visit. Shane wanted all the rats to assemble at the elementary school when the sun was high.

Jimmy's orders were to spread the word between Walnut and Center streets.

Normally, he'd welcome the chance to socialize, especially the house where Candy lived. But not today. He knew the rats would bitch and moan at Shane's demand that they hide in the catacombs. A few of the older ones might even refuse to go. Most of them would get mad at him for delivering the message.

Still, he would get to see Candy, and he hoped she wouldn't be too angry. Walking along Center Street, he struggled to understand why going to Candy's house made him feel all weird inside. In the last few months, he taken to stopping by his old classmate's home more often than necessary, only to get all twisted up and not being able to talk or explain why. *Hell*, he thought, *What is going on with me?*

He had known the girl ever since he could remember, growing up only a few blocks away. They had started in kindergarten together, progressing through elementary school. The classes were tiny in a small town, which meant all the kids knew each other. Still, Candy was the only one that made him feel all warm inside.

Lately, he'd even taken to making special trips to her house after a successful hunt, delivering her ration of the meat personally, building up his manly exploits as a provider. Jimmy shook his head, feeling stupid about how he'd been acting.

The last few times he'd visited Candy, some odd, previously unknown part of his brain had taken control. It had been so strange, like some other person had welled up inside him. He had felt an overwhelming desire to impress the blonde-headed lass, to let her know how strong and worldly he had become. *You were showing off*, he thought.

He'd even gone so far as to give her extra portions of feral pork, boasting about the size and the ferocity of the dangerous beasts he'd bested on the hunt. In reality, the pigs were getting smaller and smaller, the "extra cut" actually his personal share of the meat.

He didn't mind eating only corn for a few extra days – seeing Candy's face light up at the extra meat made his belly feel fuller than any meal.

Embarrassed, worried Shane and the other guys would tease him to high heaven if they noticed, Jimmy resolved himself to deliver his message and then leave Candy's porch as soon as possible. This was serious business, the strangers a real threat.

He pushed open the gate, not even noticing the overgrown yard now as high as the surrounding white picket fence. Bounding up the two steps leading to the front porch, he rapped hard on the screen door's frame.

No one answered. He repeated the knock, following by a loud, "Candy? Candy, it's Jimmy."

Panic tore through his gut. Were the strangers already in town? Had they taken Candy? Memories popped into Jimmy's head, terrible images of the last time vicious, bullying men had entered Riley. He hadn't understood why, didn't realize what it all had meant at the time.

There had been only a handful of the town's men left alive when the strangers had appeared. Most of the adults had succumbed to the sickness by then; many more killing each other, or perishing in the crossfires and battles with trespassers.

Jimmy remembered waking up one morning, his aunt crying hysterically. His older cousin Darla was missing, as were a handful of the more mature girls.

They had found the pitiful teens three days later, six of them locked in a tiny storeroom. Jimmy had gone with the men to storm the church, the building having been overrun and occupied by the raiders.

He could still remember Shane's words, "Kill them all, just like they were wild pigs or rabbits. Don't hesitate or think about it. Put those evil animals in your sights and pull the trigger. Blow 'em to bits. We don't have any choice; we'll never be safe while they draw breath."

And they had.

But those five newcomers hadn't gone down without a fight. Jimmy remembered helping Shane and the others carry a bunch of bodies to the grave trench. He'd lost count of how many they had loaded onto the wagon.

Then they had pulled the raiders out of the church, dragging their remains behind Mr. Baker's horse without respect, their heads and arms bouncing across the washboard road on the way to the field. He'd never seen Shane's face look so... so... so wicked as he lit the pile of wood under the stacked bodies. He tended the fire while the few remaining men had stood and watched those corpses burn. Jimmy would never forget the crackling and hissing of people-fat... the gross smell of burning human flesh.

Jimmy hadn't understood why they had found the girls naked, wide-eyed, and sobbing. He hadn't been old enough to grasp why the older women had wrapped them in blankets and hustled them off without a word. No one had clarified the connection to a seemingly unrelated event a few weeks later when two of the rescued sisters had hung themselves in the loft of their garage.

It wasn't until months later, when Shane had explained it to them all, that the events set in motion by the kidnappers became clear to Jimmy. Now, Candy was missing, and those memories all came boiling back up, conveying rage and fury with them.

Pulling the rifle off his shoulder, Jimmy worked the bolt and chambered one of the few bullets Shane had left. He'd kill the strangers... shoot them dead if they had hurt Candy.

He pulled open the screen door, stepping inside the house as quietly as possible. He'd shot men before, this wouldn't be any harder.

He found the living room empty, as was the bedroom and dining area. He was sneaking his way to the kitchen when he heard Candy's voice through the backdoor screen.

Rushing out with his rifle ready, Jimmy stopped short. Candy and her little sister were strolling across the backyard, a dozen bottles of water dangling from the two girls' shoulders via an assortment of shoestrings, twine, and rope.

Exhaling, Jimmy slumped in relief. "Shit," he whispered, "they were only down at the creek getting water. Thank God."

Candy peered up, spotting him standing on the back porch. "Hey, Jimmy," her musical voice sounded. "Did you get another pig this morning?"

He didn't answer immediately, wanting to enjoy her smile for a minute before he delivered the bad news. Moving down the steps, he trotted out to help the two girls with their heavy load.

Once they had set the water jugs on the porch, Jimmy explained, "I've got bad news. We found some strangers just outside of town, and Shane wants everyone to move into the catacombs right away."

The alarm that painted Candy's face distressed him. "Are they sickos? Are they acting crazy?" she asked with dread in her voice.

"No. No, they seemed normal enough. I don't think they've been here long enough to catch the sickness. But Shane doesn't want to take any chances. He wants everyone to gather at the elementary school when the sun is high. Bring as much food and water as you can carry."

Candy was clearly worried, but didn't react like Jimmy expected. "Okay," she agreed, pacing back and forth on the creaking planks of the outside decking. "We'll be there. Any idea how long we'll be gone?"

Jimmy tilted his head, a little surprised she hadn't protested the move. "No, there's no telling, but I can't imagine the strangers will stay long if there isn't anything here for them."

The older girl swayed close, reaching up to touch Jimmy's arm. "You're going to stay with us, aren't you?" she asked, a pleading look in her eyes. "I mean… I… *we'll* be safe as long as you are there."

For once, Jimmy was thankful there wasn't any breeze blowing, sure that even the slightest stirring of air would knock him over. The sensation of her hand on his forearm made his knees feel all watery, the look in her eyes causing his muscles to turn to putty.

"I'll be there," he managed to stammer. "I'll make sure nothing bad happens," he added, hefting his rifle.

Her eyes managed to be frightened, yet brave at the same time. Staring down at his weapon, she probed, "Jimmy, what will happen if they don't leave? What will happen if they go crazy like all the other grownups or if they're evil people like that last bunch? We can't stay down in those caves forever."

He thought her fear would rip his chest apart, the emotions he suddenly felt almost unbearable. Through a tight throat and dry mouth he replied, "If they don't head out in a couple of days, then Shane and I and the guys will go kill them. Just like we have all

140

the others."

Candy seemed to accept that, nodding slightly and gazing back into his eyes. "Be careful, Jimmy. I don't know what I'd do if something happened to you."

The line of bicycles, wagons, and backpack-laden kids stretched the entire length of the elementary school. Shane stood at the front of the parade formation, like a teacher readying the student body to reenter the building after recess. For a moment, the young man felt a sense of pride as he looked over the rag-tag collection. They were resilient, adaptable... and would survive. He was reminded of the stories an old uncle used to share, sordid tales about the man's tours in Vietnam.

"The North Vietnamese Regulars moved mountains using only bicycles," his uncle had said. "They moved heavy artillery pieces up steep hills, and attacked the French at a place called Dien Bien Phu. They moved entire divisions south through the jungle on bicycles. They were a two-wheel army, and we couldn't stop'em."

"We may not have much," Shane whispered to himself. "But sure as shit we have bikes."

"Everybody is here," reported one of the older boys.

"Are you sure? Did you count twice?" Shane asked.

The preteen spat on the sidewalk, a rebellious display of discontent over being challenged. "I can count, Shane. Besides, I walked up and down the line twice. There's 34 of 'em here, just like there should be."

"Okay," came the leader's response. "If you're sure, then let's move out."

Shane assumed the strangers would stay on Indian Ridge, the only high ground for 30 miles in any direction. That's where

Jimmy and the hunting party had found them this morning; that's probably where they would stay. He had selected a route to the co-op that would keep them mostly hidden from anyone watching from that elevation.

Letting one of the Herbert twins lead the way, Shane stood and watched the procession of children pass.

What a bunch of little rag muffins, he thought, the moving multitude reminding him of what life had been like just a few, short years before.

He had been enjoying the bachelor life, playing the field while hunting and fishing as he pleased. He worked part-time at the co-op in the winter, all the hours he wanted during the harvests. He could weld a little, lift his share of feedbags, and drive any tractor or combine in the county. It had been a good life.

When the financial collapse of the country occurred, only the lack of cold beer had bothered him at first. Since the bank had closed, making the payment on his house trailer wasn't an issue. No one had electricity, so there wasn't a bill to be paid. He had well water, plenty of fish and game at his disposal, and a keg in the shed. The apocalypse? No big deal.

The trailer's air conditioner didn't work half the time anyway, so sleeping in the heat didn't require any adjustment. He had learned to hose down the roof a few hours before sunset, and that seemed to cool the interior enough to doze off.

There was an eight-year-old GMC pickup in the driveway, the body rusted through here and there, but the engine was still strong. The title was in the glove box.

There was plenty of firewood for the smoker and grill out back. He had two good deer rifles, a couple of bird guns under the bed, a .357 magnum pistol in the nightstand drawer. He always bought ammo and cigarettes in bulk, stocking up via his larger-than-normal paychecks from the harvest. The freezer contained zero food, the space entirely consumed with red and white cartons of Marlboros. What more could a man ask?

He'd made one mistake in life, deciding to drive to the Shell Station after running low on ice one evening. He'd had a few beers too many, and evidently it showed. At first, he'd thought the flashing blue lights of the highway patrol officer weren't meant for him. Pulling to the shoulder to allow the cop to pass by, Shane was a little surprised to see the cruiser pull in behind him.

He'd blown a few points over the legal limit and had been sentenced to 60 days in Huntsville after he'd told the judge he didn't have enough money to pay any fine. It had changed his life forever.

Still, his lot in Riley, Texas hadn't been so bad.

Even after the electricity had flickered out, no one living in the small village had been effected much. There was a virtually unlimited supply of food at the co-op, the huge, skyscraper silos full to the brim with corn.

The town had maintained a large tank of gasoline for the water tower's pump, the provision a result of the destructive tornados that ripped through the Texas Panhandle and neighboring Oklahoma every year. Riley had learned that weeks, even a month or more, could pass before electrical power was restored after the worst of the summer storms tore through.

With water and food available, only the lack of air conditioning bothered the town folk. But what could they do? What little news had made it through made Riley seem like a paradise. Few of the town's residents were in any hurry to leave.

A little over 60 days had passed before the first refugees from Amarillo had wandered into town. Nearly dead from dehydration and starvation, the kindly folks of Riley had slowly nursed the small group of vagabonds back to health.

Stories of looting, violence, and murder in the closest big city had spread like wildfire through the community. It was every man for himself in Amarillo, according to the newcomers. Complete anarchy. A total breakdown in the rule of law.

Still, as time passed, most of Riley's residents held out hope that things would get back to normal. The months dragged by, the village holding things together and helping each other out.

All along, the co-op was the town's savior. The feral hogs normally so prominent in the area, migrated south that first winter. A few months later, the deer population plummeted, the doe-eyed beauties hunted almost to extinction. The closest branch of the Red River had never been much for fishing, the few local farm ponds quickly depleted of their stock.

But the mammoth silos of the town's reserves remained full of life-giving corn. It was a pure accident of geography that such an out-of-the way place as Riley had been blessed with the facility.

The Texas panhandle is marked with flat, featureless terrain, better suited for raising crops than grazing cattle. Mile upon endless mile of fields dominated the region prior to society's collapse, the fertile breadbasket reaching into Oklahoma and then Iowa, Nebraska, and beyond.

Due to the settlement's close proximity to massive farms, an unused spur from an old rail line, and a low average humidity, Riley had been chosen to house what was destined to become one of the largest grain storage depots in the nation.

Ten years ago, the sleepy town had suddenly come alive with construction. A rail car marshalling yard had been built first, the existing spur expanded and improved.

An entire concrete factory sprouted from the prairie, specifically designed to produce material for the half-mile long row of silos that were to tower above the quiet town. Below ground, over a mile of connecting conduits, rail car unloading bins, and transfer conveyers had been poured. Over time, the locals had taken to calling this massive subterranean complex the "catacombs."

Solar powered circulation units, acoustic cleaners, and state of the art oxygen control systems had been installed. Over two years later, without electrical power or any maintenance, the corn was still as fresh as if it had been harvested yesterday.

The people of Riley became experts on ways to consume the food so prevalent in their own backyards and cheap in their supermarkets. Cornbread, corndogs, corn soup, corn pancakes; the human palate demanded variety, and the culinary artists of Riley had tested every possible recipe for preparing the plant. And to make matters worse, the silos held seed corn. It wasn't even sweet. Shane shook his head, yet again swearing that when things got back to normal, he'd never eat corn again.

As he watched the child-convoy pass, Shane detected the dread on most of their faces. The underground, concrete-walled world they were about to enter was a dreary, colorless place. It was hot in the day and cold at night. There wasn't anything to do but sit and watch the time go by. But it was more than that.

The children had hidden there before, finding refuge in the seemingly endless maze as they sought to escape the sickness. Shane didn't blame them; he shared their anxiety.

When the gasoline tank powering the town's water pump ran dry, the result had been more than just thirsty residents. Shane had always suspected it had something to do with human waste or the lack of bathing that had caused the sickness. Additionally, the local gardens no longer offered fresh fruit and vegetables, having dried and shriveled to brown, lifeless patches of scorched earth. The corn became more than a staple; it was their lifeline.

Whatever the reason, the adults had started behaving erratically. They simply seemed to act normally one day, and the next they were insane. There wasn't any other way to describe it.

Reverend Butler had been the first, the town's people waking up one morning to find the local preacher strolling down Main Street, naked as a jaybird and singing an old Neil Diamond hit "Sweet Caroline." Growing violent as the concerned citizens tried to help, it was clear to all that the man had snapped. Most speculated it was due to the stress associated with living in a post-collapse world, others believing the man of God had always been a little "touched."

A few days later, some passersby noticed Mr. Ash had locked himself in the local savings and loan without food or water, never leaving the building again. And then another of the townspeople began to show odd behavior.... After that, the sickness began to spread rapidly.

While different people reacted in diverse ways, one thing was for certain. They all lost touch with reality. Some became delusional, others sitting on the street corner and mumbling as if they were speaking in tongues. Most turned violent sooner or later.

Shootings, stabbings, brawls, and arson ravaged the adult population, sometimes the killings numbering three or four per day. Only the children and young adults seemed immune.

No one knew what was causing the illness, medical care from the town's two doctors unavailable, as both had been murdered by rampaging patients early in the outbreak. People hunkered down in their homes, standing guard against their unstable neighbors. A few innocents had been shot by mistake.

The teenagers didn't understand it all, but one thing was for certain. The adults, including their parents, were out of control... had left the reservation... and were to be avoided at all costs. The older adolescents started herding the younger children into the catacombs, the only place that was safe from the marauding grownups.

Shane, along with a few other 20-somethings, hadn't contracted the disease, or virus, or bug, or whatever it was. After a few months, the children and young adults were the only survivors residing in Riley, Texas.

One little girl stepped out of line, her tiny face gazing up at Shane. "Are the monsters going to come again?"

"No," he replied, looking down at the still-innocent face. "No, I'm not going to let the monsters come any more."

"Okay," she responded and scurried off to retake her place.

"At least I hope not," Shane whispered.

The monsters. It's what the older children had told the younger ones to get them to cooperate, to remain quiet and hide. Shane shook his head, a small twinge of guilt over having used the exact same lie – more than once.

In reality, the "monsters" were the raiders, looters and other nomadic desperados who had descended upon Riley over the years. Time and again, the fiends visited their little community. Sometimes small groups of invaders disrupted their world. Occasionally, a sole traveler, wandering from town to town, salvaging whatever he could to survive. Most were shy, avoiding people and remaining in the shadows. Others were bold, placing little value on human life, having no issue with killing anyone or anything to get what they needed. When the adults had still controlled the town, they fought to protect the community. Gun battles with the rovers claimed almost as many as the sickness.

146

Later, when only Shane and a handful of the other younger men and women remained, their plan had been the same – fight and either kill or chase away the evil-hearted.

One day, after burying a friend who had been ambushed while picking blackberries, Shane suddenly realized he was the only person left who had seen 20 or more years. He was now the default father, mayor, uncle, and priest to over 30 children. It changed his life.

Sure, many of the older teenagers had stepped in as caretaker for their younger siblings after mom and dad were dead. Others of the orphaned kids had simply moved to the next occupied household. The extra mouth to feed wasn't any big deal with tons of corn nearby. And besides, where else could they go?

The younger boys picked up their parents' weapons or those left behind by dead bandits. All of the children grew up quickly, the harsh life of a post-apocalyptic world leaving them no choice.

Shane shook his head, dismissing those bad memories. He started jogging, quickly catching up with the front of the line. As they trekked through the streets of Riley, he felt a little like the Pied Piper, leading the children away from their homes and into the unknown.

Bishop moved to the edge of the wood line, staying low on the off chance that he was being watched. He had borrowed Kevin's sniper rifle while the team's best shot had taken his turn in the rack. Grim was also catching some sleep, the contractor snoring away in Bishop's net-hammock.

He'd told Cory to hang back and observe the camp, violating his own rules about operating alone. Still, he wasn't going far, and the sleeping men were far more vulnerable.

It was another hour before sunset, and Bishop wanted to take a detailed look at the town before they moved in after dark. The scope on Kevin's rifle offered the most powerful magnification available.

Bishop steadied the rifle on a tree limb, turning the focus knob until the details of Riley cleared. The first things that drew his eye were the grain silos.

Dwarfing the rest of the structures in the area, the complex of buildings, tracks, roads, and towering structures was amazing. If the grain elevators were as full of seed corn as their source claimed, the Alliance could begin replanting thousands and thousands of acres, while at the same time making a significant dent in the imminent food shortages.

There was no way to tell if the silos were actually full from Bishop's vantage. He would have to wait until Cory inspected the storage areas. Still, it was exciting to be a part of something that could change so many lives for the better – perhaps even save the Alliance.

Satisfied with his review of the night's objective, Bishop lowered the rifle and sat back to relax for a few moments. The sun was just touching the western horizon, low enough that a man could view it without hurting his eyes. It was going to be a clear night, his watch indicating a quarter moon.

Those conditions would offset the advantage of their electronically enhanced night vision, but not enough to delay the trip to town.

Bishop took a moment to marvel at the beauty of the remote Texas countryside. The birds, chirping and singing, obviously didn't care about the apocalypse. He spied a rabbit emerging from its burrow, the long-eared jack preparing for a nocturnal graze.

"We're the only species that gives a shit," Bishop whispered. "We built it up, let it fall down, and now we're struggling with the consequences. Every other life form on this ball of rock could care less. Maybe we should be more like them."

It wasn't the first time the Texan's mind had traveled in that direction. Was mankind's reorganization really the best move? Was society, rule of law, and all of its trimmings really the best strategy?

There was a streak of Darwinism in Bishop. A line of thinking that conjectured that the human race had asked for much of what happened because it had bypassed survival of the fittest, circumvented nature's rule that only the strongest survive. Yes, the species had prolonged life, made the less successful more comfortable, and propagated the population to billions and billions of individuals. But had the collapse really been unavoidable? Had the downfall been set in motion by the habits of men? Habits that violated the rules followed by every other creature on the planet.

Bishop traveled back in time, to Houston, when everything started falling apart. He wished he knew then what was so obvious now. Terri and he had gotten lucky, and in so many ways. They always overstocked their pantry in case of hurricanes. They had secured a bug-out location. They had managed to scavenge fuel from Bishop's employer when it was no longer available to the general public.

Without that set of parameters, his wife and he would have ended up no better than the starving masses that now depended on the Army for their every need. And the military was running on empty.

And then there was Meraton, Texas… a small, less affluent community that had naturally developed and grown as a self-reliant entity - out of necessity. Part of that mindset sprouted naturally from the adjacent, sprawling ranches whose owners had learned 150 years ago that they could ultimately depend on no one but themselves. For them, the fall of society hadn't really meant that much.

Often, he'd pondered what the situation would be like if the population of Houston had been as self-reliant as the residents of Meraton. It the state's largest cities had been dotted with gardens, backup water supplies, and fruit trees, would so many lives have been lost?

If the government, education system, and society had embraced a more autonomous lifestyle, would the nation have survived intact? Instead of social safety nets provided by Big Brother, the American people might have embraced an attitude from yesteryear, a motto simply stating, "I am responsible for my own survival." Would the collapse have killed so many?

149

Even if the world hadn't slid over the edge, would the hurricanes, tornados, floods, earthquakes, and other natural disasters have been so devastating to the American economy and her people?

Bishop grunted, an interesting thought popping into his mind. "Are we repeating the same mistake?" he whispered to the birds. If the council's plan to utilize the grain stored in the giant silos below worked, wouldn't the Alliance be substituting one system of dependency with another? Would bailing out all those people east of the Alliance render null and void the severe reality of how fragile society had become?

Bishop remembered his grandparents, survivors of the first Great Depression. He recalled how they had never trusted the government, neighbors or anyone else to put bread on the table. They had learned the hard way, experienced true hunger, and changed their lives to make sure it never happened again.

But that lesson's value had faded over the years. A vast majority of Americans pursued wealth, big screen televisions, and a lifestyle of convenience instead of being able to sustain their families independently. What is worse, they mocked the unassuming souls who supported the tenets of a self-reliant lifestyle.

Bishop shook his head, the line of thought triggering a pounding in his temples. He'd seen more than his share of starving people, and it wasn't pretty. Was it humane to deny people food, medical care, and security just because they had been shortsighted? Was it fair to let human beings die of starvation just because their priorities and focus hadn't been aligned with reality?

There were more than a few people in the Alliance who would have answered those questions with a resounding, "Yes!" Survival of fittest, they would argue, would strengthen the gene pool and eventually make the entire race stronger.

Sighing, Bishop knew he wasn't going to resolve these deep, contradicting philosophies that had probably plagued every leader since the beginning of time.

"Your lot is not to answer," he mumbled, "but to risk your life trying to do."

He hoped those folks in H-town and the Big D would appreciate the sacrifices made in Brighton, Alpha, Midland Station, and a hundred other towns across the country. He hoped one day the men who fought to save this nation would be remembered, and that people would be humbled from the sacrifice, maybe even learn their lessons.

"I'm going to bail you out one more time," he chuckled, heading back for the camp. "After this, you're truly on your own."

Shane made sure the last of the kids was settled in. He'd directed the older boys back to town to retrieve blankets, additional water, and a few ancillary items he realized they would need or that would make their hideout more comfortable for an extended stay. As soon as it was dark, they could start the fires and warm the meager amount of food they'd carried in with them.

As he roamed the underground labyrinth of storage rooms, dump chutes and passageways, he couldn't help but note what a pitiful lot this cluster of survivors was. It made him angry.

Hadn't they already suffered enough? Hadn't watching their parents die of insanity, hostile raiders or other acts of horrible demise been payment enough?

Yet again, they were being pushed out of the only homes they knew, huddled together in a dark place hoping to avoid discovery. At that moment, Shane couldn't understand the world or any God that watched over it. He just couldn't.

Shaking off the melancholy funk being conjured up by his emotions, he decided to tour their new home one last time. Candles had already been lit here and there, the older children trying to conserve what was becoming an increasingly rare commodity.

Some of the older kids were reading books to the very young, using the colorful drawings to lighten the mood or settle adolescent fears. Shane was always amazed when he saw such acts of maturity and caring. When he had been ten years old, the thought of tending to a kid half his age would have been unthinkable - far beyond his grasp or capability. Now, the older children routinely shared responsibility for the less capable.

Turning to enter a long, low concrete corridor, he almost bumped into a pair of older boys carrying their rifles. "Hey, Shane," they greeted, moving to one side so he could pass.

"You guys doing okay?"

"Yeah. It's our turn to stand watch in a little bit. We thought we'd give Chad and Ricky a break so they could grab a bite," one of them replied.

"Good luck then. I'll be up that way in a bit."

As Shane watched them go, pride welled in his chest. He thought the older boy was 11 or 12, the younger probably laying claim to a mere nine years on this earth. They were reporting for a job, carrying firearms, and showing compassion for their friends. How many pre-teen boys would do that?

"I sure as shit wasn't that mature," he said. "The only thing I was ever on time for was Saturday morning cartoons. I don't think I ever did a chore without my old man having to remind me. Sometimes he'd have to get pissed before I'd go do it. They're good kids – they deserve better than this."

He found Jimmy right where he thought his nephew would be, hanging around that Candy girl with those lovesick, puppy dog eyes. "Ahhh, hormones," he whispered under his breath, "It had to happen eventually."

"Hi, Shane," Jimmy said.

"Hey. You and the twins all ready for our little raiding party tonight?"

"Yeah. I was just making sure Candy and her sister were comfortable."

Shane nodded knowingly, not wanting to embarrass or trouble the kid right before they were heading out to do something dangerous. "Well, if you're ready, we need to get going."

With his team gathered at the catacomb's opening, Shane began issuing their instructions. "I think the intruders will come into town tonight. They probably have night vision, maybe even other military gear. I hope they look around, don't find anything, and leave. There's no reason for them to stay. While they're busy checking out Riley, we're going to go locate their camp. Jimmy and the other guys saw lots of food and equipment... more than they can carry. If these guys don't leave tomorrow, then we'll go back and steal their stuff. Maybe they'll get the idea and head out."

"Where do you think they are camped?" one of the boys asked.

"They'll be up on Indian Ridge, probably a little east of where Jimmy found them. We'll go around the school and behind the old church... stay on the eastern outskirts of town," Shane said.

The leader smoothed out a clear patch of dirt with his palm and then began drawing a diagram of Riley in the dirt. A few minutes later, every head was nodding in agreement. They all knew the route.

"If anybody gets lost, come back here to the catacombs. But don't get lost."

Bishop spread the map across the tailgate, his team gathering so all could see. "I want to avoid the downtown area," he began. "We'll stay to the east and circle around to the silos. There's a church right here... and the school is right here," he said, pointing to the map.

Grim shook his head, concern etching deep lines on the contractor's face. "I don't like leaving the truck here unguarded. It's our only way home."

"I know," Bishop responded. "But nobody operates alone. If I split us up, that means only two of us going into the town, and I'm uncomfortable with that. Remember, this is just a quick fact-finding excursion. We need to see what's in those silos. If they're empty, then the mission is over, and we head back home. If they're full of good stuff, then we can decide how to approach the people."

"Damned if you do; damned if you don't. This reminds me of the Army," Grim commented. "But I do have to agree... it would be better not to divide our forces on this first trip."

Bishop extended his upturned palm, a small electronic device in his hand. "This is the master relay from under the hood. They won't steal the truck without this. We might drive home hungry, but we'll not be walking."

That settled, Bishop continued, "I want a box formation, each man at a corner. Kevin, you and Cory will be at the back. Spacing is everything, and never, ever lose sight of your opposite corner. One of us being taken hostage is the worst consideration. Got it?"

The two lesser-experienced men nodded their understanding. Bishop then had each of them draw his route on the map with a finger, just to be sure they both fully understood.

Forty minutes later, the sun's last illumination faded, and the Alliance team moved out.

Their first objective was the church, the high steeple an easy landmark for navigation. He was satisfied with Cory and Kevin's spacing and noise discipline during the move, proving the two weeks of training back in Alpha a worthy investment of time and resources.

Shane and Jimmy rounded the corner of the school, the remainder of the guys spread out behind them. "I wish we had more moon," Jimmy whispered, "I can't see much."

"Shhhhh," Shane scolded. "Just scan, don't focus. Like we were stalking deer. You'll see movement before you can make out any shapes. Now hush."

The rest of the boys caught up, Shane examining the wide-eyed bunch with a critical eye. They were too noisy, and he was beginning to regret bringing them along.

He quickly reconsidered those harsh thoughts. In a way, he was proud of each and every one of them. Yes, they were on edge, and making stupid little noises while bunching up. But it wasn't fear. *I suppose even the most experienced men would be wound up tight*, he thought. *For a bunch of kids, they're doing really, really well.*

Shane had to admit, even he was nervous. Hunting at night was one thing, but this was proving to be a completely different challenge. Deer and hogs didn't shoot back. The low light made even the simplest task daunting. And worse yet, it was easy to see a threat in every pool of shadow.

They knew that armed, hostile men were in the area, and that knowledge fueled already vivid imaginations. Just in the half-mile between the silos and the school, Shane had twice thought he'd identified the outline of a man. One had ended up being a bush, the other, one of his own guys who had gotten out of line. Shane had almost shot the kid, realizing at the last second the target was a friend.

No, it was easy to be freaked and make a mistake. And he was the most experienced of the bunch.

Having second thoughts about trying to find the strangers' camp, he almost called off the excursion. But they needed to know what was happening above ground. It would help him plan and react. Maybe they just needed to go about it in a different way.

After scanning the open area between their position and the church, Shane decided to risk a little noise of his own. Pulling them all close in a huddle, he cupped his hands around his mouth and whispered, "Stay here while Jimmy and I go scout the church. One of us will come back and get you if it's clear."

After making sure everyone had heard the instructions, Jimmy and he pushed off, heading for the outline of the chapel's steeple.

Bishop and Grim stood at the edge of what had been the parking lot in front of the sanctuary, both of them scanning the area to their front with night vision and thermal optics, both hesitant to step from the soft, quiet soil onto the crunchy, noisy gravel surface.

Not detecting any threat from the building or surrounding ground, Bishop keyed his radio once, the single click telling his team it looked clear to move forward. Pausing for a moment to see if anyone objected by sounding two clicks, he then stepped out of the weed line and onto the rock surface.

Their pace slowed considerably, each man doing his best to move quietly. But the small stones under their feet made such stealth almost impossible. Halfway across, Bishop was furious with himself. They sounded like a herd of thundering cattle crossing the gravel covering. Not only did everyone for five miles know their location, they were completely exposed with zero cover for over 50 feet. *Why the hell didn't you go around this shit?* his mind cursed. *You're going to get everyone killed.*

Shane heard a crunch and put his hand into Jimmy's chest, both of them freezing in place, ears and eyes searching the darkness. His heart was beating a million miles a minute, pounding in his head and making listening even more difficult.

There it was again. The grinding of a footfall on pea gravel.

Motioning for Jimmy to stay put, Shane moved to the corner of the church, cautiously peeking around. He was only 30 feet away from Bishop, the sight of a man so close causing a cold, wet sensation to flow down his legs. For a second, he thought he'd pissed his pants.

A vague outline, distorted by the darkness, Bishop looked like a robotic killing machine. Shane could see the rifle, bulging pouches, kit, and body armor making the approaching shape appear larger and more menacing than any man.

Shane's perception of the situation deteriorated as the other men in the parking lot came into focus. His mind in a panic, he believed there were at least a dozen intruders coming to kill him. Somehow, the instincts of self-preservation kicked in, and he managed to step back. Then another half step. And then he rushed to Jimmy's side.

Motioning for the kid to join him, Shane started running back

156

toward the safety of the school and his group. Jimmy, seeing the sheer terror on his mentor's face, didn't waste any time following.

Breathless, Shane skidded to a halt next to the gathered huddle of boys. After a few deep breaths, he managed to whisper, "They're in the church's parking lot, headed this way. There's a bunch of them, like an infantry platoon or some shit."

Seeing the normally brave Shane in such a state, the boys all started glancing in the direction of the church. More than one of them clicked the safety off his rifle.

"What do you want to do, Shane?" one of the older boys asked.

The first thoughts that flashed through the leader's mind were to fight. He envisioned spreading out his guns across the school's lot and waiting on the strangers to enter their sights. As he glimpsed the eager, frightened faces waiting for his words, Shane couldn't help but wonder how many of them would be killed.

Images of those he'd already buried came flooding back, pain and trauma accompanying the gory memories of friends who'd died defending their homes. There had been so many dead. The smell of their blood and guts rose in the back of his throat with an acidic burn. *Too many*, he realized. *Too many dead.*

He turned to stare back toward the church, fully expecting to see the outsiders charging around the corner with guns blazing a deadly hail of lead. After seeing only empty ground in the moonlight, he couldn't help but wonder if that small piece of earth was worth dying for. Nothing but knee-high weeds and overgrowth met his gaze, the dilapidated church in the distance. He then glanced at the distant outline of downtown, the darkened windows and empty streets of the ghost town instilling a sense of loneliness and abandonment. Was there anything left in Riley worth the ultimate sacrifice?

There are only 30 of us left, he considered. *We're outgunned, low on ammo, and sure to lose good men. I'm sick of digging graves and listening to people cry.*

"Fall back," he whispered. "Go back to the catacombs. There's too many of them."

Bishop sighed in relief, looking up at the enormous silo outlined against the star-filled sky. Despite studying the complex since they'd arrived, he was still impressed by the size.

"Cory," he whispered, motioning his man closer. "Can you take the samples and do the tests at night?"

"Some of it, yes. The council wants to know approximately how much grain is housed here, so I'll have to climb every silo and look through the inspection hatches. I don't like heights, so I'd rather do that part during the daytime, sir."

Bishop understood completely, secretly glad it was the other man's assignment. "Can you tell if there's even any grain at all?"

Nodding, Cory motioned Bishop to follow. The two men ventured to the base of the enormous tower and began circling.

Halfway around, Cory pulled up and pointed to a steel door with an intricate looking mechanism attached to the surface. Bishop thought it looked like something that belonged on a submarine. Sliding his rifle to his back, Cory grabbed a lever with both hands, struggling to pull the rusty device down. After a grind and squeak, the machinery finally cooperated. Next, he spun a small wheel-like control. Finally, he tugged open a slight, but thick metal door and stood back.

A stream of bright, yellow kernels came shooting out of the opening, the steady flow lasting three or four seconds. Cory stuck out his hand, catching a fistful out in mid-air.

Smiling at Bishop, he raised the corn to his nose and inhaled deeply. "Smells fresh and clean," he whispered, offering his leader a sniff. "I don't detect any mold or fermentation."

Bishop obliged, inhaling the aroma and nodding his head in agreement. The scent was earthy and pleasant.

Bishop considered the possibilities - the seed, food, and opportunities this could mean for the Alliance and her people. But how many of the silos held the golden treasure? Were all the grain elevators full?

Glancing down the long line of similar towers, Bishop shook his head. This was going to take a while, especially if Cory had to climb each one.

Then he turned his gaze toward downtown Riley, realizing their discovery was but a hollow victory. The team had verified the existence of the grain and its viability. Now Bishop needed to know how difficult the local population was going to make his life.

"Take Kevin and randomly check five more silos," he whispered to Cory. Grim and I will make sure you're not disturbed. Hurry."

After watching the two men hustle off, Bishop turned to Grim and announced, "I'm going to climb up that ladder and see what's going on in Riley. Should be some candles or fires or something."

Grim nodded, positioning himself so he could keep an eye on the silo testers and Bishop at the same time.

Flipping his rifle around to his back, the Texan began his ascent up the rungs, quickly reaching a height of about 30 feet. From that vantage, he could clearly identify the outlines of roofs, structures, and light poles in the residential section of town. But the village lay in complete shadow.

Looping an arm around the vertical support so he wouldn't fall, Bishop managed to lift his rifle and again proceeded to sweep Riley with the night vision. Nothing. Not a single flame or flicker. No movement whatsoever.

When he had planted both feet firmly back on the ground, he stepped toward Grim and proclaimed, "Not a creature was stirring, not even a mouse."

"Really? No lights or anything?"

"You are welcome to try your hand with the thermal unit, but I detected neither hide nor hair nor any light source with the NVD."

"Where did they go?" Grim asked, not really expecting Bishop to know. "It's only been dark two hours. Do you think everybody hit the hay early?"

Bishop considered his response for a second. "Could be. I think it's a little weird for there not to be a single light, but it could be. We'll find out in the morning."

Two hours later, Cory returned with an ear-to-ear grin spread across his face. "Every silo I tested contained good product inside. I can't tell if the structures are nearly empty, full to the top or somewhere in between, but I do know that what is inside can offer enough food to make a substantial dent in our famine issue. No sign of any rot, mold, or fermentation."

"That's great news!" Bishop responded with an excited whisper. "Maybe this wasn't a wasted trip after all."

Grim chimed in, "Let's move the truck up here. There are a couple of little nooks we can fit it into that are very defendable. It doesn't look like the locals come this way often."

Scratching his chin, Bishop nodded. "Well, that *would* send a message, but I'm not sure if it's the right one. On the other hand, we need to complete a full inventory of this facility, and that's obviously going to take a few days. We could improve security if we weren't shuffling back and forth."

Grim motioned toward an area between two buildings, probably once dedicated to the employee of the month's reserved parking space. "If we back the truck in there, we could spend more time performing inventory and less time guarding our supplies."

Bishop scouted the spot and liked the setup. One man on top of the nearby building could cover an extensive area and provide security.

"We'll head back, break down camp, and drive in tonight. I want to be in a position to observe the residential section of town at first light. We have to establish contact with the residents. I don't want them thinking we're just going to abscond with all their grain and not provide anything in return."

Grim grunted, "Is it really their grain? That sign over there says it belongs to Mid-South Mills, Incorporated."

It was a question that constantly tested the Alliance leadership. Who owned what? Who had the rights to property, equipment, stores, and supplies? Without banks, corporate governance, or rule of law, it was an extremely difficult question.

At first, the old adage of "Possession is 9/10s of the law," was the rule of thumb. This especially held true with foodstuffs, medical supplies, and fuel.

But now that a recovery was in process, what about abandoned industrial plants and equipment? What about the motorhomes Terri and the council members used to tour the territory? Those had been discovered on a sales lot, the facility's owner, lien holder, or titles nowhere to be found.

Even in Alpha, where empty homes had been allocated to immigrants, there had been problems. Bishop knew of three or four cases where the original owner had suddenly reappeared, shocked to find occupants residing in the family homestead.

Diana had been forced to create a special review panel to settle such situations, as well as disputes that arose over pre-collapse versus post-collapse ownership. Homes were an easily resolved matter, most cases involving relocation of the new family and letting the original homeowner retake possession.

But what about equipment? Bishop recalled one dispute over a tractor. Pre-collapse, one of the valley ranchers had taken his implement into Alpha to be repaired. Post-collapse, with food production being a priority, Diana had allowed the distribution of farm equipment as needed. The repaired unit, sitting on the lot, had been taken by a neighboring rancher. A dispute soon arose.

Bishop turned to Grim and offered an option. "Maybe we should print off some business cards and put on a suit and tie. We could go to the townsfolk and claim to be executives from Mid-South Mills Incorporated, here to take possession of our property."

Grim nodded, "And how would they prove or know any different? It's no bigger lie than your telling that kid you are a Texas Ranger."

Bishop smiled, nodding at Grim's carbine, load-gear, armor, and thermal imager. "You do fit the executive prototype, my friend. I'm sure all the bean counters at Mid-South aspire to dress like that."

Scrutinizing Bishop's garb in turn, Grim smirked. "I'm sure a lot of Texas Rangers dress like *that*."

"No doubt the community has grown accustomed to thinking this grain is theirs. For all we know, those silos may contain their primary source of food. None of this will be easy, I am sure. Let's move out and get the truck back here."

Two hours later, Riley experienced a sound not heard for over a year, the running engine of a pickup. The team hustled to set up security, unpack gear, and generally make themselves at home. They found the grain elevator's office complex inhabited by spiders, rats and a thriving roach population. The interior just wasn't inviting, smelling and feeling like an Egyptian tomb.

They all set up their sleeping arrangements outside, with Bishop choosing his net while Kevin, Cory, and Grim elected to use sleeping bags in the pickup's bed.

After settling in, Bishop pointed to his watch. "Come on, Grim. It's time to observe the good people of Riley awaken."

"What are they doing?" Shane asked Jimmy.

"It looks like they're moving in. What are we going to do? They're almost on top of us," sounded the worried voice.

Since retreating from the chapel, Shane had spied the newcomers head directly to the entrance of the catacombs. He and the sentries had remained hidden, observing the strangers fiddle with the silos and wander here and there. Shane had passed the word for everyone to remain quiet and stay deep within the underground system. All fires were to be extinguished.

A couple of times, he thought they had been discovered. The guy pulling samples had stopped and stared directly at one of the entrances, but then nothing happened.

Temporary relief had come when the strangers had hiked out. He had even exited the tunnels, following behind them until they reached the city limit. But then the pickup truck had returned, shattering any thoughts of being able to return home in the morning.

When the outsiders had started setting up camp, Shane knew they were in trouble.

"We have to wait them out," he told Jimmy. "They are outfitted with better weapons and have more ammunition than we do. They would slaughter us."

"I don't like this, Shane," Jimmy replied. "We don't have enough water to stay down here very long. And where they are parked, we can't come above ground without attracting their attention. We really are a bunch of rats now. Trapped rats."

Reaching out to touch the boy's shoulder, Shane tried to reassure him. "They'll leave before long. There's no reason for them to stay unless they're the biggest corn eaters in history. They'll either catch the sickness or head out. Go tell the older kids – everyone is to hide, conserve water, and stay quiet."

Jimmy nodded and then backed down the steps into the tunnel. After he was a safe distance away from the entry, he pulled out a plastic lighter and ignited a torch. The warm red glow improved his attitude. It was amazing how fire always seemed to do that.

The kids had learned the hard way to use chalk to mark the paths. Since the younger ones couldn't read, they had drawn pictures on the doors; the sun and arrows indicating which of the corridors led to the surface.

In addition to marking the emergency exits, they had given certain tunnels names. There was Cat, Dog, Fish, and Skunk, each of the underground "streets" identified via a picture of its namesake.

Cat and Dog were sleeping areas. Fish indicated the location where the cooking was done. Skunk was the bathroom, where the children were instructed to bury their work in the sand floor. It reeked of human waste, but was the only solution they could fashion.

Jimmy knew that most of the younger kids would be asleep by now. The older rats would be hanging out in Fish, either waiting on their turn at guard duty, or getting a snack.

As he entered the tunnel, there was enough candlelight for him to extinguish the torch and conserve it for later. He ducked low and came into one of the hundreds of "rooms" scattered throughout the complex. Inside were a few of the older kids, lounging around a cardboard box that housed a lone checkerboard. A stack of feedbags, an old scruffy-looking lawn chair, and an upside-down bucket served as seating.

"Hey, Jimmy, what's up? Are the strangers still outside?" Candy asked.

His stress melted away, replaced by wonderment at how the candlelight danced in her eyes. Finally realizing he was staring, unresponsive, and looking stupid, he mumbled, "Yes, and they've set up camp."

Forcing his eyes away to look at the others, he managed to relay Shane's orders for quiet and conservation.

Candy could tell he was worried. They all were. "Any idea how long these strangers are going to stay?"

"No way to tell. Shane knows we don't have much water down here. We need to be extra, extra careful with it."

Someone asked, "What do they want, Jimmy? Why are they here?"

"We don't know, but Shane thinks they'll leave soon. You guys make sure the little rats stay quiet. If there's nobody around, and nothing worth looting, then the outsiders will move on. If they don't leave on their own, then we'll have to fight them."

Candy shook her head, the thought of more shooting and killing wrinkling her brow. "Tell Shane I've got a little one with a bad cough. She needs sunshine and fresh air. We got two others with diarrhea, and they need to drink lots."

Jimmy nodded, wondering if the general dislike of the catacombs had anything to do with the runny butt. "I know you and the others will take good care of them, Candy. We'll do our best, but I wouldn't count on us getting out of here anytime soon."

164

Bishop glanced over his shoulder at the sun and then back at Grim. They had taken up positions on the roof of what had been a dry cleaner, the single story building providing an excellent view of a significant portion of Riley's residential area.

"Nothing. Not a damn thing," Grim whispered. "Either these people are sleeping in, or there's not a soul in this town. I don't get it."

Bishop was puzzled as well. "We know there are at least... what... six or eight people living here. We've met four of them face-to-face. Where did they go?"

"Maybe your little Texas Ranger fantasy scared them off, and they hightailed it to grandma's house."

Bishop grunted, "Could be. I'm sure your threatening to slice off that boy's head had nothing to do with it."

"Either there's no one here, or they know we're up here and are hiding. One way or the other, I need to stretch and move my legs. I'm afraid this situation is going to require a little house-to-house search action."

Bishop lowered his head, the thought having already occurred to him. "You're right. God, this is going to suck."

There was nothing worse than going into a neighborhood and searching for people. Bishop had done it before with Terri in New Mexico, and it was a nail biting, ball of stress. Any rifle from any window could ruin your day. The locals knew the terrain, including every bit of good cover and hidden crannies. The Texan wasn't looking forward to the task at hand.

No longer concerned with remaining concealed, Grim stood and uncoiled his frame. Stretching and twisting at the hips, he glanced down at Bishop and grumbled, "I'm getting to old for this scout-sniper bullshit. You got any jobs that call for a plain, old, everyday stand-up gunslinger?"

Bishop soon joined his comrade, gingerly bending and flexing, every joint sounding with pops and cracks. "That's too bad, Grim. I could complete a triathlon and *then* kick your ass after I finished. You should work on your conditioning."

The only response was an exaggerated eye-roll, Grim more concerned about circulation to his legs than Bishop's sarcasm.

Soon, the duo was climbing down from the roof. "Now or never," Bishop declared, nodding toward the first street.

An hour later, the mystery had only deepened.

There was clear evidence of habitation. Two homes displayed laundry lines stretched across the backyard, one of them adorned with a colorful array of t-shirts, sporting no evidence of sun bleaching from long-term exposure. There were paths of crushed grass and weeds between some of the houses, one of the abodes decked with a slop bucket full of fresh table scraps sitting on the back porch.

Those houses that showed clear evidence of recent occupation were thoroughly searched. Bishop was surprised to find the doors unlocked, all of the windows open. *Now that's really odd*, he thought. He didn't know anyone in this post-apocalyptic world who would be so careless with their security.

Grim had noted that all of the clean laundry was clothing for children, both in size and design.

"Do you think they all moved to the school or one of the churches?" Bishop asked, scratching his head over the recently abandoned neighborhood.

"Could be. Or maybe they evacuated to somebody's farm in the rural countryside."

Bishop's response was a yawn, quickly followed by an audible rumble from his stomach. "One thing's for certain. We aren't going to find them if they're hiding. I guess we just finish our job and report back to the council. Maybe they'll show up before we head out."

Grim frowned at the concept. "Maybe they'll show up with guns blazing. They're probably out gathering reinforcements from the

166

surrounding ranches. They're no doubt readying a virtual tide of infantry to mount a full frontal assault and kick our sorry asses. We need to stay frosty, sharp, and diligent as hell."

"Amen to that, brother. Amen. Let's go get some chow and rack. You look like you could use some beauty rest."

"Not everybody can be fresh as a fucking daisy like you, oh fearless leader," Grim replied, bowing deeply at the waist.

Three days later, Cory was finally finished with his inventory, and the results were fantastic. "We're showing 28 of the silos completely full. Only one had signs of deterioration, but I can't be sure about that from such a cursory examination. Regardless, that's hundreds of tons of seed, feed, and cornbread. Now if we just had some beans to go with it," he reported.

The Alliance team was ecstatic, smiles and backslaps all around. They had no way of knowing, just a few feet away, almost beneath their boots, there was tremendous suffering and discomfort.

The water had lasted a little more than a day. Despite being underground, the daytime temperature in the catacombs was still miserable, the dank, thick air close and stale.

Candy, Shane and the older hideouts had done their best to ration, but little frames couldn't control their body temps as well as adults. Thirsty children became cranky children, and the water carried below had been consumed quickly.

The first day without H2O had been troubling, but the junior residents of Riley were tough. By midway through the third day, everyone was complaining of headaches, sore muscles, and dry throats. Shane was getting desperate.

"We're going to have to shoot it out with them," he told the gathered boys. "We can't wait any longer. We'll pop out of the opening just before dark. Steady your aim and make every bullet count. I'll go first, and try and keep them busy with my semi-auto. The more of you that get out and start shooting, the better our odds. Meet me at the entrance in one hour."

The meeting's attendees dispersed, even the youngest of the boys well aware that they didn't have much of a chance of seeing nightfall. Jimmy traveled along to Cat, finding Candy and some of the girls gathered there.

"We're going outside in an hour," Jimmy informed the assembly. "We're going to fight our way out of here."

Candy was upset, but too dehydrated to mount much of a protest. With a sniffle, and then tears running down her dirty cheeks, she answered softly, "Jimmy... I don't know what to say. I'm afraid you'll be hurt... or worse."

The young man glared down at the floor, afraid he'd start weeping if he met her gaze. "Shane is going out first. I'll be second. Maybe if we surprise them... maybe they aren't good fighters... maybe it'll be okay."

Candy shook her head, memories of all the people she'd loved who were now dead. "There has to be another way. Can't we give them a little more time to leave?"

Jimmy waved his arm around the room, the walls lined with filthy, lethargic, little faces. "We have to do it now, Candy. We have to do it for them," he said motioning at the pathetic children. "We can't just wait until they all get really sick. Everybody's thirsty and hungry. We all need sunshine and fresh air."

Frustrated by the truth, Candy started weeping in earnest. "It's just not fair, Jimmy! Why does everyone I care about have to die?"

"*I'm* not dead yet," he chuckled, trying to be brave. "But I know what you mean. I wish things were the way they used to be. I dream about that all the time."

Stretching her arms out, Candy pulled Jimmy close and held him in a tight hug, both of their bodies racked with sobs. Every child in the room understood, many of them shedding tears as well.

It was Bishop's turn to pull guard duty, dreading the boredom more than lack of sleep. His team had done an excellent job on this mission, and millions of people would benefit from their efforts.

Since there hadn't been a single sign of another human being in the area, he decided to stroll around their perimeter before climbing up the office roof. It would get the blood circulating and help him stay awake until 11 when Kevin was scheduled to relieve him.

He had walked less than 50 feet when a scraping noise made him pull up short and freeze. *Was it an animal? A rat or rabbit?* He waited for several seconds, but the sound didn't repeat.

Another two steps, and he heard it again. In the fading light, he thought he saw movement in the distance, a shadow near a pile of busted, crumbling, cinder blocks someone had discarded near the silos.

His rifle snapped up, adrenaline pouring through his veins. He scanned and swept, but couldn't identify any threat. Bishop considered waking up the guys, but then dismissed the thought. If it was a squirrel or other vermin, it wasn't worth their loss of sleep. *Besides, I can just hear Grim going on and on about his fearless leader being scared shitless by a little ol' rodent.*

Bishop stalked to the corner, popping his head around the barrier to take a quick peek. There was something moving – and it was bigger than any rabbit. *A dog? Coyote?*

Whatever it was, he decided to chase it away. His team left food lying around, and he didn't want some animal getting a free lunch.

This time he stepped around the corner with purpose, his carbine against his shoulder, just in case it was a big dog. He'd had a few encounters with such post-apocalyptic beasts before.

Stunned, Bishop stopped short. Standing 20 feet away was a tiny child. A girl by the look of the long, curly tresses. She couldn't have been more than four or five years old. And she was clearly scared to death, clutching a doll tightly against her chest.

Her face was smeared with dirt, bits of debris in her hair. Her skirt had been lime green and sky blue at one point in its life; now it mostly matched the surrounding yellowish sand. The flip-flops on her feet showed filthy toes that had tracked through miles of earth.

Lowering his weapon, he decided to start a conversation with the tiny Riley resident. "Hi there," Bishop said as gently as possible. "Where did you come from?"

"Are you going to eat me?" the weak little voice replied.

"No, I don't eat people. What's your name?"

"Are you a monster? Please don't be one of the monsters."

Bishop flashed his biggest smile and dropped to one knee. "No, I'm not a monster. I'm just a man, and a nice man, too."

"I heard the other kids talking. They said you were a Texas Ranger. Is that true?"

Bishop didn't know how to answer at first. Lying was against his nature, especially to a child. But on the other hand, the girl's tone indicated she wanted it to be true.

He thought about rushing over and catching her, but her body language made it clear she would scamper off at his slightest movement.

"Yes," he finally decided to lie. "I'm a Texas Ranger, so you don't need to be scared of me. I protect people, especially little girls like you. What's your name?"

"My name is Missy. My daddy told me that if I was ever in trouble, I could get help from policemen, firemen, or Texas Rangers."

Bishop smiled, thinking he liked Missy's dad. "Your father was right, Missy. I can help you. What kind of trouble are you in?"

"We don't have any water. All the kids are getting sick, and the older boys are getting ready to shoot at you and the other men

170

up here."

"Where are these kids at, Missy?" Bishop said, looking around. "I don't see anyone but you."

"I'm not allowed to talk about it. But if you are really a Ranger, then you'll give me water so the boys don't have to shoot their guns."

"I'll give you all the water you want, Missy," Bishop said, slowly walking toward the child.

When he was close enough, he again took a knee and offered his Camelbak tube and mouthpiece. "If you come over here, you can drink from this tube. The water is in a big canteen on my back."

Missy hesitated, looking around as if she were about to bolt. Bishop squeezed the rubber tube and a small bit of water squirted out. "See, Missy. It's good, clean, fresh water. Come on over here and you can have a drink. We'll get some water for your friends after that."

Still, the child lingered, her nervous eyes darting among Bishop's face, the water tube, and the pile of concrete rubble just a few feet away. Bishop noted her cracked, dry lips, and the vision made his chest hurt. He'd been there, and the thought of any child suffering through dehydration was simply unacceptable.

Ten feet behind Bishop, Shane, Jimmy and the rest of the boys were just arriving at the entrance. Shane heard Bishop's voice close by, so he gently slid aside the burlap bag that disguised the opening to the catacombs. When he recognized Missy, he turned to the others and hissed quietly, "What is she doing out there? How did she get past us?"

"She must have found another way out," Jimmy answered.

"She'll tell them where we are," one of the other boys sounded off.

Shane maneuvered slightly, trying to find an angle to aim his rifle at Bishop. He was almost there when Missy decided to take a drink.

The small girl moved a few feet forward, and without taking her eyes from Bishop's face, put the water tube in her mouth. "You bite the end with your teeth, and water will come out," Bishop instructed.

Shane couldn't shoot, Missy's body between the stranger and him.

For a moment, Missy's eyes opened wide with surprise, and then Bishop saw her swallowing. After several mouthfuls, she popped the tube out and almost yelled, "That's the best water I've ever tasted. Can we get more like this for the rats?"

"Rats?"

She didn't answer at first, her mouth busy at the tube. While she drank, Bishop keyed the microphone on his other shoulder. "Grim? Kevin? I need you guys over by the first silo - right now. Bring as much bottled water as you can carry. I've made contact with the locals."

It took a moment, but Kevin's voice finally sounded through his earpiece. "Sir, did you say you needed as much water as we could carry?"

"Yes," Bishop responded. "I think I know where the citizens of Riley are hiding. But hurry. My new friend thinks we're about to be attacked."

Missy again pulled the tube out of her mouth, a smile brightening her face. "Are you hungry?" Bishop asked.

"You have food, too?"

Bishop dug in his pouch, producing a small bag of beef jerky, courtesy of the Beltran Ranch. "Here, eat it slowly... chew it up real good. You'll like it." Bishop took a bite himself, hoping to convince the suspicious girl that it wasn't poison.

"Damn it!" Shane hissed. "I can't get an angle on him without hitting Missy."

"Wait, Shane," Jimmy warned. "He's giving her something to eat and drink. He's not hurting her."

"He's just doing that so she'll tell him where we are."

Bishop watched Missy chew the jerky, pleased when a smile crossed her lips. "Want some more?"

"Yes! That tastes yummy."

Letting her reach into the bag to fetch her own piece, Bishop said, "So are we friends now?"

His answer came in the form of a hug, the girl's tiny arms wrapping around his neck. Bishop scooped her up and then stood. "My friends are on the way with water," he said. "I don't want them to scare you."

Missy wanted more water, and then more jerky.

A minute later, Bishop heard his team approaching, their arms full of water and faces full of curiosity. Bishop held up a hand, warning them to keep their distance. "Hi guys, this is my new friend Missy. From what she has told me the rest of the kids are in real need of water. Can you nice men set that down right there and then head on back to the truck?"

Grim didn't like it. "How about I stay here with you, Captain Ranger? That way, if the kids need any help carrying all this water, you and I can give them a hand."

Bishop shook his head, "Thanks, Uncle Grim, but I think Missy and I can handle it. You might go high though, just to keep an eye on things."

Grim understood, the rest of the team backing away slowly.

After they had departed, Bishop turned to Missy and said, "Okay, now there is a bunch of water here. More than you can carry. What do we do with it?"

Missy, between bits of jerky, managed to point to a gap in the pile of cinder blocks. "It's okay. Shane and the other boys can carry it down to the catacombs."

Bishop realized they were probably being watched. It had never occurred to him that the grain elevator probably had significant underground machinery and storage spaces. That's where everyone had been hiding – right underneath their feet.

"Missy, do you think Shane and the others can hear me?"

173

Even though her concentration was on the water tube, the girl still managed to nod her head.

"Listen up," Bishop said loudly toward the gap. "I told you all once we didn't mean any harm. I wasn't lying. I'm going to let Missy go and walk away. You can have the water. I only ask one thing. Send someone out to talk with us. You don't have to hide and suffer. If you've got sick among you, at least send them out. We'll try to help them."

Bishop bent over, gently setting Missy on the ground. "Come out and visit me again, Missy. I like having new friends."

"Thank you, Mister Texas Ranger. Can I have some more of that meat?"

Bishop gave her the whole bag and then stood up.

"I've got him," Shane whispered, his finger tightening on the trigger.

"Shane, no!" Jimmy shouted. "He's not a raider. Don't!"

Bishop could hear the low voices, but wasn't sure what was going on. He began stepping back toward the truck without giving the suspected opening a second glance.

Shane lowered his rifle, throwing a dirty look at his second in command. "Why did you stop me?"

"Because he could have taken Missy. He could have hurt her or killed her if he wanted to. He could have ordered his men to start searching for the opening, but he didn't. He left water and asked that we talk to him. I think he *is* a Texas Ranger, and if you won't go out there, I will."

Shane glanced at the other boys gathered in the entry, trying to read their expressions. About then, Missy appeared at the opening, her arms toting a couple of bottles of water. "Look, Shane! Look what the ranger gave me! There's a lot more out there. He's a nice man."

Thirty minutes later, Bishop looked up and spotted Shane approaching the truck. The local looked like shit, but still held his head up high. "So what do you want?" he opened.

"I know you guys have seen your share of bad men. I know some of them probably hurt your town and the people who live here. But we aren't here to harm anybody. We're here to take all this corn and distribute it to farmers and ranchers so they can grow more food and feed millions of starving people."

"You can't take our corn... *we'll* starve to death without it," Shane protested, his eyes getting wild.

"No," Bishop reassured. "We won't let you starve. As a matter of fact, our intent is that your lives will improve... Riley's survivors cannot possibly consume all the corn in the silos, nor is it healthy for that to be your primary food source over time. You need so many resources that the Alliance can provide. No doubt the lives of the little children will be better. How many orphans do you have?"

Shane almost didn't answer, still hesitant to share too much information. "There are about 30 of them."

"And the adults?"

"All dead... but me."

Bishop stepped up to Shane and extended his hand as well as a sincere compliment. "Well, young man, you deserve a reward for that kind of community service," the Alliance negotiator proclaimed. "I have a newborn at home, and my wife and I struggle to keep up with him sometimes. I cannot imagine assuming responsibility for so many youngsters by myself." After a pregnant pause, Shane finally accepted the gesture. Grim, Cory and Kevin approached, each introducing themselves and shaking hands.

Twenty minutes later, the Alliance team was helping the residents of the catacombs climb to the surface, passing out water and small bits of food. Cory gathered the sickest to one side, the man showing a natural affection for children as he cleaned scraped knees and listened to coughing lungs.

"What now?" Shane asked, after they all were on the surface.

"Go home," Bishop replied. "Go back to what you were doing before we got here. In a few days, some more of our people will start arriving. I'll be right here until the details are all worked out.

We'll bring food, a doctor, and others. Work with us. We're good people. We can help you."

Bishop watched the seemingly endless line of trucks cued to fill their beds with corn. Motioning for Shane to follow, the two men walked for a bit, eventually arriving at the quieter residential area.

"You look like you've put on weight?" Bishop said.

"Yeah... probably a few pounds. The fruit and beef your people brought was the first I've had in almost two years. The kids are loving it."

Bishop was about to warn Shane to stay away from Pete's bathtub gin when the doctor sauntered over.

After exchanging greetings, the physician announced, "I have good news. We finally figured out why the adults all lost their sanity. There are no diseases or viruses hereabouts. It appears as though they were all suffering from Pellagra."

"What's that?" Bishop asked.

"It is essentially caused by a niacin deficiency, sometimes associated with a diet heavy in corn consumption... or at least corn not treated properly. Something in the maize inhibits the body from absorbing the B vitamin, and that can lead to mental instability. After the Civil War, the southern United States suffered epidemic waves of Pellagra. Another big outbreak occurred in 1907. In some adults, it can cause mental instability. Often, violence is associated with the condition."

"Never heard of it," Shane responded, "But how come I didn't come down with it? Or the kids?"

"It doesn't affect everybody. And, as an adult, you were probably eating alternative food sources, so you probably got enough niacin to avoid it. Children rarely suffer from it."

"So there's nothing contagious we have to worry about?" Bishop asked, wanting to go home and avoid being quarantined from Terri and Hunter.

"Nope, nothing to worry about. You're free to go," the doctor replied.

After the physician had continued onto his next task, Shane and Bishop strolled a bit more toward downtown Riley. It was a remarkably different place than when the Alliance team had arrived just 15 days before.

An Army-provided generator was humming in the distance, its electric output powering the town's water well and a few key buildings. Bishop grunted, remembering the day when the life-sustaining liquid had become readily available again. One of the Alliance engineers and he had proudly marched to a corner fire hydrant and opened the valve to help flush the rusty, grungy pipes.

Before long, a crowd of small faces had appeared, watching the fountain of shooting water as if it were some sort of religious miracle. Bishop had handed his rifle to someone, gathered up Missy, and then stepped into the waterfall of gloriously cool refreshment.

Missy had squealed with delight, quickly demanding to be put down, and then running back and forth through the shower. In less than a minute, all of the children were soaking wet, laughing, splashing, and playing. *Now that's what a neighborhood should sound like*, Bishop had thought.

As Shane and he continued into the small business district, the men noted the activity surrounding the church.

The parking lot was filled with school buses. Homeless, desperate people were being relocated from Dallas. The military commander there had been instructed to post "life skill openings," for residents of the Big-D who had previous experience such as law enforcement, childcare, gardening, and civil engineering. Special priority was given to young couples who wanted to adopt.

Anyone who was willing to work and wanted a fresh start away from the city was welcome to sign up. The response had been overwhelming.

177

So the Alliance had organized buses for transportation to the small village and begun the process of repopulating Riley, Texas. The bustling church now served double duty as the local welcome center.

The imports had started arriving a few days ago, the tops of the buses covered with suitcases, bags of personal items, and even a few small pieces of furniture. Ropes crisscrossed the rooftop cargo, eager faces peering out the windows at their new home and hopefully a better life.

"It's going to be weird around here," Shane noted. "All these new people and activity. I guess it's good for the kids though. Now they won't have to raise themselves."

Bishop nodded, pointing with his head at a young man and woman having a picnic with Missy and another small girl – a first step in the process of gently pairing up adults with the town's orphans.

"You did a great job," Bishop said, putting his hand on the local man's shoulder. "I don't know anyone who could have done any better. Those kids you helped keep alive will be tough as nails, smart and perceptive. They will be the next generation of leaders and help make sure nothing like the collapse ever happens again."

As the two men studied the bonding-picnic, a voice sounded out from behind. "Mr. Mayor? Mr. Mayor?" One of the Alliance volunteers called, seeking Shane's attention.

Bishop grinned at the young man's reaction, a shy frown, and flush of red at the title.

"Accept it," the Texan whispered as the volunteer approached. "There's no one better for the job. You earned it."

"The candidates for town marshal are ready for you to begin the interviews, sir. We have them seated over at the school," the Alliance coordinator informed Shane.

Turning to Bishop with a face full of helplessness, Shane shrugged and said, "No rest for the wicked. Any advice as to what I should be looking for in a lawman?"

178

Bishop grinned and shook his head, "No clue... but, if any of them are named Grim, I'd pass."

"Are you sure you don't want to be a general?" Terri asked, watching her husband check himself in the mirror for the tenth time.

Bishop grunted, flashing a shy smirk. "I haven't earned that rank. Matter of fact, I probably haven't earned the rank of captain."

Terri couldn't help herself; seeing Bishop in a vulnerable state was so rare. "How about Admiral Smarty Pants? Commodore Manly Man? Field Marshal Bishop? That's it! Field Marshal Bishop! You could hang a ton of medals and ribbons across your chest like all those tin pan dictators used to do before the collapse."

"Terri! Stop. Besides, I don't think the Texas Rangers had such ranks. Captain was about it."

Deciding she'd teased enough, she stepped beside him and toyed with the shoulder of his new jacket, her voice becoming low and sultry. "You know... I find a man in uniform incredibly sexy, regardless of his rank. After the ceremony, you could be Mark Anthony... I could be Cleopatra. You know, your butt looks great in those pants, Mark."

Bishop looked down at his adoring wife and smiled. Formally taking a knee in front of her, he bowed his head and tried his best to quote Shakespeare, "Finish, good lady; the bright day is done, and we are for the dark. I love you, my queen."

It was Terri's turn to be embarrassed. Flushing red, she lifted his head with a hand at both cheeks and looked into his eyes. "I love you, too."

He scooped her up in a blur, effortlessly carrying her to the nearby bed, ignoring her protests. Setting her down gently, he kissed her passionately, eventually pinning her to the mattress with his weight.

Terri responded to the embrace, but soon sensed an urgency building inside him. It wasn't the time. "Bishop... Bishop... the ceremony. We can't be late."

Nuzzling her neck, he whispered, "They won't mind waiting. The delay will be for a good cause. No one will blame me."

"Bishop. Stop," she giggled. "That tickles, and I have to get Hunter ready. Later, my love. I promise to be Cleopatra, and so much more - but later."

He relented, raising off her with an expression that made it clear the decision wasn't easy. "This is all such a farce," he started, reluctantly returning to the mirror. "I don't see the need for all this pomp and circumstance."

Terri stood, straightening her dress and checking her hair in the mirror. "Oh, stop being such a spoilsport. Nick and the military guys believe they owe you a debt of gratitude. I think they feel a little guilty about doubting you over that massacre. Then what happened at Brighton just deepened their remorse. Smile, be happy and enjoy the festivities."

"It just seems like a waste of resources. Instead of having a party, we should be out helping the rest of the state recover. We have a ton of work to do. Riley was just the beginning."

Terri put her hands on her hips and tilted her head, a clear indication that she wanted to be taken seriously. "We've been through this a dozen times. The people in the remote areas want and need organization. Your little white lie in Riley worked, and it got everyone to thinking. Most people respect the Texas Rangers. We've already proved rolling into those towns with force doesn't work. But the Rangers showing up... then folks might listen for a few minutes *before* they start shooting."

Bishop frowned, not buying the argument. "So just give me a little tin star, and let's get on with it. Why all the hoopla?"

Terri exhaled in frustration with his stubbornness. "We have to play the role. People desperately want to see their leaders succeeding. It shows progress and optimism, a chance at a better future. The ceremony today isn't for you, my husband; it's

180

for them. While I love that wonderful humility of yours, now isn't the time. The people need this acknowledgment of service and reward. They want you to be honored. They need to see good deeds are indeed valued and appreciated. Like it or not, we're part of leadership, and we have to act like it."

But Bishop didn't like it. "Look, all I wanted to do is head back to the ranch and take another shot at a garden. Mr. Beltran said he'd give us a few head of cattle in trade. We could start a herd. I could play with Hunter in the evenings, and maybe even start gathering the materials to build a proper house. We've done our part. We've helped as much as anyone with the recovery. I've even got the patched up holes in my body to prove it," he protested, gesturing at his injuries.

She moved close to him again, standing on her tiptoes and kissing his cheek. "I share the same dream with you, but we're committed. You should know as well as anyone that this… everything we've worked for… could all go south on a moment's notice. There's so much left to be done. I promise, swear on my mother's grave, that I'll step down, and we'll retire to the ranch as soon as I see the recovery sustaining itself."

Bishop knew the sincerity of her pledge, but doubted the job would ever be finished. That, however, was a discussion for another day.

After Bishop and Grim had returned from Riley, word of Bishop's antics as an imposter-lawman had spread like wildfire. It had been Nick who raised the concept of reconstituting the infamous Texas Rangers.

"It's perfect! Back in the old days, they were more like a paramilitary operation – part lawmen, part militia. Sheriff Watts has his hands full as it is. We need every single trained policeman we can find to reestablish rule of law in the major cities. El Paso alone is proving a challenge, and order needs to be standard throughout Alliance territory, so a unit of Rangers sounds like one hell of an idea."

So the council decided to form a new organization, roughly along the lines of the old Rangers. Bishop, despite his protests, was nominated and confirmed as the first man to be sworn in.

Bishop and his family emerged from their room at the Manor, dressed to the tee and greeting everyone with a smile. Someone had pulled a large flatbed semi-trailer in front of the famous hotel, the stage adorned with a public address system and several rows of chairs for the attending dignitaries.

Emerging from the lobby, Bishop was amazed at the number of spectators lining Main Street. As far as he could see in any direction, friendly faces, Western hats, and toothy grins packed any open spot with a view of the stage. Turning to Terri, he whispered, "Look at all these people... Pete must be running a special today on his best moonshine."

Butter and Slim were suddenly at their side, ushering Bishop, Terri, and Hunter through the tightly packed throng and making sure they reached the stairs without incident. As Bishop appeared on stage, he paused for a moment, holding up Hunter and trying to get him to wave to the crowd. A hardy cheer rose up, several folks clapping and whistling.

When Terri was at his side, Bishop leaned over and said, "They love Hunter. Listen to them clap and whistle. I told you he was a special boy."

Terri leaned back, and without breaking her smile, said, "Stop it, Bishop, or I'll kick your ass right here in front of half the Alliance."

"Now that spectacle would draw a standing ovation," he grinned.

The family was guided to a pair of seats, Hunter taking his favorite position aboard his father's knee. Soon they were joined by Nick and Diana, Bishop's best friend taking the folding chair next to the new Ranger.

"All I did was tell a little kid an innocent white lie, and now look what's happened," he complained to Nick. "Now, I'll be obligated to do an honest day's work every so often."

Laughing, the big man replied, "No good deed goes unpunished, my friend. Besides, deep down inside, you know this is a great idea. People respect the Rangers, and from what you've run into along the way, I'd say that respect will go a long way."

Before Bishop could respond, General Owens appeared onstage, quickly followed by Pete, Betty and the entire Alliance Council.

Pete, being the elected mayor of Meraton, took the podium first.

"Ladies and gentlemen, my friends, and fellow Texans," began Pete, "It is with great pride and confidence that I attend this ceremony today. Not only are we honoring one of our own, but also officially announcing what I believe will be an important step toward the recovery of our great state, perhaps a new nation."

A rousing round of applause followed the proclamation, Pete turning to wink at Bishop while he waited for the outbreak to die down. "Most of you know Terri's husband, Bishop," he began, a rolling laugh billowing from the gathering. "Many of you have fought beside him, worked with him, and know him personally. Most of you are well aware that he has performed beyond the call of duty, sacrificing himself for the greater good of our community. There are more than a few citizens of the Alliance who owe their lives to the man seated behind me."

Again, clapping hands, cheers, and shouts of encouragement erupted from the audience. "So without further ado, it is my great pleasure to introduce Diana Brown, Alpha's mayor and council representative. Miss Brown."

Pete stepped back, giving Diana center stage. After a quick tidying of her papers, Diana gazed across the throng and smiled broadly. "Good morning," she greeted, the respect and admiration clear on practically every face.

"Before we make our presentation, I want to be the first to officially inform the citizens of the Alliance that the council has officially voted to reinstitute the Texas Rangers."

This time the listeners' reaction was loud, so boisterous that Hunter was startled, turning to glance at his dad as if to make sure everything was okay. Bishop snuggled his son close, reassuring and soothing until the noise died down.

"In addition to that wonderful news, it is my great honor to swear in the first of a new breed of Texas lawman. Please welcome Bishop, the first Captain of the new Texas Rangers."

Handing Hunter over to his mother, Bishop stood and strode toward the podium. Nick rose as well, moving to Diana's side. He raised the Bible, nodding for Bishop to place his right hand on the solemn book.

Diana began reading the sworn oath, the words identical to those spoken by all Rangers since the late 1800s. Bishop sincerely repeated the promise, the irony of it all not lost on the Texan.

He was echoing a historic vow that had been born of a necessity, the need to tame a wild territory that held such promise and potential – a region and people requiring a fair, steady, and sometimes heavy hand. History, as it is so prone to do, was indeed repeating itself. It was almost predictable in a way... today's environment so similar to those early days when the world required such a specialized policing. The Rangers hadn't always been perfect, but they had done the job.

Bishop finished with the closing, "So help me, God."

While a chorus of support and clapping arose from the excited crowd, Diana fished a small box from her jacket pocket, producing a shiny silver badge, the traditional star-in-wheel design created from a Mexican silver coin.

She pinned the emblem on Bishop's lapel and then joined with the supporters, clapping and smiling as Bishop waved his thanks to the gathering.

One gruff, old cowboy on the front row turned to his friend and shouted, "I'll bet you a drink at Pete's that Terri can still kick his ass... shiny badge or not."

"No bet," came the immediate response, the remark generating a round of hearty chuckles from those nearby.

The Third Directive – Transportation

Her red and black paint was spectacular, fitting shades of pigment that projected power, prestige, and ageless elegance. Her brass was polished to a mirror-like shine, a glimmering accent reminiscent of a beautiful woman adorned with jewelry of rare metal and precious stone.

At 85 tons, she could hardly be described as dainty or petite, yet her lines and pedigree stirred men's hearts and fantasies. She was a classy dame, earning respect and deserving admiration.

Born in 1907 at the Baldwin Locomotive works, the Texas Star was far from the youngest of her breed. Despite the years, immeasurable miles, and countless tons of freight, the decline of man had extended the refined lady a new lease on life.

In a world where diesel fuel was in short supply, where her more complex and capable cousins could no longer rumble across the rails of Texas, Lady Star was once again the belle of the ball.

Before the collapse, she had been regulated to semi-retirement, hauling tourists and train buffs on a short, private track among small towns from eastern Texas to the coast. But all of that changed after the collapse.

The benefactor of loyal enthusiasts, funds from the state's budget, and adoring riders, Star had been maintained at the highest possible standards. Every week, hundreds of Americans journeyed from Boston to San Francisco and everywhere in between to travel in her cars and admire the craftsmanship and engineering so inherent in her creation.

Now, hundreds of people still arrived to ride on the rejuvenated train, but they weren't tourists. Star had once again accepted a role of prominence, serving as a critical component to the benefit of mankind.

Grim and Bishop stood at the edge of the gathered throng, both men dressed to fit in with the local population, both admiring the steam-powered locomotive with the rest of the milling humanity.

For the people of East Texas, a supply of diesel fuel was non-existent. Even with the limited refining capability of the Alliance in

24x7 operation, there simply wasn't enough of the BTU-laced liquid to go around. The rising needs of military, over-the-road trucking, and agriculture consumed every drop that could be produced.

But like so many of the survivors the Alliance was now encountering, the citizenry of the Great Piney Woods had adapted. While they didn't have the capability to refine petroleum, what they did possess was an abundance of trees. The region's handle included the words "great" and "woods" for good reason.

Even more amazing to the two men from the Alliance was the adaptation of the grand old locomotive's boilers. The Texas Star hadn't been born as a wood burner. She'd originally been engineered to consume coal, later modified to accept a more efficient and inexpensive diet of fuel oil.

But even that lesser-refined version of fuel was impossible to obtain, so clever men had modified the old girl a third time, her steam now generated by the burning of wood gas.

Bishop stepped closer, taking advantage of a gap in the mob to improve his view. The beauty and polish of the engine was completely offset by the car immediately following the old workhorse.

Looking like a moonshiner's still that had gotten out of control, the train's second car was a flatbed unit, the front half completely covered in a cacophony of steel and bronze kettles, bins, tanks and pipe.

Two of the locomotive's firemen worked the mechanical menagerie, twisting valves, checking gauges, and supervising a second crew working at the rear of the car. There, men were stacking several huge bags of what appeared to be wood chips.

"Check that out, Grim," Bishop said to his friend. "It looks more like a mad scientist's lab than anything I've ever seen on a train."

Grim nodded, seemingly unable to take his eyes off the spectacle. "Wood gas has been around for a long, long time. I heard the Germans used it when fuel was running low at the end of World War II. Over a million vehicles were powered with gasified wood by the end of the conflict."

186

Bishop nodded his understanding, and then said, "As much as I'd love to stand here all day like a little boy wanting to grow up and be a train engineer, we need to get going."

"After you, oh great and fearless leader."

The two men made their way through the crowd, the surrounding multitude reminding Bishop of the market at Meraton.

They passed a child dragging a coop occupied by two unhappy chickens, followed by two men with a side of beef hanging from the pole braced on their shoulders. Women hustled here and bustled there, some toting goods, others with their hands full of youngsters. Most everyone was armed.

While some bartering was in process around the edges of the crowd, most of the people in the vicinity were actually there to board and ride the train.

After winding through the swarm of activity, Bishop spied a man with a red armband, the serious-faced fellow sporting the same colored cloth ringing his hat and an unadorned battle rifle slung across his chest. Making sure his own weapon was pointed down and in a non-threatening position, the Texan approached what was clearly a local policeman or guard.

"I heard a man can find work around here?" Bishop inquired.

"You heard right," the guy replied. "Keep walking; you'll see a sign and a line."

And they did.

Soon, Bishop and Grim approached a tiny wooden shack; a hand painted poster above the small, booth-like window had one word, "Hiring." Just as the security man had predicted, there was a line.

The cue was comprised of a mishmash of folks, mostly men; some of the applicants looking relatively put together, others appearing to be on the brink of starvation or despair. At the front of the line, on either side of the opening, stood two rather large guards wearing the red bandanas on their arms and hats. Each looked menacing as hell and each wielded an AR15 rifle.

Slowly the line inched forward, Bishop noting some of the job seekers strolling away from the opening with a bounce in their steps, others stomping away, shaking their heads in disgust.

Before long, Bishop and Grim stepped to the window. Inside, they found a rotund, sweating man who didn't even bother to make eye contact. "Chopping wood pays 22 ounces of food per day, four of that being one variety or the other of meat. We start at 6 a.m., end at 6 p.m. Take it or leave it."

"We were looking for something in security," Bishop said.

The man on the other side of the booth finally glanced up, his eyes quickly scanning Bishop and Grim. Both of the Alliance men had "dressed down," for the mission, exchanging their personal rifles for standard issue military models, and leaving their best optics and kit behind. Nodding toward Grim, he said, "He's big enough, but I don't know about you. Military?"

Grim stepped close, eyes darting left and right to make sure no one could overhear. "We left Fort Hood a few weeks ago. Our papers weren't exactly in order."

"Deserters, huh? We see our share. Do you have ammunition for those weapons?"

"Yeah, we have enough to take care of business," Grim replied.

The response was a grunt. "I'm still not sure about the little guy," he said, scrutinizing Bishop. "Take these two passes and head 150 yards down the tracks. Ask around for Major Misery."

"Misery?" Grim questioned, accepting the two aces from a deck of playing cards.

"Are you fucking deaf?" came the impatient answer. "You can't work security if you can't hear." Then, casting a dismissive gaze over Grim's shoulder, the jerk yelled, "Next!"

The Alliance men did as they were told, hiking along the tracks in the direction indicated. "Damn," commented Bishop, "I'm six foot and 200 pounds. They must grow 'em big around here if that's too small."

"You do look a little soft around the edges. You might consider working out a little more to tone up," Grim teased.

"How about I tone you up the side of your head, *big man*?"

Before Grim could continue the banter, they reached another pair of red bandanas. "You're in the wrong fucking place," the larger of the two sentries barked. "Move your asses out of here."

Grim held up the two aces and then responded, "We were told to find a Major Misery."

Unapologetic, the man motioned over his shoulder, "You'll see a big tent down the tracks. The major is there. Don't go anywhere else."

"No way 'Misery' is this guy's real name," Grim observed as they walked, "but I like it."

"Really? You don't think so? Next thing, you'll be telling me is Grim isn't what your mama called you," Bishop chided. "I need to come up with some sort of badass handle like that. All you high-speed, low drag individuals have such cool names, like Reaper, Bull, or Grim. People hear my name and think I'm either a chess piece or a religious executive."

"Those nicknames are earned, my friend. You need to work a little harder, and perhaps one day someone will hang one on you," Grim teased.

"I'll keep that in mind," Bishop replied, a huge grin on his face. "Does it count for anything that Terri calls me Stud Muffin?"

"Yeah... that's good... We can call you Captain Muffin. I like it. Fits."

The tent appeared after another hundred yards or so. After asking another inhospitable gentleman the whereabouts of the good major, they were shown to a table where a 40ish man with a shaved head sat shuffling papers. "Yes," he said, without looking up.

"We were told to come talk to you about security positions," Grim announced, presenting the two playing cards on the table.

Major Misery examined his visitors, his eyes performing a quick evaluation of the two men standing before him. "How long were you in?" he asked.

Grim replied first, "Eighteen and counting."

Bishop followed with, "Twenty plus."

"CIBs?" fired the next question, the major wanting to know if either man had earned the coveted Combat Infantry Badge.

"Yes," they both replied at the same time.

Standing, the man in charge stamped around the table, still sizing up the candidates. Focusing on Bishop, he stated, "We do a lot of crowd control here. That normally takes a little more ass than you've been issued. That, and you're a little long in the tooth. Can you fight?"

"I've managed a scrap or two, sir," Bishop responded without hesitation.

"Would you be willing to prove that?"

Bishop was surprised by the question, not sure how to respond. He finally settled on, "No problem."

Major Misery grunted, mumbling, "We'll see about that," and then turned to the front of the tent. "Somebody get Hoss."

Returning his gaze to Bishop, he explained, "Most men find my son quite the challenge when it comes to doing it hand-to-hand. If you really want the job, we'll see how well you hold up."

A few minutes later, Bishop understood. Hoss was only an inch taller than the Texan, but a good 40 or 50 pounds heavier. The young man evidently spent all of his free time lifting weights. Bulging, broad shoulders led to thick arms, both limbs covered with veins and cords.

"You want me to *fight* him?" Bishop turned and asked the major.

Laughing, Misery responded, "You said you could handle yourself. It's not too late to change your mind. There's plenty of work available chopping wood."

Bishop shook his head, indicating he'd been misunderstood. "No sir, that's not what I meant. I was more concerned about hurting the little fella."

A few minutes later, a circle of men irascibly waited in a flat clearing next to the tent. Word had spread quickly amongst the security forces that Hoss was about to consume another victim. There was an impatient excitement in the air, the event more resembling a boxing match or afterschool fight, than any job interview Bishop had ever attended.

Grim stood with his friend to one side, both men eyeing Hoss as he removed his shirt and then flexed his considerable mass for the crowd.

"Are you sure you want to do this?" Grim asked. "He's just a tad bit smaller than a T-Rex."

"The bigger they are…" Bishop stated, unbuttoning his own shirt.

"The bigger they are, the harder they kick your ass," Grim teased. "Terri is going to be so pissed if I carry you back to Alpha without any teeth."

Major Misery appeared at their side, "To work with my team, you don't have to win. I'll judge your qualifications by how long you last and the skills you display. He's only killed two men. We were just a little slow in pulling him off on both of those occasions."

"Any rules?" Bishop asked.

"No. No rules. No holds barred."

And then it was time.

Major Misery moved to the center of the arena, and simply said, "Go."

Hoss was clearly an aggressive fellow. Charging from his corner with a growl, he moved quickly toward Bishop with extended arms and the intent to grapple.

But Bishop knew better. He understood it would be over quickly if the bigger man managed to fix a hold on any part of his body. There was no way he could match the strength of the larger foe, but that didn't concern the Texan.

Waiting until Hoss was almost upon him, Bishop ducked and sidestepped at the last moment, springing away from the outstretched arms of his opponent.

I have to wear him down, Bishop thought. *These big guys are strong as hell, but it takes a lot of oxygen and energy to move that huge body around. Wear him down.*

Bishop danced in a circle, moving to his right with the bouncing footwork of a prizefighter. Again, Hoss lunged, but his target wasn't there.

For over three minutes, Bishop avoided the behemoth, cutting right, ducking left, or simply backing away. Hoss was growing frustrated and began taunting. "Come on, you little chicken shit. Stand and fight, pussy."

Bishop ignored the words, instead focusing on the glistening coat of sweat that now covered his foe's upper body. Hoss's breathing was becoming labored, his footwork less certain.

After another minute, the crowd began to jeer, obviously bored with Bishop's constant avoidance of the hometown favorite and reigning champion. Mumblings of, "He's not going to fight," and "What a coward," rolled through the gathered mob.

On the next pass, Bishop again stepped to the side, but this time he didn't scamper off. In a blur, two sharp blows landed on Hoss's neck and head, immediately followed by a powerful kick to the back of the giant's knee. The mob cheered the contact.

Hoss wasn't unskilled. Sensing Bishop's proximity, he snapped an elbow into Bishop's hip, the numbing impact of the blow rolling the Texan across the ground.

Jesus, that hurt, Bishop thought, barely hobbling to escape the follow-on assault. His leg and side throbbed from the impact. *I've been kicked by weaker horses.*

Rage and adrenaline surged through Hoss's body as he spun, reaching out to grasp Bishop's arm. But the Texan wasn't there any longer, moving off with his never-ending, annoying little two-step.

Confident his opponent had finally decided to fight, the giant charged in again, only to land a swinging maul on empty air. Bishop just slid aside, intent on making the big fella chase him around the ring.

After two more passes, Hoss was becoming confused, his adrenaline dump now burning off, his lungs struggling to provide the oxygen needed by his tremendous mass of muscle. Deciding to change tactics, he moved to the center of the clearing and simply stood in a ready stance, as if he expected Bishop to come to him.

"Have you had enough?" Bishop asked his clearly frustrated foe.

"Fuck you," came the reply. "Come in a little closer, and I'll rip your little piss ant head off."

"Do I look stupid?" Bishop grinned.

Again, the onlookers grew impatient, their bloodlust completely unsatisfied. Unlike before, both Bishop and Hoss began receiving their share of catcalls and heckling.

"What?" Hoss said, half-turning to look at his one-time supporters with outstretched arms. "He won't fight."

It was the opening Bishop had been waiting for. With his opponent slightly distracted, the Texan took a single step and leapt, both boots landing in the center of the Goliath's chest with an audible thud.

Both men went down, but Bishop was prepared, deftly turning away and regaining his feet first.

Stunned by the attack, Hoss only managed a knee before Bishop was on him with a vengeance.

Three rabbit punches struck the back of the big man's head, quickly followed by another roundhouse kick that landed square on Hoss's nose. The sickening crush of cartilage could be heard all around.

A shower of blood exploded from the giant's face as he surged upward with a roar of pain, but Bishop had no intention of letting the attacker regain the initiative.

A savage downward kick landed on Hoss's right knee, the edge of Bishop's boot delivering the blow just above and outside the kneecap. Again, the Texan's leg coiled and flashed, repeating the strike to the same tortured flesh and tendons. The hulk toppled in a howl of agony.

Bishop, recovering his balance, started to move in on the semi-prone man at his feet. The Texan's expression was neutral, like a predator making to finish wounded prey. The effort was cut short by a shouted command, "Enough!"

Major Misery appeared between Bishop and his foe. "It's over," declared the local leader. "Stop."

A passing flash of fear crossed behind Misery's eyes. Face to face with the man who had impossibly bested his son, the older man saw something deep and primordial in Bishop's glower. For a fleeting moment, he wondered if the Texan *would* stop... doubting his ability to halt the advancing stranger.

And then Grim was there, gently guiding Bishop away from the downed man and disgruntled multitude. Hustling his friend to the side, Grim's only comment was, "What took you so long?"

Still panting hard, Bishop cleared the battle-lust from his vision while his lungs worked for air. "I need some water. Damn, that guy was strong," he eventually responded.

As they made to leave, Major Misery stepped up. "You've got the job. Report here at 0600 hours tomorrow. The pay is two pounds of food, six ounces of that being beef, and two cartridges per day. Don't be late, and I wouldn't turn my back on Hoss for a while."

Word of the Texas Star and the fantastic strides accomplished by the people of East Texas had reached the council a week before Grim and Bishop's arrival.

Terri and her entourage had been visiting Houston, meeting with the military commanders and civilian authority that now controlled what remained of the nation's fourth largest city.

The chairwoman had entered a nightmarish zone of human suffering, destruction, and general dismay. With 40% of the city

194

having burned to the ground, or been bulldozed to create a firebreak, Houston no longer resembled the hometown that Terri remembered.

During the two-day marathon of meetings, presentations and tours, she had been deeply saddened. It was more than just the physical devastation that broke her heart. Seeing the hollow mass of humanity, the once proud citizens of the Bayou City, ripped her soul like nothing she'd ever witnessed.

Terri was reminded of old pictures and black and white news reels of German cities after World War II. And it wasn't just the piles of blackened rubble and stretches of flattened lots – the people had that same blank expression of helpless defeat on their faces.

When the topic of feeding the multitudes arose, Terri had inquired about the status of Galveston and the potential for seafood to fill the ever-increasing void of food.

It was then that she had learned of the Texas Star, an inspiring tale of survivors adapting to overcome, and according to some sources, thrive.

The story had actually been interesting for more than just the potential of stocking the population's pantries.

Transportation was essential to the recovery, not only to haul goods where they were needed, but also to move people, equipment and spare parts.

Like the American West of old, the Alliance had initially considered the railways and waterways as major arteries of transportation. But the limited supply of diesel was the hamstring, especially with the massive effort underway to plant the seed corn recovered from Riley, Texas.

One solution no one had exhaustively researched was steam.

It had been decades since the iron horses of the first railroads had thundered across the land, their stacks boiling with black smoke from scorching wood or coal. Now, with modern fuels being refined at a fraction of previous production, the concept of utilizing the few remaining relics from that bygone era had commanded the Alliance's attention.

According to the stories Terri heard in Houston, the operation in East Texas was quite sophisticated and organized. A steam engine was said to pull cars full of people, homegrown produce, beef, chicken, and lumber from the Great Piney Woods of East Texas to Galveston Island.

There, the bounty of the sea, harvested from the shorelines and a few operating fishing boats, was traded in an open-air market called The Strand.

The scent of fresh fish, oysters, shrimp, and kelp followed the old locomotive on its return trip north, her cars full of the island community's bartered goods.

"Another marketplace like Meraton would boost the recovery," she'd informed Diana via the military's long-range communications net. "I've heard enough down here to warrant further investigation. I think we should send in a team to find out exactly what's going on."

When Terri had reported the supposed use of wood gas to power the locomotive, the council's interest had been piqued. The purported activity originating in the Great Piney Woods might further three directives: agriculture, energy, and transportation.

But, according to the reports, there were issues.

Like the days of old, bandits, desperados, and nefarious gangs had taken to raiding the trains, often holding passengers and crew at gunpoint and helping themselves to whatever cargo they could carry off.

The reaction was predictable, honest citizens on both ends of the run arming themselves and riding "shotgun" in an attempt to protect their livelihoods.

Over time, a third factor was rumored to have entered the drama - the barons. As the months passed, strong, aggressive men with resources and gumption began to establish themselves as local leaders. They organized, controlled, and manipulated the iron horse and its surrounding economy. Some were opportunists, simply in the right place at the right time. Others had already established themselves as local businessmen long before the collapse.

Regardless of the circumstances, the rail line was now said to be tightly controlled, having morphed from a solution benefiting many, to a thriving enterprise profiting a select few.

Given the disastrous experience at Brighton, it was decided to conduct a fact-finding mission before the council made any determination how to approach or integrate resources with whoever controlled the operation. Bishop's team had been dispatched.

"Hunter and I will meet you in Galveston," Terri had told her husband on the radio. "Bring me some good news."

"Hey, I love trains. This might be a little fun," Bishop had responded. "And you. Give Hunter a hug from his dad."

After being hired, Bishop and Grim left the security compound, trekking the two miles back to their hidden pickup. Upon arriving in the area the day before, they had driven around for three hours before identifying a suitable spot to conceal the truck. Kevin and Cory were waiting on their return.

After debriefing the other two members of the team, they sat down to consume the campfire feast Cory had prepared.

"That setup is pretty brutal," Grim began. "The pay is truly a starvation wage. I was trying to figure up what a few ounces of food and meat would come out to, and it wasn't pretty, especially for a man doing a full day's manual labor."

Bishop nodded, "I agree, but that's none of our concern. I might be tempted to get the Alliance involved if they were using slave labor of some sort, but they are paying for work performed. Maybe the business can only support that wage. And remember, no one is holding a gun to the workers' heads and forcing them work to there."

"But if the folks don't have any option," Kevin asked, "is it right to take advantage of them?"

Bishop didn't answer immediately, staring into the blaze while gathering his thoughts. "That's a good question, Kevin, one that has been debated in our country for years. I don't know if you were old enough to pay attention, but before the collapse, there were always deliberations about the minimum wage. Some people believed that corporate executives and business owners were making too much money while their personnel starved. Others believed in the free enterprise system, where if employees were treated badly, they would go elsewhere."

The youngest of the team nodded, "I remember some stuff about it, but not much. I was into Batman more than the nightly news."

Bishop sighed, unsure how deep to delve into the topic. "I'm not sure where the Alliance will come down on the issue. My gut says government should stay out of it unless people are being physically harmed or enslaved. There's probably some interference warranted where children are concerned as well. As long as a man or woman can walk away from a bad situation, they will. But the people will ultimately decide what their leaders do. That's not our place or our mission today."

Grim spoke up, seemingly more comfortable discussing something he could control. "So we work here for a few days, get a ride on the train, and then what?"

"We report back to the council with what we find. They can decide what to do with the information."

"At least we won't be chopping wood," the ex-contractor noted. "I was worried there for a minute, though. I thought Godzilla was going to pound your ass."

Bishop grunted, rubbing his sore hip at the memory. "He *was* a big ol' boy. I'm sure *you* could have taken care of business without any drama."

Grim brushed the air with a dismissive gesture, "That's why I keep you around, Captain. To handle my light work."

After a chuckle went around the campfire, Bishop became serious again. Focusing on Kevin, he said, "One of these days, you're going to be part of the leadership. You'll have to make decisions that influence people's lives. I want to tell you... from my perspective... from what I lived through, that the less

198

government is depended on, the better. The less it is involved in people's lives, the better off we'll be as a society. Yes, you have to help people who are down and out, but other than that, leave them to their own devices. The more I think about it, the more I blame the collapse on our illustrious leadership and political system and their constant interference and meddling in our lives. If *your* generation learns any lesson from this mess *my* generation made of the world, I hope that's it."

Kevin seemed sincere, but confused. "Why, sir? I'm not sure I understand the connection between the government's role and the apocalypse."

"Washington tried to make it too easy on people, Kevin," Bishop replied. "They tried to fix everything, make everything right and just. They tried to make life easier for the people who voted for them, and that ended up being a huge mistake. Human beings aren't meant to have an easy path. That's not how we're designed. We need to struggle, fight, have setbacks, and suffer consequences. When everything went to hell, the vast majority of the population wasn't ready for their support system to simply vanish. They couldn't handle it, and that made things tumble downhill far faster than they should have otherwise."

"Do you really believe the fall was due to the people being soft and pampered?" Cory asked.

"For sure, it worsened the effects of the economic collapse," Bishop nodded. "I knew my grandparents well. They survived the First Great Depression because they were able to take care of themselves. If my generation had shared some of their skills, we would've hardly noticed the grid going down. Empty grocery store shelves? My grandparents wouldn't have cared. No fuel? A minor inconvenience at worst. They were self-reliant because they had learned the hard way that they couldn't count on anybody to bail them out. Not the government, not their neighbors, not the church, not anybody. If even half the country had been like them, this last collapse would've been nothing but a minor note in the history books."

It was Kevin's turn to stare into the flames for a moment. "I get it, Captain. You're saying the government trying to make everything better for everyone spoiled them... made them soft and weak. I understand now."

Grim reached over and gave Bishop's shoulder a friendly shove, "See! The kid didn't even see you fight today, and yet he still knows you're soft."

Galveston Island, 50 miles southeast of Houston, had a history of survival and adaption. The first permanent European settlement on the barrier landmass had been constructed by pirates, with Jean Lafitte operating his own little seaside kingdom, called Campeche, for almost four years. He declared himself "head of government," and stayed until the US Navy provided an eviction notice: Leave or be destroyed. He left.

Throughout most of the 1800s, the city of Galveston had been the commercial center of Texas. A natural port with good protection and easy access to the Gulf of Mexico, the city had once rivaled New Orleans in exports of cotton and sugar cane.

As it expanded and prospered, a rich, often-colorful history of growth and culture emerged from the coastal community. All of that changed in 1900 when the most deadly natural disaster in US history struck the bustling city.

On September 8, a massive hurricane took aim at the island, killing up to 12,000 people by some estimates. The sustained winds of over 125 miles per hour would have been bad enough, but a 15-foot storm surge is credited with doing most of the damage. Practically the entire island was submerged in churning, angry waves of seawater.

But the community didn't just fade away.

By the 1930s, Galveston was again a toddling town, even though it would never regain its former luster. Prohibition meant little to the local islanders as speakeasies, gin joints, and prostitution virtually ran unchecked. The berg became known as the sin city of the gulf, with a thriving subculture of depravity that would have made Lafitte blush.

Hunter's cry interrupted Terri from the study of her destination's

200

history. Folding the book she'd been exploring, she reached into the nearby playpen, lifting her son with a grunt and then sniffing his diaper. "No problem there," she smiled, "Are you hungry? Again?"

Betty appeared from the back of the motorhome, moving to help mother with child. "It's okay," Terri said, "I think he just wants me to hold him for a while. He's been lying there watching me study, and I think he wants to help. He loves to try to turn the pages."

"Are you still reading up on Galveston?" Betty asked.

"Yes. What an... ummm... intriguing history they have there. When Bishop and I lived in Houston, we drove down on the weekend a couple of times to walk the beach or to simply have some place different to go. I never knew much about its checkered past though."

Casting a knowing look, Betty responded, "My mother was from Galveston. She's told me some incredibly sordid stories about some of the shenanigans that went on down there. I wonder how all those beach bums managed the collapse?"

Shifting Hunter to her other arm, Terri pulled a stack of papers from the table. The top page was labeled "US Army Intelligence Briefing, Galveston County, Texas."

After showing her friend and helper the title, Terri stated, "According to this report, the residents have actually fared better than almost anywhere else in the state. They have a consistent food supply from the ocean, mild weather and little social unrest."

"Really? I guess that makes sense."

"Yup. The other interesting thing the Army discovered was a market, which from its description, is bigger than Meraton's. One officer claimed it was over four square blocks in size, offering a variety of goods and services."

"Wow," Betty said, "sounds like what they have organized is practically a mini-mall. I wonder if they still sell those cute little seashell rings. I had one when I was a little girl."

A knock on the door sounded before Terri could speculate. "Come in," she called, shifting Hunter back to his favorite knee and freeing up her pistol hand.

Slim opened the door, the ever-polite bodyguard removing his hat. "Ma'am, we're ready to head to Galveston. I've interviewed three different military types who've been there. I'm still a little uncertain about this. I wish you'd take the general up on his offer to provide additional escorts."

Terri passed Hunter to Betty and then stood. Slim, catching the look in his boss's eyes, looked down, sure he was about to be scolded.

"Slim," Terri began softly, "I want to check out Galveston without anyone knowing who I am. I want an honest, unbiased look at the market, island, and community. If we go rolling in there with a column of military armor, tanks, battleships and attack helicopters, someone is going to notice and start asking questions."

"Yes, ma'am, I know but…"

Terri cut him off, "Everyone I've spoken with says there is order and calm on the island. Do you have information that contradicts that?"

"No ma'am, it's just that…"

"And Bishop and his team are supposed to meet us there as well. So there's even more Alliance protection for our side, right?"

"I know all that Miss Terri, but I'm still concerned. At least give Butter and me a day to go down there and scout around. We're going in blind, ma'am, with information that is several months old. There's only one way on and off that island, and I would feel better if at least we knew what we were getting into. Please, ma'am. I'm only asking for a day."

Terri had never seen Slim quite so nervous or stubborn. She turned and paced a few steps, finally reaching a decision. "Okay. Butter and you take what you need and go check it out. It's only an hour away. We can leave first thing in the morning once you guys verify it's safe. How's that for a compromise?"

Slim actually smiled, the man's relief evident. "Thank you, ma'am. We'll be leaving right away. I'll inform the base security that you're not to be disturbed for the rest of the afternoon."

After he left, Terri peered at Betty and sighed. "You'd think we lived in some sort of post-apocalyptic world, wouldn't ya?"

Betty smiled knowingly, "They respect you. They take their jobs seriously, and I'm glad they do. You did the right thing by letting them scout ahead."

"They wouldn't allow me to do anything if it were up to them. Our roles are in constant conflict."

"You're winning, Terri. Don't forget that... you're winning."

Grim and Bishop arrived at the anointed hour, both men strolling into the railroad's security compound five minutes early. Exactly at 6 a.m., they were standing in front of Major Misery's table.

"We run between here and Galveston. The trip takes almost eight hours each way. The train leaves one hour after daybreak. We make several stops along the way to pick up passengers. Over the last six months, we've had an increasing number of attempted robberies. The bandits are extremely clever, hitting the train using a variety of methods. Sometimes they block the track and attack in a remote, wooded area; sometimes they hit us at the towns where we stop. I've seen them try two days in a row, and other times a week or more will pass before they make an attempt. Any questions so far?"

Bishop was fascinated with the situation and couldn't keep his mouth shut. "So with all of the security men you have around here, I'm kind of surprised you're having any issue at all. Are there that many train robbers in this part of the country?"

Misery grunted, his condescending tone indicative of what he obviously considered a stupid question. "If we load the cars with my men, then we can easily fight them off. But they won't hit us if the train is full of rifles, even if we try to disguise our presence. We believe they have observers and some form of long-range

203

communications. They watch the loading here and then report how heavily guarded we are."

"I see," Bishop replied. "Have you tried to leave this station and then load up in secret further down the line?"

The major was growing annoyed by the questions, answering with an exhalation. "Yes, we've tried that a few times and even had limited success the first time. The crooks caught on though. Now, we think they have spies at each stop, watching the passengers carefully."

"Why don't you load up every trip with your men?" Grim asked.

"Because there wouldn't be room for the paying customers if we did. This entire operation runs on a shoestring. If we take up too many seats, then the trip costs more than it brings in."

Bishop rubbed his chin, not understanding the system and wondering about his specific job. "How much does it cost to ride the Texas Star?"

"Ten percent of any freight being hauled each way. For commuters, passage rates are bartered. Most people purchase their tickets with food of some sort. Ammo is also a common trade item."

Grim spoke again, "So if I want to take three chickens to Galveston for trade at the market, how much would my ticket be?"

"If you can carry it onto the locomotive and you don't take up more than one seat, then it's not freight, but luggage. The conductors, the guys who do the bartering, have exchange lists. I think a chicken buys two round-trip tickets right now, but that could change anytime. Last week, I know a one-way ticket was three 5.56 cartridges, or two .308 Winchester."

"So what's our job?" Bishop asked.

"You'll start off riding shotgun on the train. It will be leaving in an hour or so. My crew chief for today's run is Gomez. He's in charge. Do as he says, and you'll get paid tomorrow evening after the return trip."

"When was the last time the bandits hit the train?" Grim asked.

"We're due," the major replied. "As a matter of fact, we're overdue. Anything else?"

The Texan couldn't help himself, "How's Hoss's nose?"

Bishop expected a reaction of either anger or concern from the major. What he saw was fear flash behind the man's eyes. It was subtle... barely detectable, but the Texan was sure. "He'll be fine. And as I told you yesterday, I wouldn't turn my back on him for a while. He tends to hold a grudge."

Bishop and Grim, sensing their orientation was over, turned to leave, but the major wasn't finished.

"One more thing," he called. "They call me Major Misery for a reason. If you fuck up, I will avalanche an ass-load of misery on your head. Is that clear?"

After leaving the HQ tent, Bishop looked around to make sure Grim and he were alone. "Hang on a second," he said, digging in his pack. "I've got to make a phone call."

Grim grunted at the use of the term, automatically moving to block Bishop from any passersby. "Going to call the kids and let them know we'll be late for supper?"

Pulling out his radio, Bishop huddled over the small device and grinned. "Something like that."

After making the call, the two Alliance men found Gomez exactly where he was supposed to be, leaning against one of the rail cars and talking to a group of the red bandanas.

"Ah. The two new guys," he greeted.

"That's us," Grim replied.

"How much ammo do you have for those carbines?"

"We were told it would be supplied," Bishop countered, not liking his new foreman from the start.

"Well, shit," replied Gomez, peering at the other men with a sly grin. "There goes my bonus for today."

Reaching into the nearby boxcar, the crew chief pulled out a cardboard container of old GI magazines. "This is all military grade, green tip. Take six mags each. Bring them back full unless we're hit. Don't get caught with any in your pockets. I have to account for those."

After Bishop and Grim had filled their vest-pouches with mags, Gomez continued, "Since you're the new guys, you get to ride up front. I want one of you over the hitch on the platform, the other on the roof of the third car. If someone shoots at you, shoot back. If you see anything suspicious, fire."

"Why the third car?" Grim asked. "Why not all the way at the front on the engine?"

"There's an unwritten rule with the thieves. They don't shoot up the engine or the fuel car. If they did, there wouldn't be any more trains to rob. We, on the other hand, don't put men up there to act as targets."

Their new boss continued on, issuing a few other instructions, hints, and procedures. He also gave both men a pair of red kerchiefs. "There will be six of us on this run. That's a light crew, and our robber friends will most likely know our number."

After another few minutes of questions and answers, Bishop and Grim started to head for the front of the locomotive, but Gomez wasn't quite done yet.

"Just so you know, there's another reason why I want you up front. The guys up there are always killed first. Keep your eyes open."

Twenty minutes later, the Texas Star sounded her whistle twice. With a bump and a clack, a jerk and a pull, the old steamer began her journey south. Bishop, perched on the roof of the third car, loved the sensation. The morning air felt wonderful blowing across his face.

"This is just the shit!" he shouted down at Grim below him. "I'd do this for free."

The ex-contractor was beaming ear to ear as well, "No shit, Captain. Why didn't we get this assignment before now?"

Pulling a string of 13 cars, Lady Star could only reach 30 miles per hour, but to Bishop it seemed like he was racing on the wind. There was just something about a train.

It felt like little time had passed before the engineers controlling Lady Star began slowing her down. Steam blew and hissed from the wheels, a jet stream of grey and white as they were applying the brakes. A few moments later, Bishop spied people edging both sides of the tracks up ahead. They were making their first stop. Lady Star announced her arrival with two blows of her whistle.

Bishop didn't know the town's name and wondered if it were big enough to claim a spot on the map of the Lone Star State. Gomez had told them that their job was to keep people away from the engine and fuel car during the stops. Bishop climbed down from the roof, quickly joining Grim on the ground and watching for anyone who might be a highwayman, or who seemed intent on wandering close to the locomotive.

There were at least 30 people waiting to board, while only a handful got off at the stop. Bishop observed everything from rabbits to candles being carried aboard, most of the passengers a little giddy over their trip to the market. It was a system that seemed to work – a system that appeared to facilitate trade nicely.

Fifteen minutes later, Star's shrill whistle again echoed in the Texas dawn, Bishop and Grim scrambling to their positions as the iron horse again hesitated and bumped until making speed.

This time, Grim wanted to ride on top. "Only for an ounce of your paycheck," Bishop teased.

Terri sat in the front seat next to Slim, the vantage offering her a chance to sightsee as their caravan traveled south out of H-town.

They rolled down Interstate 45, passing fields of rusting, abandoned cars. Terri, after 20 minutes of the depressing scenery, was beginning to wonder if she'd made a bad decision. The entire south side of Houston had been devastated by fire, the charred remains of churches, boutiques, fast food restaurants, and master planned communities visible to the horizon.

Mother Nature had started reclaiming the territory; grass, weeds, and vines sprouting patches of green through the mangled timbers and piles of blackened brick and block. It was an empty, desolate scene.

The military had cleared a single path through the worst of the traffic snarl, most of the old cars and trucks having run out of fuel. Some had been pushed aside, others gathered in empty fields just off the roadway.

After a time, they began to see signs announcing NASA and the Johnson Space Center. This area hadn't burned, but suffered from abandonment just the same. "Guess those plans to colonize Mars are off the table for now," Terri mused.

After Clear Lake and League City, civilization thinned out, fewer empty businesses lining the road, the number of relic vehicles decreasing.

Slim guided the bulky motorcoach through the mess, a single escort Humvee in front, with two pickups surrounding Terri's temporary home.

As they continued south, Terri began to notice a change in the roadside foliage. Fewer trees, an abundance of grasses, and more than an occasional palm passed by the window. It was a welcome vista after the miles of horrific destruction.

The Galveston Causeway came into view, its span over the intercostal waterway and Galveston Bay visible from a few miles away. Soon, the motorhome's engine strained as the heavy vehicle began the ascent to the apex of the bridge.

For the first time in what seemed like an eternity, Terri was inspired by the view.

Royal blue water stretched into the distance on both sides, the island directly ahead. In the early morning sun, the counterbalance of sky and water was inspiring. She considered waking Hunter so he could see, but then realized he probably wouldn't appreciate what mom was fussing over.

They drove down the causeway, descending onto the island, and soon were passing by normal-looking city streets. Like most of Texas, all of the businesses were closed, several boarded up with hurricane shutters or sheets of plywood.

But there were a few people on the sidewalks, including the first bicycle she'd seen in a long time. *Hunter is going to need a bike one of these days*, she thought. *All kids do.*

As a result of the previous night's scouting mission, Slim had discovered what he thought was a decent hiding place for the motorhome. After traveling several blocks into Galveston proper, he turned and headed down a side street.

The warehouse came into view a short time later, one of the pickups already dispatching a man who rolled back a huge double-door into an empty interior. The cab became dark as Slim pulled inside.

"The coach will be safe in here, ma'am. I'll station two men to keep an eye on it."

Butter appeared at their side, adorned in beach shorts, a Hawaiian shirt, and flip-flops. Terri swore she smelled suntan lotion. "Well, look at you," she teased, "our very own surfer dude."

Smiling, he pulled on a floppy, straw hat. "Your taxi awaits, ma'am."

"Taxi?"

Slim pointed toward a 3-wheel bicycle arranged like the traditional Asian rickshaw, complete with padded bench seat and a small luggage rack in the back. "Yesterday, we saw a guy giving people rides in that contraption. We rented it for the day. Only cost us four MREs."

Terri walked over and inspected her chariot, a broad smile crossing her face. "You guys are so sweet! This is going to be a great trip... I just know it."

A few minutes later, Butter was strapping in Hunter's car seat from the coach while Betty inspected his work, skeptical of the transportation meeting her safety requirements.

"What if a car hits that thing while my Terri and Hunter are in there?" the frowning woman questioned.

"I haven't seen any cars hereabouts, ma'am," came the response.

"What if you have an accident... or hit a tree or something?"

"It doesn't go very fast, ma'am," Butter replied patiently. "I promise to be careful."

Reluctantly, Betty strapped Hunter in the secured car seat, the baby cooing when she shook the device to insure it was safely attached. She rattled it again, more to entertain Hunter than to test the connections.

Slim set a large duffle bag on the buggy's floorboard. "Miss Terri, you, the baby, and I will ride back here. Butter wants to peddle. He claims it will be a great workout, and quite frankly I think he needs the exercise," the cowhand winked.

"He does seem a little out of shape," Terri went along. "What's in the bag?"

"Kit for the baby, water and snacks for us, and a little helper for me... just in case."

Terri, grunting at Slim's use of the word "kit" for Hunter's diaper supplies, raised her eyebrows. "A helper?"

Slim reached inside the duffle, withdrawing a tactical 12-gauge shotgun. "Just in case, ma'am."

"Well, I'm ready when you are. I want to see this marketplace everyone keeps bragging about."

"Me, too," Betty chimed in, "But I'll walk, thank you very much."

"I've assigned one of the men to escort Miss Betty," Slim reported. "He's also been warned that she's widely known as a big spender, so he's prepared to haul assorted parcels and bags back to the coach."

Everybody laughed, including Betty, who seemed proud of her reputation. "I'm just a gal who recognizes a bargain when she sees one," she responded.

After hugging the older woman goodbye, Terri and Slim climbed in the back with Hunter. Butter, ever the cowboy, mounted the cycle's helm as if it were his trusty steed, and began peddling. It took the big man a few moments to get used to the strange machine, but soon enough, they were flying down the streets of Galveston.

"It's like a magic carpet," Terri grinned, loving the sensation.

The Strand was less than 10 blocks away, the mile passing quickly with Butter's legs pumping relentlessly at the controls. As they progressed, the Alliance team began to notice more and more people strolling along the sidewalks.

Some carried small bundles of a variety of items, a few more industrious types maneuvering small carts or wagons filled with goods. Terri noticed clothing in one such hauler; another appeared to be transporting bags of salt.

The fragrance wafting on the island breeze drew her attention next. The distinct aroma of smoldering hickory as it smoked meat, coupled with the unique scent of fish filled the air. She realized they had to be close to the exchange.

With the islanders now thickening into a crowd along the street, Butter steered to a heavy utility pole and announced, "This looks like a good place to chain our limo."

After unloading, Terri hefted a wide-eyed Hunter into her arms and said, "Don't tell daddy, sweetheart, but momma's going shopping."

A few blocks later, Terri could indeed see what all the fuss was about. Just like Meraton, tables, booths, stalls, and even a few blanket-stores were everywhere. As they began touring the ever-more crowded streets, she spied the anticipated assortment of

211

goods, as well as a few items that were unique to the seaside community.

What stood out most to the chairwoman was the variety of seafood. Oysters, packed in salt rather than ice, were common here. Fish of all varieties, shapes, colors, and sizes were also plentiful. Many appeared to have been already smoked for preservation.

Terri practically squealed with delight when she happened across the first shrimp. Turning to Butter, she announced, "I love shrimp cocktail, but I forgot to bring along anything to barter with."

Slim nodded knowingly, reaching inside the duffle and producing a small bag of ammunition. "I'm sure they'll accept these."

Terri proceeded to haggle with the old man working the booth, the homemade cocktail sauce actually costing her as much as the six shrimp. "I grow tomatoes and spices in my little garden," the vendor explained. "But to really give it flavor, you need peppers, and those are rare these days."

Moving to the side, Terri peeled her first bite, dipping it in the small plastic tub of red sauce. "Down the hatch," she said to her escorts, and then plopped the delicacy into her mouth. After chewing for a moment, she grinned, smiled, and then frowned.

Waving her hand to blow air into her mouth, she croaked "Water... hurry... water," to Slim who immediately unzipped the duffle and produced a small bottle of clear liquid.

Terri gulped several mouthfuls, and then wiped a tear from her cheek.

"Are you okay, ma'am?" a concerned Slim asked.

"I've never been better," she replied, plopping a second crustacean into her mouth. "It's just been a while since I've tasted anything spicy. These are wonderful. You have got to try a bite," she offered.

An hour later, they finished touring the expansive area, Terri absolutely inspired by what she saw. "We need more of this," she noted to Slim. "Every Alliance town should have a market. We can start hooking them together once we get electricity and fuel.

People can take what's plentiful in one area and trade it in another."

A strong breeze blew down the street, the gust prompting Slim to glance toward the sky. "Starting to cloud up a bit, ma'am. You mentioned something about showing Hunter the ocean. If we're finished here, it might be a good time to head that way."

On the return trip to the bicycle-taxi, Terri stopped and held Hunter in front of a small display of children's toys. "What draws your eye, sweetie?" she cooed to the child. "Help mommy pick something so you can have a souvenir from our trip."

Hunter reached for a small, stuffed bear, complete with a t-shirt that read, "I love Galveston." It cost Terri two cartridges to acquire the memento, but she didn't care.

The wind had grown blustery by the time they arrived at their transportation. "I'm glad you're the one peddling into this headwind," Slim teased his friend.

Butter shrugged, producing the key and unlocking the contraption. "Next stop, East Beach," he replied happily. "It's a few miles from here, so sit back and relax. Enjoy the scenery."

Bishop was back on top of the railcar as they pulled away from their third stop. Just like the previous two stations, there had been a brief exchange of passengers and freight. About the only thing interesting at this junction was the addition of a 14th car, the choreographed switching and coupling from a side-rail holding the Texan's attention. *I always wondered how they did that*, he thought.

Noting the new flatbed was piled full of split timber, he asked the passing Gomez, "Is that wood to fuel the train?"

"No, that's our primary export to Galveston. They have plenty of fish and oysters, lots of water and salt, but there's hardly a tree on the entire island. According to the stories I've heard, they smashed and burned every spare piece of furniture for firewood before we started running the train."

After Lady Star was topped off with water from a hand-powered pump, they were again on their way.

From his elevated position, the Texan could identify a bend ahead. As they had progressed south, the woods on both sides of the track had been thinning, each passing mile allowing him to relax just a bit more. He knew that if he were going to rob the train, he'd prefer the cover of dense foliage.

The combination of the new, heavy freight car full of firewood, the water, and the curvature of the tracks combined to keep their speed low. It all came together for Bishop just as he recognized the first outline of a man near the rails.

"Grim, heads up. I don't like this. East side... near that big bush."

Before his partner could look, the engineers slammed on the brakes. A quick glance ahead confirmed the Texan's suspicions; a barricade of heavy logs blocked the tracks in front of them. "Shit," Bishop hissed, throwing the safety off his rifle and going prone on the rooftop.

They came out of the forest, at least six shooters running bent at the waist. The first shot zipped over Bishop's head as the locomotive came to a halt. The Texan centered the front post on the closest man's chest and fired.

Grim's weapon barked next, his first shot causing one of the bandits to double over and fall.

The trackside raiders didn't charge the train, however. Taking cover behind a small mound of earth or the closest tree, they seemed content to simply snipe at Bishop and Grim. Given the accuracy displayed so far, Bishop wasn't very concerned.

"This is it?" Bishop shouted at Grim over the din of gunfire. "This is all they've got?"

The Texan glanced at the other side of the tracks, thinking he would find the primary attack coming from that direction. There was nothing but scattered pines and scrub. *This doesn't make sense,* he thought.

After the exchange of a few more shots, Bishop looked forward at the cowering engineers. "Back up the train!" he yelled. "Put her in reverse, and back out of this ambush. Go at least a quarter of a mile."

"It will take a minute," one of them shouted back.

Bishop nodded his understanding just as a bullet tore into the metal roof of the car, the round impacting no more than two inches from his head. *I need to get down from here*, he determined. *They're finding the range, and I'm too exposed.*

He went for the small hand-ladder, thinking of climbing down and then moving off to flank the shooters from the north. He glanced back along the length of the iron horse, wondering where Gomez and the rest of the red bandanas were. Movement caught his eye at the last, recently added car, a chunk of wood flying off the load. *What the hell?*

That first projectile was soon joined by another, and then another. Bishop stopped his descent, completely puzzled why the logs were jumping out of the car like popcorn flying out of a pan. He then saw an arm appear, followed by a tarp being pulled back. He inhaled sharply when their faces appeared, covered in handkerchief masks. At least 10 men came boiling out of what had moments ago been a simple load of timber.

"Grim! That last car we just took on is a Trojan horse! It's full of shooters!" Bishop shouted to his friend.

Before Grim could digest the words, Gomez and the other guards began running toward the engine from their station at the middle of the train. Bishop tried to wave and warn them, but it was too late.

Enough of the hidden bandits had exited their hide to engage the security detail from behind. The first volley of shots took down two of Gomez's reinforcements.

Shocked by the surprise attack from the rear, Gomez and his remaining man scurried for any cover they could find. The man dove under the train, his choice a life-ending mistake as the engineers finally got Star rolling backwards. His screams were heard over the gunfire.

215

Bishop, still on the ladder, reversed his direction as well, deciding the high ground was the better tactical position. He reached the roof, and then dashed toward the back of the train, bounding to the next car as their backward speed increased.

He wasn't the only one who realized the high ground was the superior option.

Two bullets tore through the air as he landed from his hurdle. There was no cover, no place to hide, so the Texan took a knee, aimed, and began firing at the three men moving toward him from the Trojan car.

The movement, vibration, and distance didn't bode well for accurate aim, the front post of Bishop's iron sights difficult to hold on target. He started spraying and praying.

One of the attackers went down on his second shot, the other two scrambling to lie prone.

Bishop started to do the same thing, thinking going low would allow whoever was the best shot to win the shootout, but the appearance of more heads mounting the ladder changed his mind.

Despite the train now rolling in reverse at a considerable speed, Bishop rose up and charged toward the attackers, randomly firing a round every few steps in a weak attempt to keep their heads down. He advanced three more cars before going flat and exchanging several shots with the ever-increasing number of foe at the back of the train.

Grim appeared at Bishop's side, the big guy bellowing "Coming in!" as he landed onto Bishop's car and rolled into position. In a few moments, two rifles were pumping rounds towards car thirteen.

"Nice day, ain't it?" Grim said as he popped a full magazine into his weapon.

"Little humid for me," Bishop replied, letting lose with a quick three-round burst. "We need a good downpour to cool things off."

Grim centered on a man rising to his knees and fired, the impact sending sparks and metal splinters flying, inviting the target to rethink his aggressive advance. "I didn't see the forecast for the rest of the week. Are we expecting rain?"

Three bullets thwacked into the roof between the two Alliance men, both of them scooting backwards a few feet to mess with somebody's aim. "Yeah, I think we're in for light showers tomorrow. Then it's supposed to get hot again," Bishop replied between shots.

Grim sensed the raiders were gathering for a rush. Switching his weapon's selector switch to full automatic, he sent a punishing burst into the group. After watching one of the bandits fall screaming from the roof, he matter-of-factly replied, "Well, that's good. My lawn could use a good dowsing. Is it supposed to come early or late? I was thinking about a round of golf."

Again, the attackers tried to rise as a group and advance, but Bishop was ready. His carbine barked repeatedly, sending withering, hot lead at the cluster and knocking down the man closest to him. "Damn," Bishop snapped when his bolt locked back empty. "Terri's been on me to clean the BBQ grill, or I'd go play a round with ya." Bishop rolled to his side, pulling out a fresh box of pills and jamming them home. "But we both know an unhappy wife leads to an unhappy home."

Grim kept up a steady rate of fire, but it wasn't enough to keep the attackers from advancing to the next car forward. "I could still make a tee time if you can get away. Does a body good to spend an afternoon on the links now and then."

"They're getting closer," Bishop observed, "We've got to think of something else."

"No shit. You're the captain around here. Any brilliant ideas?"

Before Bishop could answer, Gomez stuck his head up between the cars behind them. Bishop, seeing the movement, almost killed his boss. "Where the fuck have you been?" Bishop yelled. "Finally decide to join the party? We could use a little help up here."

"I managed to jump on the train," the crew chief screamed back, "But I dropped my rifle in the process."

Bishop shook his head, wondering how in the hell some people managed to tie their boots in the morning. Right at that moment, the engineers began braking again.

"We need to abandon the locomotive, or they'll kill us," Gomez declared. "I've been robbed before. They'll take the freight and anything valuable the passengers have, but nobody will die."

"People have already died, you dipshit," Bishop screamed back over the noise of Grim's rifle. "What the fuck's the matter with you?"

"Who gives a shit about a little cargo? I think we should jump off and let them have the train. There are too many of them."

Disgusted, Bishop half-turned between shots and sassed, "Why don't you go *find* a weapon? Maybe some of the passengers have managed to *not* throw down their rifles yet. Maybe one of them will loan a weapon to you so you can do your damn job."

"Who the fuck are you, giving me orders?" came the sure reply.

Grim, hearing the exchange, was clearly at his limit. Pulling the pistol from his hip, he spun around and pressed the muzzle against Gomez's forehead. "Go do as he says, you stupid fuck, or I'll kill you myself. Now get out of our way!"

"Okay! Okay!" the now-frightened foreman said. "No need to get pissy."

After watching Gomez duck down, Grim returned to trying to hold off the advancing bandits. Before he could reengage, they charged forward, advancing yet another car closer.

The shortened distance translated into more accurate fire. More and more bullets were impacting closer to the two Alliance defenders. "This ain't good," Bishop declared. "We're going to get overrun here in a bit. That... or run out of ammo."

Grim had to think about Bishop's comment for a minute, sending another string of bullets at their foe. Before he could respond, one of the attackers jerked as if he were being electrocuted, and then the report of a new, distant rifle rolled across the landscape.

"I think the kids have arrived," Bishop smiled.

The bandits were confused, looking at each other and all around, trying to figure where the bullet had originated. A cloud of red and grey mist appeared as another man's head virtually exploded.

"Looks like Kevin has his rifle zeroed in pretty well. About damn time they showed up," Grim commented, his own weapon adding to the mayhem erupting on car nine.

Bishop added another few rounds himself, and then a thought occurred to him. "How do we know they are all on top with us? What if some of them are making their way forward through the cars?"

A troubled look crossed Grim's face as he continued to pull the trigger. "Shit! That wouldn't be good."

"Looks like you guys have this under control," Bishop said. "I'll go clear the cars below."

Bishop climbed down the ladder, dropping onto the platform, entering the passenger car a few moments later. He could hear Grim's rifle finding steady work, but the rhythm wasn't panicked.

The Texan passed through a cowering group of frightened passengers, most of the wide-eyed riders huddled on the floor. Keeping his rifle at ready as he made his way through the throng, he shouted for everyone to keep down and as far away from the windows as possible. He exited out the back and was in the next car, again rushing toward the rear of the locomotive.

By the time he cleared the fourth car back, the shooting overhead was beginning to slack off. He found himself on a flatbed, climbing over the cartons of freight roped to the surface. Number six was another passenger unit.

He found the sixth unit void of bandits, and passengers. Reaching to open the door at the rear, Bishop was momentarily distracted by one of the windows exploding in a shower of glass. He crouched, scanned the area outside, and quickly determined it was nothing more than a random, misplaced shot. He opened the exit door and came face-to-face with a masked man. Before he could bring up his weapon, the guy threw a haymaker of a punch, landing the blow just above the Texan's eye.

Bishop, stunned, didn't even feel the impact as his back slammed against the floor.

Dazed, lying in the aisle, Bishop barely managed to bring up his legs as the robber dove through the air.

Catching the flying attacker's weight on the soles of his boots, Bishop managed to use the guy's forward momentum, propelling his enemy over him, landing on top of a seat.

Trying desperately to reach his feet, while at the same time bringing his weapon to bear proved to be a mistake. Just as the carbine was coming up, the recovered foe kicked at the barrel so viciously that it broke the sling, sending the carbine rattling across the floor.

Again, a sledgehammer blow landed on Bishop's jaw, the Texan staggering backwards with ringing ears and blurry vision.

Backing away while trying to recover, he was able to focus on the bandit's face. Covered from the bridge of his nose down to his neck, Bishop noticed something odd about the man's eyes. They were black and purple… almost as if he was staring at a raccoon with a mask. The thought would've have been funny if the guy wasn't kicking his ass.

Stopping his retreat, Bishop weighed in on his foe, a series of rabbit punches landing on the mask. The counter-attack did nothing but piss off his opponent further, a two-handed shove throwing the Texan against the railcar's wall with enough force to numb his spine.

Despite the pain, Bishop was recovering from the surprise and shock of the attack. He was also getting mad.

Again, he attacked the oncoming thief, throwing punches that would disable most men, kicking with every ounce of strength left in his legs. He managed to back his foe up a few steps, the opponent instinctively retreating from the flurry of fists and boots headed his way.

Bishop landed his share of blows, but they did little to slow down the aggressor. Much to his surprise, the bandit kept pressing Bishop back, one blow to the head causing his vision to go dark around the edges.

Knowing he wasn't going to last long, Bishop finally reached for the fighting knife strapped across his chest-rig.

The man facing the Texan paused when he saw the drawn blade, reaching up to adjust his mask. Bishop inhaled sharply when he recognized his attacker - it was Hoss.

"What the fuck are you doing here?" Bishop panted. "Why are you robbing the...."

It all came together - a flash of realization racing through the Alliance lawman's confused brain. Major Misery was skimming off the top by robbing the occasional load of freight. The insiders on the security team were playing both ends against the middle.

"I'm going to crush your throat and enjoy watching the eyes pop out of your head, you son of a bitch," the big man promised. "You ain't such hot shit if you don't have room to squirm away."

Bishop slashed at the charging bull, cutting deeply across Hoss's shoulder and arm, but it didn't slow the assault one bit. With his back against the wall, Bishop lunged through the air once and then again, trying to keep the huge man off him. Both attempts missed, contacting nothing but air.

On the third jab, Hoss deflected the strike, his block so powerful it knocked the blade from Bishop's hand. The Texan's last defense tumbled beyond his reach.

Hoss knew he had his prey now, stepping in close and swinging hard for Bishop's gut.

Despite the body armor, vest, and pouches across his mid-section, lightning bolts of pain shot through Bishop's torso. He swung back weakly, trying to stall death's advance, but it didn't do any good.

The Texan sensed his foe's hands closing on his throat, his mind screaming for him to punch and kick, but he was out of juice. There just wasn't anything left.

The vise on his neck began to tighten, Bishop pulling hard against the two steel-like arms crushing his windpipe.

Hoss sensed it was over, leaning in close and whispering, "And now you die."

But then the Goliath's eyes grew wide, a mixture of surprise, puzzlement, and fear crossing the hulk's face. Bishop felt the grip on his throat weakening, and then Hoss slowly slid to his knees. A moment later, he fell over, landing with his face on the Texan's boots.

Trying to clear the fog of pain and regain his composure, Bishop stared down to see his knife buried in the dead man's back. Gomez was standing in the aisle, his chest rising and falling as he worked to catch his wind.

"You okay?" the crew boss managed after a few deep breaths, "thought you might need a little help clearing the cars."

"Yeah… thanks," Bishop managed to croak, his throat dry and sore.

Bishop reached down and retrieved his knife. "You're not going to believe who this is," he declared to Gomez. "Help me turn him over."

The foreman's face filled with shock after they managed to roll Hoss onto his back. "Well, I'll be damned," was his only comment.

The sound of distant gunfire reminded the two men that they weren't out of danger just yet. Rushing to the closest window, Bishop spied a small group of masked men running for the woods. Grim, Cory and Kevin were in pursuit, chasing the failed thieves into the foliage.

"Grim has them on the run," Bishop responded, finding his rifle. "But we've still got the blockade and those other guys ahead of us. Nobody's watching the front of the train."

Leaving his boss to the task of settling down the passengers, Bishop managed a slow pace back toward the engine. Every muscle in his body ached, and he wondered if his jaw was broken. Moving from car to car, his strength gradually returned by the time he reached the fuel car.

Glancing back along the track to see how Grim was doing, he spotted the rest of his team returning from the route. From their casual body language, Bishop assumed all was well.

Judging the distance from their current location to the

obstruction, Bishop hustled forward, passing by the wood gas equipment and flagging down the engineer. "Let's return to the barricade, but stop a little further back this time. Maybe 100 to 200 yards short of the blockage. We may need some room to maneuver."

The men controlling Lady Star did as they were told, braking the iron horse almost two football fields shy of the location where the bandits had originally bushwhacked them.

Grim finally appeared, Cory and Kevin in tow. "We chased them into the woods, but they had trucks parked nearby. I didn't feel like wasting any more ammo," he reported calmly. "Now, all we have to do is take care of these clowns manning the blockade, and then we can be on our way."

Bishop quickly explained his encounter with Hoss in the passenger car, the ex-contractor recognizing the scam right away. "Nice work, Major Misery," he chuckled. "Hell of a gig if you can pull it off."

With Lady Star idling, Bishop, Grim, and Cory hopped off, moving away from the tracks and into the woods. "We'll give them a little surprise from the flank," Grim commented. "Let's see how badly they want to rob our train now."

But the thieves had abandoned their position at the wooden obstruction.

The Alliance team checked all around the area, no sign of the men who'd been shooting at them just a few minutes before. "Evidently, they bugged out," Bishop said. "They did their part and then hit the road."

"Or they saw me kick those other guys' asses and decided I was too bad a man to mess with," Grim replied with a grin.

They returned to the iron giant, informing the engineer and firemen that it was safe for them to clear the log pile. Several passengers disembarked to help.

While the clean-up was in progress, Bishop thanked Cory and Kevin for helping. "I want you guys to continue on south. Make sure there are no more surprises in store for us."

"Yes, sir," they replied, and hustled off to retrieve the stashed pickup.

Gomez found his rifle, the weapon unharmed despite being dropped. Bishop still had his doubts about the man, but kept them to himself. After all, he had saved the Texan's life.

"The Baron is going to go frigging nuts when he hears his own man was behind all the train robberies. We'll probably have a proper hanging when we get back," Gomez observed.

"If Misery is still there," Bishop replied. "He'll get word that we foiled this attempt before we get back. I bet he heads for greener pastures."

With a fair share of grunting and sweat, the track was cleared in 20 minutes. Lady Star again sounded her whistle, letting all aboard know she was bound and determined to make it to Galveston.

Butter's legs held out, delivering Terri and her protectors to the East Beach. Along the way, the skies had grown increasingly dark and overcast, blasts of wind rolling in from the gulf.

"Ma'am, I don't think it's a good idea for us to stay long. It looks like the weather is going to get nasty here in a bit," Slim commented, studying the sky.

"That's okay," Terri smiled. "I just wanted Hunter to see the ocean… and to tell the truth, I kind of wanted to see it again as well."

With her escorts in tow, Terri braved the blustery air and descended the seawall's stairs. She kicked off her shoes and began heading toward the distant water, half walking and half sinking in the shifting sand, carrying Hunter and pointing toward the Gulf of Mexico. Slim and Butter struggled to keep up.

By the time they reached the shoreline, the waves were rolling in dark and angry. "Definitely not a good day for a swim," she informed the infant. "One of these days though, we'll come back, and you'll love it… I promise."

Out of pure stubbornness, Terri insisted on sticking at least her toe in the water. Handing the baby to Butter, she dashed forward in the white foamy waves, managing to get ankle deep before retreating to higher ground, chased by an incoming roller – laughing all the way.

"Okay, guys. Sorry to drag you out here for just that little bit of sightseeing. Maybe the weather will be better tomorrow."

It started raining on the way back, the boiling clouds finally producing moisture. Terri did her best to keep Hunter from getting wet, the rest of the party quickly getting soaked.

Their reverse course was easier, the wind at Butter's back. Five blocks away from the beach, the big man slowed his pace, one very worried word coming from his lips, "Slim."

There were six of them, all holding shoulder-fired long guns and spread across the road. Behind each man was a saddled horse. Their target was clear, all eyes staring at Butter's taxi.

"Get us out of here! Now!" Slim responded, reaching for the duffle bag and its shotgun. Terri's 9mm was already drawn, her body bending to shield Hunter.

Butter cut hard left, accelerating the heavy cycle-taxi with pumping legs. Slim's attention was over his shoulder, watching to observe the reaction of the riders.

After two blocks, it became clear that the horses were faster than the best Butter could milk out of the taxi. "Faster!" yelled Slim, seeing the pursuers gaining.

"It won't go any faster," replied the already breathless peddler.

Slim was on the radio, calling for support. After listening to the reply, he shouted back into the microphone, "This will be over in 3 minutes. Move your asses now!"

Disgusted and cursing himself, Slim turned to Terri and said, "They have to move the big coach out of the way so one of the trucks can get out. I should have thought about that."

Not waiting on a response, Slim again checked behind and grimaced. "Butter, cut down this alley ahead. We can't outrun them; let's buy some time via maneuvering."

The big man made the turn, and for a second Terri thought they were going to flip over. She swore the carriage took the corner on two wheels.

Down a narrow alley they shot, the pavement much rougher, causing the thin wheels to bounce and thump the passengers in the seats.

Terri could hear the sound of horses' hooves behind them. She turned to see the nearest rider less than 100 feet away and gaining quickly. She raised her pistol, thinking to slow them down, but Slim grabbed her arm and shook his head no. "Nobody's fired just yet, ma'am. They may want to take us alive or just rob us. It's not a good idea to shoot first unless you have the most guns."

Nodding, Terri agreed. "As rough as this ride is, I couldn't hit anything anyway."

Butter came to another cross street, but had to abandon the alleyway. Two junk cars blocked the entrance, forcing another hair-raising turn onto the crossing surface street.

Slim spied one of those self-storage businesses just ahead, row after row of low buildings covering the grounds. "Pull in that place. Maybe we can lose them for a bit and buy some time."

Braking just enough to negotiate the turn, they flew down the driveway toward the maze of mini warehouses. Evidently, their pursuers didn't approve of the idea, a single shot ringing out, quickly followed by a shouted "Stop! Stop or we'll shoot."

But Butter didn't stop.

"It was only a warning shot," Slim tried to reassure Terri. "It was way high."

They sped past three rows of the buildings, some of the garage doors open, other closed and padlocked. "Cut right here," Slim instructed. "Stop as soon as you're around the corner."

Butter did as he was told, Slim hopping out of the back before the wheels had stopped rolling. He ran to the corner, peeking around to see the horsemen following, now less than 50 feet behind. Shouldering the 12-gauge, he jumped out in front of the charging pursuers and let loose with a blast, intentionally aiming high.

He watched long enough to see the lead horse rear up, a terrified shrill coming from the animal's throat. Before the front hooves had returned to earth, Slim was running back to the bicycle.

"That should slow them down," he was saying as he jumped back into the seat. "Go! Go! Go!"

In a few seconds, they were again flying past the garage door-fronted bins. "Turn here, then turn again as fast as you can," Slim instructed from the back seat, never taking his eyes off their tail.

After the second zigzag, Slim barked for Butter to stop. "Ma'am, I want you to take the baby and go hide in that unit right there," Slim said, pointing at an opening that showed furniture, boxes and a rack of clothing scattered inside. "Stay out of sight until our men arrive. I'll come back and get you. Now please, hurry!"

Terri got it, the idea of shielding Hunter from a gunfight overriding her desire to help confront the bandits. In a few seconds, she was out of the carriage, running with her pistol in one hand, Hunter's car seat in the other.

Having another thought, Slim pulled his radio from his vest, tossing the unit to Terri. "Guide in our cavalry. It's already on the right frequency."

Once he was sure she was out of sight, Slim yelled, "Go!"

It wasn't much of a maze. In fact, the buildings were laid out in a relatively simple set of rows that failed to offer many hiding places. Finally, reaching the back fence of the complex, Slim pointed toward a corner. "Pull in over there. We'll see if we can keep them busy until the guys get here."

Butter turned the handlebars, pushing Terri's security team down the last short line of openings.

A man flew out of one of the empty bins, his diving tackle knocking Butter off his seat, sending the two men tumbling across the pavement.

The now-pilotless cycle flipped on its side, spilling Slim out the back. He landed badly, pinned under the heavy carriage.

The man ambushing Butter was soon joined by a second fellow. In less than 10 seconds, both bushwhackers wished they had two or three more friends in the fight.

Grasping the man who'd knocked him free of the bike, Butter tossed the hapless attacker over his hip, driving his foe to the ground with bone crushing force. The second tried to grab the big guy's arm, and that was a mistake he'd never forget.

Instead of twisting the limb to Butter's back, he found himself holding an unmovable length of iron. Grinning at the surprised look on his attacker's face, Butter effortlessly twisted free of the grip, slamming his palm into the man's solar plexus with rib-breaking velocity.

Both of his opponents out of the fight, Butter turned to assist his partner and froze. Slim was lying on the ground, two men looming over him with their rifles pointing at his head.

"That'll be enough," said one of the gunmen. "Knock it off, or I'll aerate your buddy's skull."

Seeing that they finally had the upper hand, the spokesman's partner patted down Butter, checking to see if their prisoner was armed. After determining that Butter was weaponless, he then bent to lend aid to the two stunned men still lying on the ground.

"Where's the woman?" the man in charge asked.

Butter and Slim, now on their knees with their hands behind their heads, just stared back - neither of them feeling talkative at the moment.

Shaking his head as if tired of the whole affair, the lead bandit pulled back the hammer of his lever-action rifle and said, "I don't have time for this shit. I'm going to ask one more time. If your jaws don't start flapping, I'm going to put a bullet in the big guy's knee. He'll never walk without a limp again. So... where's the woman?"

When no answer came, the man raised his rifle and aimed, but a new voice cut him off. "No need for that, Murph," said an older man, appearing from around the corner.

He stepped forward, two more armed escorts bookending the new arrival, making it clear who was in charge. "Help them up, and make sure they're okay," he said to his bodyguards, pointing to the two men Butter had disabled.

"Look, fellas, we only want to talk to the lady. What's her name? Terri? We know who and what she is," the boss began. "My name is Corky, and I'm kind of the city manager around here."

Again, the two captives remained silent, their stubbornness causing Corky to frown.

"I know you've got help on the way. I left ten men at this establishment's gate to stop them. Besides, this facility is not so big that we won't find her in a few minutes anyway, and the weather is turning bad fast. So let's avoid anyone else getting hurt. No one wants to have a big gun battle. Please tell me where the lady is hiding. I only want to talk to her."

"I'm right here," Terri said from the shadows.

Corky turned to find himself staring into the barrel of the lady's pistol. He grinned and shook his head, "Well now, don't we have just a regular, old Mexican standoff."

The rain began seriously pelting the gathering, the drizzle turning into a cold, steady downpour.

Corky seemed to ignore the discomfort, eyeing Terri closely before speaking. "I apologize for how we went about introducing ourselves, but I had to be sure who you were. One of my men claims to have met you once, and I wanted him to get a good look before I approached you. Your security men, however, reacted faster than we anticipated."

"So, now you know who I am. Say what you have to say. I've got to get this baby out of the rain before he catches his death of cold," she said looking down at Hunter's car seat. "Let's either talk, or start the killing - you decide."

229

Corky laughed, an honest chuckle coming up from his belly. "So what I've heard is true," he replied, grinning widely. "I want to invite your men and you to my captain's brunch. I have a good idea why you're here, and think we should talk sooner rather than later. Please be my honored guest."

"Forgive me, sir. While I have heard of a 'shotgun wedding,' I have never received a brunch invite at gunpoint. I suppose I can concede that social protocols changed some two years ago, but call me old fashioned, I would just prefer to bypass these strong arm tactics in our future dealings," the Alliance leader announced, lowering her weapon. "Lucky for you," she continued, "I *do* have a weakness for those little cocktail shrimp. Now, more importantly, what would a guest of honor wear to such a soiree? I left my heels back in Meraton."

Terri was just changing into some dry clothes when the coach's door flew open, a grumbling, drenched Betty cursing the world for a lack of umbrellas.

After towel drying her waterlogged locks, she asked, "When is Bishop supposed to arrive?"

"He should be here today or tomorrow," Terri answered. "But you never know with him. Trouble seems to find my husband."

Brushing more of the liquid humidity out of her hair, Betty smirked at the remark. "He's not the only one in your family that seems to be a magnet for drama. What's up with you guys, anyway?"

Terri laughed, checking her own tresses in the mirror. It took Betty a moment before she realized Terri was dressing a little more formally than normal. "Are you getting gussied up for Bishop?"

"Don't be silly," Terri replied waving off her friend. "Bishop will probably waltz in here smelling like a goat, wanting to sleep for two days straight. I have a lunch date."

"Oh really," came the response, Betty's curiosity now pegged. "Some muscular, blonde-headed surfer you met at the beach? A well-tanned, cabana boy-type you bumped into while strolling along the sand?"

"No, and no. I'm meeting with Captain Landreneau, aboard his private yacht."

Betty didn't buy it, but wanted to play along. "My, my, what a forward young lady you've become. Your husband is due in town any moment now, and you're being whisked off to share caviar with some mystery man on his yacht? Given Bishop's history, I hope this gentleman has a private army in his employ."

Terri snorted at the remark, her outburst completely destroying any attempt at playing coy. "Actually, this captain's name is Corky, and he's at least 60 years old. While the man is quite charming, he is hardly my prime candidate for a fling. Besides, his yacht is actually a tow boat, and lunch is more apt to be oyster stew."

Betty, now having fun, decided to reverse their little game. "Not that I would whisper a word to Bishop, mind you, but I must ask why you are meeting this man. He must be extremely wealthy. Did he promise you lavish gifts? I wonder if diamonds are still a girl's best friend? Are you turning into a gold digger right before my very eyes?"

Putting a finger to her lips and striking a pose, Terri did her best to imitate a bimbo. "Could be," she squeaked.

"Okay," Betty frowned, tired of the diversion. "Let's have it…. Why are you meeting with some strange man?"

"Because he runs the island we're standing on, and he requested I meet with him. He said please. I thought it only polite to attend, and besides, he promised me the best grilled shrimp on the Gulf Coast. How could a girl say no to that?"

"I was, as the old song says, truly born on the Bayou," Corky stated, the pronouncement causing his guest's eyebrows to peak.

"My parents had been staying at a remote fishing camp when my mother had announced that I was about to make an early debut. My father made a heroic effort, tirelessly rowing an old pirogue across the black waters of Bayou Boeuf in the middle of the night. It was 21 miles to the doctor in Morgan City, Louisiana. They didn't make it."

"Amazing," responded Terri.

"I guess I decided to enter the world while afloat, and it was a telling sign. Since that day, over 61 years ago, I've rarely seen fit to leave the water."

There was a polite chuckle around the table, the gathered men having never seen their leader so open and talkative. No one was quite sure what to make of the conversation, with the majority of the men deciding the beautiful lady visiting with their leader had loosened his tongue.

"While other children were learning to ride bicycles and skateboards, I was docking boats," Corky continued. "My driver's education class consisted of piloting a 20,000-ton tow boat through the Mississippi locks outside New Orleans. The captain of that old rust-bucket had taken a liking to me, and gave me an unprecedented turn at the wheel."

A steward appeared from the galley, a fresh plate of grilled shrimp delivered onto the middle of the table. A few of the seated guests immediately reached to refill their plates, others remained fixed on their boss at the head of the table.

It was the weekly captain's meeting, a tradition Corky had initiated over 30 years ago. Despite the apocalypse, regardless of the circumstances just outside the docked tug's superstructure, he had demanded that tradition be maintained whenever possible.

Every man seated around the dining table had attended these gatherings since coming into Corky's employ. Some had been doing so for decades, others just a few years. But none of them had ever heard the boss carrying on with personal stories and details like he was now. *Women and their wily ways*, they all thought. *Perhaps the old man is smitten*.

A small man in statue, Corky held the respect of everyone in his employ, but none more so than the actual captains who commanded his fleet of towboats.

His skills in pushing a barge through the brown waters of the Gulf Coast waterways were legendary. Most of those seated today had witnessed Corky's capabilities first hand, events which elevated their appreciation of his nautical skillset to the level of awe-struck.

No one could handle a towboat like Corky. It was said he could stop a 70,000-ton barge on a barrel without using any reverse thrust. Others claimed to have seen him keep an explosive load of butane off the rocks after a hitch line had failed. He was the only man in history to ever push a side-by-side load up the narrow Bayou Mardi, a stump-lined, propeller bending, hull breaching passage that few men would attempt with a single load. He was, as the old timers say, a natural.

Before he was 20, Corky knew every eddy, silt bank, foul, and shoal on the Intercostal Waterway from Brownsville, Texas to Pensacola, Florida. He could decipher a river's surface tensions as well as captains three times his age and experience.

But there was more to him than just extraordinary seamanship and piloting skills. Like most successful waterborne entrepreneurs – Corky had a natural affiliation with things mechanical.

"I purchased my first tow boat at the tender age of 25, that old, rusting hulk's diesel motor smoking like a coal-fired boiler. My pappy and I rebuilt the cranky, old machine using a cypress tree as a winch and buying parts from salvage dealers. Those were the days, gentlemen… those were the days."

Raising his glass in a toast, Corky brought the foaming head of homemade beer to his lips. It was cold; it was being served with the best food he could find for his guests. That's all that mattered.

Pushing barges full of commodities ranging from soybeans to cement mix, Corky quickly developed a reputation as a trustworthy captain and savvy businessman. His loads arrived on time, at the right destination, and for a fair price.

He purchased his second boat before he turned 30. By the end of the next decade, his growing company owned seven such vessels. The number in his fleet had doubled ten years later.

There had never been a Mrs. Landreneau. Corky spent most of his days on the water, pushing loads from Houston to Mobile, running the great river north as far as Chicago.

Like most men of the sea, he'd had his share of queenies, the French Quarter in New Orleans his favorite place to eat, drink, and make merry during the rare break from the helm. Bankers, brokers, and freight forwarders didn't like meeting on the bridge of his tow. They required his presence ashore to sign papers, negotiate agreements, and execute contracts. New Orleans was the place to conduct business… including monkey business.

There just hadn't been time for romance or courting. Besides, Corky knew his true love – the water.

By the time the terrorists attacked the United States, the aging Cajun was a millionaire several times over. The pressing needs of a growing empire allowed for fewer and fewer trips at the helm, a frustrating fact of life for a man who felt an ever-growing sense of isolation and loneliness.

It was pure coincidence that Corky was experiencing a mid-life crisis when society fell. The dawning realization that he was in the last third of his life and claimed no family, friends or children fueled a rather radical change in his outlook.

Still occupying an expanded, heavily modified, captain's quarters on one of his towboats, Corky had purchased his first car at 58 years of age. A 1956 Ford Thunderbird convertible, it was vintage just like the captain. He'd met a pretty woman during a shipper's conference in Galveston and took to wooing her with his generosity. He'd even approached a real estate agent about buying a home… on land… with a garage to house his luxury vehicle… as long as it was a beach property.

And then everything had gone to hell.

Not one to follow the national news, Corky's first sense that something was really, really wrong occurred when one of his best captains had called in, reporting that there wasn't anyone at the Port of Houston to unload the 30,000 metric tons of natural gas he'd just docked.

An hour later, another of his tows reported in from Corpus Christi, stranded at a fuel pier that seemed to be closed. No attendants, no staff... it was like a ghost town.

When he and his office staff started making calls, they found the phone systems across half the gulf were down, the attempts that did manage to ring through were rarely answered. Over the next few days, the size of the disaster became apparent. All up and down the Gulf Coast, his boats were arriving full of cargo, only to encounter empty docks, burning cities, and downed communications systems.

Sophisticated radio equipment, powered by onboard diesel generators, allowed some measure of command and control over his fleet. Not knowing what else to do, he began ordering his captains back to Galveston.

He'd gone into the city proper, trying to find information, help, or advice. He soon learned the local government was overwhelmed. It seemed as though there was a statewide lack of electrical power. Houston was suffering from an out-of-control fire, and Austin had already experienced the first food riots.

There hadn't been anything else left to do but ride it out, hunkering down on his boat and drinking coffee with his frightened captains, crew and office staff.

"I told someone recently that the apocalypse had passed me by," Corky stated. "I had everything I needed right here aboard the *Morgan City Queen*. A freezer full of food, 5,000 gallons of diesel fuel, and a yard full of barges, all filled with grain and other valuable cargo. What apocalypse? I didn't see any such end of the world."

Again, a light chuckle came from the seated guests.

"It wasn't until the galley ran out of flour that I realized everything had changed. I hiked into Galveston, and what I found there... well... you all saw what was happening. People were starving, attacking each other.... An attitude of "Each man for himself," prevailed. I couldn't just stand by and let that happen. No good

235

man could. I had to try and change things for the better, and I believe we've succeeded."

Heads nodded in agreement all around, a few glasses of beer raised in salute.

"But now, gentlemen, now we are faced with yet another change. This morning, I was informed that we had a secret, special visitor to our island. One of our men noticed a fancy motorhome, complete with escorts and armed guards. Another of our people recognized the leader of an organization called the Alliance, out of West Texas."

The old captain's eyes became very serious, moving from man to man around the table to make sure he held their attention.

"We've known of this group for some months. We've heard some fantastic stories of their escapades, intercepted radio traffic among their cities and villages, and interviewed refugees who have made some unbelievable claims. It seems the military has recently joined their ranks, and now they are marching east."

"Maybe this leader of theirs needed a vacation," teased one of the younger men. The joke fell flat, so much so that his mate scooted his half-full mug of beer away, out of his reach.

Shaking his head, Corky dismissed the suggestion. "No, our sources in Houston tell me that she's here to scout our operation. The Alliance has the intention of spreading recovery throughout the entire state. Some people even talk of recreating the Republic of Texas as an independent nation."

"She?" inquired one of the old captains. "Did you say this leader is a 'she,' sir?"

"Yes, and I would like to introduce you to her. Gentlemen, please welcome Ms. Terri, Chairwoman of the ruling Council, and Ambassador of the Alliance of West Texas."

Terri smiled around the room, several of the men openly showing their surprise.

Corky paused, giving his men time to consider the ramifications of the information. "Before we sat down to eat, I had the most interesting conversation with this insightful young lady. I was worried she led conquerors, bound and determined to take territory and impose their will on the population. She has convinced me that is not the case."

Taking another sip, Corky continued, "My next concern was of our plentiful resources being seized and distributed to less fortunate parts of the state. Again, she has confirmed the Alliance has no intention of conducting business in that manner."

Terri, for the first time, spoke up. "We believe in free trade. Our governing body only gets involved to facilitate exchange."

"And finally," Corky continued, "I was worried about democracy and representation. Again, I've been assured that the Alliance has, and will continue to have, elections. Our city will have fair representation in the system they are creating."

Several heads nodded around the table, smiles and toasts in anticipation of a new day.

"So, do we resist? Try to isolate ourselves? Or do we join forces with this Alliance and pledge our loyalty? I wanted all of you involved in this decision, gentlemen. Change is riding a fast current, headed directly at our bow."

One of the most senior men at the table cleared his throat, "Captain Landreneau, I have a hundred questions, as I'm sure do my colleagues. When the time is right, will we have the opportunity to receive answers?"

Before Terri could answer, there was a knock at the door. The first mate entered the room, quietly whispering something in Corky's ear. Soon, the message was repeated to Terri.

Standing, Terri gazed around the table, smiling and making eye contact with each seated man. "I can assure all of you, we will do our best to address your questions. I'm positive we'll have a few of our own. We will be in contact and then send a team of our experts to coordinate with you. In the meantime, I understand the weather is quickly deteriorating, and I should return to my home."

Gomez made a decision which surprised both Bishop and Grim.

"I've been thinking about this," he announced out of the blue, "and I don't reckon it's a good idea for us to make any more of the scheduled stops."

"Why's that?" Grim asked.

"Major Misery's men must have trucks and fuel. Lady Star is only making about 35 miles per hour, and it would be easy for those guys to get in front of us and lay in wait. We should just roll on through and head to Galveston."

"And what stops them from just driving to Galveston and waiting on us there?"

"No. No. No," the foreman shook his head. "The island is a boundary. It's controlled by a different man with his own security people. If the major sent his people in there, they wouldn't be welcomed at all. Only the guards on the train are allowed."

Thoughts of Terri and Hunter immediately flooded Bishop's mind. "You make it sound like some sort of mafia or organized crime syndicate?"

Gomez shrugged, "How can you tell the difference between a don and a successful businessman rebuilding his empire? Especially these days."

"And who is this man that controls Galveston?" Bishop inquired.

Gomez grinned, "He calls himself Corky. I hear he's a crafty, old Cajun who owned a bunch of barges and towboats. Story goes he organized the people down there by seizing the cargo on his craft and using that as leverage. I've heard he had hundreds of tons of grain, fuel and other freight sitting on his decks when everything went to hell."

Bishop didn't doubt it. It wouldn't be the first time he'd seen a local businessman step forward and fill the vacuum created after the government collapsed or was unable to provide solutions. Sometimes such men provided the best possible answer, other times ultimate power corrupted.

"If you think it's safer to go directly to the island, then my all means, let's skip the rest of the stops. I've had enough fun for one day."

Looking at the sun, Gomez said, "It will take at least three hours off our trip. I'm going forward and letting the engineer know."

"Looks like you might get to see Terri sooner, rather than later," Grim announced.

"I could use a day off at the beach," Bishop responded with a grin, "to work on my tan."

His friend motioned toward the south, a squall line of ominous clouds stirring on the horizon. "Doesn't look like the best time to be squishing sand between your toes."

"Figures," Bishop observed. "At least we'll be done with this assignment. I think we have enough information to create a good report for the council. Think Gomez will be sorry to see us go?"

Laughing at the thought, Grim indicated he did not. "Gomez wouldn't be sorry to see his own mother go."

"We'll tell him he can have our pay for the day's work. That ought to cheer him up."

Major Misery heard the ruckus before the two frightened, dirty faces appeared at the command tent. He knew immediately something had gone very wrong.

"Where's Hoss?" was the father's first question, the state of the men in front of him already telling of a failed robbery.

Looking down at the ground and shuffling his feet, the older of the two bandanas replied with a low voice. "He didn't make it.

239

He's dead, sir."

Both of the messengers expected an explosive tirade from their boss, the man's temper well known and respected. Much to their shock and relief, the major merely stared off into empty space and sat down slowly, as if finding his land legs after a long sea voyage.

After a few moments, Misery whispered, "How?"

"That new guy that Hoss fought yesterday... the little one... he killed him while we were shooting it out with the other guards on the roof."

"Did you see him kill my son?"

"No, but I saw Hoss's body before we took off. When I slid down the ladder, I peeked inside and saw him lying dead inside the car. That new guy was pulling his knife out of Hoss's back."

Both of the major's fists slammed onto the table, the outburst startling the messengers. The display was quickly brought under control, Misery continuing with a low voice. "So I assume our little Trojan horse caper didn't work out so well?"

"It would've, but those new guys fought like nothing we've ever seen. They were better shots and more disciplined than anything we've ever gone up against."

Major Misery was no longer in the tent, at least not mentally. His physical body rose, briefly pacing around the room, but it was evident his mind was elsewhere.

"How many men did we lose?"

"Ten... ten out of fourteen, plus two more of the forward team."

Finally, the major's eyes focused. "Did you recover my son's body?"

The frightened glance exchanged between the two visitors answered the question long before one of them mumbled, "No."

Veins appeared in the major's forehead, his body trembling in anger. Pivoting sharply on his heels and pointing a shaking finger, he hissed, "If they have Hoss's body, you know what that means. It means the fucking Lady Star is no longer a gravy train for us. It means the baron is going to come after us vigorously. It means you two, and all the rest of you worthless idiots are going to either hang, or go back to eating squirrel stew out in the woods."

Both of the messengers nodded, "What do you want us to do, boss?"

Major Misery managed to calm himself down with great effort, finally rubbing his chin in thought. "Gather everyone. All the ammo and weapons we can muster. We'll make sure that locomotive doesn't make it back here tomorrow. We'll stop it just north of the island. Now get going."

Corky, after escorting his guests off the ship, strolled onto the bridge, his experienced eye scanning the conditions outside the thick glass enclosure, his brow wrinkling in a frown. "Quite the blow," he remarked to the first mate.

"Yes, sir, it surely is. I've been watching the wind speed, and things appear to be getting serious out there. I've seen gusts at 60, pretty constant at 40."

"And the barometric pressure?"

Sighing, the man keeping watch replied, "Our barometer is down, sir. I can't monitor the pressure."

Corky motioned to a nearby docked tow, the *Morgan City Angel* restless in her berth less than 30 feet away. "Have you contacted *Angel* to check the pressure?"

"Their radio is down, Captain."

Corky grunted, remembering the issue being reported yesterday. There were no spare parts available. No new radio could be purchased, shipped, or installed. "Send a man over and ask Captain Miller for a reading."

"Yes, sir."

While he waited, Corky mentally inventoried the list of broken equipment in need of repair or replacement. Given it had been over two years, the items weren't significant. Still, it seemed like things were breaking more often, their needs growing every day.

"Maybe that's why we can't stand on our own," he whispered to the empty bridge. "Maybe that's why we should join whatever government eventually forms."

But it was more than radios and equipment.

Watching the deckhand pull on his raingear in preparation to brave the weather, Corky realized part of the reason why he welcomed the Alliance so openly was that he was getting tired. He'd worked so hard to organize the city's people, putting together The Strand and arming his men to provide security and protection. It was a thankless job, a never-ending river of problems, issues, and snags requiring more diligence than any cargo haul he'd ever attempted.

He'd been raised living off the land, and at first, couldn't understand how anyone residing so close to the water could go hungry. Under his guidance, fishing, shrimping, oyster harvesting, and even the gathering of edible seaweeds had been systematized throughout the island.

It had been one of his engineers who taught the locals how to evaporate seawater to isolate the salt.

But it was exhausting work with little reward. No one was going hungry - there was little organized violence in his realm, but other than that, Galveston simply wasn't making much progress.

The trade agreement with the train operators had pushed the standard of living a little higher. Now there was wood, beef, and a wider assortment of vegetables available to the people. Classrooms had been formed, the island's children at least learning to read.

He'd formed neighborhood committees, centralized what little medical care they could provide, and tried to organize the fishing fleets.

"Everything went to hell right as I was starting to enjoy life," he said, waiting on the mate to return. "Doesn't seem fair – but then no one promised our time on this earth would be fair."

A minute later, the drenched deckhand returned. "Sir, Captain Miller reports we are at 29.58 inches of mercury and falling."

Corky whistled, looking at his first mate. "That's not good... not good at all. I want every tow and barge double-lined immediately. Looks like we have a serious tropical system moving in, and I don't want any of our craft pulling free from her moorings."

"Right away, Captain. I'll radio and send messengers."

Corky turned his attention back to the windows, a new worry now dominating his thoughts. A tropical depression would measure 29.54, a Category 1 hurricane 28.95. A big hurricane could go as low as 28.06.

Turning back to his second in command, Corky said, "I want to be advised of the pressure every hour. If it dips below 29 inches, I want to be notified immediately."

"Yes, Captain."

Terri heard the wind and rain roaring against the warehouse's roof and walls. Even inside the coach, the storm sounded ferocious.

Pacing to the window, she glanced into the cavernous building, catching a glimpse of the torrent through the partially opened door. It looked as if the rain was blowing near horizontally. "Heck of a squall," she commented to Betty, casting a worried look toward the older woman.

"They have them down here," came the immediate response. "All that wide open ocean gives the weather plenty of time to build. That's why only palm trees thrive along the coast."

Slim, complete with glistening poncho and rifle, stepped into her view. His hair was soaking wet. He looked cold.

Terri knew her security men wouldn't leave their posts, no matter how bad the weather turned. Given her protector's imitation of a soaked rat, Terri realized the sentries were probably patrolling the outside of the warehouse as well as the interior. "I'm going to make a pot of coffee for the guys," Terri declared. "They look miserable out there."

"Let me help," Betty said, moving toward the kitchen counter.

Coffee had become one of the most valuable commodities in the Alliance. Existing stores had been depleted early on, with only the occasional new stash being discovered. Pete, it was rumored, had a secret supplier from Mexico. The deliveries were said to be made late at night, the Meraton bar owner and mayor supposedly trading his best moonshine for the precious beans.

Pete would neither confirm, nor deny the accusations.

When the pot had finished brewing, Betty produced a tray of cups. There wasn't any sugar, but cow's milk had been plentiful at the time they had left Alpha.

Slipping on her own raincoat, Terri checked her sleeping son before taking the tray of steaming joe to the door. Betty helped her down the steps, frowning at the constant growl of the storm against their shelter.

The chairwoman found Butter first, the big fellow keeping his vigil just inside the large, doublewide door they had driven through. "Hey there," she said over the bedlam outside, "I brought you something hot to drink."

"Is that coffee, Miss Terri?"

"Sure is. Now you have to promise not to tell Bishop I shared his secret stash," she teased.

Reaching for one of the cups, Butter smelled the liquid like a wine taster approaching a rare vintage. "That smells extra amazing," he replied.

"Where are Slim and the rest of the guys? I have some for them, too."

"They're down at the far end of the building, ma'am. I can't leave this door, but if you walk about 50 yards that direction, you should run into them. And thank you, Miss Terri. You don't know how good this tastes."

Butter handed her his flashlight, "You should take this with you. It keeps getting darker by the minute."

Terri glanced around, peeking outside at the drenched street and town beyond. It was shocking how dark it was given the mid-afternoon time of day.

A minute later, Terri found the other security men. They were huddled in a corner, their attention drawn to the only clear window in the entire building. Everything else had been boarded up years ago.

"Hi guys," she greeted. "Anybody want a cup of coffee?"

"Did you say coffee? As in real, down-to-earth joe? Yesssss, ma'am!"

Grinning, Terri set the tray on a nearby stool, the only piece of furniture she'd seen in the whole place. After watching the team take turns pouring, she turned to Slim and nodded toward the window. "What were you guys watching out there?"

"The storm, ma'am. One of the guys used to live here in Galveston back in the day. He said this is one of the worst he's ever seen."

Terri scanned the building around them, "Are we safe here?"

"As safe as anywhere I can think of at the moment. There's no way we could drive the RV in this wind... at least no safe way. The streets are already filling with standing water here and there."

Terri walked to the window, absentmindedly relaxing her hand against the glass. She couldn't see much, the blowing rain, dark clouds and dirty window all serving to obscure the view. She perceived another gust of wind bluster against the building, and then quickly pulled her hand away from the glass where it had been resting. Turning, she exclaimed, "I felt the wind push the glass in! It actually bowed inward!"

Slim nodded calmly, motioning to the building with his eyes. "These walls are poured concrete, every window but this one has been long gone and replaced with plywood. The rafters are 12x12 hardwoods that have survived every storm for the last 80 years. Odds are it will survive another."

Turning back to the glass again, Terri watched the rain for a few more moments and then said, "You don't think this is a hurricane, do you?"

Slim frowned, "Actually, ma'am, that's exactly what we were just talking about. It's very frustrating not knowing. There's no Emergency Alert System, Weather Channel, satellite photos, or even equipment to measure the wind speed or barometric pressure. And really, it doesn't matter. We can't leave in these conditions, so we've got to ride this out, no matter what type of storm it is."

"If it is, what about all those people? I remember the island flooding during Hurricane Ike, but everyone had been warned and a lot of people had evacuated for the mainland."

Clearly concerned about the possibility, Slim's response carried a tone of helplessness. "I can't think of any way to warn everyone. I don't like it, but there's nothing we can do."

Terri didn't like it either, her mind filled with images of the happy, productive residents she'd seen earlier at The Strand and on the way to the beach. Galveston was proving to be one of the few places she'd visited that held optimism for the future – that would be able to contribute to the recovery of the entire region.

It angered her that Mother Nature might be taking aim at one of humanity's few bright spots, but as Slim had noted, she couldn't think of any action or move that would help the situation.

Like the ocean pounding the seawall just a few miles away, waves of helplessness rolled over Terri. She could only hope it wasn't a hurricane, or that it was a small one.

The rain began pelting Bishop just after Gomez announced they were two hours outside Galveston. Keeping his station on the first car's platform, he'd been watching the dark line of clouds heading their direction for some time. When the first drops fell, he was ready with a poncho.

The steady rhythm of the iron horse made diligence difficult at best, some sections of the rail almost rocking him to sleep. For the "nth time," he pined for a cup of coffee.

They were heading almost due west now, the deep forests behind them now replaced with open, coastal plains. He knew they were nearing Houston, the route taking them to the eastern edge of the city where they'd turn south for the final run to Galveston.

Bishop had no desire to see Houston. He'd heard enough reports, talked to enough people to know his former home wasn't anything at all like he remembered.

Checking the terrain ahead and seeing nothing more threatening than a couple of goats grazing along the line, Bishop allowed his mind to wander back to the last time he'd seen Houston proper before all hell had broken loose.

Before this latest assignment, Terri and he had talked about visiting their home, or at least what might be left of it. While the couple didn't have any reason to believe it had burned, they both assumed it would've been weather-damaged and overgrown at a minimum, looted at worse.

"I can't, Bishop," Terri had declared. "I just can't. I remember it the way we left it, and I want to keep that vision. That life is gone, and I can't see any reason to stir up all that emotion again."

It seems like it was so long ago, Bishop thought. Their first home together, worrying about the electric bill, the price of groceries, and struggling to make the payments on both a mortgage and a new truck.

247

He could almost smell the coffee percolating in the kitchen as the rays of the morning sun streamed through the kitchen window. He remembered watching Major League Baseball games in the den, and how Terri fussed over the finger foods for the Super Bowl.

They had so much then and didn't even know it. There were always cold cuts in the fridge, at least a pound of bacon ready for the pan. Fresh fruit, eggs, chips and salsa... little things that they took for granted at the time. Now, even a cup of coffee was considered an extravagance to most.

The rainfall increased its annoying intensity, now stinging Bishop's face as Lady Star sliced through the blow. Ducking inside the car, Bishop tried his best to do his job and keep watch through the streams and rivulets that ran down the glass. The rhythm of the rails tempted him to close his eyes, but he didn't dare reduce the intensity of his vigil. Gomez was probably right about Major Misery.

As usual, he had to agree with Terri's desire not to visit their home. Returning to the old neighborhood would indeed conjure up a head full of bad memories.

But it wasn't the potential despair over a lost abode or looted china that bothered Bishop. What he feared had nothing to do with possessions or physical things. No, what troubled the Texan the most was losing the battle that raged inside him. He feared that visiting their first home would add fuel to a flame that he barely managed to contain.

The more he fought, witnessed, and suffered in this new world, the angrier he became at the loss of the old one. Every man he'd been forced to kill added to the fury. Every orphaned child, starving wretch and street lined with empty homes caused the ire to build.

He was constantly suppressing the urge to lash out at something, to make someone pay for all of the pain and suffering. His internal ferocity was barely contained, and if it triumphed in this conflict, his morality would disappear forever.

At first, he'd been completely occupied with simple survival. Staying alive had consumed all of his energy and time.

But as things stabilized, there was more mental bandwidth available to analyze, observe, and remember. Without the need to spend every waking moment of every day focused on providing nourishment, Bishop began second-guessing their lot, searching for answers.

Those answers troubled the Texan. For the first time in his life, he began to lose faith in his fellow man. Despite all of the conflict, treachery, cruelty, and exhibitions of pure evil he'd encountered, Bishop had always held hope and faith. Holding onto those values was becoming more and more difficult.

The dark forces within his soul spoke tantalizing words, tempting phrases that glorified withdrawal. They whispered of the imperfection of men. They pointed to the weakness, guile, and inferiority in others. People weren't worth helping. It was useless to save others. They would only repeat the same mistakes. Leave all this pain and suffering behind. Take Terri and retreat back to the ranch… it's the only path to light and salvation.

"Leave them to their own devices," the voices said. "Let the animals that surround you work it out," they tempted. "You know taking your family back to the ranch and isolation is righteous, just, and moral. Impose your will. Make Terri do it. The others deserve whatever fate comes their way."

Bishop shook his head, the conscious effort to push those thoughts aside requiring tremendous focus. "I'm losing it," he whispered to the rain-streaked window. "Becoming a hermit seems like a great career path. I could put sociopath and isolationist on my resume."

The door flew open, startling Bishop out of his trance. A soaking wet Grim appeared in the opening, hustling inside to escape the rain. Shaking off like a drenched dog, he said, "Damn that's getting nasty out there. You okay?"

"Yeah, I'm fine. Why?" Bishop responded.

"It looked like I snuck up on you, which is weird. That and the fact that you haven't made a smartass joke or remark since the ambush, which is even weirder. That big fella knocked you around pretty good… maybe you should take a break?"

"No, I'm cool. I'll take a little time off after we get to Galveston.

Maybe go to the beach with Terri and Hunter."

"I'd find some rot-gut whisky and get stumbling, falling down drunk if I were you. Hell, I'll help you drink it, and then roll you out of your own puke."

Bishop grinned, "What a guy you are, Grim. How can a fella go wrong with friends like you around?"

The knock interrupted his reading. Corky closed his book and removed the now-necessary reading glasses. Peering up at his cabin door, he instructed, "Come in."

His second in command entered, a serious look painted on his face. "Sir, the barometric pressure continues to fall. It just dipped below 29.00."

Corky didn't react immediately. Instead, he looked down at *The Old Man and the Sea*, and thought of the irony. *What an appropriate title*, he mused.

"Have the additional lines been secured?"

"Yes, Captain. We've got several rain-drenched deck rats on our hands, but the secondary moorings have been implemented."

"Wind speeds?"

"We are seeing sustained winds out of the northeast at 65 miles per hour. We've had two gusts over 80."

"Shit! You know what this means, don't you?"

"Yes, sir. We are most likely looking at a Category 1 hurricane."

"Or worse," Corky replied, his mind already thinking about the next steps.

"Have two men take the heavy fork-lifts from the port. Issue them both radios. I want one of them patrolling the seawall. If it looks like the storm surge is going to breach it, we need to know. I want you to give the other tractor driver that police bullhorn we found. Have him start going through the residential areas and warning people to get to high ground. The taller buildings along The Strand should provide some shelter. Make sure they are unlocked. My gut tells me we're in for a rough ride."

"It's not much warning, Captain. The people at the east end of the island won't have much chance of getting to high ground."

"It's all we can do. God help us if this is a big one."

Bright, glistening-yellow slickers covered the two shapes as they scrambled off the gangplank and onto the concrete surface of the pier. Half bent and struggling in the face of the wind, it was an exhausting effort negotiating the 150 yards to the tractors.

Side-by-side, the machines were giants of their kind. Unlike the typical small forklifts that toiled and rumbled through warehouse aisles across the land, these units sported tires higher than a man's head, four wheel drive, and diesel engines that could power the largest of trucks.

They had been designed to move, stack, and arrange steel shipping containers after the weighty storage boxes had been unloaded from cargo ships. Consisting of a huge motor, stout hydraulic system, fork, and a cab, they were high off the ground and offered little resistance to the wind. Just about the perfect machines to pilot during a hurricane – if such a thing existed.

Both drivers climbed for the small cabs, the slick rungs reaching over 12 feet into the air. A short time later, the rumble of two powerful diesel motors sounded across the docks, soon followed by the bright beams of headlights.

Sounding more like an enormous farm tractor than any forklift, unit #1 rolled out of the pier area, its destination the access road fronting the seawall.

251

Not to be left behind, unit #2 quickly followed, heading toward the east end of the island, set on prowling the residential streets and delivering a warning.

"Goodnight moon," Terri read to Hunter, the classic children's book one of his favorites. The absence of her own voice let the ceaseless roar of the storm dominate the coach, just as worry dominated the mother's thoughts.

She bent and kissed the top of her son's head, his spittle-soaked fingers leaving his mouth and reaching to touch an illustration. Pulling the always-present towel from her other knee, Terri wiped the tiny hand before letting him play with the page. Books were hard to come by, and they weren't making them anymore.

"Sounds like it's getting worse out there," Betty observed as she set down her knitting needles. Terri recognized her friend was nervous. She had marveled how the older woman once created an entire afghan with nothing more than a substantial supply of yarn, a couple of knitting needles and an unhealthy abundance of worry. It seemed the only time Betty occupied her hands with the hobby was when anxiety threatened to control her.

Terri hefted Hunter and stood, pacing again to the front of the coach and staring out the windshield. Despite the mid-afternoon hour, the warehouse was almost completely dark. Through the murkiness, she couldn't even identify any of the guards.

A sense of cabin fever overwhelmed Terri. That, combined with a frustrating sense of inaction prompted her to pass Hunter to Betty. "I want to go check and see how things are going. I'm getting a little stir crazy in here."

"Be careful, love," the older woman replied, knowing it wouldn't do any good to protest. "Don't sneak up on the guys. They probably can't hear very well with the wind, and that tends to make those types extremely jumpy."

Smiling down at her friend, Terri nodded. "Wise advise as usual.

252

Don't worry; I'll be careful. Back in a few minutes."

Pulling on her raincoat and grabbing a flashlight, Terri opened the RV's door and was momentarily taken aback by the volume of the howling outside.

"Maybe this isn't such a good idea," she said aloud, hardly able to identify her own voice. But the thought of retreating inside the confined spaces of the camper seemed worse.

With her flashlight's beam sweeping the area, Terri made for the double door where she knew one of the security men was always stationed. It was Butter.

"Is everything okay, ma'am?" he shouted over the constant scream of the storm.

"Yes! Everything's fine. I just needed some fresh air!" she yelled back.

She approached the narrow opening Butter was using to keep watch, the outside only slightly more illuminated than the warehouse's interior.

The avenue beyond was visible through the sheets of blowing rain, but just barely. There was a mid-sized row of palm trees along the median, their ferns bending to the force of Mother Nature. Terri could see standing water in the street, every gust of wind creating a small wave that washed over the curb. The sound was like standing next to a railroad as a freight train thundered by.

A rumble and bang sounded, a sizable sheet of metal blowing past, slamming into one of the palms and then tumbling through the air again. Terri couldn't tell if the object was part of someone's roof or a sign of some sort. Other debris followed in its wake, a trash can lid... a child's toy... what appeared to be shingles. And all the while, the deafening growl of wind and rain provided the background music. Terri shuddered, feeling tiny and insignificant next to the power of the storm.

Butter met her frightened gaze, the large man showing his own concerns. "It keeps getting worse!" he yelled. "I'm seeing more garbage and projectiles blowing past. I hope it doesn't last much longer."

Terri started to answer, but Butter held up a hand to stop her. Turning away from the noisy opening, he pushed the earpiece tight with his hand, intently listening to a broadcast.

"No copy," he shouted into his microphone. "I do not copy!"

Stepping further away from the door, Butter's face was covered in a pained grimace, his ear trying to identify the dispatch. There was more conversation, but she couldn't recognize the words.

A few moments later, he turned back to Terri, a smile on his face. "That was your husband, Miss Terri. The train is coming over the causeway. They will be on the island in a few minutes."

For a moment, relief flowed through Terri's veins, the sensation quickly replaced with concern as a strong gust tore through the street outside. "Can you tell him to turn around and go back?" she yelled. "I don't think it's safe for him to be here!"

Butter frowned, innocently asking, "Can they turn a train around?"

From Bishop's perspective, they were traveling through nothing more than a blustery tropical storm. With the wind pushing at the locomotive's back, he was unaware of the true severity of the situation ahead.

All of that began to change as they rolled around the last bend leading to the Galveston Causeway. Bishop could see some distance across the open waters, the island's high-rise buildings a vague, barely visible outline in the distance.

Not only did the now-broadside winds begin to shake the train, the bay waters below the bridge were frothy white and angry.

The open spaces also provided more perspective to the density of the rain, clearly defined sheets blowing with such velocity, the scene looked more like a winter blizzard than any rainstorm the Texan had ever witnessed.

254

But it was too late to stop now.

As they traveled further from shore, Bishop felt the car he was riding shift from side to side. His mind filled with terrifying visions of a huge gust blowing the iron horse off her tracks and into the violent seas below.

But the Lady Star kept chugging, pulling the frightened passengers and cars of freight into the maelstrom. Crossing that bridge was the most frightening three minutes Bishop could ever remember.

The presence of wonderfully solid earth beneath the locomotive helped settle his nerves somewhat, but soon he was wondering if they hadn't jumped from the frying pan into the fire.

Bishop heard Cory's voice in his ear, "Captain... Captain, do you read me?" came the static-filled, hollow sounding transmission.

Keying his microphone, Bishop replied, "I copy... but barely. What's wrong, Cory?"

"Sir, we're going to be late reaching the island. The road we're on is flooded out, and it's going to take a while to backtrack."

"Stay off the island and find shelter, Cory. Repeat, stay off the island and find shelter. The weather is worse here."

But there was no response.

"Trouble with the kids?" Grim asked, scrutinizing the frown on his friend's face.

"They're blocked by a washout. I told them to stay put and find shelter, but I'm not sure if they heard me. We went out of range before they could acknowledge."

As the train rolled through the industrial area, Bishop saw hunks of debris blowing through the air, some of the missiles quite large and potentially damaging.

More out of habit than need, the engineers sounded Star's whistle, the signal intended to let the local dock workers know she had arrived.

"What happens now?" Bishop asked Gomez.

"There is a turn-around ahead on the line. We'll go real slow around a tight loop and end up facing back the way we came."

Bishop watched as they passed into a more residential area, the lack of electric crossing signals requiring the constant use of the shrill whistle. In the howling wind, the Texan wondered if anyone could hear the warning.

As they traveled further to the southeast, he began to notice flooding. The streets they crossed were inundated, standing water covering the sidewalks here and there. At one point, he thought he saw a strange-looking tractor passing between two houses, but the image quickly faded, obscured by the downpour.

"This isn't good," Grim announced from his side of the car. "I don't think that's rainwater."

The statement compelled all three men to turn toward the east, the understatement of Grim's observation sending a chill through Bishop's soul. There were people running toward the train, a three-foot high wall of water chasing after them.

The locomotive's route blocked their view, none of the men able to see the results of the race, all of them realizing they were going to be passing back the same way after the loop.

"What was that?" Grim questioned. "Is there a river or dam in that direction that overflowed or gave way?"

"I think the seawall has been breached," Bishop replied. "I'll bet my day's pay we have just rolled into the middle of a hurricane."

Corky was called to the bridge, the first mate's tone making it clear he should hurry.

"The barometric pressure just dipped again, sir. We are now officially in a Category 2 storm, and the mercury is still falling."

"Shit," hissed the captain. "I was worried about this. Any word

256

from our patrols?"

"No, sir, not yet. I'm concerned their radios aren't powerful enough to penetrate the storm."

Corky thought about that for a moment, unsure if the rain-thick air would hinder transmission distances. It gave him an idea.

Turning to a sophisticated electronic panel, he flipped two switches and then focused on one of the three television-like screens mounted flush in the helm.

A few moments later, a colorful image of a map appeared, a solid line sweeping in a circle like the second hand of a watch. "Sir, the radar is for surface objects. Without the NOAH feed, it won't show weather patterns, will it?"

Grunting, Corky began adjusting the knob, tweaking the control labeled, "Gain."

"A wise old Cajun once told me that a ship's radar was like a guitar, some men could coax it to sing like an orchestra, others could only make noise. When you're caught in a Biloxi fog on a dark night, and you know there are freighters about that can crush your hull like a twig, you learn to make this little instrument perform like the Philharmonic."

He then touched the screen and said, "I'm switching to the 72 nautical mile range with a very low gain. I used to be able to pick out squall lines on the old models. I'm not sure about these new digital units."

As he adjusted the control, the display changed drastically. The solid mass of green returns, the radar's energy beams bouncing back off of the rain, began to fade, eventually turning into a fuzzy image similar to the snow on an old black and white television.

Now barely manipulating the knobs, Corky arrived at a configuration he felt provided the most accurate picture. The next sweep of the phased array antenna made the experienced seaman inhale sharply.

"We're in trouble," he mumbled, causing his second in command to peek over his shoulder.

"God help us," was the whispered reaction.

Out in the gulf, the radar painted a clear picture of a simple half-circle. There, 60 miles offshore, the gentle, soft-green fuzz of precipitation thickened, becoming a clear, solid shape like a quarter moon. The eye-wall. The center of a well-defined hurricane. The most deadly, ferocious part of the storm, and it was headed directly at them.

The display in front of the captain provided a cascade of answers to questions he never wanted to ask. He knew the direction of the storm from the wind and rain, now he could judge its girth. It wasn't a monster – he'd seen bigger. But the eye was tight, compact and moving quickly – a sign of ferocity. His equipment informed him of the storm's speed – 26 knots. It would slam into the island in two hours.

"Warn the crews and the tractors," he ordered.

"Aye, aye, sir."

"And I would broadcast a warning on all frequencies. Maybe the military in Houston will have time to save a few people... move them out of the low-lying areas."

"Affirmative, sir."

He returned to the window, knowing the radar wasn't going to change its story. In the pre-collapse days, they would've had warning – perhaps days. Now, it was too late. The thick glass protecting their little cocoon of calm was misleading. There wasn't the equipment available to move people off the island, yet the storm-surge would most likely submerge the entire land mass with several feet of water.

He didn't have buses, not that they would be able to leave now. No one had gasoline for private vehicles, and the roads were already flooded.

The mate reached for the radio, but a voice sounded before he could raise the microphone. "*Queen, Queen*, this is unit two; the train just arrived."

Corky rubbed his eyes, more from stress than fatigue. "This just keeps getting better and better."

258

Small puddles of water began pooling on the coach's floor, runoff from the raingear of the men hastily summoned for an emergency meeting.

Terri's RV was the only place quiet enough for everyone to be heard, the wind's constant wail making conversation nearly impossible in the warehouse.

"We need to go retrieve my husband and his team," Terri opened. "How do we do that?"

Slim looked around the gathered men, knowing his boss wasn't going to like the answer. "Our trucks are 4-wheel drive, ma'am, but that won't help with high water. There's no way we can drive this coach in that wind."

"Can they walk here? Should we send someone to guide them in?"

Again, it was up to Slim to deliver the bad news. "I had to pull the foot patrols inside just ten minutes ago, ma'am. One of our men was almost hit by a flying sheet of plywood. You can't walk out there."

Butter spoke up, "We've got the Humvee. It has that raised exhaust stack. Aren't they supposed to be able to handle really deep water?"

"It's an up-armored version... heavy as hell... I don't think the wind would move it much," another man added.

But Slim didn't like it. "That vehicle is the only thing we have that can get Miss Terri and the baby out of here if the water continues to rise. I was holding it back in reserve in case we had to get them to high ground. What if something happened to the Humvee on the way to the depot? We would be out of options if the water continues to rise."

Terri turned away, not wanting to show the men her fear. After reigning in her emotions, she said, "So I guess we leave them on

259

the train until the storm passes? It sounds like they might be better off there anyway."

"There's no way to know, ma'am," Slim began. "They might..."

All four of the gathered security team straightened, as if an electrical charge had passed through them all at once. Two moved their hands to their ears, pressing in the small speaker attached to the radios. In a blur, Slim unplugged his unit so everyone could hear the broadcast.

"I repeat," came the static voice, "All stations. All stations. This is the *Morgan City Queen*. Galveston Island is directly in the path of an approaching, Category 3 hurricane. This has been confirmed by radar. The eye of the storm is approximately 60 miles southeast of the island, moving north by northwest at 26 knots. It is projected to make landfall in two hours. All residents should seek shelter on high ground as soon as possible. Move to the upper floors of secure buildings. Avoid low-lying areas. We anticipate the seawall will not hold. Godspeed. Out."

To everyone gathered inside the coach, the roar of the storm seemed to intensify in the silence that followed the transmission. Terri was the first to move, scooping up Hunter, and holding him close. She was also the first to speak. "Do we stay or do we try and find some place safer?"

"We can't move, ma'am. I just don't see a way. The taller buildings are almost a mile away. The causeway is further than that, even if we drive out. I think we just have to hunker down and ride it out. I don't see any other option."

No one had anything else to add. As the meeting broke up, Slim remained behind, waiting on the others to leave. "Please put together the bug-out bags, Miss Terri. One for yourself, the child, and Miss Betty. If things get really, really bad, then I'll get you out of here, even if I have to drive that Humvee like it's a submarine."

Bishop and Grim had both heard the same radio transmission.

260

Shortly after receiving the bad news, the Lady Star came to a stop at the yard, the area full of a series of side-rails and dozens of empty cars. There was already standing water all around.

The train's lack of motion soon proved even more unsettling for the occupants, the floor moving underfoot as the gale blasted against the now-leeward side of the cars.

Bishop spied a man and a woman carrying two children in their arms, the couple struggling with the wind and knee-deep water. He watched as they scrambled to climb inside an unused boxcar, the raised rail-bed, and elevation above the track providing shelter. Hands reached out of the dark interior, faces appearing as they were helped aboard. Before the door was closed behind the new arrivals, he could see that several other refugees of the storm were housed inside.

Smart, Bishop thought. *The cars are heavy, and the steel walls would protect against blowing debris. As long as the water doesn't get too deep, they should be okay.*

Movement from the front of the locomotive drew his attention. He watched the engineer hop down from the cab, the man practically bowled over by a gust. He recovered, hustling back and climbing aboard the car occupied by the security team. Grim opened the door for the soaked fellow, pulling him inside.

"We normally unhook the freight cars here before rolling back into town to pick up passengers for the return trip. I don't know what to do."

Bishop informed the engineer what they'd heard over the radio. After recovering from the shock, the train's captain reminded all present that they still had four cars full of passengers. "We need to get those people off this island," he insisted. "They're my responsibility."

"Where's the highest point of the rail line?" Bishop asked, an idea forming in his head.

"The grade peaks next to downtown. It's not much of a difference, maybe a foot higher."

The statement gave Bishop an idea. "Can you still unhook the freight cars and maybe attach more empty units? Those boxcars

261

over there are already filling up with people. I've got a feeling we're not the only ones who would like to get off this sand bar."

The man pondered Bishop's words for a moment. "We've got to hurry. If the wind gets much stronger, it can blow us off the track. I can pull her back to downtown... there's a huge warehouse complex that might shelter us from some of the wind."

Grim piped in, "Won't a hurricane blow the whole train to kingdom come? I think I like my odds taking a swim rather than sinking to the bottom of the gulf in one of these steel coffins."

The engineer responded, "There's no way to tell. I was crossed by a tornado once - up in Iowa. Now that was a blow. We kept our entire load on the tracks. But I've also seen full cars tossed around like cardboard boxes. You just never know."

"Does anybody have a better idea?" Bishop asked, surveying the gathered faces. When no one volunteered an alternative, he said, "Let's do it."

The wave crashed into the 16-foot high seawall and rolled over the top, a virtual river of saltwater running across the beachfront street being patrolled by tractor #1.

The driver watched the natural retreat of the water, noting the pavement beginning to crumble from the abuse. The once wide stretch of sand between the road and the gulf was now completely submerged, the ocean's level up several feet.

He drove his powerful machine over the breach, eyes toward the sea so he wouldn't get caught broadside by another big one.

Water was already standing for as far as he could see inland. The east end of Galveston Island was now a lake of troubled, churning saltwater, and it was getting deeper by the minute.

He drove another quarter mile before another giant wall of water crashed over the wall. It receded, only to be followed by another.

262

The water levels were rising, now exceeding the protective barrier on a regular basis. If this kept up, every wave would soon be rolling into the homes, businesses, and streets now protected by the seawall. While many of the residences were built on stilts, even that level of protection would eventually succumb to the power of the angry gulf.

He continued east, watching the distant geysers of water erupting into the dark skies as more and more waves crashed headlong into the manmade wall. It was foreboding, frightening, and yet awe-inspiring at the same time. The power of the ocean was like no other on the planet.

So enthralled by the sheer magnitude of the scene, he wasn't paying careful attention to his own position. As the tractor rolled along, the hint of a shadow made his head snap seaward.

Inhaling deeply with an involuntary tightening of every muscle, he braced as a towering leviathan of solid water curled over the top of his cab. He felt his machine physically move, pushed sideways by the tremendous force of the wave.

The cab went dark, a lightless tomb as the water roared over the top. Thinking he was going to die, his eyes could only find the white and green instruments still glowing on the dash.

And then the grey light of the sky flooded in.

As the water drained away from the cab's glass, he found his machine had been pushed almost 20 yards further inland. He felt the diesel engine sputter and hesitate, saying a prayer that it would continue to run.

He pumped the gas gently, hoping to milk a recovery from the drenched power source. Again, a hesitation, a surge, a then a sputter.

A series of engine gasps and coughs sounded over the now-constant growl of the wind. Another darkening... and then the road in front of him disappeared in a flash of black water and white foam. That one had just missed.

Finally, the mechanical gods smiled upon his chariot. Full power reached all four wheels, and the tractor-lift surged forward, again rolling with authority.

He immediately turned inland, desperately wanting to escape the random ambushes of the high waves. He reached for his radio microphone and pushed to talk.

"Queen, Queen. This is unit one, do you copy?"

For a moment his heart stopped, thinking the storm was blocking his radio's transmitter. Static filled the cab, empty air and the sound of his own heartbeat overriding the diesel and wind.

Then a voice responded, "We read you, unit one. Status?"

"I can't stay out here any longer. I almost lost the tractor. There are two to three waves per minute rolling over the seawall. The base ocean level is three feet below the top. It will be completely overwhelmed in the next hour. I'm heading back to the port while I still can."

"We copy, unit one. Come on back."

Working his way inland, #1 was happy to put as much distance between the omnipotent gulf and his machine as possible. He plowed through standing water, sometimes over the hood of the relic cars parked here and there. It was difficult to negotiate the streets when houses or buildings didn't line the edges; twice he felt himself running up on a curb. Parking meters, where present, were his makeshift channel buoys.

Every now and then, he found himself facing a strong current. One street in particular was a river flowing through a residential neighborhood, some force of hydrodynamics channeling a swift flow of water – but just at that single crossing.

He sat briefly at the intersection, watching a refrigerator float past, almost immediately followed by a horse that had been claimed by the swirling sea. Like a multi-car pile-up during rush hour, his attempt to cross was further delayed by an empty mini-van being carried downstream by the rushing waters.

The scene was so surreal, watching the four-wheeled boat for a few moments. Traveling in a straight line, as if someone were behind the wheel and steering, the SS Soccer Mom sailed past like a ghost ship on a moonless night. "You ran the stop sign," he grunted.

As he headed to drive across the inland river, movement drew his attention back toward the mini-van. The third house on the left... on top of the garage... there were people. "What the hell are they doing up there?"

Looking for oncoming traffic, he turned into the street-current, the big forklift hardly affected at all. As he pulled in front of the home, all of the folks on the roof began waving their arms, pleading for help. He counted 14 stranded, soaked, miserable-looking refugees.

"They look like a bunch of shipwrecked survivors," he whispered, unsure of how to get them down, or what to do with them once he did.

The current here was too brisk for any but the strongest person to manage. There were young mothers clutching the hands of small children and elderly among the rooftop mix – walking to safety would be impossible.

Looking around for any possible solution, the answer came from the next home down. Someone had evidently been remodeling or renovating the place, a large dumpster used for construction trash on the premises. The unit was now pinned by the torrent against a fence and a telephone pole.

He unbuttoned the cab's window, a blast of cold rain blowing into his space. Sticking his arm out the opening, he held up one finger. *I'll be back in a minute,* he mouthed to the storm's soaked evacuees.

The dumpster was a light load for #1, the forks sliding under the long, green container and lifting it easily. Once he had raised it above the water line, he reversed course and returned to the castaways.

He maneuvered to the garage roof, raising the steel salvation container to the gutter. They got the idea immediately, some sliding down the slick shingles and jumping in, then turning to help their less nimble friends aboard.

Now what to do with them?

Backing into the street-river, he proceeded along his original route, sure the water had risen another foot during the rescue effort, positive the wind had grown even stronger.

Twice more he spied stranded people, both families pushed onto their roofs by the rising waters and hanging on for dear life in the wind. The dumpster became crowded.

A few blocks later, he was crossing another street when a dim, dark, line appeared on the distant horizon. His heart stopped, thinking a tidal wave was approaching through the blowing rain and whipped up sea foam. They were all going to die, crushed under a tsunami that was at least 10 feet high.

Then the driver realized the wave wasn't coming any closer. The air cleared, a small gap between the bands of rain and wind, and he saw it was the Texas Star, not a wave of destruction.

It took a bit for his heart to slow. Shaking his head over the incident, he was more than a little embarrassed that his nerves were now causing hallucinations. Glancing again at what he thought was certain death, he noted the locomotive was moving.

Wait a minute, he thought. *If the train is moving, that means the tracks are high and dry. I can set my passengers down there, and they'll be safe.* Executing a quick left turn, he began chasing the engine.

It didn't take long to catch up, as the iron horse had come to a halt. Approaching closer, he realized several of the boxcars were loading people aboard. "Next stop, Grand Flooded Station," he said to the unhearing dumpster riders. "At least the boxcars will keep the wind and rain off your head."

"Watch this," Slim yelled at Terri. "Watch the water level."

Peeking out the barely open warehouse door, she did as instructed, focusing on what appeared to be a six-inch high wave rolling down the street outside. It looked perfect for a Barbie doll-sized surfer.

The disturbance rolled past the entrance to the warehouse, heading west to some unknown destination. At Slim's behest, she'd identified a visual marker, a piece of reflective tape on a newspaper box, just above the waterline. After the wave had passed, the tape was gone, now submerged in the rising flood.

"It's rising that fast?" Terri shouted back.

"That was a little one. Three minutes ago, one of those waves tumbled past that was at least two feet high," Slim explained at the top of his lungs. "We have to get out of here. Look," he said, pointing a flashlight at the warehouse floor just 15 feet away. There was water running in from some unknown source, already an inch deep across the smooth concrete floor.

Terri returned her gaze to the outside, just in time to witness a trailer full of lawnmowers and yard equipment swirl past. The current was stronger than it looked.

They returned to the RV, the interior still providing enough sound barrier to have a reasonable conversation. "We need to go, and go now," Slim insisted. "Another five minutes, and I don't know if the Humvee will make it through."

"What about the men?" Terri asked, concern all over her face.

"There are nine people total in our party. The Humvee holds five, six tops. The guys we leave here can shelter on top of the RV or lash themselves to a pole if it gets bad.

Terri didn't like it. The men that worked for Slim risked their lives for her safety. "We don't leave anyone behind," she argued. "That's not our way."

"Ma'am, with all due respect, this isn't the Army or Marine Corps. I have sworn an oath to protect you and your son, and I'm going to do whatever it takes to keep that promise. Please get your things, Miss Terri."

Crossing her arms in defiance, Terri said, "I won't. We aren't going to leave anyone behind. There has to be another way."

"Ma'am, please don't make me throw you over my shoulder and carry you out to that Humvee," Slim responded, his voice as resolute as hers.

"You wouldn't dare!" She protested, backing one step away. "Bishop would kill you in a heartbeat."

Slim shook his head, "No, ma'am, he wouldn't. I know the type of man your husband is, and he would buy me a drink and offer me a cigar. He would be thankful to any man who saved his wife and son, regardless of any loss of dignity required for the rescue."

Terri reached for his pistol, but Betty's voice stopped her. "Terri! Stop! What are you doing? Are you really going to shoot him?"

The Alliance ambassador stopped, her hand shaking as she removed it from the weapon's grip. "Oh, Slim," she whispered, "Oh, I'm so sorry."

The tears clouding her eyes didn't match the anger in Terri's voice. "But there has to be a better way... something other than lashing people to... that's it!"

"Ma'am? What's it?"

"Why can't we lash them to the Humvee? What would be the difference? They could last until we reached someplace safer... until we find higher ground."

Slim's first reaction was to shake his head no, but then he thought about it for a moment. "You know, that's not a bad idea. Hopefully, we won't have to travel far."

He turned to bounce the idea off his team, pausing for a moment to add, "Please get ready, ma'am. We need to leave right away. I'll be back to help both of you and the child get loaded in just a minute."

And then he was gone.

They pulled out of the warehouse, all nine members of the Alliance aboard. With Slim driving, Butter in the front seat, Betty, Terri and another man across the back seat. Hunter's car seat rested on Terri's lap.

Another rider squeezed himself into the small cargo area behind the rear seat, leaving two volunteers to ride on the back bumper. Each man had lashed himself to the vehicle in his own way, knowing not only the risk, but also the punishment he could expect to endure from the cold water, biting rain, and blistering wind.

The water had risen another foot by the time they'd reached a decision. Twice Slim had to pause before pulling into the deepest part of the street, once due to what appeared to be a lifeguard stand rushing past, the other to avoid hitting a dead body bobbing down the street-river.

Terri inhaled deeply as the water churned over the hood. When the cold liquid started running in from under and around the door, she almost screamed.

"It's designed to take on water," the man beside her stated, trying to keep everyone calm. "The water will weigh it down so it doesn't float away."

Slim drove slowly, keeping his eye out for debris and doing his best to avoid any submerged objects.

When the cold water reached Betty's butt, she yelped as if she'd been bitten, trying to rise above the chilling sensation. Finally giving up, she sat back down, a look of disgust and fear spreading across her face.

Terri's arms were getting tired, trying to hold Hunter high and dry. The man next to her… Garcia was his name… offered to hold the car seat while she rested her limbs.

He was going to lash himself to a tree so I could live, Terri thought. *Where does Nick find these guys?*

Despite the windshield wipers running full blast, Slim still had trouble seeing. The combination of the outside rain and too many humans inside resulted in fogged windows and low visibility. The anxious occupants shivered from the water now up to their waists, the hot air from the defrosters doing little to offset the chill as the cold seawater filled the cab.

"I have to pee," Betty said, her terrified voice making it through the storm's din.

Before Terri could respond, the front of the Humvee dipped down, the vehicle tilting badly toward the front. They jerked to a halt. Terri couldn't see what, or why... it was as if they'd hit a wall.

Over the roaring wind and slashing rain, she heard Slim yell, "Fuck!"

She could see the concerned look on Butter's face in the passenger seat, and then the water was above her window. She grabbed Hunter's seat.

In it came, raw, frigid seawater rising above her stomach, then her breasts and finally her throat. She somehow managed to open her seatbelt, push down with her feet, and raise her head to the roof to gasp for air. Every muscle in her body strained to hold Hunter's seat against the roof, a bare few inches of cool, precious air left in the gap. She couldn't tell if her son's head was above the water or not.

But soon it didn't matter.

With her lips pinned to the metal roof, pulling in the last thin layer of air, she felt the water roll into her mouth. It was a natural reaction to seal her only source of breath.

She held that last lungful, still holding Hunter as high as she could, moving him over her head to where something in her brain reasoned an air pocket might be. It was eerily quiet under the water, the first time in hours she hadn't heard the storm.

Her chest began hurting, every cell in her being screaming for oxygen, her lungs on fire. It was a dark, quiet place; the only sound she recognized was the ever-faster beating of her own heart.

I'm so sorry, Bishop, she thought. *I love you. Hunter and I will see you in heaven.*

A calm came over her, the empty, harsh feeling in her lungs seeming to dissipate. She felt her jaw beginning to unlock, knew that her mouth would open by involuntary reaction as soon as her brain ceased to function. She felt a warm, floating sensation. It was a welcome replacement over the cold, bone chilling numbing of the water.

Terri saw what she thought were the wings of an angel spreading to lift her away. There was a glow and the sound of rumbling drums. She felt a weightlessness as she was lifted upward toward the skies.

The celestial being was massive, much larger than she'd ever imagined, the illumination of brilliant white light surrounding her in a sensation of warmth and safety. She was in God's hands.

He'd seen the Humvee rolling through the water, curious where the driver thought he was going, interested in how deep the military vehicle could dive.

The two men strapped to the back bumper made the spectacle even more appealing.

He'd shouted from #1's cab, a worthless use of lungs and energy given the constant, thunderous volume of the storm. Still, he tried, screaming to warn the driver that he was about to run into a ditch. The hood went under, then the cab. He watched as the two guys tied to the back tried to free themselves, frustrated when their heads disappeared under the surface.

He set the empty dumpster down, his makeshift flood-bus having just delivered its third load of people to the locomotive. It was his best guess where the Humvee was, only a small ripple of water showing on the surface over the submerged transport.

Down went the forks, diving into the depths of brownish water until he felt them hit the pavement below. He inched forward, estimating where the vehicle went under. His guess was good, the hydraulic rams lifting the biggest fish he'd ever caught. *That's a keeper*, he mused, the gallows humor having become necessary to retain his sanity. A moment later, the wheels of the Humvee cleared the surface.

Like every other load of victims, he couldn't think of any other destination but the train.

Three blocks later, he was setting the still-draining Humvee down beside the tracks. Opening his window, he got the attention of a man helping people climb out of a flat bottom boat that had just arrived at high ground. "I'm not sure they're alive," he shouted, pointing at his delivery. "I watched them go completely under."

Saluting, the guy wading through the water below yelled back, "I'll check them out."

"I can't do any more. I'm about out of fuel, and the water's too deep for this rig in places. I'm heading back. Good luck!"

Bishop slogged through the water, rushing to the Humvee as fast as his waterlogged legs could pump. He opened the driver's door first, the water gushing out telling him the interior had been completely inundated. The driver was there behind the wheel... pale, grey skin and closed eyes.

Bishop reached to slap the man's cheeks, the effort causing the victim's head to roll. The Texan recognized Slim immediately. "Terri!" he shouted, thrusting his head inside the cab to search.

There were bodies everywhere. In the low light, he couldn't discern any faces, but the sight of a child's car seat handle made his gut turn to ice.

He flung open the rear door, turning to yell to Grim. "These are our people! It's Terri and Hunter! Get help! Now!"

He pulled Hunter's car seat out first, the image of his son's closed eyes and soaked blankets sending bolts of agony through his skull. He unfastened the restraints, pulling the tiny body free and moving to the hood. He tilted his own child's head back, ready to pinch the tiny nose... remembering his CPR training and how to only blow the smallest "puff" into the babe's mouth.

He sensed more than saw Grim pull Terri out of the back seat. Other men and women were flying by, racing to get access to the victims. He bent to place his mouth over his son's, when Hunter's arms jerked... then a cough. A weak, raspy sound... and then another cough. Ten seconds later, Hunter vomited and began crying. His father did, too.

Handing off the infant to a nearby man, Bishop rushed to find Grim's ear right above Terri's mouth. "She's breathing!" he shouted over the storm, "I can feel her breathing!"

Evacuees, many of them just rescued themselves, were bustling all around the injured Humvee. Bishop saw Butter stand on his own, still projecting the dazed look of a badly confused man. It took a helper under each arm to move the huge fellow toward the train.

The storm raged all around Bishop, but he didn't notice. Carrying a ragdoll-limp Terri like a baby laid across his arms, he barreled through the deepening water to the nearest boxcar. Bishop pulled his blowout bag from his vest, tossing the contents onto the floor until he found the emergency blanket.

A miracle of modern science, the small package unfolded into a twin-sized sheet that resembled common kitchen tin foil. After Hunter's wet clothes had been removed, Bishop wrapped his son and wife in the metal-like material that was supposed to reflect over 90% of their body heat. They were both breathing, as warm as he could make them. Mental exhaustion consumed him, and he couldn't fathom any other emergency care for his loved ones.

Working as quickly as he could, Bishop turned to see more of the Humvee's victims being laid out on the floor of the boxcar. Grim, carrying Betty, gave the Texan a sad look and shook his head. She hadn't made it. There were other casualties as well, their bodies laid out at the other end of the car.

And then the door was pushed shut to keep out the wind and rain.

It was completely dark inside. He was so tired, it took a supreme effort to raise his arm and pull the flashlight off his chest-rig. He somehow managed, illuminating the interior with a faint glow.

He looked down to see Terri's eyes staring up at him. Her lips

273

moved, but he couldn't understand a word. Bending closer, he heard her ask, "Am I dead? Is this heaven?"

"No, you're not dead," he said, brushing back her hair and rubbing her cheek.

"Hunter?" she asked, fear filling her eyes at the potential for bad news as the memories came flooding back.

Bishop lifted their son, turning him enough so that Terri could see his eyes were open and clearly full of life. She tried to reach for her baby, but the blanket and her own weakness defeated the movement. Bishop unfolded Terri's cover, placing Hunter in his mother's embrace, helping her hold him in the nook of her arm.

"Betty?" Terri's voice cracked with the dreaded question.

"I'm not sure, babe," Bishop managed over the storm's wail, not having the heart to tell her the truth.

"And the others? Slim? Butter?"

Bishop shook his head, putting his finger to her lips. "Shhhhh. Rest. Keep Hunter warm. That's all you can do right now."

Terri seemed to accept that, closing her eyes and pulling the now sleepy-warm Hunter even closer.

Bishop leaned back, his ears immune to the wailing storm outside of the metal walls of their sanctuary. He closed his eyes, exhausted from fighting with water, wind, and men for the last 16 hours.

The storm continued to pound the iron horse, the gale so strong the entire car swayed back and forth. To the exhausted, waterlogged, and shivering people inside, the motion was like the rocking of a baby's cradle.

Bishop fell asleep.

274

The sliding freight door flung open, brilliant sunlight flooding the interior of the car. Bishop blinked, lifting his hand to block the obnoxious intrusion.

"What the fuck…"

Grim's head appeared, peering inside. "There you are. I thought you'd fallen to Neptune's trident."

"What?" the still confused Bishop asked.

"Wake up, Sleeping Beauty. We've got a decision to make."

Shaking his head, Bishop managed to stand, limping to the opening on shaky legs. The scene outside the boxcar was undoubtedly one of the most unusual he'd ever seen.

The sky was cloudless, a shade of blue unlike any the Texan had ever witnessed. The sheer beauty overhead was in stark contrast to the horizon where a line of midnight dark, swirling clouds was visible in all directions.

"Has the hurricane passed?" Bishop asked, jumping down into the knee-deep water lapping at the iron wheels.

"No," Grim stated, sweeping a circle with his hand, "we're in the eye."

"No shit?" Bishop observed, spinning all around to verify Grim's claim. "So what's the decision?"

"The engineer says the back side of the hurricane will reverse the winds. He says when the far wall slams into us, the flooding will be worse. He wants us to get the people out of the cars and take them some place safer."

Again, Bishop scanned the area. "Where? Everything is flooded. There is no place safer."

Grim held up both hands, "I'm just the messenger."

"Come on, let's go talk to this guy," Bishop said, pissed, tired and angry.

They found the engineer adjusting Lady Star's valves and reading her gauges. "When the back side of that storm hits, the wind is going to come from the southwest. The cars almost blew over before; no way will they stay upright with gusts coming from the other direction. That, and I expect the flood waters to rise even more on this side of the island."

"Then move the train. Get us on the mainland while you can still cross the causeway," Bishop instructed, the solution sounding logical enough. "There's no place here to move all these people."

"We can't do that," the man objected. "We don't know the condition of the tracks on the other side."

Bishop wasn't in the mood for a debate or discussion. "It can't be any worse over there than it is over here – can it? Move the damn train. The further inland we get, the less we have to worry about flooding. From what you have said, we face certain death if we stay put. What choice do we have anyway?"

A discussion ensued between one of the firemen and the engineer, the new participant agreeing with Bishop. The Texan watched and listened for two minutes, his mood growing foul with the inaction. Finally, he flung his rifle around to his chest, chambered a round and demanded, "I am a captain in the Texas Rangers. Move the fucking train. Right now."

The two stunned railroaders froze, their faces painted in disbelief. Bishop reached inside a pouch on his kit and produced the badge he'd been issued just a few weeks before. "Now move the damn train before we lose this weather."

Nodding, the engineer began to issue orders, his crew hustling to ready Lady Star.

Bishop turned to check on his family, Grim hustling to catch up. "Sure do hope you're right about the mainland," he whispered. "If the track is blocked, or the causeway is impassable, this is going to suck."

"Thanks for the support, deputy. I appreciate your confidence," Bishop replied, not in the mood to engage in banter now.

After returning to let a still-sleepy Terri know what was going on, Bishop climbed aboard the first passenger car, intent on monitoring the crew's progress.

276

Five minutes later, they began rolling through the floodwater covering the tracks, the white concrete of the distant causeway clearly visible against the coal black sky beyond.

"We have to go slow through standing water," one of the firemen informed Bishop. "Even a locomotive as heavy as the Lady Star can hydroplane off the tracks."

To the Texan's eye, it was a surreal ride, a wake of water passing away from the train just like a boat crossing a glass-smooth lake.

The closer they drew to the causeway, the higher the track's elevation. Soon, they were climbing up and out of the flood, the entire crew showing relief.

The next potential obstacle in their path, a blocked or washed-out causeway, never materialized. At the apex of the bridge, Bishop looked back over his shoulder, inhaling sharply at how fast the solid black wall of the storm's eye was catching up with them. "Pour the coal to her, boys," he whispered. "Let's see Lady Star kick some ass."

It was an uphill grade coming off the island, but that was all right with every man aboard. Each mile gave them precious elevation above sea level... reduced the chances of being caught in the flood.

Both sides of the line showed standing water, downed trees and toppled utility poles. As they passed over a small stream, Bishop held his breath. The water was already over the bridge supporting the tracks, and there was no way to know if the supports had been weakened by the flow.

Like a bloodthirsty leviathan, the back wall of the storm chased them across the landscape. Taller and taller the dark, churning wall of clouds grew, eating away at the escapees' head start with every passing minute.

Turning to look at their pursuer, Bishop yelled at Grim, "Now I know what an insect sees right before a tire squishes his ass."

They rolled north by northeast, every mile giving them a better chance of riding out the other half of the hurricane. Just when Bishop was starting to feel confident with his decision, the iron horse began to slow, and then the engineer hit the brakes hard.

Craning his neck to see what the problem was, Bishop finally spied a pile of rubble across the tracks. Trying to figure out the source of the debris proved frustrating. There wasn't anything around that could have collapsed or fallen over. "Where did that come from?" he turned and asked Grim.

Wood erupted from a wall behind the ex-contractor, three bullets tearing into the surface. Automatically ducking, Bishop spun to see men with rifles scrambling alongside the barrier blocking their path.

More bullets whacked and thwacked all around the two Alliance men, both of them going low, trying to bring their weapons into the fight.

"We're being robbed again?" Bishop yelled at Grim. "What is the problem around here with trains?"

"Who the hell stages a hold-up in the middle of a hurricane?" Grim shouted back, his burst of return fire sending two attackers scrambling for cover.

Bishop knew the answer as he centered on his first target. The man in his sights wore a red bandana around his hat. Major Misery and the boys had evidently decided to retrieve Hoss's body... and eliminate any witnesses.

"It's Misery's security men!" Grim shouted, arriving at the same conclusion. "They want your hide nailed on a barn door for killing Hoss. Probably want to keep us from snitching on them to the baron, too."

Bishop evaluated the situation quickly, taking little time in reaching the determination that there were too many of them for just Grim and him to handle.

"Back the train out of here!" Bishop yelled to the cowering engineer. "Get us out of here!"

Instead of leaping to the controls, like Bishop wanted, the engineer pointed toward the back of the train. Bishop had to stick his head out to see, a slight bend in the tracks revealing a group of men behind them piling blocks and timbers across their retreat.

278

They were hemmed in.

"They are going to overrun us in about two minutes," Grim announced, firing his rifle at a staccato pace. "We need help."

Bishop pondered where Gomez was, wondering what excuse the man had for avoiding the fight this time. He knew Butter and a couple of Terri's security team had been recovered from the Humvee, but didn't think they'd be in any condition to do much fighting.

He was wrong. Multiple rifles sounded from the back of the train, Gomez and others evidently alerted by the stop.

More rounds tore into the car, hunks of the structure smarting exposed skin. Bishop made a decision, "We're going to abandon the train," he called to Grim. "It's you and me they want. I don't think they'll kill the refugees. If we make for those woods over there, they'll be sure to follow us. We can lose them in there."

"What about Terri and the baby?" Grim called back.

"Shit!" he yelled, disgusted with his lack of thinking, "Never mind. I will not leave them here, and there is no way she can make that trip with Hunter in the condition she's in. Shit!"

Three men rose up from the barricade, their timing corresponding to a blistering barrage of fire from their friends. They began charging toward the locomotive, a dozen rifles throwing everything they had at the train's defenders.

Bishop, hugging the platform for dear life, almost didn't spot the maneuver. Despite the dozens of bullets snapping just inches over his head, he managed to aim his carbine and send several rounds directly into the rushing team's midst. Two of them went down, the third retreating to the barricade.

"That was close," Bishop screamed over Grim's barking weapon. "Another one of those, and we're toast."

Before his partner could respond, the daylight seemed to vanish, like someone had drawn the hotel blackout curtains. Bishop felt the wind, could see the surrounding vegetation bending in the breeze. The storm had caught up.

Like a steamroller, the weather moved across the landscape. In a matter of moments, the calm air was filled with howling gusts. Less than a minute later, the sky opened up with a deluge, horizontal sheets of nearly solid water plowing through the atmosphere.

The air began to scream, a thousand howling wolves voicing their rage. In a minute, the gusts topped 100 mph, three minutes later they were approaching 160... and then 200.

Bishop and Grim were somewhat sheltered from the assault, the passenger car at their back serving to block direct exposure. Still, both men had to wrap their arms and legs around the railing, praying the old iron bolts wouldn't give way.

Through squinting, barely open eyes, Bishop saw the storm pick up one of the attackers and toss him at least 20 feet through the air before being slammed back to the earth. The Texan watched as the stunned fellow was rolled, pushed, scooted, and scraped across the field and into the tree line beyond.

The air became thick with missiles. Blended with the stinging drops of precipitation was an airborne litter of tree limbs, baseball-sized rocks, sheets of metal, and chunks of buildings. Bishop saw a highway sign larger than a king size bed blow past, the sheet of steel burying itself in the soaked earth for a few moments before being whisked away.

Rocketing projectiles thumped and rattled against the cars, some hitting the sides, other large masses rumbling across the roofs of the battered boxcars.

Lady Star and her cars shuddered and moaned under the assault, the Alliance men sensing the movement of their anchorage as the passenger car underneath them rocked and swayed. Between passing bands of rain, Bishop thought of Terri, looking back along the line of cars, watching as a boxcar was pushed up on one set of wheels before returning to the tracks.

At times, the Texan couldn't hear, see, or feel anything but the burning in his muscles as he held on with all he had left.

And then the wall had passed.

The winds began to diminish, the noise and blowing clutter less volatile and dangerous. It was still a life-threatening, powerful storm, but nothing like the violence of the eye's wall.

Bishop relaxed his cramped grip on the rail, managing to lift his head to test the wind. While it was still blowing so hard that walking upright was out of the question, a death grip was no longer required to avoid becoming a human cannon ball. "I don't think we're in Kansas anymore," was all he could think to say.

The rain continued to pelt the Alliance men, sending cold rivers of liquid running across their already soaked bodies. Bishop lifted his head again, looking toward the barricade to ensure none of the assaulters were secretly advancing on them.

He couldn't see a soul.

Determined to remain diligent, Grim and Bishop huddled under the small awning, their ponchos pulled tight, weapons across their laps.

Neither man had the energy or will to speak, only the occasional moment of eye contact shared between them. It was a shivering, wet, miserable stint of guard duty.

Bishop lost track of the time, unsure of how much had lapsed before Grim finally spoke. "Looks like it's died down enough for us to check out that barricade."

"Ya think?" Bishop responded, not sure his legs would function.

"I bet they hightailed it out of here when the storm hit."

"Could be. Could be they'll be back."

Grim shrugged, "Best to check it out now while there's still a little light left. I don't know how much longer I can stay awake."

The two men rose, stiff from exertion and cold. They climbed down from the ravaged front of the passenger car, hardly an inch of the tortured surface void of battle damage.

Bishop knew he should have his weapon up and ready, but his arms were too tired. Some corner of his brain registered that his spacing sucked, but fixing it would require trudging through the mud. *Not an option*, he thought, barely managing to put one foot in front of the other. *I'll just stay up here... nice and dry next to the rails and gravel.*

They finally arrived at a low embankment, a drainage ditch being used by the majority of Major Misery's men as cover. It was completely void of hostile, or formally hostile humans.

The other side of the barricade proved the same; even the bodies of the two men Bishop had put down were nowhere to be found.

They continued their tour, separating to search a debris cluttered field and wood line beyond. Bishop found the first body, the red bandana around the corpse's arm, indicating he was one of the attackers. The man was lying in the mud, his neck at an unnatural angle.

Grim uncovered the next victim, Major Misery himself. A pickup truck, looking like it had been in a major freeway accident, held the man's body. The roof was smashed almost flat, as if the vehicle had been rolled over dozens of times. Misery was hanging halfway out the passenger side door, his body practically severed in half.

Finally reaching the woods, it soon became clear to both men that no threat remained. They found the majority of Misery's raiders here, deposited by the wind, often in an extremely violent manner. One man was a good 12 feet up in a tree, a wrist-sized branch protruding from his chest.

Some of the dead looked as if they'd simply laid down and given up. Bishop turned one man over with his boot, the victim's arms flopping oddly, as if every bone had been pulverized. The Texan shuddered.

Others were warped in grotesque, peculiar positions. Bishop had seen enough.

"Let's head back," he radioed the nearby Grim, too tired to walk the short distance.

"Roger that," came the response. "The storm did more damage than our blasters."

Bishop hadn't taken two steps when his radio sounded with a new voice. "Captain? Captain Bishop, is that you?"

"Kevin? Yes, it's me. Where are you?"

"We're under an overpass. I don't know exactly where. We pulled the truck under here to ride out the storm. It was the only place we could find," broadcast the excited young man.

Bishop grinned, one less worry on his mind. "Is the truck's heater working?"

"Yes, sir, but we've got better than that. There were some old trash barrels filled with wood. It was dry enough to light. We just finished a hot meal."

"Do you have any hot coffee?"

Cory's voice sounded the response, "Why of course we do, sir. Can you describe where you are?"

The wagons pulling the three caskets were neither designed, nor designated for a funeral procession, but no one noticed or cared. All eyes were on the flag-draped boxes, each covered with a bouquet of flowers from the Manor's gardens.

Main Street was packed, hundreds of solemn onlookers four deep in many places. For the first time since its inception, Meraton's market was closed, as was Pete's, and every other business in town.

Lining both sides of the pavement, slightly in front of the subdued crowd, were uniformed men. Each stood statue straight at parade rest, a sign of respect for the deceased. Some were Army officers, resplendent in their dress uniforms, attending from Fort Bliss and Fort Hood. Others were members of Nick's militia, two of their own among the fallen. Sheriff Watt's deputies, impeccably outfitted, were also in attendance.

A single horse pulled the first small wagon, its saddle empty, Pete grasping the reigns. Terri, in a plain black dress, a veil covering her face, plodded numbly alongside. Her left hand rested on Betty's casket. Bishop walked beside his wife, steadying her gait with one arm about her waist and newborn Hunter snuggled in the crook of his opposite arm. They were soon joined by Diana, District Attorney Gibson and a medley of mourners, drawing from the Alliance leadership, local business leaders, the women's church league, and the local garden club. It seemed everyone knew and loved the spunky hotel manager.

"Teeeeen hut!" a voice ordered, all in uniform snapping a smart, crisp salute as Betty's body passed.

Next sauntered Mr. Beltran, leading the riderless horse that pulled Slim's remains. Butter trudged next to the pine box, his hand resting gently on his lifelong friend's casket. The big man's shoulders were slumped, his eyes red with grief. The open expression of anguish was heartbreaking.

The final victim was a man most hadn't known well, Charles Henry Garcia. Recently relocated to the Alliance, his service, both to the United States Armed Forces and the Alliance Militia, was known to have been exemplary. He had been one of the elite men assigned to Terri's security detail, the trip back east his first, and last operation with the team.

Nick led Mr. Garcia's horse, a grieving widow and two children each steadying a hand on the family man's casket.

The three wagons stopped in front of the Manor, the sound of sniffling and soft tears rising from the gathering. With her head on Bishop's shoulder, Terri sobbed, "It feels like I've buried two mothers in one lifetime. Betty was so good to me... she treated me like one of her own children. I loved her, Bishop."

"She was a good woman. We were blessed to have known her for as long as we did," Bishop replied.

Three soldiers marched forward, followed by their commanding officer. The sun reflected off the ranking military leader's saber as his voice rang out, "Ready!"

In unison, the three riflemen stepped forward with their left heels, rifles briskly brought to their shoulders.

"Aim!"

"Fire!"

Three times, they executed the sequence, one volley for each of the fallen. After the final report had echoed off the distant Glass Mountains, another order sounded.

"Present. Arms!"

Three synchronized rifles followed the two-count command, the underside of the weapon facing the honored, fully extended in presentation. Pete moved closer to Terri and Bishop in an attempt to better control the now stirring mare, unaccustomed to the noise. Another soldier appeared, a highly polished trumpet in his gloved hand. The lonely, desolate sound of "Taps" soon drifted over the saddened community.

As if on cue, a single tear slipped down the Meraton mayor's cheek with the first trumpeted note, his darkened mood an obvious indicator of the depth of his suffering and grief. Around town, it was an unmentioned, but commonly known fact that Betty held Pete's eye. Something, it seemed, was always getting in the way of the two making a go at a relationship. And now it was too late.

"I am going to miss her so much," Pete whispered, barely holding it together. When Terri embraced him in a hug, the dam burst, uncontrollable sobs racking his frame. Within moments, both of them succumbed to the torrent of emotion, weeping openly, leaning on each other for support.

When the horn fell silent, the officer's voice boomed again. "Order. Arms!"

"Port. Arms!"

"Right face!"

"Forward, march!"

As the three riflemen stepped away, the officer bent and began collecting the spent shell casings. It was dishonorable to leave them on the ground. One by one, he approached each of the coffins, offering a sample of the brass to the closest friends and family of the deceased.

Bishop accepted two, one for Hunter, the other for his wife. One day, when he was old enough, the father would share the story and keepsake with his son. Good people had died honorably, in service to others – an important lesson for any young person.

Staring at the empty cartridges in his hand, the meaning of the tradition crystalized in Bishop's troubled mind. In death, the body was an empty shell, the soul having moved on to a better place. Watching his wife with Pete, he couldn't help but wonder if Terri wasn't ready to move on to a better, safer place. Not in death, but in life.

He was worried how Terri would deal with the tragedy in Galveston. Not only had she lost two people she held dearly, the fact that Hunter had almost perished was casting doubt, forcing his wife to reevaluate her priorities. Since the incident, she had mentioned turning over her position on the council to someone else and moving back to the ranch. Even this morning, she'd casually asked who he would have supported to take over as chairperson if she'd hadn't survived the storm.

He watched her stroll over to Mr. Beltran and Butter, virtually repeating the same scene that had just occurred with Pete.

"My wonderful, optimistic, passionate, Terri," Bishop whispered. "The apocalypse made you realize you were so very, very much more. It enabled you... forced you - kicking and screaming - to realize your potential. And now? Now has that been taken back?"

He resolved to support her, no matter how the events that unfolded during the hurricane affected his wife. If she wanted to retire, resign her position with the Alliance, he'd support that move 100%. More than once, he'd had the same thoughts and desires. He loved Terri, believed she was a great mother and the best lifelong companion any man could ask for. He respected the sacrifices she made every day and her heartfelt desire to help her fellow human beings. She was a true leader, exactly what the Alliance needed.

But there was only so much any one individual could endure. Was his wife at her limit?

"I'll leave it up to you," he decided. "You'll know what's best. And no matter what it is, I've got your back."

Epilogue

The Gathering
by D.A.L.H.

Mesmerized by what the future might bring,
Immobilized by the fear of how it might present itself.
Gathering together to wait and watch.
Unable to change its ominous approach.
Unable to look away.

Able to pray.

Gray and purple above.
Rotating, shifting, unpredictable.

Gray and blue below.
Crashing, boiling, certain.

They gathered together,
Great in number,
Each soul standing alone.

The storm gathered together,
Great in its solidarity
But weak against the faith of each staring from the shore.

Two weeks after the hurricane...

Corky leaned against the shovel's handle, taking a short break to wipe the perspiration from his brow. As he refolded the handkerchief, one of his men approached, a portable radio in his hand.

"Sir, a lookout is reporting that several vehicles are crossing the causeway. He indicates there are at least a dozen."

"Military?"

"No, sir, an assortment of civilian trucks, buses, and semis."

The leader of the island community scrutinized the mounting

287

tangle of rubble and grunted. "We're not quite ready for company just yet; the place is still a mess."

Passing the long-handled tool to another, Corky looked around, wondering if they would ever be ready. Piles of debris, sand, and mud still clogged many of the streets. While the odor of rotting flesh had helped them locate most of the victims, the occasional cadaver was still being unearthed.

Corky shook his head, admiring the gang of volunteers working to clear whatever street he was standing on. For a moment, he was embarrassed over having forgotten the name, but the feeling soon passed. There were still dozens and dozens of areas that needed to be searched, cleared, and cleaned up if possible.

Most of the people working around him were missing family members, friends, or neighbors. He'd lost count of how many of the dead they had buried, no idea how many were listed as missing.

There had been a few bright spots. A few survivors had been found alive, buried in wreckage or trapped wherever they'd hunkered down. A few, but not nearly enough.

At least 50% of the homes were damaged to the extent that occupation was no longer an option. That was a secondary consideration, given the substantial drop in Galveston's current population.

Still, they kept at it. Block by block, street by street, they worked. There wasn't much fuel for the heavy equipment left on the island. What little gas and diesel they did have needed to be reserved for the boats. Without the shrimpers, oyster boats and offshore fishermen, he'd be burying the victims of starvation alongside the storm's fatalities.

More than once since the hurricane, Corky had considered powering up the *Morgan City Queen* and sailing off into the sunrise. There *had* to be some place better to tie up - *had* to be a new home out there that wasn't full of the misery, stench, and desperation that now held Galveston in their collective grips.

But he didn't.

He couldn't bring himself to abandon the people that had come to

288

depend on him... on his men... on the bulk supplies carried in the hulls of his barges.

Even some of those had been causalities of the storm. Two of their precious boats had blown loose in the tempest and sunk, irreplaceable tanks of propane in one, thousands of pounds of wheat flour in the other.

The rumble of engine noise brought the Cajun out of his melancholy contemplation. Shielding his eyes from the sun, he spied the line of trucks approaching from the north. It was quite the collection. A fleeting thought flashed through his mind – *What if they have ill intent? What if they are invaders?*

"I'll let them have the place without a fight," he mused. "Maybe they can do better than we have."

A block away, two pickup trucks rolled to a stop, armed men piling out of the back of each.

"Oh, shit," Corky worried. "I was only joking. I didn't *really* think anybody would invade."

The next vehicle was a large, deluxe motor coach, the kind Corky had seen carrying famous country and western stars across the nation while on tour.

It too rolled to a stop, the bus-like door hissing open a few moments later.

Several people stepped down from the RV, one of the distant faces vaguely familiar. Corky smiled, remembering Terri from the day of the maelstrom, almost having forgotten her visit. She was traveling with an entourage.

Corky stepped forward to welcome the new arrivals. Terri noticed the captain, immediately moving to meet him halfway, raising her arm to wave a friendly greeting.

"Hello," Corky said, extending his dirty palm after wiping it on his pants leg. "I wasn't expecting honored guests. I'm afraid I've been a little busy lately," he added, sweeping the surrounding area with his arm.

Terri laughed, her smile clear and bright. "We thought you might need some help. That, and we have a few hundred of your citizens that have been clamoring to return home."

She pointed, just as one of the buses began unloading a stream of people. "They escaped on the train with us, right as the worst of the hurricane hit. It took us a while to gather up the resources to bring them back to the island."

Corky watched as more and more people disembarked from the transports, several of them looking around at the surreal landscape with stunned expressions on their faces.

One of the nearby workers dropped his shovel, tentatively approaching the growing crowd of returning residents. "Kim? Kim, is that you? Oh, thank God... I thought we'd lost you," the man said, running the last few steps to embrace a smiling woman.

Terri and her host stood and watched the joyful reunion for a minute, both of them relishing in the uplifting event. "That's what it's all about," Corky observed. "That's what keeps me climbing out of bed these days."

"Well, maybe I can add a little more cheer to your mornings," Terri said. "We've brought fuel, as many blankets and medical supplies as I could gather, and a few pieces of heavy equipment. We figured you could use some bulldozers to help with the cleanup."

Emotion welled up inside the Cajun, his eyes turning wet with joy. "I didn't think we'd get any help. No way. I had just about given up hope of anyone even realizing our plight."

Terri hooked arms with the overjoyed man, the two strolling back toward the still-arriving Alliance caravan.

"We'll have the Texas Star running in another week. The plan is to open additional lines and stations following that. With your seafood production, you should be able to trade for most of what you need. We are screening over 10,000 volunteers from Houston who want to relocate... move down here to help rebuild the island. Welcome to the Alliance of Texas."

"Membership has its rewards," Corky managed to tease.

"Come on, let me introduce you to my husband and son," Terri beamed. "One of them is cute, the other quite charming. I'll let you decide which is which."